THE CONTEST

THE CONTEST

K.E. GANSHERT

Cover Design by Courtney Walsh

Map Illustration by Audrey St. Amant

For Betsy

For believing in this story when I didn't and encouraging me to keep going when I wanted to call it quits.

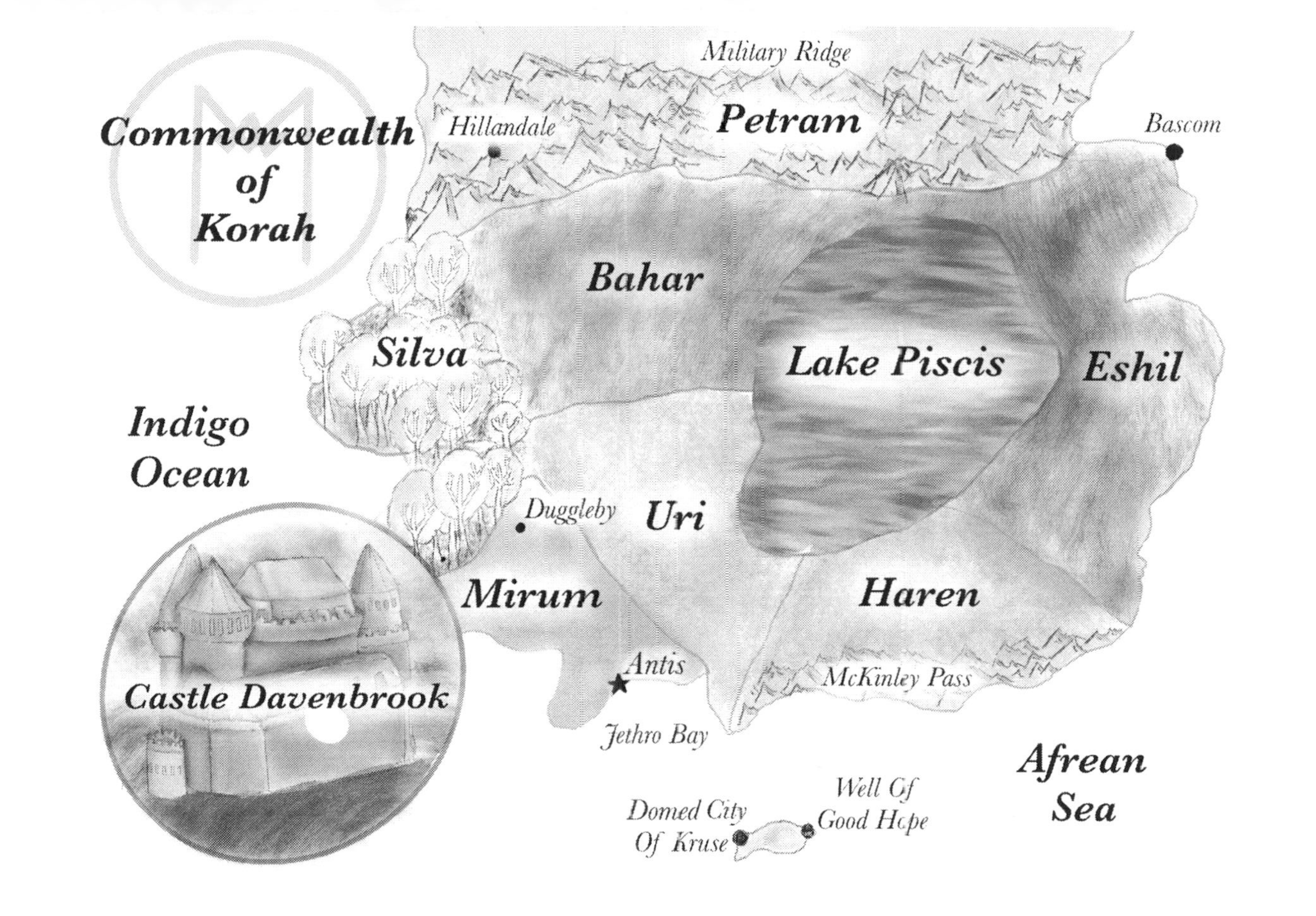
Commonwealth
of
Korah
Military Ridge
Petram
Hillandale
Bascom
Bahar
Silva
Lake Piscis
Eshil
Indigo
Ocean
Duggleby
Uri
Mirum
Haren
Castle Davenbrook
Antis
McKinley Pass
Jethro Bay
Afrean
Sea
Well Of
Good Hope
Domed City
Of Kruse

PROLOGUE

The wish came early like some wishes do.

The desperate ones.

The dying ones.

Those come the earliest.

This one arrived on the cusp of a plan just as it was being set in motion. A glimpse of the future, throbbing like a heartbeat in the old man's palm. Though the night was calm and quiet, he could feel the panic of another. Fire licking up the stands. Smoke filling the air. Thunder and lightning and screaming all around as spectator trampled spectator in a desperate attempt to escape. The scene swept through him as if he were in the center of the chaos, as if he *were* the boy.

Standing on the dais, unmoving as the destruction unfolded, his eyes fastened on the girl.

Then the locket.

Destroy it.

The boy wished for that destruction with every fiber of his being.

For only then could she be killed.

THE PACT

YEAR OF KORAH: 483

LENA

Magic was forbidden. Lena knew that as surely as she knew her mama baked the best beef pie on this side of the island. Flower petals weren't supposed to dance in the sky, not without the wind to carry them. Even then, they didn't choreograph themselves in a dazzling display of hearts and loop-de-loops.

Perhaps, if Lena's friend had asked, Lena would have said no. They shouldn't.

But Phoebe was not the sort of girl to ask.

So Lena watched—at once delighted and terrified. For if her parents had taught her anything in her eight years of life, it was the danger of *this*. Not just kid-dangerous either, but adult-dangerous. The kind that could topple governments. The kind that could sow anarchy. The kind that got people killed. Like the woman who used to live at the end of the lane. She had a niece like Phoebe. According to Lena's parents, Magic had turned the girl strange. The woman died when Mama was swollen with pregnancy, two weeks before Lena would come writhing and screaming into the world. Her parents spared her the details of this gruesome death. All Lena knew was that it had been unnatural and though there was no proof that the woman's niece had done it, everybody knew that she had and not a single soul objected when she was taken to the mainland and put in a home for troubled girls.

Still, Lena turned in a circle, her eyes wide as a multitude of white blossoms swirled in a waltz around her, dancing with the strands of dark hair that had come loose from her school day plait. She stood in a whirlwind of sweet perfume as sunlight dappled through the leaves overhead. If Mama saw—if Papa saw—they would forbid Lena from ever seeing Phoebe again. Lena knew this, too. Even without having ever seen, Lena's parents already encouraged her to make friends with other girls. But compared to Phoebe, those girls were dull, rainy days after weeks of blue sky. And how could anyone catch them, all the way out here, so deep under the cover of the forest outside their obscure little village?

"People are afraid of what they don't understand,"

Phoebe liked to say. "According to my papa, *that's* the danger. Not Magic. But the fear of it."

Like most people, Lena didn't understand Magic. She only knew that out of all the girls in their village, Phoebe had chosen her. She'd trusted Lena with the biggest secret in the whole world and Lena would not forsake her. She would take that secret to her grave.

Lifting her arms, she twirled with the petals as they spun faster and faster. An enchanting, feather-light cyclone. She laughed. Phoebe laughed too as the petals fell to the ground and she raced ahead. It took Lena a moment to catch her breath. Then she made chase, running deeper into the woods where the cover was so thick, the dappling sunlight disappeared altogether.

"W-wait!" Lena called, her cheeks flushed.

Phoebe stopped, peering up at a peculiar tree covered in something like silver veins.

"Wh-what is it?" Lena asked, approaching hesitantly as Phoebe walked around the thick trunk, eyes trained upward, fingertips grazing the bark.

"It's a Vine Tree," Phoebe finally said, her tone soaked in reverence. "They're dead rare. Mama says almost all of 'em got chopped during The Purge."

The Purge.

Another reminder that Magic was dangerous.

Back then, a simple accusation was a death sentence.

And sympathizers were guilty, too.

"Why were they ch-chopped down?" Lena asked, wanting to touch the tree herself. She reached out tentatively, head cocked as she examined the thin veins that weren't really veins at all, but vines. They reminded her of the ivy that grew up the north side of their schoolhouse, only these were silver without any foliage.

"People think they're Magic."

Lena pulled her hand back, capturing her bottom lip between her teeth.

"I wonder how old it is," Phoebe said, walking around the tree a second time. Then she stopped, cleared her throat, and in a theatrical voice that had a bird taking flight, asked, "What is your age, Good Sir?"

Lena cupped her hand over her mouth to trap a giggle.

Phoebe pressed her ear against the bark. After a beat, her eyes rounded.

"What d-did it say?" Lena asked, forgetting herself.

Trees didn't talk.

"*He* said that he's as old as the Well of Good Hope."

The Well of Good Hope.

That was as old as time itself.

Lena looked up to its highest branch. It was a beautiful tree, but not the tallest. Nor the widest. There were bigger trees around them. It was hard to believe that this one could be so old. Before she could say so, Phoebe did something very silly. She gave the tree a hug, her arms only long enough to reach halfway around.

Lena's trapped giggle escaped.

"C'mon," Phoebe said.

Lena hesitated before joining her friend.

When she did, the two girls could spread their arms just far enough for their fingers to touch.

"What are we doing?" Lena asked, her cheek pressed up against the vines.

"Shh!" Phoebe shushed.

There was a still quiet, as if the forest held its breath.

Or maybe that was Lena.

"Can you hear it?" Phoebe whispered.

Lena strained, wanting to hear whatever it was Phoebe heard. But unless her friend was talking about the chirping of birds, Lena could hear nothing. "Hear what?" she finally whispered back.

"He wants us to make a pact."

"The t-tree?"

"To love and protect each other always. Like true sisters. Until the day we're dead."

True sisters.

The idea delighted Lena, for she had always wanted a sister, and despite any reservations her parents might have, she was positive there'd be none better than Phoebe.

"We've got to close our eyes and make a wish. That nothing will ever separate us."

Lena scrunched up her face and wished to the Wish Keeper himself. "I wish it," she said.

"Do you promise?"

"I promise."

"Me too," Phoebe said back, giving Lena's fingers a squeeze.

Then Phoebe let go. She crouched down and pulled out the small switchblade she kept tucked inside her left boot. When she stood, she addressed the tree with all the gravity of the High King taking a royal oath. "Do I have your permission, Good Sir?" she asked, holding the blade next to one of its vines. When the tree neither objected nor concurred, Phoebe cut off a length.

Lena gasped as the severed vine on the tree grew back into wholeness, reconnecting itself right before their eyes. "H-how did it d-do that?"

Phoebe didn't answer. She took the vine in her hand, cut it in two, and held the pieces apart. They grew toward one another as if they weren't meant to be separated. Phoebe placed one half of the vine against her forearm. Gently, almost tenderly, it wrapped itself around her wrist like a delicate bracelet made of silver. Phoebe held up the other half and touched the vine to Lena's skin. It felt warm and smooth and a little tingly as it circled her wrist.

The two girls examined their new accessory.

"Friendship bracelets," Lena said.

"*Sister* bracelets," Phoebe corrected.

Lena smiled as a sound came from behind them. The

girls turned, and there, north of the tree, was a rabbit caught in a snare.

"Trappers!" Phoebe exclaimed. "Blast those varmints!"

As she approached, the poor rabbit cowered in her shadow. At the sight of its broken, bleeding paw, a great sadness overtook Lena, the kind that filled up her entire chest and made her want to cry.

"It's okay, little friend," Phoebe said, her voice gentle and soft. The kind of voice she'd used with Lena the first time she caught her crying after Tucker Thompson and his buddies made fun of her stutter. It was not the voice she'd used with Tucker. "We're going to get you out of there. But first, I need you to promise not to run away. Otherwise, your paw will get infected and you could get awful sick."

Slowly, with her hands held in such a way so the animal could see every movement, Phoebe pried open the trap. The rabbit didn't hop away. It stayed in place. Phoebe picked it up and cradled it in her arms. She kissed it softly on the head, closed her eyes, and began to sing. It was the softest, most beautiful song Lena had ever heard. The kind that turned all the sadness in her chest into something hopeful.

Overhead, the leaves began to rustle.

Branches began to sway.

A rush of warmth enveloped Lena, so noticeable she gasped. And when she looked down at her friend, she saw that the rabbit's paw was no longer broken or bleeding. But completely healed.

Phoebe set it on the ground.

Its nose twitched.

Once.

Twice.

A third time.

Then it hopped away, disappearing into a bush.

Phoebe stood and dusted off her hands. Her face was pale. Her eyes, cloudy. This was the first time Lena had seen Magic take any toll on her friend. But then, this was the first time she'd seen her friend do anything so powerful.

"A-a-are you okay?" Lena asked.

Phoebe smiled a tired smile, and together, the two girls left the forest, the pact of their sisterhood wrapped around their wrists, a resoluteness solidifying in Lena's eight-year old heart. She wasn't sure about Magic. But she was sure about Phoebe. Her friend wasn't dangerous. No matter what her parents said, no matter what anyone would ever say, she knew this to be true. Phoebe was too good—too filled with light and happiness—to be anything other than perfectly safe.

CHAPTER 1

BRIAR

"I hate them."

The words escaped between clenched teeth in a cloud of hazy white. They belonged to one Briar Bishop, a golden-eyed, raven-haired, seventeen-year-old girl who hated a great many things. Parox, for starters, and the devastation the illness wrought on innocent lives. The commonwealth's nobility, and the blind eye it turned to so much suffering. Guillotine Square, and the executions that took place there every Red Moon. Magic, and the havoc it brought upon her family. And the Illustrians. The nauseating Illustrians, to whom her hatred was currently directed. She watched with slitted eyes as a group of them made their way through The Skid—finely-dressed as always, sticking out like peacocks in a flock of sparrows.

They came on any day of the week, but Nuach seemed

to be the most popular. Extra aggravating as that particular day was already overcrowded, which was probably why the Illustrians preferred visiting on Nuach. The Skid's inhabitants weren't scattered throughout the capital city of Antis working laboriously, but condensed and on full display—hanging laundry out to dry, bargaining for food with the peddlers who sold vegetables and dried fish and butchered meat, hauling bags of water from a well north of the railroad tracks—while the Illustrians filtered through in tightly-knit groups, led by a tour guide, flanked by a constable. They gawked and they gaped and they pointed, capturing bits and pieces with their sleek technology like sightseers at a menagerie, wrinkling their noses anytime a breeze swept up the slum's main artery and stirred up the trademark scent of raw sewage. It was a scent Briar no longer noticed. The Illustrians, however? She never failed to notice them, no matter how commonplace they had become.

"I wouldn't mind being one of them," Lyric said.

This was Briar's brother. At thirteen, Lyric was growing like pulled taffy with never enough food to feed him. Like his sister, he had black hair and golden eyes. Unlike his sister, he didn't hate the Illustrians; he envied them. Sometimes Briar suspected he admired them. A fact that made her stomach twist into a knot. There was so much Lyric didn't understand. And a significant amount he didn't know.

Overhead and to the east, the morning sun stretched across the rooftops of shanties so squished together that from above, they resembled a patchwork quilt of rusty browns. The light extended to meet the very edge of one rooftop in particular—Rosco's booth.

Briar hated Rosco's booth.

At the moment, Briar also *needed* Rosco's booth.

A moral quandary she had faced too many times in her young life. A moral quandary that had her wrinkling her nose more aggressively than the despicable Illustrians.

The breeze returned, tugging a strand of hair from her braid. It caught in the corner of her mouth. She pulled it away and tucked it behind her ear with the hand she hid inside a black, fingerless glove. Two men on a motorized scooter zoomed past—calling out a curse as they went—swerving so close they practically ran over Lyric's boots. Briar grabbed her brother by the elbow and yanked him back, nearly tumbling over the vendor behind them.

"Oi!" the proprietor shouted. "Watch where you're going, would you?"

She steadied herself, straightened her well-worn parka, and with a lift of her chin, wove her way through the crowded thoroughfare toward the booth she hated. An outbreak of Parox was spreading through The Skid like wildfire, polluting the nights with a violent chorus of wheezing and hacking that left without treatment, almost always concluded in death by asphyxiation. Their neighbor—Mrs. Simmons, a woman who had been like a grandmother to them these past couple years had fallen victim. Recently, she'd grown so weak she couldn't go into work—a death sentence in and of itself. The herbal remedies found at local apothecary stalls would no longer do. Mrs. Simmons needed an antibiotic. Those were not sold in places like The Skid. Nobody could afford them.

Unless …

It was Lyric's *unless*, spoken with raised eyebrows as he wiggled the rolled-up parchment in the air. Last month, Rosco had given her brother the parchment, as well as a set of oils, and ever since, a pile of bright paintings had been accumulating on their rickety-table-for-two, as out of place as the Illustrians.

A generous gift, Lyric had said.

More like a strategic temptation, Briar had thought.

"When will that brother of yours quit breaking his back at the Docks and join me here?" It was the same question Rosco had been asking ever since he caught Lyric spray-painting the side of a broken-down taxi van with his friend, Jet. And while it was true—her brother did have a gift—he would not be an apprentice to a drunkard. Nor would he build his livelihood on the very people so happy to exploit them. This was the bigger issue in Briar's mind. The one she couldn't stomach. Every day, Rosco laughed with the Illustrians. Rosco posed for their insulting pictures. Then he took their money with his greasy hands, encouraging the exploitation, for the Illustrians could leave The Skid pleased with themselves for supporting local business.

More like lining the pockets of a local sot.

And yet here Briar was, stepping inside Rosco's booth, ready to hand over one of Lyric's paintings. She could smell the alcohol on Rosco even now, well before noon. Not only did he accept money from the Illustrians, he proved to each one that their tightly held prejudices were true. People like them—ciphers all throughout the commonwealth of Korah—were depraved degenerates. Any destitution they faced lay on their shoulders and their shoulders alone. That one whiff of alcohol negated centuries' worth of injustice and oppression.

As soon as Rosco turned around and saw them standing there with the painting in hand, his jaundiced eyes went bright. "Are my sights deceiving me?"

Lyric smiled his lopsided smile. "We finally broke her down, Rosc."

Briar shot him a dark look. He might be half a foot taller, but she was and would always be four years older, and for all intents and purposes, more of a mother than a sister, given the fact that she'd raised him these past ten years. "It's one painting, Lyric. Just one. For Mrs. Simmons."

"I hear she's sick with the cough." Rosco took the painting. This one, a dreamlike cottage nestled in the woods with beams of ethereal sunlight dappling through the trees. It was a scene Lyric had never laid his eyes upon. A creation in his mind, inspired from the stories he charmed Briar into telling. Stories she hardly remembered herself. And yet somehow, her little brother brought the vague memories to life with such astounding clarity, she had a hard time looking at them. Rosco held the parchment flat between his outstretched hands. "If it's medicine you're wanting, this will more than get it for her."

"How soon do you think it will sell?" Lyric asked, an unmistakable note of excitement in his voice.

"If I was a betting man, and I am—" He shot them a wink. "Before the end of the day, I'd wager."

Lyric went taller, prouder beside her.

Briar nodded matter-of-factly. "We'll be back later, then."

"He's welcome to stay if he'd like."

"And pose for pictures with the Illustrians? No thank you." She took Lyric by the arm and pulled him from the booth, out into the crowd.

"Why can't I stay?" he protested as she drew him along.

"Why do you think Rosco fills his belly with rotgut every night after he closes?"

"It's a cheap way to fill his belly?"

"To dull his conscience. He knows what he's doing is wrong."

"Wrong? According to who—Briar the Judge?"

Briar rounded on him. "I'm no judge, Lyric." She slid a glance at the constable on the corner, then stepped closer and lowered her voice. "It's called having standards. And dignity. Rosco has neither."

"Rosco is harmless."

Briar closed her eyes. Rosco wasn't harmless. Rosco was part of the problem. And now, so were they. Just like they'd been before. And yet, Mrs. Simmons needed that antibiotic. With a sigh, she gave her shoulders a weary lift. She was in no mood for a debate. "I'll go back before sundown. If Rosco is right, then I might be able to get the medicine before curfew."

They walked the rest of the way in silence, Lyric brooding, Briar lost in thought. So much so that when she pushed through the corrugated metal door of their shanty, she didn't notice the strange and mysterious envelope on the dirt floor. Lyric tromped over the threshold, the sole of his boot leaving a dusty print on its gold lettering. He plopped down on their tattered sofa, its springs squeaking in protest, and began fiddling with their crank receiver—turning the lever, fiddling with the wires—until the fuzzy squawks gave way to a program with decent reception. On the table, the oils and parchment sat beside a pile of artwork so vivid and beautiful, it pinched at something deep inside Briar's chest. Her brother was a talented artist. There was no denying it. But what was the point of such a gift here, in this place that demanded practicality?

"This becomes the latest in a string of death defying stunts, leaving the world to wonder—is this a cry for help, or is Prince Leo simply sowing his wild oats?"

Briar's ears perked.

The program host was talking about the High Prince. She'd seen footage of him yesterday, projected on a holographic simulcast near Guillotine Square on her commute home from the Docks. She could still picture him—tall and broad, dark-haired and blue-eyed, arms spread wide as he soared like an eagle in full dive down the face of a cliff with a wing-like contraption strapped to his back. Briar's stomach had swooped at the sight.

"That's right, Ed. Old wounds are hard to heal. Which leads to another question on everyone's mind. Will the High Prince be in attendance at today's executions? He hasn't set foot inside the Square since his mother's murderer was brought to swift justice ten years ago—"

"Turn it off." Briar's voice whipped across the room like a snapped bowstring.

"But it's the prince," Lyric said. "You *looove* the prince. Or you hate him. I can never tell."

She marched over, grabbed the receiver, and twisted the dial herself, Lyric's teasing words echoing in the sudden silence.

"What'd you do that for?" he asked.

Briar didn't answer. Her voice was stuck in her throat, trapped behind a rising tide of memories every bit as confusing now as they ever were.

A darkening sky.

Swirling clouds.

Mama's fury.

Papa yelling at her to run.

"Briar?"

She opened her eyes, unsure when she'd closed them.

Lyric stood in front of her, his hand on her shoulder, concern tugging down the corners of his mouth. "You okay?"

"I'm fine, I just ..." She blinked several times, her gloved hand curling around the locket resting in the dip of her clavicle. At times, she wanted to rip it off. Throw it away. But it was the last thing she had of her parents and taking it off might mean forgetting. And if she forgot, the monster that got her mother might get her, too. Briar couldn't let that happen. She turned to the sink—a metal basin perched on top of a wooden barrel. "People's heads are being loped off on national simulcast and *this* is what the media cares about—whether or not the High Prince will be in attendance?"

She poured lukewarm water from a large pitcher into the basin and began scrubbing a tin cup with hands that trembled. "Excuse me for not having the stomach for it."

What she said was true enough.

"What's this?" Lyric asked, moving to the entryway. He scooped something up from the ground—the strange and mysterious envelope. Sunlight from one of their small windows reflected off the gold, looping cursive beneath the dust of Lyric's boot print. *To Miss Briar Bishop.* "I didn't think couriers came to The Skid."

"They don't," Briar said, taking the odd delivery from her brother.

She turned it over to a wax seal stamped with the letter W. She sliced it open and pulled out the most peculiar parchment she had ever seen. Stiff, like a hardy card stock, but smoother than silk against her fingertips, and iridescent, like it couldn't decide on one color and so chose to display a dazzling array of them. There were words in the same looping cursive as her name. The same color, too, as if they'd been stitched with golden thread.

The Honor of Your Presence is Requested

In the Capital City of Antis

On the Fifteenth Day of the Third Month.

Please Arrive Ten Minutes Before the Bell Tolls Midnight

Outside the Gates of the Squire Estate.

"The Squire Estate?" Lyric said, reading the words over her shoulder.

Lyric never had a formal education. Ciphers typically didn't. But Briar's father taught her to read when she was very young. She had done her best to pass that knowledge along. She and her brother saw the Squire Estate every day when they worked at the Docks. It had been boarded up and closed to the public for longer than she'd been alive. Curious, she turned the invitation over and found three lines, followed by a signature so absurd, she laughed.

There is something you want.

A wish you would die for.

Come and see how it might be granted.

"Sincerely, the Wish Keeper," Lyric read, his voice brimming with the same excitement he'd used inside Rosco's booth.

Briar rolled her eyes. "This isn't real."

"How do you know?"

"Because the Wish Keeper doesn't exist." It was nothing more than legend. There wasn't actually a person out there somewhere in Korah, collecting and granting wishes. The whole thing was made-up, a story passed from parents to children, one she foolishly believed once upon a time. One that was as *harmless* as Rosco, only instead of perpetuating stereotypes and feeding oppression, it spread false hope and disillusionment.

"Lots of people believe otherwise."

"Just because lots of people believe in something doesn't make it true." She tossed the invitation on the table next to Lyric's paintings.

"You have to go," he said.

"No, I don't."

Her brother looked incredulous.

"I'm sure it's a prank, Lyric."

"Who would play a prank on us?"

"I don't know—Jet?"

"Jet would play a prank on *me*, not you. And he wouldn't have the patience to wait a month and a half to see if we'd fall for it. Besides, he doesn't have anything so fancy to play a prank with. Nobody we know does." Lyric ran his fingertips across the curious, and no doubt *fancy* parchment with such a sense of wonder, it made her chest pinch in the same way his paintings did. "You really don't want to find out if it's real?"

"If it's real, it's wrong."

Lyric scoffed. "You're telling me there's *nothing* you want?"

"Of course there are things I want." Almost more than the things she hated. "An ethical King, for starters. A better life for everyone stuck here in The Skid. Dignity for our people. Fair wages, equal access to education, affordable medicine—"

"Is that all?" he asked, quirking his eyebrow.

"I want those things, little brother of mine. But they're never going to happen." Certainly not from any wish she might make. Briar learned long ago that her wishes fell on deaf ears. She couldn't change the world, but she *could* take care of Lyric. That was her duty.

"As long as people keep thinking that way, it never will."

She turned back to the sink, away from her brother's disappointment, her brother's words—and the aching way they made her think of their father—while Mrs. Simmons' hacking cough pierced the walls from next door.

CHAPTER 2
LEO

Leo Davenbrook was tempted to jump. Strip naked and dive right off the cliff into the crashing sea below. Let the meddlesome media document *that* for the public. He knew they were out there, lurking in the distance with their cutting-edge equipment, eager to turn a profit on the images they captured. He could shake his bodyguards, but he could never shake them. They always managed to find him. As far back as Leo could remember. No matter the circumstance. No matter the situation. There they were, exploiting every piece of his life for the public's eager consumption. As if he were nothing more than a collection of atoms that existed for the sole purpose of fetishizing, idolizing, critiquing. Sometimes, Leo believed it. Sometimes, he only remembered he was real when adrenaline coursed through his veins. This jump would make him feel real.

He leaned forward, staring down the cliff's craggy face as the wind tousled his dark hair. He doubted anyone would live to boast about the thrill. Assuming the jumper could survive the sheer height, they would still have to contend with the rocks at the bottom. And there were plenty of those.

A chirp sounded behind him—an aggravation that tempted Leo all the more.

The royal stewards were summoning him via his cousin's vox.

Leo had long since slipped his own off and tucked it away.

"You are so dead." A thrill of excitement shaped Hawk's words. Leo's rebellion never ceased to amuse him. "So am I if I don't answer."

Death was inevitable, then. For him and his cousin. He'd rather meet it in a thrilling jump than at the hands of his father.

"Leo."

His name came like a croon poured softly into his ear. He turned and pulled back his chin, surprised by Sabrina's presence beside him. Her face swam in his vision, doubling as her hair danced in the wind. His lips turned up at the corners—a lazy, inebriated grin. "Sweet, sanguine Sabrina."

The s's felt funny on his tongue. He found himself elongating them.

"Sanguine is a fancy word to use when you're drunk. Now come on. Let's get you away from here."

"I could make it, you know. This jump." He leaned forward, calculating the exact place he'd have to land.

"I'm sure you think you can." Sabrina took his hand.

If the tabloids captured this, they'd love her more than they already did.

"I should marry you right now. Give the people what they want. I think even my dad would approve." Which spoke highly of Sabrina's likability. Leo's dad *never* approved. At least not when it came to Leo.

"Your wife should be someone you can kiss."

"We've kissed."

"Once, and I believe your exact words were 'this feels incestuous'."

Leo sighed. Unfortunately, it had. Perhaps because the two of them had been running around together in diapers, when her grandfather acted as senior chamberlain to his. His attention slid down her backside as she led him away from the drop. "Sightly, sublime Sabrina. Keeping me alive since we were kids."

"It's been a full time job. One nobody else is bothering to help me with." She pointed her words at Hawk.

"He doesn't care if I die," Leo said.

"Of course he does."

Leo snorted. If he died, Hawk would be that much closer to taking the throne. He'd just have to eliminate his own father and his older brother and he'd officially be next in line. While such a fate had become a millstone around Leo's neck, it was a tasty morsel to Hawk, one that made him salivate. Sabrina sat Leo in the grass beside his cousin, a safe distance away from the drop. Hawk cradled a bottle in his lap.

His vox blinked in the dark and began chirping again.

"Turn it off before I throw it into the sea!" Leo clamped his mouth shut and looked sideways at nobody in particular. He was fairly certain he slurred the words, which meant he'd gone too far—bypassing the pleasant buzz of tipsiness and plummeting into inebriated misery. According to Sabrina, he brooded when he was drunk.

"If the sightly, sublime Sabrina really wanted to keep you alive," Hawk said, "she should have made sure you went to Guillotine Square."

The alcohol in Leo's gut soured.

"I don't understand why you didn't just go."

The very idea of Guillotine Square slicked his palms with sweat, stirring up memories he didn't want stirred. Dark, viscous sea monsters lurking in the deep. He grabbed Hawk's bottle and took a long drink.

"There are far less tedious duties," Hawk pressed. "At least the executions are somewhat entertaining. You should start picking your battles. Stop poking an angry bear over ciphers."

His cousin's callous words made Leo want to stand

back up and sprint headlong off the cliff. Sometimes he didn't understand how they were related. But then, Leo was related to his father. "My mother was a cipher."

"Your mother was murdered by a cipher."

Leo frowned. She was. But she'd been one, too. A long time ago. He stared at the horizon, beyond Jethro Bay where the Afrean Sea stretched from east to west. "She was born out there, you know."

He could feel Sabrina looking at him.

Of course she knew.

So did Hawk.

His mother had been born on the Forbidden Isle formerly known as Cambria. The disaster had killed her parents and forced her to evacuate when she was seventeen. Somehow, the destruction of her homeland made her that much more unreachable. As if the chasm of death could be widened by his inability to visit the place that knew her first.

Sabrina sat beside him and wrapped her arms around her knees. "I heard there were—Are there really—" She pulled a face, like she wasn't exactly sure how to ask the question. "*Creatures* there?"

"Radioactive mutants." Hawk wiggled his fingers and widened his eyes. They sparkled deviously. "My brother used to tell me they were attracted to the scent of urine, and if I didn't stop wetting the bed, they would swim across the sea and gobble me up in my sleep."

Sabrina shuddered. "That's horrible."

"It worked, though. I never wet the bed again."

"And never slept again, either." Leo finished the remains inside Hawk's bottle, then drew back his arm and whipped it into the great abyss.

"They can't really just ... swim across the sea, can they?"

Silly, solicitous Sabrina.

The Forbidden Isle was home to the Domed City, once a fortress city. A military city. With a wall surrounding it. The epicenter of the disaster. As soon as it was evacuated, first responders erected a dome to keep the contamination within. "If there are mutants, they'll be stuck inside until they die."

"*If* they die."

Leo jabbed his cousin with his elbow as the sound of footsteps approached behind, falling in perfect unison. Leo swore under his breath. His father had used Hawk's vox to track them down, and judging by the number of footsteps, he'd sent an entire detachment to apprehend him.

An hour later, Leo was home—his mood black, his head splitting.

The grand atrium was still and quiet, but not unoccupied. Uniformed guards stood at attention inside like they did everywhere throughout the palace—as still as statues with their eyes trained straight ahead. It was as if they weren't real.

It was as if they were him. A fresh throb of pain stopped him in his tracks. He winced. The problem with drinking was, the distraction never lasted. And he always paid for it later.

Tenfold.

The soft sound of footfalls captured his ear.

He glanced over his shoulder at a young maidservant. She jerked to an awkward stop and fell into a curtsy, the gold shackle on her wrist shiny and new. A slave, just like every other servant inside the castle. Judging by the slightness of her build and the tremble in her shoulders, she was a young and terrified one.

Leo waited, curious if she'd speak.

Apparently, she needed some prompting.

"May I help you?"

The girl's cheeks went from pink to pale. She started and stammered. Curtsied a second time. Then finally found her voice. "I apologize, Your Highness. I came to see how I might serve *you*."

Her accent was born far away from the capital city of Antis, from the whole province of Mirum. By the way she rounded her vowels and shortened each R, she came from somewhere north. "You're new."

"Yes, Your Highness."

"What is your name?"

She blinked at him, looking as though he'd just asked her to explain a complicated math equation.

"It's not a trap. I'm simply inquiring after your name." It was, of course, a misleading statement. There was nothing simple about inquiring after a slave's name. As soon as they sold themselves, they were stripped of their names, stripped of their identities, stripped of their fealties. As if doing so would also strip them of their ability to think for themselves, and thus eliminate any threat that might otherwise gather in secret. Like it had once before. A fact Leo would be wise to remember.

The girl's attention slid to the nearest guard. "Nothing of significance, my Lord."

"That's a long sort of name, isn't it?"

A blush rose in her cheeks.

"If I'm any connoisseur of accents, then I'd say you're from ..." He waffled between two options, then settled on the province further north. "Bahar?"

Her head came up quickly, her eyes bright with surprise.

He'd guessed correctly. Before he could say so, the far doors to the atrium swung open. His father entered sans his usual entourage. His staccato footsteps echoed in the large chamber, his face a mask of cold, contained fury.

The poor girl shoved her hand into the air. "Izar!" she choked.

His father frowned, then asked her to leave in a voice so low and ominous, she couldn't scuttle away fast enough.

When she was gone, the High King turned his ire upon his son. "Flirting with the slaves again, I see."

"If flirting is being kind, then yes, Father. I guess I am."

The king closed the gap between them in two long strides. He reached into the front pocket of Leo's coat and yanked out the small circular band hidden inside. Leo's vox. "So you *do* still own one."

"I forgot to turn it on."

"The public expected you at the executions today. Instead, they will no doubt see footage of you carousing on the cliffs with your foolish cousin."

"We were still celebrating my birthday. I'm sure the public will understand."

"The public will speculate."

"Then let them speculate."

Quicker than a viper, his father struck. He grabbed Leo by the collar of his coat and shoved him against the wall, his face thrust so close, Leo could see the vein throbbing in his temple. Only he did not yell. He never yelled. His voice came out eerily calm while rage swirled in his frosty blue eyes. "If the public thinks I cannot control my own son, then what is to stop them from thinking I cannot control *them*?"

Leo clenched his teeth, nose-to-nose with the man who was no longer taller.

"I have been more than indulgent. But here it ends. You're eighteen now, which means playtime is over. You will be at the next execution, even if I have to drag you there myself. Is that understood?"

Leo held his tongue.

His father pulled him forward and slammed him against the wall. So hard, spots of light danced in the periphery of his vision. "I said *is ... that ... understood*?"

"Yes, *my lord*," Leo replied, gritting the words between his teeth.

"Good. Now clean yourself up and meet me in the Chamber of Lords in one hour." His father let go, returned the vox to Leo's front pocket, and swept out of the room, leaving his son alone with the unmoving guards. Would they have stepped in if the king's rage got the best of him? Or would they have stood there like statues watching while it happened?

Leo turned in the opposite direction and strode toward the east wing. When he reached his chambers, he flung open the doors and slammed them shut. He marched to his dressing table and in a surge of frustration, swept his arm across the surface, sending an array of items crashing to the floor. He spread his hands wide against the cool marble and looked at his reflection in the gilded mirror.

His hair was a windswept mess. Stubble shadowed his jaw. The thirty-six hour birthday binge had purpled the skin beneath his eyes, making the blue of his irises all the bluer. He'd reached his father's height of six foot two. His shoulders and chest—once skinny in youth—had grown broad with muscle. He had—the public liked to say—the face and physique of a god.

He glared at the glass, searching for a trace of *her*.

But after ten years, her face was growing increasingly difficult to recall.

All Leo saw was *him*.

A cold and heartless king.

He yanked at the collar of his shirt, pulling it down to reveal the mark above his heart. The Davenbrook family crest—the national symbol of Korah—every bit as neat and distinct as it ever was. Even after eighteen years of growth, the scar remained unaltered. The law forbid Magic, and yet here it was. Etched on Leo's chest. There was no stretching it. No distorting it. No changing it. A perfect picture of his destiny. The reason he was here and his mother was dead. This scar that trapped her. Trapped him. Bound his life to the throne. Anger swelled like waves. He dragged his hand down his face, then noticed something in the mirror's reflection. Something that didn't belong.

An envelope lay in front of his door.

He turned around. Mail wasn't surreptitiously slipped under the doors of private chambers. Not official mail anyway. This certainly looked official. Moving closer, he found his name written in golden script sans his royal title. It said simply *To Mr. Leopold Davenbrook*. A traitorous act, if he cared. He slid his finger beneath the seal and broke it, then pulled out the card inside which shimmered as it caught the light.

There is something you want.

A wish you would die for.

Come and see how it might be granted.

CHAPTER 3

BRIAR

Rosco wagered wrong. When Briar returned later that evening, the painting had not sold.

Nor did it sell the next day.

On the third day, Lyric and his friend, Jet, left for a short-term gig at an oil rig out in the countryside. It was labor-intensive work. Hard to reach, too. Ciphers weren't allowed to travel underground. That was a perk reserved only for Illustrians. And getting anywhere outside of the capital city of Antis via public transport required time and money and more than a bit of luck. So Lyric decided to stay out in the countryside. It was the longest stretch of time he and Briar had ever been apart. But it paid better than their work at the Docks, and getting that medicine for Mrs. Simmons grew increasingly paramount, for the coughing stole her life by the hour. Which was why, after a long and grueling shift at the Docks, Briar returned for the fifth day in a row to Rosco's booth.

Despite the sinking sun and the commonly held fear amongst Illustrians about The Skid at night, the booth wasn't empty. Rosco had a customer. A spindly, well-dressed gentleman with a carefully manicured goatee stood inside examining her brother's painting.

"He's had no formal training?" she heard the man ask.

To which Rosco responded with a bark of laughter that quickly turned into a fit of coughing. He pounded his chest like a violent thwack might clear his lungs.

The man leaned away with pinched lips.

Parox, Briar thought with a sinking heart. As much as she disagreed with Rosco, she didn't wish him ill; she didn't want him to die.

"Sorry 'bout that," Rosco said, wiping his lips dry with a dirtied handkerchief. He spotted Briar in the booth's entrance and gave his hands a clap. "Well, if this isn't happy timing! Sir Wellington Ferris, this is Briar, the artist's guardian. Briar, this is Sir Wellington. He's a curator visiting from Petram."

"An extremely wealthy, influential curator." Sir Wellington clasped his hands behind his back, his posture stiff, his mouth pursed as his attention flicked from the crown of Briar's shabby woolen cap to the soles of her muddy boots.

The feeling is mutual, she thought. Briar swallowed the acrimonious words and said instead in a voice as bland as porridge, "You've come a long way."

It was an understatement. Petram was the northernmost province of Korah—thousands of miles from the city of Antis, which sat on the southern coast. For someone who'd only been as far as Silva—and those memories were so long ago Lyric had to paint them to make them real—Petram might as well have been a made-up land from a story book.

Rosco tucked his dirty handkerchief into his back pocket. "Sir Wellington is interested in your brother's painting."

"I'm interested in more, actually."

"What do you mean?" Briar asked.

"I haven't seen artwork of this caliber in a very long time." The man's attention returned to Lyric's art and the purse in his lips smoothed away. "I'm interested in sponsoring him."

"For?"

"*L'Eclat Ecole D'Art*."

She exchanged a confused glance with Rosco.

"It's an art school in the city of Hillandale," Sir Wellington said. "The most prestigious in all of Korah. All the greats—both contemporary and of old—have trained there."

"Hillandale is in Petram."

The man raised his eyebrows as if to ask her point.

"My brother and I can't move to Petram."

"I'm not inviting *you*. *L'Eclat Ecole D'Art* is a boarding school."

"Filled with Illustrians, no doubt."

"Of course." He gave her an odd look, like he didn't understand what to make of her comment, or the tone in which she delivered it. "There will be skepticism at first. That's to be expected. *L'Eclat Ecole D'Art* is not accustomed to opening its doors to riffraff. But once they see your brother's gift, I am certain the board will more than come around. In fact, I am certain that between his raw talent, the school's prestigious training, and my influence, his artwork will hang in every Illustrian home across the commonwealth. Even Castle Davenbrook."

Rosco made a funny sound—something between a hiccup and a yelp.

"As his sponsor, I will cover the full cost of tuition, provide room and board on holidays, teach him proper etiquette, introduce him to all of the right people. For a mere ... " He twiddled his long fingers in the air like a spider wrapping up its prey. "Sixty percent royalty on all artwork sold herewith. I realize it's a generous offer. A risky investment, if you will. But it's one I'm willing to take."

The air had gone stagnant in Rosco's booth. This man.

This man wanted to spirit her brother thousands of miles away. He wanted to take Lyric from her, send him to a school filled with rich, entitled brats whose families lived in shameful excess. He wanted to bring Lyric into his home—this prideful, arrogant man—and teach her brother *etiquette*, which might as well be code for snobbery and disdain. Even if there weren't other issues to consider —issues that made Sir Wellington's offer impossible to accept—Briar could never allow this man—this haughty, peacock-feathered man—to turn her brother into such a tool.

One who had *risen above* the conditions he was born into, and if he could do it, then so could anyone else. But it was a lie. One that perpetuated their oppression and comforted their oppressors. There was no rising above, not unless one possessed a talent that could make an Illustrian money. Sir Wellington Ferris didn't care about Lyric. He cared about the profit he could make off of Lyric, and yet he looked at her now as if fully expecting her to fall over herself with gratitude.

"You don't look pleased," he said.

"We just want to sell his painting."

"And I am offering you more. What fool goes looking for an apple only to complain when he happens upon an entire tree of them?"

Briar's blood boiled. His tree was rotten.

"Why don't you speak with your brother. See what *he*

wants. If I were you, I'd be in touch sooner rather than later. You never know when an opportunity will be lost." Sir Wellington removed a small card from his pocket, jotted an address on the back with a silver pen, and handed the card to her. "I'm staying in Antis through the week. This is where you can find me."

He turned to leave.

"Wait!" Briar took a lurching step forward.

Sir Wellington stopped.

"Aren't you going to buy his painting?"

"I don't want the painting, girl. Not without the artist."

She watched him go, his card in her hand while Rosco danced a jig, then fell into another round of coughing.

Briar ground her teeth. "You told me you would sell his painting."

"I'd say we did more than that."

"We need money, Rosco. Not business cards."

He drew back like a man gobsmacked.

"From now on, keep our names out of it. Just sell the painting." Before the shock could let go of the old man, before he could spread anymore of his germs with that cough, Briar turned on her heel and left his booth.

It had started to rain. A drizzle at first that thickened into cold, fat drops that soaked through her parka. She ran the rest of the way and as she slipped inside her front door, the clouds unleashed completely. Warfare on the tin roof.

She shuddered, then got to work setting out buckets in

the usual places where the water leaked through. When she finished, she went to the wood stove and started a fire. She took off her woolen mittens. She rubbed her hands together in front of the flames, hoping to thaw her fingers. Instead, she found herself staring at the back of her left hand—at the scar tissue that pulled and puckered and pinched her skin into a swirl of deformity. With a knot in her throat, she shoved her hand into her black glove and pulled out the card from her pocket.

Sir Wellington J. Ferris

Hillandale Art Museum

Senior Curator

Briar shook her head. She had worked so hard—so incredibly hard—to get herself and Lyric to a place of stability. They had a roof over their heads and food—albeit never enough—in their bellies, which was more than most in The Skid. She had done everything possible to ensure that she and her brother would no longer have to steal to survive or depend on exploitative men like Sir Wellington Ferris. They were doing fine, too. Until Parox struck Mrs. Simmons. Proving that poverty was merciless. Stability, a soap bubble.

The door swung open behind her, sending Briar's heart into a series of jarring backflips. She spun around, ready to lunge at the bold intruder, but found Lyric instead. He stepped all the way inside, shaking rain from his hair like a wet dog.

"You're home," she said, her palm flat against her chest. She wasn't expecting him until tomorrow evening.

"They made us work through some of the nights so we could finish before the weather rolled in." And he didn't look at all sad about it. In fact, he looked buoyant and carefree as he strolled to their makeshift sink and swept back the curtain Briar had hung beneath, behind which hid their savings.

"What's that?" he asked, nodding at her hand.

With a jolt, she tucked the business card into her pocket. "Nothing."

Lyric eyed her suspiciously.

She laughed nervously. "It's good to see you."

Smiling, he stepped forward and wrapped her in a hug, nearly lifting her off the ground. With a swell of emotion, she hugged him back, resting her head against his chest, relishing the steady beat of his heart, the smell of rain and something else that was undeniably *Lyric*, wishing they could stay this way forever—she and him against the world. She hadn't slept well while he was away. She liked him right here with her. But he was thirteen and not inclined to tolerate prolonged affection.

When he stepped away, his smile had turned devious. He wiggled something in his hand.

Briar's heart skipped a beat. "Give that back."

But Lyric was taller, and he held it straight up in the air, laughing as she swiped at it. "Why—is it a love note?" He opened the folded parchment above his head, then promptly brought it back down, revealing not Sir Wellington's business card, but the strange and mysterious invitation.

She exhaled—a swoosh of relief.

Lyric had gone for the wrong pocket.

Earlier this morning, for reasons Briar couldn't quite understand, she'd folded it up and taken it with her.

"Did you change your mind?" Lyric asked with a note of anticipation. "Are you gonna go?"

"Are you that eager for me to die?"

He rolled his eyes and sat down at one of the kitchen chairs, propping his wet boots on their table. "It doesn't say you're going to die. It just says that you have a wish you're willing to die for."

She plucked the invite from him. "And we've already established that I don't."

Lyric folded his hands behind his head. "I'd die to get out of here."

His declaration twisted like a knife in her gut. Lyric didn't have to die for that to happen. The wish was his to take, right there in her *other* pocket. *See what he wants*, Sir Wellington had said. Briar already knew. Lyric wanted out, and here was his ticket—one far worse than selling paintings in Rosco's booth. Worse than pandering to the Illustrians. Her brother would become one. And what if in such a transformation, someone found out who he was. There was a bounty on their heads—one he didn't even know about—and while it might have become a long-forgotten thing, it was still out there—a reality that set the level of her vigilance on a constant state of high alert. She pushed at Lyric's heavy boots. "Feet off the table. And for the love of all that is good and right, please stop taking things from people's pockets."

"You taught me how."

"Back when we needed it to survive. We don't anymore."

A dark cloud rolled across her brother's face. "Right. We're living in the lap of luxury."

As if to punctuate his sudden bout of bitter scorn, a sharp round of hacking wheezes filtered through the thin walls of their shanty.

He grimaced at the sound. "Did Rosco sell my painting?"

"Nnnot yet."

It wasn't a lie.

Not technically.

Lyric picked up the stack of parchment on the table—exquisite, arresting artwork—and huffed. "I guess I'm not as good as the old man thought."

Oh, but he was.

He was even better.

So good, in fact, his paintings could hang in Castle Davenbrook.

She wanted to take him by the arms and tell him so.

But he stood from his chair, grabbed a dry cap hanging by the wood stove, and shoved it over his head. "I'm going out."

"In the rain?"

"It stopped."

Oh. Right.

The warfare on the tin roof had gone silent. Water no longer dripped into the buckets. Briar worried her bottom lip. What if Lyric ran into Rosco? He would never keep Sir Wellington Ferris to himself. He would tell Lyric upon sight. But Rosco was always eager to close up his booth when the last of the Illustrians left. From what Briar could tell, Sir Wellington had been the last, which meant Rosco would be long gone by now, emptying his pockets for a fresh bottle of moonshine. "Where are you going?"

More wheezing and coughing sounded from next door.

"Somewhere quiet." Lyric stomped to the door.

"Wait!"

He stopped on the threshold.

Tell him, Briar.

Just tell him.

It was right there, on the tip of her tongue—the power to change her brother's mood back round again. But fear was there, too. It pulsed through her body like an electric shock. As soon as she told him, he would want to go. But he couldn't go. And he wouldn't understand why. So Briar bit back the words and said instead, "Make sure you're back by curfew."

He tossed her an acerbic salute, then slammed the door behind him.

CHAPTER 4

BRIAR

Briar paced from one bucket to the other while the time ticked closer to curfew. Over the past thirty minutes, she'd been operating under the assumption that at any second, Lyric would come home. He knew better than to break curfew. He knew they couldn't afford the fine, and if they couldn't pay the fine, much worse could happen. Surely, her brother wouldn't be so foolish.

But then, Lyric was thirteen.

The height of foolishness.

Briar shot another glance at the clock. If she left now, there remained a chance of finding him and bringing him home before official nightfall. She put on her woolen mittens, her coat that had dried by the wood stove, and stepped out into the encroaching darkness. If they had to work the next ten Nuachs because of her silly brother, she would never let him hear the end of it.

She stopped at Jet's first. Although if Lyric really did want to go somewhere quiet, it would be far from here, where the pandemonium was so loud, she could hear it ten shanties away.

Jet's mother answered with a red-faced, wailing infant in one arm and a thrashing toddler in the other. Behind her—in a home no bigger than Briar's—three young boys wrestled, a mad scramble of sharp elbows and knobby knees. Jet was the oldest of six, all of them boys and all of them gaunt with malnourishment. His mother could barely feed one child, let alone half a dozen. And yet, she kept having them. None of whom came by the same father. Like too many women in The Skid, Jet's mother sold herself in order to feed her children, and in so doing, had more children in need of feeding. And around and round the cycle went.

"Yeah?" she hollered above the din.

"I'm looking for Lyric."

One of the three boys came tearing past. His mother—having lost her grip on the squirming toddler—snagged him by the ear and yanked him to such a sudden stop, he let out a howl five times louder than the baby's. "Oi, you. Where'd your brother and that friend of his run off to?"

He clawed at his mother's hand. "They ain't never tell me nothing!"

She let go.

The boy clutched his poor ear and darted away.

"No help, I'm afraid. But if you find Jet," she said, her bushy eyebrows set in a severe line. "Tell him to get his hide home before I tan it from here to Duggleby."

Briar nodded and hurried off, trying to guess where Lyric might have gone. The train yard? Rosco's booth? She made her way toward The Skid's main thoroughfare. Shops were closing or already closed. The streets were practically empty. All was quiet. Almost eerily so. Until an echoing, guttural sound punctuated the air.

Briar stopped.

The sound came again, more distinct.

It was—she realized—a human sound. A loud, agonizing grunt. Like someone getting every last ounce of breath knocked right out of them.

She started moving again, faster this time, and found a crowd gathering around the bend in the road. There was a sickening thud. Another pain-soaked *oomph*. Briar ran toward the commotion only to be stopped by Jet on the edge of the gathering—his thin face twisted in horror.

"It's Lyric," he said. "He's being arrested!"

Briar's heart slammed into her throat. She shoved through the mass of people, all of them watching in horrified, helpless silence as a constable beat her bloodied brother with his baton. She rushed out into the open space and grabbed the man's thick arm, but he brought it down with a backhand so violent, it lifted her off her feet and sent her sprawling into a puddle of muck and rainwater.

"Briar!" Lyric yelled, attempting to get to her, so zeroed in on his sister that he didn't notice the baton flying at his face.

It cracked against his cheekbone. His head whipped violently.

Briar screamed as his eyes rolled and he collapsed into an unconscious heap and the constable grabbed his arms and dragged him away.

She scrambled to her feet. But another constable blocked her, shoving her back down into the muck.

"Please," she cried, clambering to her knees. "Where are you taking him?"

"Same place we take all dirty, rotten thieves."

She shook her head, unwilling to hear it.

But the man said it anyway. "Shard."

He might as well have sucker punched her with his baton. Shard Prison was a death trap, a place plagued by diseases much deadlier than Parox. Lyric couldn't go there. He wouldn't survive. "He's only thirteen."

"A thief's a thief, no matter the age."

Briar tried to push past him, but he shoved her to the ground once again, his fingers wrapped around the handle of his baton, the badge on his chest glinting like sharpened incisors. Every constable wore one. Two stark M's, one large and upright, overlayed by another that was small and inverted. The symbol of Korah.

Eleos Partim Pentho Omnis.

Mercy for some. Misery for all.

Her stomach heaved.

Before she could get up and throw herself at this hateful man, Jet grabbed her left arm. Someone else grabbed her right. They dragged her away like the constable had dragged Lyric. Only she wasn't unconscious like her brother. She bucked and she kicked and she scratched, ten times wilder than all of Jet's brothers.

"Stop it now, lass." The voice belonged to Rosco. "Stop it before they arrest you, too."

"Let them arrest me!"

"What good will that do yer brother?"

It was the only question that could have calmed her.

Briar's body went still.

"If they arrest you, then yer both locked up for good."

The constable glared at the three of them, then pointed his ire at the crowd. "Get home if you know what's smart. Or we'll fine the lot of you!"

Onlookers scattered until all that remained was Rosco and Lyric's best friend.

Briar grabbed him by his emaciated shoulders. "What happened, Jet? What did he do?"

"He wouldn't stop going on about money. About there never being enough. About Mrs. Simmons needing medicine. But none of us have money. Ain't nobody here but the constables."

Briar closed her eyes.

No.

No, no, no.

Lyric couldn't have been so senseless.

So reckless.

Jet twisted his cap in his hands. "I tried talking him out of it. I swear, I tried. But he wouldn't listen."

Briar sank to her knees.

Her brother hadn't been caught stealing from just anybody. He'd been caught stealing from a government official. People went to Guillotine Square for much less than that.

CHAPTER 5

BRIAR

Briar pounded on the door, setting off a chorus of barking dogs up and down the lamp-lit street. She didn't care. She wouldn't stop. Not until somebody on the other side answered.

Lights flooded the first floor windows. A bolt turned. The door opened and a reedy, hawk-nosed woman appeared on the other side. Her gaze shifted from Briar to the dark night and back again. It was well beyond curfew. Briar had slunk and slithered past the constables until she reached the outskirts of The Skid, where the curfew ceased to apply. Then she ran. She ran so fast, she was huffing and puffing now, holding the stitch in her side as her breath escaped in clouds of white. She could only imagine how she looked, with one side of her body covered in mud from head to toe, her dark hair a mess and half-loose from its braid, her cheek swollen and bruised from the constable and his knuckles.

"What is the meaning of this?" the woman asked indignantly.

"Please, I need to speak with Sir Wellington Ferris. He gave me this address. He said he was staying here." Briar reached inside her pocket.

The lady pulled back, her face filled with alarm, like maybe Briar was reaching for a knife. When she pulled out a business card, the woman scrunched her beakish nose as if Briar held out a dead rat.

"Who is it?" a male voice called from inside.

"Some *street urchin* with your contact card."

Sir Wellington appeared over the woman's shoulder, taking in Briar's half-crazed appearance.

"What are you doing, giving out my address to people like this?" the woman demanded.

"Relax, dear cousin. This is the girl I was telling you about. The sister of the artist I discovered at that drunken man's booth today."

"The one in The Skid?"

"Please," Briar interrupted. "I need to speak with you."

"Come back in the morning," the woman said. "The audacity, coming here at such an hour. Doesn't The Skid have a curfew?" She began to shut the door.

Briar stopped it with her hand.

The woman gasped.

"He'll go to Petram!" she shouted. Sir Wellington could have his investment. He could have more than sixty percent, if he wished. The risk had grown into something small and insignificant compared to Shard. "He will attend your school."

The woman attempted to strongarm the door closed.

But Briar was stronger.

"It's okay, Verity," Sir Wellington said. "I will speak with the girl tonight."

"Not inside my house, you won't."

"I have no intention of inviting her in."

The woman sneered at Briar, then turned and left, muttering under her breath as she went.

Sir Wellington stepped outside. The door shut behind him. He stood in the front garden, studying Briar curiously beneath the glow of the streetlight. "Your brother will come with me to Petram?"

"Yes."

"And might I ask what led to the change of heart? Forgive me, but I got the distinct impression that you weren't very interested."

"I'm not. But Lyric will be. And right now he's—" She stopped, unsure whether to say it. Whether doing so would dig their grave. But she had to, didn't she? The whole reason she came was to get Lyric out of trouble, which meant she had to tell Sir Wellington that her brother was currently *in* it. "He requires your help."

She could see the shadow sliding down his face. The wariness, like shutters slowly closing.

"Our neighbor is sick. Deathly ill with Parox. My brother cares about her, Sir. He was simply trying to get money so he could purchase medicine."

Sir Wellington arched a carefully manicured eyebrow. "And how, exactly, did he go about getting this money?"

Briar hesitated.

His eyebrow lifted higher.

"He took it. Out of desperation. To keep someone alive."

She waited, watching for some trace of understanding. Some glimpse of compassion. She'd even take pity, as much as she hated it. But none of it came. His expression had gone cold and uncaring, not that he ever really cared to begin with. But even the spark of greed was gone.

"They took him to Shard. I'm sure if you went there, if a man like you could vouch for him—"

"I do not vouch for criminals."

"But—"

"And I can assure you, *L'Eclat Ecole D'Art* will not accept them either. I had hoped your brother was different. What a pity to see such talent go to waste." Without giving her time to argue, he stepped inside and slammed the door in Briar's face.

Eleos Partim Pentho Omnis.

Not even the promise of profit could override it.

~

The world was on fire.

She choked on the thick, black smoke curling from the flames.

She choked on the heat as she gripped her brother's hand, flesh melting off her own.

He flailed above the inferno, her ability to hold on his one and only hope.

She squeezed her eyes tight and screamed.

Somebody help me!

But there was nobody there.

It was just her and him and if she let go, he would die.

She couldn't hold on any longer.

The pain won.

She jerked back and watched as her brother clawed the air and fell toward the flames, his dilated eyes never leaving hers. Just like their father's when he yelled at her to run.

Briar jolted awake, sucking in a loud, long gasp.

She sat upright on the dilapidated couch, soaked in her own sweat, her lungs heaving as morning sunlight filtered inside the small window of their shanty. Somehow, she'd fallen asleep. She didn't think she would. She thought she would lay awake throughout the entirety of the night, plagued with thoughts of Lyric inside that prison as Mrs. Simmons coughed and wheezed next door. A dark, dank cell. A cold, stone floor. Huddled in the corner, alone and afraid with nothing to drink but dirty water ridden with bacteria.

She couldn't bear it.

She had to save him.

She couldn't fail him.

She clambered off the couch and stopped in front of the table piled with Lyric's paintings.

I guess I'm not as good as Rosco thought.

The memory of those words pierced her straight through. How could she have let him leave thinking they were true? His artwork wasn't just good. It was worthy of a palace. And she hadn't told him. He never would have left if she'd told him. He never would have done something so reckless and desperate. Her gloved hand tightened into a fist. She gritted her teeth and snatched up the pile of artwork.

With her cheek smarting and her hair still a mess, she squeezed inside one of the city's public taxi-vans. Graffitied vehicles so jam-packed with bodies, some commuters stood on the fenders, others hung out the doors. She took the taxi-van in the opposite direction of the way she usually went. She would lose her wages for missing work, but at the moment, none of that mattered. Nothing mattered but getting to Lyric.

She switched transportation in three different spots. Paid three different fares. And an hour later, stood outside the stone fence that hemmed in the menacing facility that was Shard Prison, with its high, windowless walls made of concrete. The wrought iron gate was manned by two members of the First Guard. Each of them brandished weapons alarming in size and eyed her distrustfully under tasseled hats.

She hated the way her insides quivered. She wanted to grind her fear into pulp and spit it on their polished boots. Instead, she pulled back her shoulders and told herself to stand straight. "I'm here to see Lyric. Lyric—" She stopped short. There were plenty of Bishops in Korah. It was a common enough surname but she made a habit of not giving hers out and had taught her brother to do the same.

The guards looked at each other, smirks tucked into the corners of their mouths like she'd been sent to entertain them.

"He was brought here last night. About this tall." She held her hand up above her head. "A boy. Only thirteen."

Unconscious.

Beaten to a pulp.

"Half a dozen reprobates were brought here last night," one of the guards said. "I don't know any of their names, heights, or ages. And none of them are allowed visitors."

She knew they would say this. She knew this was Shard's policy. She knew this was a fool's errand. And yet, she'd come anyway. With trembling hands, she unrolled the outer parchment from the bundle she'd haphazardly gathered. "Please. This is his artwork. An Illustrian curator from Petram said it's good enough to hang in every home across the commonwealth. Even Castle Davenbrook."

The two guards looked at her for a silent moment, then erupted in laughter.

Heat surged up her neck, but she kept going, pressing past the humiliation. "Eighty percent! You can have eighty percent of every piece sold. More, if you'd like."

Their cackling only grew louder. And Sir Wellington Ferris's words turned into a ghost that would haunt her forever.

You never know when an opportunity will be lost.

Yesterday, she couldn't bear the thought of Lyric going to Petram.

It was too dangerous.

She couldn't bear to lose him.

And now today ...

She would give anything to pack him up and see him off herself.

"Please. He's my brother." The only one she had left. "Please, just let me see him."

"Yeah, sure. You can see him."

Her body flooded with hope. It rushed up her legs. Tingled in her scalp. "Really?"

"At the next Red Moon," said one.

"In Guillotine Square," said the other.

Incinerating all hope.

Bile rose up her throat.

"Now get out of here, girl, before we throw you into a cell, too."

What if they did? Could she get to Lyric? Could she somehow find him inside, and together, could they escape? It was a ridiculous thought. Nobody escaped Shard. Not even the most skilled escape artists.

Briar wanted to scream. She wanted to pull out her hair and gnash her teeth. She wanted to grab the two guards by their fur-lined coats and make them listen. She would not lose her brother. Not when she'd already lost another. Her heart squeezed. She couldn't fail Lyric like she failed Echo. But the words were futile; the display of grief, a shout in the void. They didn't care. They didn't have to. To them, she was nothing more than a fly to swat. With her hands limp by her sides, Briar shuffled away, Echo's words taunting her from the grave.

I saw it happen, Briar. You're going to be the hero. You're going to save us all.

It had been nothing more than a pain-induced hallucination.

Bitter icing on a cruel cake.

She couldn't save Echo.

And now it seemed that she couldn't save Lyric either.

Halfway home, something slipped free from between two of the paintings. It drifted one way, then the other, and landed on the cement as she waited for the next taxi-van to arrive. She stared—bleary-eyed—at the gold lettering reflecting in the sunlight.

There is something you want.

A wish you would die for.

Come and see how it might be granted.

SPLIT IN TWO

YEAR OF KORAH: 488

LENA

The day that Phoebe and Lena looked forward to every year for as long as they could remember was finally upon them. Merivus Eve. Merivus itself was a national holiday, wherein all the shops would close and the High King would make a grand speech and pop open a bottle of sparkling wine and every citizen over the age of sixteen would lift a glass—even if that glass was filled with nothing but cheap hootch—and toast their forefathers, who had led them out of civil unrest into the dawn of a new era. One marked by peace and security.

Whether the new era was truly marked by such things mattered little to Phoebe and Lena. They simply cared that every Merivus Eve, the carnival came to town. The girls would ride the rides until they couldn't stand up straight and eat the food until their stomachs felt like they might explode and Lena always bought a whole bag of pulled taffy. This year's excitement landed on the fifth day of the week, which meant school first. And Phoebe was nowhere. Her desk remained empty all morning long as the teacher tried teaching a bunch of overstimulated, overexcited seventh years. Lena and Phoebe weren't the only ones who loved the carnival. Everyone did. Even Lena's parents, and they hardly got excited about anything.

But Phoebe wasn't at school. And at lunch, Lena heard Tucker Thompson saying things about her missing friend from all the way across the commissary. Mean things. The kind of things that would've had Phoebe feeding Tucker Thompson a knuckle sandwich, just like she did once before, when his mean words were aimed at Lena. Not only had Phoebe risen to Lena's defense, she'd spent the next three years helping Lena overcome her stutter. Now it was mostly gone—a rare thing that only resurfaced when Lena's emotions were exceptionally strong. But Tucker Thompson was still a jerk who got away with it because he was handsome and the best at *snag*, a favorite after-school sport most of the boys at school played. Tucker could even beat the eighth years. Lena consoled herself with the knowledge that Tucker talked bad about everyone. He didn't actually know anything about Phoebe or her secret, even if he was dancing uncomfortably close to it.

As the afternoon came and went, Lena could not quench the ominous feeling that something was wrong. By the time the bell rang, her nerves had worked themselves up into a frenzy. While her classmates cheered and rushed out of the north exit—where they would head straight to the carnival—Lena gathered up her things and made a beeline for the south. She needed to check on Phoebe, even if Lena wasn't allowed to go to Phoebe's house. She stepped out into the sunlight, books clutched against her chest, and saw something that had all of her anxious breath swooshing away. Her friend—her *sister*—standing like a slip against the brick facade. As though waiting just for her.

"Phoebe!" Lena exclaimed.

Phoebe turned, and Lena's short-lived relief vanished. Phoebe's eyes were puffy and red, as though she'd spent the day crying.

Phoebe never cried.

Unease tied into a knot in Lena's chest. "What's the matter?"

Phoebe looked over her shoulder in a paranoid sort of way, like she was checking to make sure nobody else was nearby. But of course nobody was nearby. Everybody had gone the opposite direction. Casting a final glance behind her, Phoebe took a step closer as if whatever she was about to say was something shameful. "Mama's pregnant."

Lena blinked. She wasn't sure what she expected, what her tightening muscles had braced for. But it wasn't that. A confused sort of lightness fell over her. Wonder with a tinge of jealousy too. Lena had always wanted a sibling. Now Phoebe would get one. Perhaps her friend was worried that this would change things between them somehow. A silly thought, really. The girls were thirteen. A sibling so much younger could not compete with a friendship like theirs. Lena stepped forward and took Phoebe's hands. Even now, five years later, she could feel her bracelet pulling, stretching. As if the vine wrapped around her wrist remembered that it had once been part of the vine wrapped around Phoebe's. Proof that nothing could separate them. Not even a sibling. Lena smiled reassuringly. "A baby will be fun."

"*Two* babies."

And there it was.

The bomb.

The warmth in Lena's cheeks drained away. She tried to find her voice. Ask for clarity. But her voice was stuck. Two. Twins. Only women who were Magic could conceive them. A tremble began in Lena's middle, then worked its way into her arms. Not very long ago, families with twins were hunted down and executed in an attempt to eradicate Magic from Korah. It was a topic they'd learned about in school. The Purge was a bloody time in the commonwealth's history, one that ended only two years before the girls were born. And while The Purge had come to an end, twins were still forbidden. Now Phoebe's mother was pregnant with them.

Phoebe dragged her hand across her eyes. "Mama says we have to go."

"When?"

"Pa's already packing."

The girls stood staring at one another, a heavy hush all around.

"Where are you going?" Lena finally asked.

"I don't know." Phoebe shook her head and turned away, her hands balling into fists. When she turned back around, her eyes blazed like fire. "They won't tell me."

"Why not?"

"Because they don't want me to tell you. They don't want anyone to know."

"I won't tell anyone."

"That's what I said. But they think it's too risky."

"How long will you be gone?" It was a foolish question. One Lena knew the answer to before she asked it. If Phoebe's mother was pregnant with twins, they could not come back. Not ever. Lena's eyes began pooling with tears the same as Phoebe's. "H-how will I write you?"

Without an address, she couldn't.

The girls would be cut off completely.

Oh, how Lena's parents would rejoice.

As if reading her thoughts, Phoebe stepped forward and wrapped Lena in a fierce hug. "*I* will write to *you*," she whispered with all the conviction in the world. "Every day, I'll write. Until I'm eighteen. Then I'll come back and we'll be together again."

"S-swear it?"

"Swear."

Lena held on tight—to her friend, to the promise—knowing that when she let go, nothing would be the same. Not Merivus. Not the carnival. Not school or the woods outside their village. Not even the bracelet around her wrist. Phoebe made everything better. Now Phoebe was going away. And Lena's heart was breaking in two.

CHAPTER 6

LEO

The moon shone bright and full over the palace, lighting up the grounds like an obnoxious guest who didn't know when to leave. Leo craved the dark, not the moon, especially after doing the hard work of escaping the castle. Not only had he evaded the unmoving guards lining nearly every corridor, he deftly avoided every slave and surveillance monitor, a minor miracle, as the palace was overflowing with both. Now he was outside, crouched low beneath a bush with the pristinely landscaped courtyard before him, hemmed in by the protective wall that ran around the perimeter. There were monitors on the wall, too, and the worst of the media on the other side stationed near the exits at all hours of the day and night.

Leo stared out at the manicured maze of gardens and paths and planned the most covert route. He couldn't use one of the exits. That was obvious. The wall had plenty of ivy, so climbing it was always a cinch. The tricky part would be avoiding the moonlight and monitors and the possibility of reporters waiting for him on the other side. He'd snuck out before, but never when the stakes felt so ridiculously high. Ridiculous because seventy-five percent of him was sure this was a practical joke and Hawk would tease him relentlessly when he arrived.

For the last month and a half, the invitation had been tucked away in the locked bottom drawer of his desk. Out of sight, but far from out of mind. Now it was the fifteenth day of the third month, and he hadn't told anybody where he was going. Not even Sabrina. If his father knew, he would be livid. He would have taken one look at the invitation and ripped it to shreds, then ordered a battalion to ambush 'the ambush' for that's absolutely what his father would assume this was—a trap to dispatch the High Prince. The rebirth of a ten-year-old plot to take out the royal family and here Leo was, combat-crawling his way right into it. Leo had to concede that assassination was a distinct possibility. So, too, was the slightly more nauseating, less extreme prospect that this was a scheme executed by one of his more ardent admirers. Should he not stumble upon Hawk at the gate, the chances were high that he'd stumble upon a fan who paid off a guard to slip the invite under his door. Given the option, Leo might choose the assassin.

Either way, sneaking out without his guard, without any of his friends, without even his vox was the definition of foolhardy. He'd even erased all evidence of his research, for that would give his location away as surely as anything else. The media accused him of being reckless, so reckless he was determined to be. The epitome of the self-fulfilling prophecy. And yet, he pressed onward like a man impossibly compelled. Now that he was eighteen, he had to sit in on meetings with parliament and judiciaries, going over matters of national security and foreign affairs and criminal reform and economic policy, all of it so mind-numbingly dull Leo thought he might rot of boredom. Every day he felt more and more trapped, more and more suffocated. If he didn't do something soon, he might crawl out of his own skin. So here he was, creeping through King's Bounty, the palace's most renowned rose garden.

When he finally reached the northwest corner of the lawn, he paused to survey the grounds, then grabbed the ivy and began to climb. He used it like a rope, pulling himself up with ease until he reached the top. Careful to stay low, he peeked over the battlement, searching for any signs of life on the other side. He detected nothing but a hooting owl and two squirrels scampering up the side of a tree. If word ever got out that Leo had snuck over the wall into this particular patch of woods, reporters would station themselves in this precise spot forevermore. Thankfully, Leo had never bothered to sneak out in this exact way before, and over the past month and a half, he'd done his best to be on good behavior, lulling the media hounds into a false sense of complacency. He dangled off the ledge, then let go of the ivy and dropped.

He'd done it.

Leo was outside the castle walls.

Next stop, the Squire Estate—home to the mysterious and reclusive Ambrose Squire, a person Leo had come to learn a great deal about these last several weeks. Through diligent research, he'd collected a plethora of interesting facts, one of the most notable being the tragic loss of his wife and son in the Cambria Disaster, the very same one that orphaned Leo's mother. Reportedly, the loss had driven Ambrose mad with grief. The once generous philanthropist, host to the finest parties in Antis, shut up his estate and hadn't opened it again. Now, he was claiming to be Wish Keeper, a title shrouded in speculation.

It wasn't until Leo investigated the actual words from the invitation that he came upon information too tantalizing to resist. All the more reason to believe this had to be a prank. Hawk would have known that Leo would do his research and in so doing, would stumble upon the information he'd stumbled upon, and thus, anticipate the appeal such an invite would hold. Leo fully expected to arrive at the gate only to find his cousin laughing at his gullibility. Still, even the prospect of such an adventure drew him like a moth to flame.

Underground travel was cleaner, safer, and faster. It was also heavily monitored. So he made his way aboveground. He moved quickly and quietly, sticking to empty side streets until he reached the entry road that would carry him up a steep hill to the estate above—a mansion that rivaled the castle in size, perched on the cliffs overlooking Jethro Bay. Leo didn't use the road, but the woods surrounding it. He stayed hidden in the trees, careful to keep his footsteps silent. If Hawk really was waiting for him at the gate, Leo would not give him the satisfaction of arriving in plain sight. Or on time.

As he neared, the sound of voices filtered through the dark.

He crept closer, peeking through the trees, and counted nine waiting outside the iron gate. Five stood in a group talking. The other four loitered on the fringes. Leo moved a low hanging branch from his line of vision and spotted a man dressed in uniform. An officer of the First Guard with dark brown skin like the people from Korah's easternmost provinces—Haren and Eshil. And on either side of him, two people Leo recognized. Nile Gentry, an infamous politician making headlines, and a girl with a crown of intricately braided hair, her skin a shade between the politician's and the officer's. She was a classmate. They didn't run in the same circles, but Leo knew her. In grade school, she brought pictures of her family for Show and Share. Everyone wanted to know why she didn't match her parents. It was the first time he'd learned about adoption. It had been the year his mother died and his grandfather, shortly after. The year his father became king. Leo had spent the rest of that school day fantasizing about adoption. Now here she was—Aurora, was it?—talking with the officer and the politician and two more. A rosy-cheeked gentleman wearing a clergyman's collar and a girl occupying most of the moonlight. She had legs like a stork and she was dressed like ...

Leo cocked his head.

She was dressed like a cipher. So was the kid behind her—a skinny ghost of a boy with hair so blonde it glowed white in the moonlight and a port wine birthmark staining one half of his face. Not far from him, another girl shuffled her feet. She had slouched shoulders and flaming red hair and a tattered scarf that covered her mouth and chin. Hawk disdained ciphers. Leo leaned forward, trying to catch what they were saying. But all he could make out was the nasally pitch of the moonlit girl's voice and the officer's eastern drawl. The girl held up something familiar.

The invitation.

Movement in Leo's periphery caught his attention. Another female, crouched in the trees like himself, with shiny black hair and a pointy chin. She had spotted him before he spotted her and she was staring at him now like a coiled snake, as if deciding whether to strike or slither fast away. There was venom in her eyes—a venom so fierce and penetrating, Leo drew back. Perhaps this *was* a plot to assassinate him, and here was his assassin. But then, her attention swiveled to the group, and for a second, he thought she was going to sound an alarm. Jump out and warn them all to scatter. Like *he* was the enemy who'd come to assassinate *them*.

Leo's heart beat faster.

What in the world was going on?

As if in response to his unspoken question, the iron gate let out a loud groan. With brazen complaint, it grumbled open as though its hinges hadn't been disturbed these past twenty years. Maybe they hadn't. Maybe whoever helped feed and care for the man and his large estate entered through a back entrance. The gate came to a stop. After a moment of silence—bloated with anticipation—an old man stepped out into the open.

Ambrose Squire.

According to Leo's research, this was the first time anyone had seen him since the disappearance of his second wife twenty-two years ago. The images Leo found were even older, showcasing a healthy, middle-aged, brown-eyed man with wavy hair the color of chestnuts, a matching horseshoe mustache, and a fondness for tweed jackets. Time and grief had turned him pale and thin, his cheeks sunken beneath a scruffy goatee that had gone silvery gray. His hair, too, now shoulder-length and unkempt. He donned, of all things, a tartan robe over a nightshirt and matching slippers. As he spread wide his arms in welcome, Leo noticed a subtle warp to the shape of his hands, like an object beneath a layer of clear, rippling water.

It was a shield.

Leo leaned back. Ambrose Squire was using the same type of electromagnetic shield his father used whenever he gave speeches to the public. Leo could spot them anywhere, and here one was now. Protecting this old recluse of a man. From what, Leo wondered. He glanced at the venom-eyed girl hiding to his left, but she had ducked further into shadow.

"I am pleased you have come." Squire's voice was as out of use as the iron gate. He gave it a loud clear, then continued. "It's been some time since I've entertained company, so you will have to excuse me in advance if my conversational skills prove out of use. I am very glad that you have accepted my invitation. Now if you will join me inside."

Leo stared, mouth agape.

Several feet inside the grounds, Squire stopped. Nobody was following him. The nine guests standing out in the open remained behind, their only movement the exchange of suspicious glances. Squire scratched his sunken cheek. Rings decorated several of his fingers—none of which could be mistaken for a vox. To nobody in particular, he spoke again. "I understand your wariness.

But I must insist on this gate closing in half a minute's time. If you wish to participate, I advise you to make your decision very quickly."

"Are you really the Wish Keeper?" the nasally-voiced girl blurted.

Squire gave his bushy eyebrows a daring lift, then continued on his way without another word, the trail of his robe dragging behind him.

Leo stifled a disbelieving laugh.

The man was clearly a nutter.

And this was clearly not a joke.

Hawk was no mastermind. Nor was he a particularly persuasive salesman. There was no way he had convinced a hermit going on twenty-three years of solitude to open his estate to one of the most eclectic groups of people Leo had ever seen. A disgraced politician. A classmate they barely knew. An officer of the First Guard. A clergyman. A smartly-dressed woman with a doctor's pin. And a smattering of ciphers whom Hawk did not associate with, which would have to mean he'd hired performers. Never in all of their years had Leo's cousin gone to such lengths—expelled such effort—on anything. Not even a well-executed prank.

Everything had just become wildly interesting. More interesting than anything Leo had experienced in a long time. The nine guests shuffled uncertainly inside. Leo peeked again at the girl in shadow. She stared intently at the gate, which let out a warning groan. With a rustling of leaves, she sprang out into the open. So, too, did someone else. Another young man hiding in the woods. Both of them startled. The young man recovered first, slipping inside just as the gate began to close. The girl cast a glance over her shoulder at Leo. Something about her face, so much clearer in the moonlight, struck a familiar chord. Before he could place how or why, she hurried in after the others.

CHAPTER 7
BRIAR

Conspiracy.

Entrapment.

Danger.

The words raced through Briar's mind. Her heart crashed in her ears. She didn't know what to expect when she came here tonight. A clandestine meeting with a rich and powerful man? A crooked request in exchange for her brother's freedom? She only knew that desperation drove her. And now it seemed the last month and a half had finally broken her. Forty-five days of agony—the purest kind—with Lyric locked up in Shard, headed for Guillotine Square, and nothing she could do. No person she could speak with. No money or influence she could wield. Never mind setting him free. She couldn't even get past the front gate. She had no idea if he was sick. No idea if he was dying. She only knew that he wasn't yet dead. For every evening after work, she went to the prison gate to check the list of the deceased. So far, Lyric's name was not among them. And now here she was, answering an invitation she didn't even believe, entertaining the delusions of an old man who thought himself the Wish Keeper, hallucinating just like Echo had in the end.

This couldn't be real. This couldn't be happening. The High Prince of Korah wasn't really hiding in the woods outside the Squire Estate. The gate clanged shut behind her and latched with resounding finality. Briar took a deep breath, slowly gathering her courage, fully expecting to turn around to nothing but wrought iron. But when she did, the hallucination remained. There he was, standing inside the grounds. Not on the cover of a tabloid or projected as a hologram, but in the flesh.

His Majesty, the High Prince.

Briar did not raise her arm and shout, "Izar!" as was protocol. She did not curtsy or bow or give any salute at all. She simply stood there, too shocked to do anything but blink in frozen stupidity as he cocked his head and stared back at her in a way that resembled amusement. After ten years, she was seeing him in person once again. Only he was no longer the scared, grieving boy he'd been that horrible day on the dais inside Guillotine Square—the youngest member of a royal trio projected on a large screen above a platform where her parents were shackled.

There were some moments too profound, too life

altering to forget. That had been one of them. The day the sky went dark and the clouds went swirling and the monster won and Papa shouted at her to run. She remembered the prince's face with crystal clarity, like a frozen image in her mind. A boy not much older than herself. A boy who had lost his mother and now Briar was about to lose hers. She was being put to death for killing his. A boy with the same raven dark hair as Briar's, but eyes as blue as the Afrean Sea in the dead of winter. A boy living a life so foreign from hers that she couldn't begin to fathom it. She'd spent the last ten years seeing his face on simulcasts and tabloids—morphing from a sad eight-year old kid to the wild, devil-may-care young man he was now.

And now, here he was. Studying *her*.

Cold sweat broke out under her arms. She wanted to run. To flee. To sprint far and fast away and never come back to this place again. And yet, love for Lyric bid her to stay. Even if this was a trick—a trap—she had no choice but to walk right into it, for she had exhausted every other avenue of rescue. So she swallowed her fear and told herself that he didn't know her. He'd never seen her. She'd been hiding that day, and when the decree went out through Korah in search of the missing children, there had been no images to go with it. Within the first five days, they found Briar's grandparents. They found Briar's uncles. But somehow, they did not find Briar or her brothers. Days turned into weeks. Weeks into months. Months into years.

Until the decree was forgotten. The High Prince couldn't know who she was. And yet, her stomach twisted and her heart hammered, her attempts at self-assurance falling drastically short.

He reached inside his coat pocket.

Every muscle in Briar's body went rigid.

Slowly—carefully—as if trying not to scare away a frightened rabbit, he pulled out a familiar envelope. The bile churning in her gut lurched up her throat. She swallowed again—harder this time—her jaw taut as she stared at the invitation, a world's worth of incredulity digging into her shoulders. *He* had received an invite? This boy who'd grown up in the lap of luxury with the best education, the best health care, the best opportunities and resources? Meanwhile, she'd spent the better part of her life scraping and scrapping to put food in her belly, food in Lyric's. What wish could he possibly have that he couldn't grant himself?

"Did you get one, too?" he asked with an infuriating hint of mirth.

Before she could find her voice—if that was even possible in a moment such as this one—a loud *ahem* carried through the night. Ambrose Squire. A man claiming to be Wish Keeper. Delusional, obviously. But rich, too. The kind of rich that could buy her brother's freedom. He stood with the others up ahead, in front of a large fountain. Briar could hear the sound of trickling water from where she stood, far enough away that the other guests could not have realized who she was standing with. From this distance, the two of them would be nothing more than shadowed figures inside the gate.

Eager to get away—far, far away—Briar strode up the path. It took effort not to run, especially when he followed. But as she approached, something strange began to happen. The closer she got, the more her frantic, disjointed thoughts fell quiet and still. Until they stopped completely, and somehow, there was nothing but this strange fountain before her. Beautiful. Magnetic. With crystal clear water and a golden statue in the center of a young boy and a young girl holding hands. Like Lyric's artwork, it plucked something deep inside Briar's chest—a wistful cord that vibrated through her soul as the air throbbed with energy. An electrical current she could not see but was undeniably there. The locket around her neck thrummed. Briar's panic returned. Doubled.

Conspiracy.

Entrapment.

Danger.

The words tumbled through her mind again as the man dressed in uniform stepped forward and thrust his hand into the air like a proper citizen of Korah. An officer of the First Guard. An officer like the ones stationed outside Shard. "Izar!" he said in a deep, booming voice.

The others quickly joined. All except a pale boy with

one half of his face stained red, and Ambrose Squire himself, who did raise his arms, but not in salute. "That will be quite enough, thank you."

The others looked around—confused, uncertain.

The High Prince of Korah was here.

Duty required them to salute.

But the High Prince didn't object, so they brought their arms down hesitantly, some hiding their awe and disbelief better than others.

Ambrose folded his hands, rings glinting on his fingers, and looked at each of them in turn with a solemnity that sharpened the hollow of his cheeks. Briar wasn't sure if it was her imagination, but he seemed to stare at her the longest, his attention dipping to the place her locket pulsed, strangely warm beneath her shabby tunic.

Conspiracy.

Entrapment.

Danger.

Magic.

She could sense it here, next to this fountain. The monster that stole her mother.

"If we are to do this correctly," the old man said, "we must agree to leave societal hierarchy behind."

"Do *what* correctly?" the birthmarked boy interjected.

"How do I get my wish?" a nasally-voice girl asked.

"Both worthy questions," Ambrose replied. "Ones I will

be more than willing to answer once we've had a good night's rest."

A good night's rest?

Briar gaped.

She hadn't come here to sleep.

"We're staying overnight?" the officer asked.

"My parents will be worried," the girl beside him said.

"I didn't pack anything for overnight," another added.

"There was no reason for you to pack anything," Ambrose replied. "All that you might need is here. Unfortunately, I can do nothing to assuage worry. Be it parental or otherwise."

"What about rage?" the prince asked, his blue eyes dancing in a way that made Briar want to snarl. To him, maybe this was a joke. To her, this was life and death. "Can you assuage that?"

"I'm afraid I cannot assuage that either." For a moment, Ambrose did look afraid. Or at least, troubled. As if his inability to alleviate such emotions genuinely disturbed him. "If you wish to continue, this is a factor you must consider. You cannot tell anyone where you are or what you are doing, which may produce worry or concern or *rage* in those to whom you are closest."

The only person close to Briar was locked in a cell. Lyric knew about the invitation. Did he know she'd responded to it? Did he know she was doing everything she could to set him free? She couldn't stop thinking about him. Forty-five days in a cell. Her optimistic, quick-to-laugh Lyric. Alone. Afraid. Already too thin when the constables dragged him away. Was he skeletal now?

"I do ask that you consider quickly, for the night is no longer young and I'm eager to retire."

"If you didn't intend to explain anything tonight," a woman said, "why didn't you invite us in the morning?"

The old man's attention lifted to the sky. "The moon is bright, but never so bright as the sun." Then, without any reason Briar could observe, he clutched one hand to his chest, his bony knuckles whitening. He squeezed his eyes shut, his cheeks blanching even whiter than his scruffy goatee. For a moment, Briar thought he might collapse right there in the dead of night in front of his bizarre fountain and this odd collection of guests. But then his cheeks puffed with air and he exhaled slowly, his shoulders slumping. "That one was quite ... strong."

Perplexed, Briar followed the old man's gaze.

He was staring at the floor of the fountain. A gold coin shimmered at the bottom, the refraction of moonlight through the water warping its appearance.

Briar narrowed her eyes.

When she arrived, the fountain bed had been empty.

A ROYAL WEDDING

YEAR OF KORAH: 497

PHOEBE

All of Korah had the day off and it wasn't Nuach. It wasn't even Merivus. A rare treat for so many accustomed to working twelve-hour shifts six days out of seven, week after week after week. The air all around buzzed with excitement—one Phoebe didn't feel.

"Hurry up or we'll miss it!" Jenna called over her shoulder as she hurried ahead beside Jalene. The two young women were as giddy as school girls. They had talked Phoebe into coming with them, and judging by the crowded streets, everyone else was doing the same. Leaving their tiny villages for town in order to partake in the festivities.

"It's going to drag on all day," Phoebe said.

"We don't want to miss the beginning! That's the best part," Jenna replied. "Now come on. I'm sure we'll get loads of ideas for *your* wedding."

Phoebe scoffed. Her wedding would be nothing like the one about to unfold. And Jenna didn't really want to watch to get ideas. She wanted to watch the same reason everybody else wanted to watch. To see the new princess—the mystery woman who had managed to evade the media thus far. The mystery woman who had captured the prince's heart. A union that had tongues wagging all throughout the commonwealth. A union that felt very much to Phoebe like one of King Casimir's calculated moves.

His disdain for ciphers was making it all the more impossible to climb out of the hole they'd been born into. The poor were tired of being poor. Ciphers were finally beginning to rally. Some had even organized revolts. They were, of course, quickly and emphatically squashed by the First Guard. But the unrest was there and it was growing.

Ah, but now ...

Now everything had been thrown into question. How could the king possibly disdain ciphers when he was letting his son marry one?

Phoebe wasn't fooled.

Nor was Flynn.

Her body flushed with pleasure at the mere thought of him.

Her love. Her beau. And now, her fiancé. She couldn't wait to marry Flynn. Handsome, kind, brave, eternally optimistic Flynn. Unafraid of who she was. *Loved* who she was. Every piece, even the secret, forbidden ones.

"What do you think she will look like?" Jenna asked.

"She must be very beautiful to have caught his attention so thoroughly," Jalene replied.

"Can you even imagine? A cipher like us catching the eye of the High Prince?"

Jalene practically swooned. "Living in a palace?"

"Parties and food and dresses."

"Servants waiting on you hand and foot."

"You mean slaves," Phoebe muttered, though not low enough to go unheard.

"*Servants*," Jenna shot back, casting Phoebe a scandalized look before glancing quickly at Jalene, who had probably gone pale. It was an insensitive thing to say. Jalene's oldest brother sold himself six months prior. The sum of money went to his family who sorely needed it, and Jalene hadn't seen her brother since. Nobody had. Nor would they probably ever.

"There aren't slaves at the castle. They hire their help." Jenna hooked her arm around Jalene's like the best of bosom buddies. It was a friendship Phoebe could never quite crack. In large part because she didn't care to.

The three young women reached their destination—Snoots, an unassuming noshery that didn't charge an arm and a leg for an afternoon pick-me-up or a good-morning muffin. Phoebe regretted coming. She'd much rather be deep in the forest with Flynn and her father, chopping and gathering wood for a home that would soon be theirs. She held the thought close, relishing its warmth as they joined the crowd gathering outside to watch the wedding festivities on Snoot's simulcaster through the storefront window.

It was a long-standing rule—even at a place like Snoots. Only paying customers were allowed in. So when Jenna pulled open the door, Phoebe didn't budge. She wasn't going to spend her hard-earned money. Not for this.

"Come on," Jenna said. "My treat."

"*Jenna.*"

Jenna responded with an exaggerated eye roll. "Consider it an early wedding present. Now hurry. I've been saving for this and I'd really like to enjoy it."

With a heavy sigh, Phoebe followed her friends inside.

She and Jalene snagged the last remaining table while Jenna went to the counter. She returned with three drinks. She set one in front of Jalene, one in front of Phoebe, and scooted out a chair for herself. Phoebe stared down into the mug, her heart pinching tight.

"What now?" Jenna asked, the question soaked in exasperation.

"It's fizzy lemonade."

"Did you expect something fancier?"

"No, it's just ..." Phoebe bit the inside of her cheek. The last time she drank fizzy lemonade was ten years ago at the Merivus Carnival.

"A simple thank you would suffice."

"Thank you," Phoebe replied quickly, the gratitude tumbling forth in a breathless rush.

If Jenna or Jalene noticed the thickness in her voice when she said it, neither let on. Their attention moved to the screen mounted in the corner of the shop and remained there, impossibly glued as Phoebe took small sips of the familiar drink. The sweet treat slid past the lump in her throat as even sweeter memories swelled in her heart. Lena. Precious, wonderful Lena, who had loved every piece of Phoebe, too. Just like Flynn.

For four years, Phoebe wrote to her knowing Lena couldn't write back. Lena didn't know where they'd gone. For four years, Phoebe trusted those letters were reaching her friend. Her confidante. Her sister. For four years, she counted down the days until she would be old enough to return and reunite with Lena again.

Then tragedy struck.

Lena and her family had been listed among the dead.

Even five years later, Phoebe couldn't seem to adjust. Her dear friend had become a phantom limb that still pricked and tingled even though it no longer existed. Just like the village Phoebe had grown up in no longer existed.

The Cambria Disaster wiped it all away, ushering in a fresh wave of persecution, for authorities blamed all of that death and destruction on Magic. By the time Phoebe turned eighteen, the promise she made Lena had become null and void. There'd been nothing and nobody to return to.

In want of a distraction, Phoebe turned her attention to the simulcast where the wedding celebration unfolded, all of it dripping with wealth and grandeur. The opulent cathedral. The royal orchestra. The guests dressed in their finery.

"Would you just look at him," Jalene said on a sigh, her chin propped in her hands. "He's so dreamy."

The footage panned to the groom, King Casimir's eldest son.

"He's so in love," Jenna added.

It was a fact not even Phoebe could deny. If this marriage was a ploy to squash the rebellion rising amongst the proletariat, the king had at least found a bride with whom the High Prince was truly besotted. The truth of his feelings was written all over his face, which was indeed handsome even if Phoebe didn't want to admit it.

A line of trumpeters blasted their horns as the cathedral doors slowly opened. The bride appeared on the other side, swathed in ivory and lace. Jenna, who had taken hold of Phoebe and Jalene's arms, squeezed Phoebe's —a reaction to the dress, no doubt, so perfectly tailored, it was as if each stitch had been woven with the woman inside of it. The orchestra began to play, and Korah's soon-to-be princess made her way down the aisle.

"Just think if you could wear something like that," Jenna said.

"The train alone would bankrupt an Illustrian," Phoebe replied.

Jenna swatted the air. Illustrians didn't go bankrupt. "And those flowers. Have you ever seen anything like them?"

"They look like tiny white butterflies," Jalene said.

"They're laceleaf," Phoebe replied, her voice lifting in surprise.

She could feel her friends looking at her.

Phoebe was no connoisseur of flowers.

But these she knew. They'd grown in the Forbidden Isle formerly known as Cambria. In the woods outside her village. Jalene was right. They looked like butterflies. So much so that on multiple occasions, Phoebe had sent them fluttering about in the air as if they were.

The young bride stopped at the end of the long aisle.

The guests remained standing.

As was custom, the stern-faced King Casimir stepped forward to lift the veil. All of Korah seemed to hold its breath. Everyone in Snoots, anyway. Even Phoebe found herself leaning in, curiosity getting the best of her.

The veil was lifted.

And Phoebe nearly spewed the last of her fizzy lemonade. She stared. Wide-eyed. Unable to believe what she was seeing. *Who* she was seeing. Beside her, Jenna and Jalene jabbered away. Commenting on the young woman's beauty—her striking features, her flawless form. But they might as well have been doing so from behind a thick oak wall.

"Phoebe? Are you okay?"

She couldn't answer.

She couldn't talk.

She couldn't look away from the screen.

Nine years.

It had been nine, long years.

Yet Phoebe would recognize her face anywhere. And even if she couldn't, the bracelet wrapped around the bride's wrist was as familiar to Phoebe as the sun. She wore the same one around her own. Phoebe covered it with her hand, remembering the pact they made when they were little girls in the woods. To love and protect one another. But Phoebe hadn't been able to. Her friend died. Perished in the Cambria Disaster alongside her parents. Alongside so many others. But how could that be true when here she was? Plain as day. Not dead. But very much alive. Staring up with wonder at her groom. The High Prince of Korah.

Here was Prince Alaric's mysterious bride.

Her Lena—a cipher who would soon become Princess Helena.

CHAPTER 8

BRIAR

The echo of her father's cry followed her into consciousness.

Run Briar! Run!

She bolted upright in a strange room beside a stranger bed—white and fluffy like a cloud lined with silk. After a lifetime of sleeping on the hard ground and sagging couches, that bed was entirely foreign. She had tossed and turned, her mind an incessant beehive of buzzing, unable to sleep until she dragged the comforter to the floor. Even then, sleep had been fitful—haunted by monsters and fountains and executions and a blue-eyed, eight-year old prince. Now she was awake, wearing the same clothes she came in the night before. She hadn't bothered changing into nightwear, despite an impressive selection in the wardrobe. The morning had not come easily, but it had come nonetheless.

It was time for answers.

She needed to find Ambrose Squire in order to get them.

Briar made quick use of the washroom—splashing her face, rinsing out her mouth—trying not to think too hard about the luxury of clean, running water that went warm at the simple twist of a nozzle while her brother languished in Shard. She bypassed the wardrobe with day clothes, too, all tailored to her exact size, a fact she found every bit as disconcerting as the prophetic invitation—and stepped out into the corridor.

One of the other guests stood nearby, gazing up at the masterfully painted ceiling—a collection of scenes that spanned the length of the hallway. Briar had studied some herself the night before while Ambrose led them each to their sleeping quarters.

"It tells a story," the girl said in a voice as soft as the bed. She pointed at a battle scene—a platoon of soldiers beneath a dark and threatening sky. "If you follow the illustrations in a certain way, they tell a tale. A sad one, I think."

The girl looked at Briar. She appeared similar in age with almond skin and a dusting of freckles across her upturned nose, her hair a thick crown of intricate braids. Her clothes were Illustrian and they weren't from any wardrobe either. She'd been wearing them last night. There was a delicateness to her hands, a softness to her frame that flew in the face of hard labor. The girl was unmistakably high society and yet she smiled at Briar, who was unmistakably not.

"I'm Aurora," the girl said. "Aurora DuMont."

Aurora *DuMont*.

Her name dripped Illustrian, too.

Briar shifted. "I'm Briar," she said. "Just ... Briar."

"It's nice to meet you, *Just* Briar." Aurora's smile turned conspiratorial, like a wink without actually winking. "Should we join the others in the dining room? Several went that way already. A nice lady escorted them. I stayed here, though, to figure out the ceiling." She looked up again, a serene expression falling across her face.

Briar found herself looking up, too. Lyric would love this ceiling. He'd probably study it for hours, every bit as fascinated as Aurora DuMont. A part of Briar wanted to ask Aurora what she thought about the prince's presence, about Ambrose Squire, about the invitation. Instead, she cleared her throat and said, "The dining room would be great."

Aurora folded her hands behind her back and set off at a leisurely pace. "Are you from Antis?" she asked.

"I live in The Skid," Briar said—boldly, almost brazenly, waiting for Aurora's reaction. The Skid was the largest slum in the entire commonwealth. If there'd been any mistaking Briar's status, there wouldn't be any longer.

"I was supposed to do a research paper on The Skid last year in school," Aurora said. "My professor suggested I take a tour. I didn't realize people took tours. The idea was so peculiar to me that I decided to change the topic of my paper to Ethics and Exploitation. My professor didn't have any more suggestions after that."

Briar blinked dumbly, not at all sure what to make of this girl beside her.

"I think this must be it." Aurora stopped.

They'd reached a large room with a table inside, longer than any other table Briar had ever seen. And on it, an intricate centerpiece made of silver and more food than Briar had probably eaten in her entire life. Her mouth watered—an unwelcome reaction. Lyric was undoubtedly starving and here she was, in the presence of a feast. Her heart squeezed. If only her brother could be here, too, for once filling his belly instead of pacifying it.

This seemed to be the mission of the boy with the red stain on his face. He sat in one of the chairs with his arm curled possessively around a plate piled high, his cheeks stuffed like chipmunks as he forked more inside. He seemed to think the bounty before him might disappear at any second and he better ingest as much as possible before it did. His white-blonde hair fell into his eyes, which darted about distrustfully, like the others might snatch his plate of food. Two chairs down from him sat the girl who talked through her nose, eating a much more reasonable portion, looking at Briar with her right eye while her left one wandered. Unlike Briar, Aurora, and the birthmarked boy, she had swapped out her clothes for an ostentatious outfit. Only instead of looking like a sophisticated Illustrian, she looked like a sparrow trying on peacock feathers.

The officer—still in uniform—stood with his elbow propped against the ledge of one of a dozen tall windows lining the far wall, sunlight illuminating his umber skin. He was shorter in stature but powerfully built, his frame almost exaggerated with muscle. When Briar first arrived last night, his presence had been the most alarming. Up until Shard, she'd never interacted with an officer from the First Guard before. They didn't make a habit of visiting The Skid. That was patrolled by lower-ranking constables and she was always careful to avoid them. Then she spotted the High Prince in the woods, and all apprehension about the officer was completely overshadowed.

With the prince's absence, he once again became the most formidable in the room.

"Where is ...?" Briar's question deflated. She wasn't sure what to call him out loud. *Old man* wouldn't do. *Ambrose* was much too familiar. Sir Squire seemed acceptable, but then, *Sir Squire* insisted on leaving societal hierarchy behind.

"He's a slippery fish, dear," a lady said, bustling inside behind her. She replaced an empty platter with a plate of golden waffles and a tureen of strawberries and cream. She was pink-cheeked and frizzy-haired and bright-eyed, as if she'd spent all night bent over a hot stove and couldn't be more delighted about it. "He'll turn up soon enough. He always does. Until then, he said to feed you well, and I have every intention of doing just that."

"Did he leave?"

"Oh, heavens no." The woman swatted the air, as if batting the question away. "He never leaves." With the empty platters in hand, she gave Briar's shoulder a maternal pat and swept out of the room, humming a tune as she went.

Aurora helped herself to a waffle.

Briar remained in the entryway. "I thought he was going to answer our questions," she said to nobody in particular.

"Us too," the officer replied, his voice a deep baritone.

"Nobody's seen him?" she asked.

He shook his head. "Nor have we seen anyone else."

"The gent beside me was still sleeping when I left my room," announced the girl with the wandering eye. "I could hear him snoring through the walls."

"The gentleman beside you was Nile Gentry," the officer said.

Nile Gentry.

The name was familiar.

“He’s been making the headlines lately,” the officer added.

Right.

Nile Gentry was the Governor of Duggleby. The youngest in Korah’s history. He’d been making an impressive run for a seat in parliament when he was caught lining the coffers of influential Illustrians in exchange for votes. Perhaps that would have been forgivable had he not also been caught having an illicit affair with one of their wives.

“What’s he doing here?” Briar wondered aloud.

“Getting a wish, I suppose,” Aurora replied, dabbing the corners of her mouth with a linen napkin. “Maybe he wants a second chance.”

“You think Ambrose Squire has the ability to grant such a wish?”

“He’s the Wish Keeper, isn’t he?”

“He claims to be the Wish Keeper.”

“You don’t believe him?”

“You do?”

Aurora shrugged. “I don’t have any reason not to.”

Other than the Wish Keeper didn’t exist.

But then Briar remembered the fountain outside. The thrumming heartbeat in the air. The way her locket had responded. The sudden appearance of the mysterious coin.

She stuffed the possibility down. The Wish Keeper

didn't exist. Ambrose Squire was a hermit of an old man who'd clearly lost his marbles.

Another guest arrived, interrupting the stilted silence. He wore the familiar collar of a clergyman, reminding Briar of another. This one was younger with a rounder, cherry-cheeked face. He introduced himself in a voice that lilted upward, as if he wasn't quite sure but he thought his name might be Sam Poe.

Aurora returned the introduction.

Then the officer—Titus Ferro.

Then the girl with the wandering eye. Iris Grout was her name, and this was the first time in her entire life that she'd been invited to anything. The way she said it reminded Briar of the way the birthmarked boy wrapped his arm possessively around his plate of food, as if the rest of them were vultures threatening what was tenuously hers.

The boy went next. Garrick Wick. He spoke in a clipped tone as he stood to serve himself more food and when he finished, only Briar was left. *Just* Briar. If anybody noticed the omission of her last name, they didn't comment. Of much greater interest was the High Prince. Iris's good eye kept flicking past Briar to the hallway behind, as if waiting for him to appear while everyone discussed his shocking arrival the night before.

Two more moseyed in.

Nile, the philandering politician, and a woman named Dr. Margaret Geremond.

Briar wasn't interested in any more introductions or speculations. Lyric was waiting and the Red Moon was approaching. She grabbed a croissant to appease her rumbling stomach and slipped out of the dining room in search for answers.

CHAPTER 9

BRIAR

Briar didn't find answers. She did, however, find the boy whose eight-year old self had starred in her dreams last night. Ran into him actually, and nearly choked on her croissant. When he reached out to steady her, she jerked away.

He held up his hands like a man under arrest—tabloid-cover ready with his full lips arranged in a crooked grin and his dark hair a mess in that sleep-tousled way that made all the girls swoon. He was wearing the same well-cut trousers and casual pullover he came in the night before, sans the charcoal gray coat he'd donned over top. He smelled expensive—a subtle but enticing fragrance she couldn't place and had been too shocked to notice yesterday.

She swallowed her bite, her brain short-circuiting. It was one thing to be under the cover of night, then keeping her distance as Ambrose showed them each to a room. It was quite another to be here in the brightness of day with sunlight streaming in through the windows and the prince staring down at her with an alarming hint of recognition.

"It's the wooded assassin," he said.

"The *what*?" she choked.

"In the woods last night. You looked like you wanted to murder me." He studied her for a prolonged moment, his head cocked. "I'm sorry, but ... have we met before?"

Briar's heart leapt into her throat. "When would we have ever met?"

"I don't know." His attention swept her body, down to her tattered boots and back up to her face, causing an onslaught of heat to surge up her neck and pool in her cheeks. "On one of my tours? Last summer my cousin and I went to every district in Mirum."

"Do you make a habit of mingling with ciphers while on tour?" she asked, her tone so acidic it could melt the stomach of a goat. Echo used to joke that fear turned her into a feral cat. Give her a fright and out came the claws, up went the hackles.

The prince raised his eyebrows. "You really don't like me."

"I really don't know you."

"Most people think they do." A flicker of annoyance flitted across his brow—there and gone again—quicker than a blink. He nodded at her croissant. "You found food."

"It wasn't hard. There's an absurd amount in the dining room."

"Does an absurd amount of food usually make you so angry?"

"When there are people starving in The Skid, it does."

"Is that where you're from?"

She pressed her lips together, trying to get a handle on her pounding heart. It was a discombobulating thing, being in the presence of a young man who'd grown up in front of the whole commonwealth. A young man who could order her dead if he had any clue who she was. She took a deep breath. The less he knew about her, the better. And besides, how could she expect him—a prince whose entire life screamed exorbitance—to understand the offense she might take at such excess? "The dining room is that way," she said, nodding in the direction she'd come, then moving to step past him.

To her dismay, he moved with her. "So what's your take on all this?"

"All what?"

"This. Us. The invitation. Ambrose Squire."

"I think he has a lot of money."

"That's it?"

What else was there? He had money which equaled influence and enough of that could get her brother out of Shard with his head still safely on his neck.

"Do you think he's going to have a contest?" the prince asked.

"A what?"

"A contest."

Her brow puckered. She had no idea what he was talking about.

"When I researched the invitation, I came across a few obscure articles. Apparently, a long time ago there used to be these contests and the winner was granted a wish."

Briar narrowed her eyes. Was that what was happening here? Her mind darted from the High Prince to Officer Ferro to the lilting clergyman named Sam and all the rest. Were they her competitors? Eleven people standing between her and her brother's life. If this was the case—if she was entering some sort of contest—what exactly was going to be tested? Strength? Agility? Intelligence? "Contests involving *what*?"

"I'm not sure. The whole thing was very secretive. All I could find out is that each one began with mysterious invites that would arrive on random doorsteps. They used to happen once a year, then one of the contestants *died* and they slowed down to every five. The last one was *sixty* years ago." He spoke like the prospect of death was thrilling.

Briar scowled.

She had seen too much of it.

Was she going to see more at the next Red Moon?

Her heart squeezed. With desperation. With longing. All of this had to be a dream. A prolonged nightmare. She wasn't really here, walking through the Squire Estate with the blasted High Prince of Korah. Any second, she would wake up. Lyric wouldn't be in Shard but sleeping on his bedroll in the corner of their shanty, mouth wide open like it always was when he slept. She'd ball up her ratty blanket and toss it at him from the couch—his morning alarm clock. Then she'd entertain him with the strangest, most awful dream of her life as they got ready for another long shift at the Docks.

She and the prince rounded a corner.

Briar lengthened her stride.

"What's your name?" he asked, sliding his hands casually into his pockets.

"Why?"

"It's not every day I meet a hostile stranger."

The heat in her cheeks spread to her ears.

"You didn't bow or salute last night," he said.

And here it was. She didn't exalt the High Prince as was custom, and now he was going to make her pay. Which meant she had to plead with the boy whose family had eradicated hers and might yet kill Lyric, too. She opened her mouth to make her excuses, but he beat her to it.

"It was refreshing."

Her step faltered.

"So are you going to tell me or do I have to guess?"

She shot him a sideways glance.

He raised his eyebrows, waiting.

"Briar," she said. There was no harm in sharing it. When the search went out for the missing children, their names had never been divulged, nor their likeness.

"Briar," he repeated, turning the two syllables over as if tasting the sound of them on his tongue. It made the heat in her ears all the hotter. "It's pretty."

"It means thorn patch."

He laughed—a rich, carefree sound—his eyes glittering like they had last night. Like this was all an amusing game. "Bristly, blazing Briar."

She glared.

"Bearish, belligerent Briar."

"*Belligerent*?" She ground to a halt.

"I thought you'd take more offense to bearish."

"How can I be belligerent when I've hardly said anything?"

"Trust me, your face says plenty." One corner of his mouth quirked, pulling in the deep dimple in his left cheek, the very one she'd seen hundreds of times on the covers of hundreds of tabloids. Only this time he wasn't smiling for the masses; he was smiling at her. "What is it about me exactly that repulses you so thoroughly?"

She folded her arms.

"You have permission to speak frankly."

"I can hardly speak frankly with someone who has the power to send me to Guillotine Square."

"I don't send people to Guillotine Square."

"Your father does."

"It's a good thing I'm not my father, then."

The conversation had gone low, ominous. Absent was the charming prince the media loved to capture, replaced now by a young man whose blue eyes had gone dark. This was her cue to stop. Bite her tongue. Swallow the words. He was no longer kidding around and despite what Ambrose said, societal hierarchy would always exist in Korah. But it was as if a dam had given way—ten years of hardship and helplessness and injustice in the making. A reservoir of hurt and anger came gushing past the breach and there was nothing she could do to stop it. "You have power and influence like him, though. Only you don't use it. Not for good anyway. You live your life in the lap of luxury, partying and playing while real people die of preventable diseases. While real people die in Shard Prison."

"*Criminals* die in Shard Prison."

"Lyric is no criminal!" She clamped her mouth shut as soon as the words flew, but it was too late. They were impossible to retrieve.

The prince tilted his head. "Who's Lyric?"

Briar tucked a lock of hair behind her ear. She considered telling him. Maybe this was her chance. Maybe some piece of that eight-year old boy who knew what it was like to lose someone he loved would be moved enough to help her. Or maybe the High Prince would look at her the same way Sir Wellington Ferris had the second she told him Lyric had been caught stealing.

In the end, someone else decided for her.

Another guest.

The red-headed girl who wore a scarf on the bottom half of her face. Last night, her clothes had stunk like she'd washed them in pig slop. As soon as they stepped inside the manor, Briar had smelled them, for the open sea air could no longer conceal the stench. She came tearing down the hall in different clothes now, even a different scarf, and yet traces of the smell remained as if it were baked into her skin. She ground to a halt, then toppled clumsily. Straight into the prince.

Briar expected him to shove the girl away in disgust.

Instead, he steadied her, then gently let go.

The girl stepped back quickly. Skittishly. She didn't shout *Izar*, but she did sink into a deep bow and raise her arm in salute, her bright copper hair a matted mess.

"Are you all right?" the prince asked, looking past her like he expected someone to come barreling after her in hot pursuit.

The girl pointed in the direction she'd come. When they didn't react, she began gesticulating wildly, her hands a whirl of motion. When that didn't garner the right response either, she took Briar's elbow and waved for them to follow.

They did so without hesitation. The girl's urgency was so sharp, Briar half-expected to come upon a dead body. Instead, they stopped in front of a dimly lit chamber where all was quiet, but not still. There was a pulse in the air. Briar could feel it throbbing against her ear drums—the same invisible something she'd felt at the fountain outside. She looked at the prince, wondering if he could feel it, too. His face was caught somewhere between confusion and curiosity as the girl waved them inside.

Warning bells pealed in Briar's mind, but a piece of her was irresistibly drawn.

Shelves filled the chamber. They stretched from floor to ceiling. Rows upon rows of them, all lined with ...

"Jars," Briar said.

The prince stepped further inside. "With coins."

It was such a strange way to keep money. *So much money*. Like the feast in the dining room. More than Briar had ever seen.

"They have names."

The prince was right.

Names were etched on the front of every jar.

The girl tugged Briar's sleeve. She walked quickly, purposefully through the maze, not stopping until they reached one jar in particular, inscribed with the name

Posey Travert. The girl pointed at the jar, then jabbed her thumb at her chest.

"Is that you?" Briar asked.

She nodded emphatically, then pantomimed a request. She wanted Briar to take a coin. Briar hesitated, then rose up on tiptoe to get a better look inside. The coins were gold but not Korish. Or at least, not exactly. For these were only half-finished. Instead of bearing the two M's that made up the familiar symbol, they bore only one. Alone and upright.

Posey insisted.

So Briar took.

As soon as her fingers touched the gold, a surge of pain shot up her arm and exploded in her shoulder. It came with such force, such violence, Briar dropped the coin almost as soon as she picked it up. She yanked her arm back and clutched her accosted hand, her half-eaten croissant falling to the ground.

"What happened?" the prince asked.

"I—I don't know." Briar pressed her gloved palm against her clavicle where the locket hid beneath her tunic. The pain hadn't been physical. More like a searing emotion, one so acute she had felt it physically.

The prince turned to Posey. "May I?"

She didn't object, and despite Briar's strong reaction, he didn't hesitate. He picked up the coin she dropped and held on much longer than Briar had, his face twisted in concentration, as if keeping hold of it required great effort. And then, when it seemed he could bear it no longer, he let go with a great convulsion, his chest rising and falling as if he'd just sprinted several laps around the manor. "What was that?"

Posey fiddled with the hem of her top.

She couldn't answer, at least not with words. Her inability to speak had become obvious.

"Did you know that would happen?" he pressed, dipping his head in an attempt to catch Posey's eye.

She shrugged.

The prince wrapped his hand around the back of his neck, looking up and down the aisle in which they currently stood—so many jars. So many coins. "What is this place?" he asked.

Briar's skin prickled.

She had no idea.

"Do you think *we* have jars in here?"

There was only one way to find out.

The room was impossibly large. Truly impossible. The mind-bending logistics of it had the warning bells caterwauling inside Briar's head. Impossible things were forbidden things. Impossible things were dangerous things. She turned in a direction opposite of Posey and the prince, eager to get away from him. She walked quickly toward the exit, reading only the names on the jars that sat at eye level. She didn't plan on wandering. She didn't plan on tarrying. Until she came upon a name that stopped her dead.

Leopold Davenbrook.

Briar stood in the silence, so hauntingly quiet it was as if nobody else existed. Despite the unpleasantness that had been Posey's coin, she found herself wanting to touch again. Her fingers twitched by her side, the desire growing so strong it morphed into a need. She cast a look over one shoulder, then the other, then reached inside the prince's jar and picked one up.

It came like a lightning strike—an image illuminated in the dark. A crumpled figure on the floor, unfamiliar hands held out in front of her as if they were her own, and a sweep of dawning terror—so strong and poignant, the sharp scent of it filled her nostrils.

Nobody can know.

The thought crashed like a clap of thunder.

Her whole body jolted.

She lurched back with such force, she stumbled and landed on the floor.

Her breathing rose and fell in frantic jerks, and suddenly, the chamber ceased being quiet. All of those coins in all of those jars came screaming to life. Crying and wailing—all of them at once—reaching a crescendo that had Briar scrambling to her feet and doing what her instincts had told her to do when she first came upon this chamber.

She ran.

Down the aisle, up another. Into the open and out of the room into the corridor, where she screeched to a stop. The man she'd been looking for—the man with the answers—stood in front of her holding two coins in his palm. Briar recoiled like they might start screaming at her too.

"There you are," he said, as if he'd been wandering his manor looking specifically for her. His hair was just as unkempt as the night before, his goatee just as scruffy. But gone was the robe and nightshirt, replaced by a pair of black trousers, a matching collared shirt, a gray velvet vest and a deep green pinstriped jacket with elbow patches. "Is everything okay?"

Realizing she still had possession of the coin from the prince's jar, Briar dropped it quickly into her pocket and the screaming chaos came to a jarring halt. "I just—I saw —" But she didn't know how to finish. What exactly had she seen? That awful feeling of terrified paranoia tingled in her fingertips, making her mind race in disjointed circles. What were these coins? What was this place?

"You picked up a coin?"

"Yes," she said, her attention trained on the two in his hand.

"Do you mind if I ask what happened?" He looked curious. Intensely so. Like her answer was of great importance.

"It felt like a memory."

The answer didn't belong to Briar.

She turned around.

The prince stood behind her. He scratched his ear, the signet ring he wore on his pinkie finger catching a stream of sunlight. The hands held out in front of her when she held the coin from his jar had been wearing the same one. "A very odd, disturbing memory."

Ambrose seemed to inspect his answer, turning it over to get a view from every angle. When his examination was complete, he nodded with apparent satisfaction. "I'm sure you have questions."

"Loads," the prince said.

"I will answer any that I'm able as soon as I finish attending to these." He lifted the coins in his hand. "If you'll excuse me for just a moment."

As soon as he disappeared inside the chamber, Briar looked at the prince who was staring after Ambrose. She couldn't stop seeing what she'd seen. It kept flashing like a blinking light in her mind. *Nobody can know*. If those coins were somehow tied to memories, what did Prince Leopold Davenbrook do that nobody could know? And who had he done it to?

"Where's Posey?" she asked.

"Still inside, I guess." He turned his attention on her, his eyes narrow. Suspicious. "You ran past me like someone was chasing you. I came to see if you were all right."

"I'm fine," she said. But her heart pounded.

"Did you see the scars on his palms?"

"I was more preoccupied with the coins." She thought of the one that had appeared last night in the fountain. Her thoughts began to spin. Around the invitation. Around wishes and the legend of the Wish Keeper and this member of the royal family standing before her. Around Magic. For the past ten years, she'd done everything possible to keep that monster in the closet. But somehow, in the process of trying to save Lyric, she'd stepped inside of it, only to discover that the High Prince was standing with her. Of all people, why in the world had Ambrose Squire invited him?

The prince rubbed his chest.

And around the corner stepped another guest.

The young man who startled her last night. She hadn't noticed him hiding in the woods until he stepped out into the open. This time, he seemed startled by her. Or the prince. Or both. He ground to a halt, then seeming to recover, strode forward to join them. He was fair-skinned with dark eyes, and while his gait carried a sophistication common to Illustrians, his clothes were simple.

Briar had a hard time placing him.

"Good morning," he said in a heavily accented voice. "I am searching for the master of the house."

"You came to the right place then," the prince replied. "He just went inside. Said he'd return shortly."

The young man's attention flitted to the chamber entrance.

Briar shivered, wishing they could move further away.

"You are the prince of Korah," he said.

"Unfortunately," Leo replied.

The flippant response seemed to catch the young man off guard. He jerked his head back. His mouth opened, then shut. Then opened again. Frowning, he glanced at Briar, then ran his hands down the front of his pants. "Forgive me, but I am unsure how to introduce myself to a prince."

"A handshake will do." Leo offered his.

The young man peered at it for a moment longer than comfortable. He was a couple inches shorter than the prince, still plenty taller than Briar, with a slightly crooked nose and a cleft chin, which he scratched before shaking Leo's hand. "My name is Evander."

"Do you come from Nigal, Evander?"

Briar blinked at the prince. Nigal wasn't part of the commonwealth. The country bordered Korah to the north, just beyond Military Ridge. Well past the city of Hillandale in the northernmost province of Petram.

"You are good with accents," Evander said.

Leo shrugged.

"You got an invitation all the way up in Nigal?" Briar exclaimed.

"I did," he said.

Before she could make any more inquiries—like how had his invitation arrived—the master of the house returned looking noticeably lighter exiting the chamber than he had upon entering.

"Ah," he said. "Evander. Splendid."

The foreigner did not return the easy greeting. He looked at the old man with wariness in his midnight eyes. It was a wariness Briar felt, too. She didn't trust any of this either, especially not now after that room. Behind him, the prince motioned silently. He pointed at Ambrose's hands. Sure enough, there was a scar on each one—the exact same size and shape as the half-finished Korish symbol stamped on the coins.

CHAPTER 10

LEO

Leo stretched his fingers like he might be able to stretch away the lingering feelings from Posey Travert's coin. The crushing fear. The wretched despair. And that image. That awful image. It came with a loud and clear plea that filled his mind—*Make it stop! Please, she's dying!* If that coin really was a memory, then Posey Travert had been horribly abused, for when he held it, he'd watched the abuse unfold. It was as though he'd been the one begging for her life. Leo shook his head. This was crazy. All of it. Coins didn't hold memories.

Not without Magic.

His mind buzzed. Magic was forbidden. Outlawed. It was the reason his mother was dead. It had also etched the unchanging scar on his chest that bound his life to the throne. Didn't it stand to reason, then, that Magic could unbind him, too? The buzzing grew louder. He came here for an adventure. He came because he was bored out of his skull. He didn't actually think Ambrose Squire might be the Wish Keeper. Now, however? What else explained such a room? What else were those coins? *Make it stop! Please, she's dying!* A memory. But a wish, too. He pictured the half-finished symbol of Korah stamped into the gold. An upside down M, or a right side up W? The same as the scar marking both of Squire's palms. If the old man was playing a game, he was taking it to the extreme.

Then there was the girl.

The wooded assassin.

Why was she familiar?

Leo slowed his pace so he might walk beside her, but she only quickened hers. It was an entertaining game. He'd slow down. She'd speed up. He'd speed up. She'd slow down. All the while radiating an impressive amount of animosity. Briar, the thorn patch, with dark, shiny hair braided long over her shoulder, a pointy chin, and eyes like liquid gold. Never in his life had his presence been so obviously unwelcome, and that was saying something, given the near constant disapproval emanating from his father. That train wreck-of-a-relationship had been years in the making, but this girl—*bitter, biting Briar*—hated him on principle. She accused him of abusing his power by not using his power, making the false assumption that he had any power. She fascinated him almost as much as Ambrose Squire and his invitation.

The old man walked ahead of them brusquely, the foreigner named Evander close behind, his hands balled into fists, every bit on edge as Briar. Squire invited them inside a cozy study. Warm, earthy hues with a crackling fire and floor-to-ceiling bookcases crowded with spines that stood straight as soldiers, as if attempting to make more room when there was no more room to be had. Evidenced by the extras piled in horizontal stacks, obscuring the titles behind them. The upholstery smelled like mothballs and traces of chimney smoke and mounted on the wall behind a beautiful mahogany desk crowded with trinkets and ink pots was a life-sized portrait of a woman and a child.

Squire motioned to three cushy chairs—a perfect number.

Leo took the one in the middle, giving Thorn Patch Briar no choice but to sit next to him.

"Is that your wife, Anna?" he asked, making himself comfortable.

Squire smiled sadly at the portrait, then eased onto the wing-backed chair behind his desk. "And my son, Collin, rendered when he was quite young."

"And your second wife," Evander said. "Do you have a portrait of her?"

The foreigner had just played some of his cards. He was letting Leo know that he'd done his research, too. Enough of it that he'd learned about Squire's much more obscure second wife.

"Unfortunately, I was never able to get a portrait of her made." The fire in the grate reflected in the old man's eyes as he studied Evander intently. Then he folded his hands on top of the desk. "The three of you were looking for me."

"Yes," they said, in near perfect unison.

"You want to know how to get your wish."

"Yes," they said again.

"As I will explain to the others shortly, I'm holding a contest."

A prickling warmth ballooned inside Leo's chest. He could feel the heat of the girl's stare on the side of his face —there and gone again as she shifted beside him.

"The champion gets a wish," Squire continued.

"*Any* wish?" Briar asked.

The old man gave her a steady, singular nod.

A log popped in the fireplace followed by a thick and heavy silence that fell over the room.

They sat staring at one another, waiting for someone else to speak first. To ask the obvious question. Namely, *how?* How did he have the power to grant *any* wish unless he was actually the Wish Keeper? Unless Magic was involved? Leo glanced at Briar, but she wasn't asking the obvious question. In fact, judging by the painful set of her mouth, it looked like she was determined *not* to ask it. Leo opened his own, but the obvious question wasn't what came. "Why are you having a contest now, after sixty years?"

Squire scratched his grizzled whiskers, his attention shifting slowly from Leo to Briar to Evander. "I was never fond of these contests. My father was the one who hosted them. He thought they were exciting. When he died, I had no interest in carrying on the tradition. Unfortunately, necessity has forced my hand. And while I understand you have your *hows* and your *whys*, I hope you can understand that I have my reasons for not answering them."

"How does someone win?" Briar asked.

"By passing a series of trials designed to test certain qualities. Attributes, if you will."

"Like?"

"Bravery. Discernment. The ability to think on one's feet." Squire opened the top, middle drawer of his desk and removed a small stack of parchment and three feathered quills. "I must warn you that these trials will be very dangerous. Perhaps even deadly."

Deadly.

Like it was once before.

Leo couldn't find any details about how the contestant had died, only that she'd been a university student at Antis Academy just short of graduating with a degree in botany.

"I implore you not to enter lightly or under compulsion, but of sober mind and your own volition. If you decide to move forward, you will need to write your wish down. I recommend being specific but succinct. Brevity requires less blood."

"Blood?" Leo blurted just as Squire set not an ink pot beside the quills but a pin cushion, along with three porcelain saucers.

"You want us to write our wish using our own blood?" Briar said.

"Another necessity, I am afraid."

The fire crackled.

This entire thing had become very cloak-and-dagger, leaving Leo to wonder if this wasn't a prank after all. Maybe there were recorders hidden in the walls and the whole commonwealth of Korah was tuned in and eagerly watching to see whether or not the High Prince was gullible enough to take one of the pins, prick his own finger, and scribble his wish in blood. But then, certain rituals required blood. Leo knew this better than anyone. He had the scar to prove it. He rubbed the spot on his chest. He could feel his mother's arms around him. He could feel her chin resting on the crown of his head as she rocked him back and forth like a baby. Only he wasn't a baby. He'd been eight years old. Too big for such rocking, too young to understand her sadness. He only knew his mother was crying and saying things that scared him. She didn't want to stay in the castle anymore. She wanted to run away. She wanted to escape. But Leo couldn't. Not with any permanency. His scar trapped him. So his mother stayed because *he* had to. Then she died.

He grabbed a pin. He stuck his pointer finger and

squeezed three fat drops onto a saucer. He took a piece of parchment and a quill, dipped it into the small pool of his own making, and wrote down his mother's wish, making it his own. Specific, succinct words slashing across the parchment in blood red. He folded it in half as Briar and Evander began writing their own. When they finished, Squire handed them each a bandage and collected the parchments. He rolled them into tiny scrolls that he tied with pieces of twine.

"When do we start?" Briar asked, wrapping her finger.

"After dinner tonight. Attire will be provided. Please arrive in the dining hall by seven o'clock." He stood from his seat and turned his back to them, opening a small safe perched on a stack of books on one of the shelves, where he placed the tiny scrolls inside and locked them up. "If you'll excuse me, I must find the others."

Back out in the corridor, the air felt cold.

Leo watched Squire stride away from them, then turn a corner out of sight.

Briar turned to Leo. "What else do you know about this contest?"

"I told you everything I know."

She narrowed her eyes at him.

He tipped his chin at Evander. "What about you? You obviously did your research."

"I am no more informed than you."

Leo didn't believe him.

Just like Briar didn't believe Leo.

They were no longer showing their cards but holding them tight to their chests.

They were competitors, after all.

Excitement thrummed through Leo's veins. He loved a good competition.

CHAPTER 11

LEO

Leo buttoned the cuffs of his tailored suit. When he'd come to his chamber to get ready, he'd found it carefully laid out on the bed. He checked his reflection in the mirror, running a careless hand through his hair, then headed toward the dining hall, eager to arrive before anyone else. He wanted to size up his competition and avoid the fuss of salutes and shouts of *Izar* upon his entrance.

All day, he'd been itching for his vox. There was so much more he wanted to research. Coins that held memories. Coins that were wishes? The scarred symbol on Squire's palms. Strange chambers filled with jars. The names of the contestants he'd met so far. Not to mention what was happening outside this estate. Did the world know yet about his disappearance? Or was his disgruntled father keeping it under wraps, privately interrogating

Hawk and Sabrina and the castle guards? With every passing hour, Leo's anticipation grew. He kept waiting for a battalion of officers to knock down the front doors of this idiosyncratic manor and take him away. So far, nobody had come. A fact that had him wanting his vox all the more. This was real. He was participating in a contest that might actually end with his freedom. The ability to walk away with his life intact. His life his own.

He was dying to tell Sabrina.

But he had no way of contacting her. Ambrose wasn't wearing a vox. Neither were any of the other contestants Leo ran into throughout the course of the day. Over lunch, he inquired after a tabloid, but Peg—the grandmotherly lady serving the food—regretted to inform him that the master of the house didn't subscribe to any. There was, however, a large library, where Leo spent several hours flipping through thick, obscure titles dusty with neglect, hoping to find something relevant or useful. His search had been futile. When he finished, he went looking for Briar the Thorn Patch, then the odd chamber full of jars, but both seemed to have vanished into thin air.

Leo stepped into the dining hall only to discover that someone had beat him. The pale boy with white-blonde hair and the port wine birthmark. Like the night before, he didn't salute, but remained in place looking laughably uncomfortable as he yanked at his collar, knocking his crooked tie further askew. Leo gave him a dismissive nod and made a quick scan of the room.

Over lunch, the tall windows spanning the length of the west-facing wall had been bright with sunlight. Now the windows offered a stunning view of a pink sun setting over the Afrean Sea. Two large paintings of illuminated watchtowers hung in ornate frames on the north and south facing walls. The spread of finger food at lunch had been replaced by thirteen fancy settings with crystal goblets filled with what appeared to be mulled wine and placards with names written in the same gold ink as the invitation. Stretched long beside all sets of eating utensils but one were twelve twine bracelets, each encircling a *coin*. Leo touched the closest, and for a split second, he was back inside Squire's study, writing blood red words in a hard-to-read script that wasn't his.

I wish to discover a cure.

He jerked his hand away and blinked.

Somehow, the wishes they'd written in blood had become coins on this table.

The white-haired boy watched him suspiciously. Leo shoved his hands into his pockets, heart thudding. He'd been contemplating the coins off and on throughout the day. They didn't have to be Magic. It could be an advanced form of technology, like the invisible shield his father used. Like the invisible shield Squire had used. But how could technology turn a wish into a coin? Twisting his lips to the side, he found his place on the opposite end of the table between placards for Titus and Aurora, the officer and his classmate. Throughout the day, his path had crossed several times with the latter. She seemed to be spending her time strolling the hallways, admiring the ceiling. He'd met the former over lunch and through conversation, learned that the young and formal Titus Ferro had been stationed at Military Ridge, but received his invitation while on an extended furlough in Bascom, a port city on the northeast coast in the province of Eshil. Across from Titus was Evander. And next to Evander, Briar. Impulsively, Leo switched his placard with the foreigner's. The twine bracelets, too—careful not to touch either of the coins as he did.

"What are you doing?" the white-haired boy asked. The name on his placard was Garrick.

"Improvising." Leo winked, then straightened his tie and sat down in his new seat feeling almost giddy as two contestants walked inside—the clergyman and the doctor. The doctor sat down in front of the coin Leo had touched. Somehow, because of that touch, Leo knew that Margaret the Doctor was searching for a cure. He touched his own and a longing for freedom welled in his soul.

He considered touching Briar's, but her entrance distracted him.

She was no longer dressed like a cipher, but in a gown that matched her eyes and showcased a startlingly attractive figure previously hidden beneath bedraggled clothes. An appreciative heat stirred in his belly. Briar was full of surprises. He took in the long, dark braid hanging over her bare shoulder, a silver locket that didn't match her dress, and a fingerless glove that did. She'd been wearing a black one earlier. He assumed it was a fashion preference—the perfect accent to her tough-as-nails exterior. Now he wondered if she was hiding something like Posey was with her scarf. He doubted Briar owned fingerless gloves in different colors, which meant Squire provided hand wear. He watched eagerly as she surveyed the settings and found hers beside his. She stopped, her cheeks blooming with color, her golden eyes narrowing into slits

Leo grinned.

Briar scowled.

He was no stranger to critics. He had his fair share of haters. They just weren't typically young females. And should one from that particular subgroup dislike him, it was never *because* of his position. But rather, in spite of it. Like *caustic, carnal Contessa*, who only hated him now because she'd failed to turn their summer fling into something more permanent. If it wasn't his position she was after, he might have felt more remorse.

"Good evening," he said when Briar made her reluctant way around the table. "You look stunning."

Her blush deepened. She tugged at her dress, every bit as uncomfortable as the white-haired Garrick, then sat down on the edge of her chair as far from him as possible while Aurora sat across from them in an iridescent dress that changed color with the lighting and multicolored flower petals in her crown of braids. Posey came next in an olive-green frock with a matching shrug and a silk scarf for her face—her bright red hair an unfortunate beacon for a girl so painfully timid. In drastic contradiction came the girl who followed, fluttering and preening the feathered scarf draped across her shoulders like a little girl playing dress up, every movement flamboyantly exaggerated, her good eye roving the room until it landed with hunger upon him. Nile Gentry, the infamous politician from Duggleby, was the last of the twelve to arrive and avoided Leo's stare as determinedly as Briar. The only seat that remained empty was at the head of the table, and that belonged to the old man.

Leo assessed his competition. A disgraced politician. A hostile cipher. An observant foreigner. An officer of the First Guard. A clergyman. A doctor. A mute. An adopted Illustrian. And three others. By Leo's estimation, the foreigner and the officer would pose the greatest physical threat. Intellectually, he'd guess the doctor. When it came to grit and ferocity? The hostile cipher, hands down. With eyes like a lioness and the attitude of one, too. He was pretty sure she lived in The Skid, which meant she was scrappy. She cared deeply about someone in Shard, which meant she ran with criminals. Leo wondered if this prisoner named Lyric was her lover. He studied her openly, his attention snagging on the silver locket resting in the dip of her clavicle. It struck a familiar chord—like her face—but her rigid posture angled away from him, making closer inspection impossible. She couldn't weigh much more than gaunt, ghostly Garrick. But Leo would be a fool to dismiss her.

He needed no further proof that appearances could be deceiving than the dining room in which he now sat. Should the Royal Guard choose this moment to break down the doors of Squire's manor, they would assume Leo was having dinner with a room full of Illustrians. If Hawk came with them, he'd recognize Aurora. Side-eye Nile. Assume Posey wore her scarf for religious reasons. And probably wonder why the flamboyantly dressed Iris hadn't bothered to have her eye surgically repaired. He would have no idea that almost half of them were ciphers. How quickly the right clothing could erase a lifetime of prejudice and disdain.

The grandmotherly woman Leo met over lunch entered carrying a silver tray on which sat an array of tiny covered platters. Her name was Peg. "Good evening," she said, her cheeks flushing as the small talk ceased and twelve pairs of curious eyes swiveled in her direction. "I've brought you something to get started. Master Squire insisted upon it."

She set the small platters in front of them—her movements so efficient, she'd gone halfway around the table and reached Leo by the time she finished speaking.

"Where *is* Master Squire?" he asked.

"On his way, I'm sure. Or getting to that point, I hope." She smiled kindly and bustled past, not stopping until everyone had a platter of their own. When nobody lifted the lid to see what was inside, she gave her chubby hands a decisive clap. "Go on now. The quicker you get to it, the quicker I can bring you something that will actually fill your bellies."

This was all the prompting Garrick needed.

He lifted the cover to reveal a petite, crescent shaped biscuit.

A wise cracker—the kind that entertained little children at festivals and parades.

Garrick's thin face fell.

"Not to worry, dears, I'll be right back." She whisked out of the room, leaving them alone with the unconventional hors d'oeuvres. Curious, Leo cracked his open and pulled out the slip of paper inside. So did everyone else. "A dubious friend might be an enemy in disguise," he read aloud. "Think it's talking about you?"

He quirked his eyebrow at Briar, but she didn't respond.

Her face had lost all of its color.

Leo peeked at the fortune she held in her hand.

"Beware of holding on too tight. Sometimes the key is surrender?"

She crumpled the slip of paper in her fist. Across the table, Aurora read hers with a laugh. "It says that the answers I seek come from above. I spent most of the day doing just that."

"Summoning a higher power?" Evander asked with a thick roll over each R.

"Reading the story on the ceiling."

The foreigner frowned. "It tells a story?

"A very fascinating one."

Leo glanced at the slip of paper on Evander's plate.

It's never too late to change your mind.

Peg swept back into the room. She quickly cleared the tiny platters and replaced them with normal-sized ones. Plates full of quohog, their shells the color of rich cream.

"What are these?" Garrick asked, trying to stab one with a fork.

Leo explained the delicacy, demonstrating how to pry them open with a knife. He'd eaten quohog plenty, so he was an expert. Everyone else struggled to get to the meat inside, even the Illustrians. He found himself watching Briar the most, curious whether the succulent, surprisingly sweet taste would offend or delight her.

"Care for some help?" he offered.

She shot him an irritated look, then returned to her shell with stiffly-set shoulders. When she finally succeeded, Leo had no idea what to make of her reaction. As soon as she tasted, her fingers fluttered to her lips and for a moment he thought she might cry. Then she set down her knife and pushed her plate away and didn't eat anymore. Perhaps her mind had gone to the starving people in The Skid.

The next platter of food was every bit as indulgent as the quohog. A skillet of coconut cod with a warm, buttered baguette. The mulled wine wasn't something typically paired with such a dish, but it had a unique spice to it that was addictive. Leo swirled the drink in his goblet as his competitors found a conversational rhythm—sharing and speculating, some more than others. He learned that Dr. Margaret was a researcher studying infectious disease. Iris Grout with the lazy eye cleaned dormitories at Antis Academy. The cherry-cheeked Sam Poe was a chaplain there. Garrick was a roustabout who traveled with the circus. When Iris tactlessly asked if he was in it, the unmarked half of Garrick's face flushed to match the port wine stain. They discussed their belief or lack thereof in a Wish Keeper—Briar's scowl deepening as they did so—and danced around their wishes, hinting but not sharing, until Leo finished the last of his wine and the man of the hour finally arrived.

He was smartly dressed in a plum dinner jacket with velvet lapels, his unkempt hair no longer unkempt, but combed and neatly curled around his shoulders. He placed a pouch on the table. The contents inside clinked like glass and when he sat down, everyone but Garrick stopped eating.

"My sincerest apologies for my late arrival. The arrangements took longer than I expected." He smiled, but there was little joy in it. He looked tired and drawn, stretched thin and squeezed dry, as if these arrangements had zapped him of all energy. "You all look lovely."

Peg returned with another covered platter. She set it in front of him as he unfolded his linen napkin and tucked it into his collar like a bib. When he lifted the lid, he did not do so to quohog or cod skillet, but a mound of steaming green beans. An entire plate of them.

He picked up his fork and knife. "This looks delightful, Peg. Thank you."

She muttered something under her breath while collecting an impressively tall and tottering stack of dinnerware.

Squire cut a bean in half and pierced one end with his fork. He ate the small bite, then moved on to another as Peg exited the room. "The contest, as you now all know, will be a series of trials."

Leo sat up straighter.

Briar did the same beside him.

Squire continued as if he'd naturally segued into the topic instead of plunging right in. "They will be very grueling.

Designed to stretch—perhaps even break—you mentally, emotionally, and physically. Your goal is to avoid elimination, which can occur in one of four ways: failure to complete a trial in a specified amount of time, serious injury, and or death."

Stillness fell over the room.

The old man cut apart a second bean and took another bite.

"What's the fourth?" Leo finally asked.

"Misplacing your coin."

Leo looked at the twine bracelet near his hand.

"Whoever passes each trial and submits their coin first will win."

"Submit it how?" Briar asked.

"You will receive clear instructions when the time comes. Until then, do not lose it. Do not let anyone steal it away." Squire set his silverware down and placed his hands on either side of his plate, his palms flat against the table. Dark circles pooled beneath his eyes. The hollows of his cheeks were impossibly deep. He was a man marked by grief. No amount of hair combing or dressing up could erase it. Magic was responsible for the death of his first wife and son, just like Magic was responsible for the death of Leo's mother. And yet the man appeared to have a Magic room and Magic coins, just like Leo had a Magic scar. Squire stared at them all beseechingly, his knuckles whitening. "If you have any doubt, any uncertainty that you should continue, I implore you to reconsider before it's too late."

Leo looked around the table, a shiver curling up his spine. The media accused him of having a death wish. But the media was wrong. None of the thrills he sought were truly life-threatening. Paraflying through canyons and diving off bridges was scary, yes. But not dangerous. Not with a team of professionals inspecting every thrill before he could take it. This was different. There were no bodyguards. No inspectors. No safety nets.

All twelve of them remained in their seats.

With a heavy sigh, Squire pulled open the pouch he'd bought with him and removed a vial filled with green liquid.

"What is that?" Dr. Margaret asked.

"A serum each of you will take."

"Not before they've had dessert." Peg was back, rolling in a cart filled with slices of creamcake drizzled with berry compote. She set one in front of Leo and refilled his goblet with wine.

"Of course not," Squire said. "You will wait until you've returned to your bedchamber and changed into the clothing provided. Think carefully before you drink, for once you do, the contest will begin and the only way out will be elimination."

Peg circled the table and set the final plate in front of Briar.

"I would like to make a toast." The old man lifted his goblet into the air.

Everyone else, too, sliding looks at one another as they did.

"This contest will be a reflection of life. There will be times of great peril. Moments of tremendous uncertainty. When you find yourself in such an occasion, when you're unsure which way to turn, remember to look to the light. Not the night."

Nobody said *cheers*.

They simply lifted their goblets higher and drank.

Squire brought his to his lips. He inhaled deeply though his nose, then stopped Peg before she could wheel the dessert cart from the room. "If you would please pour this down the drain." He handed her his cup. "I'm afraid it's been poisoned."

CHAPTER 12

BRIAR

P*oison.*

Somebody put poison in Ambrose Squire's goblet. The exchange had happened so casually, so nonchalantly, as if the event was an everyday occurrence and indeed, Ambrose affirmed that it had been happening more often. He said it like one commenting on an increasingly common, but minor inconvenience, like a tweak in his knee.

Meanwhile, the urge to flee had been all-consuming. Briar wanted to stand from her seat and race from the room—race from the manor—before the High Prince realized why she was familiar. Surely poison would be the catalyst that jogged the puzzle piece into place. She was not one of his swooning subjects he'd met while on tour. She was Briar *Bishop*, a girl who bore an uncanny resemblance to her mother—the woman who killed his.

With poison.

Briar worked hard to keep that truth and all of its implications locked inside a box and buried deep. But now? It resurrected itself like a screaming banshee, filling her with the same emotions that shot up her arm when she picked up Prince Leo's coin. *Nobody can know.* She still didn't know what to make of it. Perhaps one of his stunts had gone awry and somebody got hurt. Or perhaps he'd simply done something awful like Briar's mother. It was impossible to tell. She only knew that as soon as Ambrose asked the cook to dump the contents of his goblet, those three words screamed as loudly as that banshee of a truth.

Nobody can know!

Somehow, she remained in her seat. The prince did not pin her down with an accusing stare. In fact, he stopped staring at her altogether. Now dinner was over. Briar was free to go—to flee to her room, away from the danger. Instead, she was pursuing it.

The advice inside her wise cracker was a load of hogwash. If she surrendered, Lyric would die. If she failed, he would fall. Which meant she had to try every door, exhaust every possibility. Even if it meant meeting the same fate as her parents.

She found the prince around the next corner, dressed in his perfectly tailored suit, standing in the middle of the corridor running his palm against a barren wall.

"What are you doing?" she asked.

He turned—his dark hair messy per usual, his equally dark eyebrows pulled together, the contrast of his blue eyes arresting—stirring in Briar a quagmire of emotion. Fear, because of all that he could do. Resentment, because of all that he didn't. Guilt, because of what her mother *had* done. And running beneath all of it, a current of disquieting attraction. It was one Lyric loved to tease her about. Her little brother didn't know the truth. He'd been three when it happened. By then, Briar and Echo had gotten so good at hiding the fact that they were twins, Lyric grew up not realizing they were. For his own protection, they saw no reason to tell him otherwise. He knew their parents were dead. But he had no idea they'd been executed for the murder of Princess Helena. No idea their mother had been Magic, and thus, her children, too. Lyric thought his sister had a closet crush on the High Prince. But her attraction had nothing to do with silly feelings and everything to do with the decade-old image in her mind. A young boy sandwiched between two moguls with everything in the world but his mother, watching the execution of hers while the whole world watched him. Briar couldn't look away because she couldn't stop trying to rectify the two—the sad eight-year old boy in her mind with the reckless, flirtatious heartthrob he'd become. The two seemed like entirely separate beings and yet somehow, they were one and the same.

"Trying to find the entrance to that chamber," he said,

running his hand again over the smooth wall. "It should be right here."

"You must have the hallways confused." It was easy enough to do. They all looked the same.

"I don't."

"That's arrogant of you."

He rolled his eyes, then stepped closer and pointed to a scene on the ceiling of a man lying prostrate before another in front of what appeared to be the fountain outside. "I know because of that. I noticed it before because of the crown. The man on the ground is wearing it."

Briar tilted her head. The crown bore the Korish symbol, which meant the man on the ground wasn't just a king, but the King of Korah. She could understand why it caught Leo's attention. It wasn't every day they prostrated themselves. "Maybe the painting is a double," she said, her words catching as she looked from the painting to the prince.

He was standing startlingly close. So much so, she could see each individual eyelash in the thick fan of them.

"Or the chamber entrance disappeared." Before she could laugh nervously and insist entrances didn't disappear, his attention dipped to her clavicle and there remained. He cocked his head. "What is that made out of?"

"What?"

"The material of your necklace."

Briar pressed her hand over the locket. "Why?"

"My mother had a bracelet I think might be made from the same material."

Briar's skittering pulse seized.

"She always used to wear it. I haven't been able to figure out what it's made of. I've never seen it anywhere else." His blue eyes had taken on a curious glow—sounding off the alarm in Briar's mind again. Loud clanging bells.

Her father's voice echoed from the grave.

Run Briar! Run!

But she was frozen in place. The locket she wore had been fashioned from a bracelet on Briar's fifth birthday. Her mother had given Briar the locket as a gift. Was it possible that Princess Helena had something so similar?

"Where did you get it?" he asked.

She scrambled for a lie. Something that would erase any connection he might make between her and his mother. "A friend gave it to me."

He quirked his eyebrow.

"I didn't steal it, if that's what you're implying."

The prince held up his hands. "I didn't imply anything."

"I know what you're thinking, though. I'm a cipher, so of course I must be a thief." But she was, wasn't she? Or at least, she had been. For too long, it was steal or starve. She worked relentlessly to rise above such a choice, but in the end, none of it mattered. Lyric still ended up in Shard for pickpocketing. Maybe this was retribution—some cosmic karma for taking from the one person who had given them so much. The clergyman. Not Sam Poe. But another. One who had taken Briar and her brothers in when they were on the brink of starvation. She wondered where the clergyman was now, if his sick wife had ever gotten better. If he still made a habit of taking orphans off the streets, or if he'd lost faith in such charity after she and her brothers robbed him and ran. Briar swallowed the shameful memory. "A friend found it at a scrap market. She traded it for eggs and gave it to me for my birthday."

"She got that locket at a scrap market?" he asked doubtfully.

"Have you ever been inside a scrap market?"

He shoved his fingers in his hair and shook his head. "This place. It's like a giant mind trick."

She couldn't help but agree.

That room.

The fountain.

The coins.

And an old man who insisted he was Wish Keeper. Back inside the study, when Ambrose told them about the contest, Briar had wanted more than anything to ask him why. If he really was Wish Keeper, why had he ignored all of her wishes? But she'd bit back the question, refusing to ask it. Doing so would be conceding that the Wish Keeper was real. It was easier to believe her wishes had fallen on imaginary ears than indifferent ones.

The prince looked again at the wall with no door. “Did you notice the shield Squire was wearing last night?”

“What shield?”

“It was electromagnetic. If you don’t know what you’re looking for it’s mostly invisible. My father wears one every time he’s out in public. Squire was wearing one last night. And just now at dinner ...” His eyes went cloudy, his voice far away. “That poison.”

Danger.

Danger.

Danger!

“My mother died of poison.” His attention lingered on her gloved hand, which was still covering her locket. “But you know that.”

She made a choking sound, quickly followed by a strangled laugh. “Why would I know that?”

“I thought everybody did.”

Heat rose in her cheeks.

Of course everybody knows. Briar, you idiot.

“Her murderers were put to death. In Guillotine Square, actually.” He shot her a rueful look, no doubt recalling the accusations she’d flung at him about that particular place. “My grandfather was murdered shortly after. Apparently, there was a plot to take out my entire family, so every single staff member inside the castle was exiled and replaced by slaves." The crinkle in his brow deepened. "Surely, you know about it?"

"Yes. Of course." Briar tugged at her dress. It was like nothing else she'd ever worn, so form-fitting she could hardly breathe. Meanwhile, the prince stood there looking perfectly at home in his suit.

He tucked his hands into his pockets. "Why are you wearing it?"

"What?"

"The dress. You obviously hate it. You're obviously not comfortable. So why did you bother?"

"I wasn't going to be disqualified for something as ridiculous as clothing."

"You thought you were going to be disqualified?"

"I didn't know the rules. Our host wasn't exactly clear about the parameters until dinner." She tugged at her dress again and gathered her courage. She'd come looking for him for a reason and it wasn't to discuss attire. She squared her shoulders and took a steadying breath. "I'd like to speak with you."

"Isn't that what we're already doing?"

"It's about my wish."

"And this fellow named Lyric."

Hearing her brother's name on his lips was every bit as jarring as hearing her own. She hadn't expected him to remember her outburst, especially not in light of the incredibly bizarre events that followed.

He raised his eyebrows. "The *non* criminal in Shard."

"Yes."

"Is he your lover?"

"No!" Briar made another choking sound, her face catching fire. "He's my brother."

"Oh."

"And he shouldn't be there."

"He didn't commit a crime?"

"He was trying to get medicine for our neighbor but we didn't have enough money, so ... he took it."

"Took?"

"Stole."

"Ah."

Her jaw hardened. "To save an old woman's life." An old woman who was now dead. Mrs. Simmons passed one week to the day after Lyric's arrest. "And now he's going to pay with his." And the royal family would officially kill off what remained of hers.

"He's being sent to Guillotine Square?"

"At the next Red Moon."

His expression soured. "Why are you telling me this?"

"You're the prince. I was hoping you might do something."

"If you think I can stop your brother from going to the guillotines, then you don't know anything about my father."

"Won't he listen to you?"

He scoffed. "If I so much as suggest mercy, he will take your brother to Guillotine Square himself and have him executed while I watch."

"He's that cruel?"

It was a treasonous question. One that could—at the very least—solicit a slap across the face. But the prince did not raise his hand. "He wasn't always," he said with a frown, then dragged his hand across his jaw. "I'm sorry, but I can't grant your wish. If you want your brother free, you will have to win the contest."

Briar deflated.

That was it, then.

He wasn't going to help her.

If she was going to save Lyric, she would have to do it herself.

But then, hadn't that always been the way of things?

She stretched her fingers inside her glove, the scars she hid a constant reminder of her failure.

She would not fail again.

She would do whatever it took to win.

Leo stood in the guest chamber contest-ready in the provided attire—a custom-fit, one-piece athletic suit the color and shine of obsidian and a pair of black combat boots—his mood dark. It had nothing to do with the mulled wine and everything to do with Briar's request, the disappearing chamber, the poisoned goblet. Rolling the vial of serum between his thumb and forefinger, he stared morosely at the bracelet puddled on top of the dresser.

His father gave it to him on his eighteenth birthday in a rare moment of civility.

"She would have wanted you to have this," he'd said gruffly, then cleared the thickness from his throat and quickly exited the room. Leo had stood there dumbfounded. Seeing something so familiar—so much a part of his mother after all this time had come like a shock. A piece of her soul resurrected.

Ever since, he carried that piece of soul around inside his pocket like a talisman, pulling it out from time to time to examine the strange material. Delicate, as if spun from a spider's web and dipped in melted silver. Malleable, too. Hence, the puddle it created on top of this dresser. Odd, because in Leo's memory, it had wrapped itself thrice around his mother's wrist in such a way that did not suggest malleability. He hadn't been able to figure out the substance. He only knew he'd never seen it before.

Until tonight.

Only he'd left his talisman here in his chamber. Even without being able to directly compare the two, he was positive Briar's locket was made of the same material. He didn't notice until she was standing directly in front of him. According to the wooded assassin, a friend had traded it for eggs at a scrap market. Surely such material was worth more than eggs. He picked up the bracelet and let the chain sink though the spaces between his fingers. He thought of Briar's story. Her brother in Shard Prison headed for Guillotine Square all because he stole to get medicine. Noble, perhaps. But if they were really so desperate, why not trade in the necklace and come by the money honestly?

The question might as well have belonged to his father. Mercy was a slippery slope, one the king must never slide down. For if the king extended mercy for stealing, what would stop him from extending mercy for whatever came next?

Eleos Partim Pentho Omnis.

It was an oath he would take upon his coronation.

A duty he would have to uphold.

An inevitable future carved into his chest during a secret ceremony when he was but seven days old.

Leo closed his eyes, remembering the lavender scent of his mother's skin, the sound of her heartbeat as she held him tight and wished them both free. She said there was poison in the walls. Had she meant literal poison? Did she know she was in danger? His hand curled into a fist. He hated that she was dead. He hated the chambermaid for killing her. He hated that he had to grieve such a loss so publicly. But most of all, he hated the scar on his chest—

the Magic that trapped him and in so doing, trapped her, too.

He wanted that scar gone.

He wanted the freedom to choose his own future.

He dropped his mother's bracelet inside his pocket. He wrapped a different one around his wrist—made of twine, encircling a coin. Then he lifted the vial into the air. "Bottoms up," he said to the empty room, then tipped back his head and poured the serum down his throat.

REUNITED

YEAR OF KORAH: 506

PHOEBE

For three days, Phoebe worked over a hot stove as an official kitchen maid of the palace. Long hours away from her children. Away from her husband. In the den of the dragon, as Flynn liked to say. He was uncomfortable with his wife's obsession, especially when that obsession put her inside a castle that was actively trying to exterminate people like her. But Flynn's sleep had not been haunted these past six years. Phoebe's, however? Lena's face plagued her dreams. She couldn't stop seeing it the way she had six years ago, when her oldest and dearest friend presented her first born son to the watching world.

Korah's favorite couple were finally going to be parents. The long-anticipated announcement of a pregnancy sent the public into a swooning, ecstatic frenzy only to have their hopes quickly dashed. There would be no watching Princess Helena's stomach grow. The royal doctor informed the media that the princess was very sick, her pregnancy in grave peril. And so, she would be remaining in bed behind the high, fortified walls of Castle Davenbrook.

The crestfallen public had to set aside their fervor for the sake of the princess's health and that of the child. Even the media seemed to respect the family's need for privacy during such a time. It was as if the smallest of stresses might push that perilous pregnancy over the edge, and nobody wanted that. Phoebe had grown increasingly unsettled. She'd gone from seeing her long lost friend on the cover of every tabloid since the royal wedding to not seeing her at all. Phoebe thought she'd be every bit as eager as the public to see Lena and her new child, but by the time the announcement came that the princess had given birth to a healthy boy, Phoebe's concern had been redirected to an issue much closer to home.

Which was why—when everyone throughout the commonwealth was gathering in excited groups to watch the simulcast, busting at the seams to see the princess and her new babe—Phoebe found herself all alone, sitting on the floor of her and Flynn's cottage, her heart not quite in it. She was packing up their meager belongings, getting ready to leave this place that had become their home, this cottage Flynn had built with his own two hands. They would have to say goodbye to Phoebe's mother, her father, her dear brothers who had just turned eleven—a celebration they could only ever have in secret. She would say goodbye to them as she'd said goodbye to Lena all those years ago in Cambria—without hope of ever seeing them again. While media crews gathered in the castle courtyard, along with the public elect—Illustrians rich enough to line the pockets of the most influential members of parliament—Phoebe battled tears. Not over Lena, but her own precarious predicament.

Then suddenly, there they were on the small monitor of their rudimentary simulcast set—the princess and her son. A pink-cheeked cherub swaddled in a ceremonial shawl with a cap of dark hair. He was the picture of health and perfection, and yet, Phoebe's sad heart crashed into her stomach. Even had Lena spent the whole of her pregnancy retching into a basin, it did not explain *this*. Phoebe got up from her spot on the floor, abandoning the pile of folded kitchen towels, and kneeled in front of the screen.

Something was wrong.

She could sense it as assuredly as she could sense life growing inside her womb. She could see it, too. Fear, trembling in Lena's smile. Grief, pooled in her eyes. What had happened to put it there? The longing to go to Lena right then, to find a way through the rigamarole of security swept through her like a fearsome wave. But it was impossible. She could not go to her old friend, for Phoebe was not simply carrying one life inside of her, but two. *Twins.* Just like her little brothers. Which was why she and Flynn had to move away, go into hiding. For how long she didn't know. While Phoebe could sense the twins, she had no way of telling whether or not they were identical. Should that be the case, they might have to hide forever.

Thank the Keeper, the twins were not identical.

The first was a girl. She came screaming into the world with a head full of black hair.

Flynn had whooped, ecstatic at the sight of her. "That explains the heart burn!"

Then came the boy—his hair not as thick but just as dark with a body much smaller than his sister's.

His smallness was alarming. The quietness of his cry, too. But his skin was pink, his body warm. And so, Flynn and Phoebe named them. Briar and Echo. By the time Phoebe fell pregnant again, the twins were four. Echo was no longer alarmingly small, but a couple inches taller than his sister. Nobody would ever suspect the siblings were twins. And this time, only one life grew in her womb. They did not need to remain in hiding; they could move back to the cottage Flynn had built before their own wedding day. But the memory of Lena's face holding her own babe continued to haunt Phoebe's sleep. She'd promised to love and protect Lena. They'd made a pact. And while it was foolish to think a cipher like herself could possibly help a member of the royal family, Phoebe had been compelled to try.

"She's the daughter-in-law of King Casimir," Flynn had said. "He began his reign with The Purge. The Cambria Disaster only intensified his loathing of Magic." Flynn stepped closer and wrapped her in his arms, enveloping her in the familiar scent of cedar and pine. "This need of yours, my love. This obsession to see her. It isn't safe."

"But something is wrong, Flynn." The pictures she'd seen since had only confirmed it. For while Princess Helena's dark circles had faded, while her coloring had returned, the grief remained. The fear, too. It was the latter that worried Phoebe the most. "I know it deep down in my bones."

"You're Magic, Phoebs. You're Magic, and she knows."

Phoebe pressed her ear against the deep rumble of Flynn's voice. "Yes."

"What if she turns you in?"

"She would never."

That's all it took. Flynn believed her, supported her. They moved with their three children to Antis—a shocking change of location compared to the quiet and solitude to which they'd grown accustomed—and Phoebe spent the last two years applying for work in the castle—a tediously ambitious task, for they vetted castle employees most rigorously. Finally, Phoebe got her wish. And now here she was. Three days bent over a hot stove, feeling as far away from Lena as she had back in Silva.

It wasn't like the princess came into the kitchens, and it wasn't like the kitchen staff brought food out to the royal family. There were other servants for that, which meant Phoebe would have to get creative. Halfway through her third day she got her opportunity. When a boy not more than sixteen dressed in servant's attire took a platter of croissants from one of the kitchen tables, Phoebe quickly excused herself for a bathroom break. She intercepted the boy and with a matter-of-factness that could not be doubted, told him the Executive Kitchen Maid needed him at once and she looked rather cross. Phoebe would be happy to take the platter for him. The boy's face turned a bright pink as he rushed off without question.

Phoebe fixed her flyaway hair, disheveled from the heat of the stove. She left her apron puddled on a step and made her way up the winding staircase, pleased that her plan had worked so well. Until she got to the top and realized she had no idea where the dining hall even was. She waited an awkward moment, afraid of being caught, until another servant bustled up the stairwell with a platter of fresh fruit. Phoebe followed him through a wide, elaborate foyer and stopped short in the dining room entrance.

There she was.

Sitting at the table, her brown hair pinned into an

elegant chignon, her clothes fine, her posture straight and regal, combing her fingers through the young prince's hair as the two of them bent over a story book. The young boy had been named Leopold—after his father's given name. The public called him Prince Leo. He was a handsome little boy, perpetually captured by the tabloids in adorable jumpers, always holding his mother's hand. Across from them sat Lena's husband—the High Prince Alaric, who'd always gone by his middle name. A tribute to his grandfather, the former High King assassinated thirty-six years prior. He read from the Antis Gazette. And on the far side of the table, the devil himself. His Royal Majesty, King Casimir.

Phoebe might be adamant, but she wasn't a fool. She never objected to Flynn's concerns. She acknowledged their validity and pressed on anyway. Which was why every muscle in her body coiled now. Truly, she was in the dragon's den.

With steps so quiet they were nearly silent, she approached the table.

Look up, Lena. Please look up.

The tray rattled in her hand. Sweat broke out under her arms. She felt at once like a giddy schoolgirl and a terrified gazelle. It had been eighteen years since the two had looked at one another—when they were thirteen year old girls exchanging tearful goodbyes—and while Phoebe had the privilege of seeing Lena on the news since the royal wedding almost ten years earlier, Lena had not. Would she recognize Phoebe after such a long time?

She set the tray down.

Lena didn't look.

But the young prince did. Everybody fawned over what a little miniature he was of his father, with dark hair and olive skin and full lips and eyes as blue as the sea. But his smile—that was all Lena. His dimples, too. So much so, Phoebe couldn't help but love him instantly. "Croissants are my favorite," he said, with the barest hint of a lisp.

Lena looked up.

If there was any question as to whether or not she would recognize Phoebe as quickly as Phoebe had recognized her, it vanished into dust. Lena blinked once. Twice. Her eyes filled with equal parts dawning recognition and shocked disbelief. She drew up her hand, as if to cover the gasp tumbling past her lips, and as she did, it connected with the plate in front of her. Fork and knife and a bit of egg clattered to the floor. The legs of Lena's chair scrapped against the marble and for one panicked moment, Phoebe was certain Lena was going to stand and wrap Phoebe in a hug. Phoebe had not spent the past two years studying every detail of royal etiquette to let her friend make such a blunder now. Nor was she willing to answer the questions that would surely follow.

Quickly, she ducked to the ground—saving them both.

She gathered the fork and the bits of egg as the princess ducked beneath the table too and their eyes connected.

"What in the blazes are you doing?" King Casimir barked. "Let the drudge clean the mess."

Slowly, Phoebe took the knife from her friend's hand and gave her an encouraging nod.

Lena stood and straightened her gown.

"You're a clumsy cat, Mommy," young Leo quipped.

"Yes, dearest," Lena replied, running her hand over his hair. "I-I sure am."

Phoebe set the silverware and bits of egg on the plate.

"Are you feeling all right, darling?" the High Prince asked, his eyes clouding with concern. "You look pale."

Lena cupped her forehead. "I do feel a bit shaky."

Princess Helena's chambermaid came forward; she'd been standing silently, almost invisibly off to the side. "I can escort you to your chamber, Highness."

"No, actually. I ... well, I'd like this one to escort me."

Everyone in the room stared.

"But she's not your chambermaid," the High Prince replied.

"Yes, I know. But—well, I'd like a new chambermaid, you see. Someone who ..." Phoebe tried not to wince as Lena scrambled for an excuse. "Someone who is m-my size."

"Your size?"

"You know how dull I find all the fittings. I was

thinking it would be nice if my chambermaid could stand in for me, and this one looks to be the perfect build."

There was a long moment of silence. Phoebe kept her head bowed.

"All right, then," the High Prince finally said. "What shall we do with the chambermaid you have now?"

Phoebe peeked at the chambermaid under discussion. The poor girl's face had blanched white. Lena must have noticed.

"Oh. She'd be a wonderful nursemaid for Leo. He just adores her. Don't you, sweetheart?"

The little prince looked up at his mother's chambermaid like he wasn't sure.

"Leo already has a nursemaid."

"Yes, but she's getting quite old, and two's better than one." Lena looked down at her son. "Don't you think so, love?"

That was all the convincing he needed.

Little Leo popped up from his seat and took the hand of his mother's former chambermaid.

A loud bang, followed by the sharp rattle of plates filled the room.

Leo jumped.

King Casimir had pounded his fist against the table and glared—not at Leo—but at his son.

Prince Alaric's jaw went tight. "How many times must I remind you, son," he said. "You do not hold hands with your nursemaid. You simply walk to your room and she will follow."

Leo dropped the girl's hand sheepishly. Then with an uncertain smile, he waved at her to come.

The young girl curtsied—confused—and did as she was told.

Lena excused herself, too. She cast a glance at Phoebe, then walked out of the dining hall. Phoebe followed two steps behind, both of them in silence. There was no sound at all but the echoing of their footsteps.

As soon as they reached the princess's chamber, Lena shut the doors behind them, and with tears brimming in her eyes, threw her arms around Phoebe and held on for dear life, her entire body trembling.

CHAPTER 13

BRIAR

creaming.

Panic.

Fear.

All of it oozed into Briar's pores and swirled in her stomach as the sky turned black as pitch and the clouds boiled overhead. Her hair was unbraided. The wind blew it every which way as King Casimir's voice rang through the square—amplified. He accused Mama of having darkness in her heart. Briar didn't want to believe it was true. But how could she deny it when that darkness was seeping out now, swirling in the sky?

Stop it, Mama! She wanted to scream. *Please stop!*

But Mama didn't stop.

Briar could feel the Magic growing, seething, thrumming like a heartbeat as the crowd pushed and shoved in an attempt to flee.

The wind blew harder.

Briar begged the Keeper to save them. But the Keeper wasn't there. The Keeper never was. Papa yelled at Briar to run and the sound of the blade came slicing down.

Her eyes flew open and the nightmare vanished.

She tried moving but couldn't.

Her feet were wet. Standing water soaked through her boots and rope bound her to a metal chair. She wasn't alone. The other contestants were bound with her. Only two chairs were unoccupied. A pile of rope lay in the water-logged floor in front of them.

The serum must have put Briar into a deep sleep. Judging by the dryness of her tongue, she'd been so for a significant time. Ambrose had moved them while unconscious, and now here they were, inside a room without corners, the walls and floor and ceiling the same metallic gray as the steel chairs. A matching podium stood in the center of their oblong circle and above it—hovering in the air like a projection—red, digitalized numbers ticking down the time from five minutes and two seconds.

"Good morning," the prince said across from her, his voice calm, his face a mask of concentration. He was wearing the same athletic suit that she was. All of them were. Except she and the prince were the only ones awake in them.

Her attention zeroed in on the two empty chairs. "Where are Nile and Evander?"

"They were gone when I woke up." The muscles in his shoulders worked like he was attempting to free his hands from behind his back.

Briar got to work on her own, grappling with the lock near her wrist, the twine bracelet and the rope chaffing against her skin. "Where'd the water come from?"

"Another mystery."

Her eyes lifted to the clock.

Four minutes and fifty-one seconds.

Would they all be eliminated when it reached zero?

She struggled harder, working her fingers frantically, but the restraints were impossibly tight. The other contestants began to stir, then awake in varying states of confusion. The lazy-eyed Iris Grout, worst of all, her discombobulation slamming straight into panic. As soon as she realized she was bound, she thrashed and screamed, her shrill voice echoing off the metal walls, waking up whoever wasn't already.

Briar squeezed her eyes tight in an attempt to shut out the sound. Wasn't this the kind of thing Ambrose was testing? The ability to think quickly. The ability to keep a clear head. Nile and Evander had already escaped, which meant escape was possible. She opened her eyes and scanned the room. The ticking clock. The water on the floor. The podium in the center. And something on top of it. She strained upward to get a better look. A piece of driftwood attached to a pick. She straightened her legs, her boots rising above the water, and stretched as far as she could. But her feet fell discouragingly short of the podium.

The clock ticked down to three minutes.

Iris screamed louder.

She was claustrophobic, she said.

She couldn't breathe, she wailed.

"Shut up!" Garrick yelled, attempting to squirm his way free. He was the smallest of them all. If anyone could escape, it should be him. "How did they get out of this?"

"Maybe waking up first came with an advantage," Leo answered.

"Or maybe they got a hold of that pick," Briar said. She nodded at the podium.

Officer Ferro stretched one powerfully built leg toward it, the cords in his thick neck bulging as he strained and failed.

The clock ticked down to two minutes.

"What happens when it reaches zero?" Iris screamed—louder this time, as if they all knew the answer but were withholding it from her and if she just raised her voice to the right decibel, they might finally explain.

"I'm guessing elimination." Leo stretched his leg long, too. But he wasn't tall enough either. None of them were.

Briar began to buck and kick, refusing to let this be it. She didn't write her wish in blood and dress up in that stupid gown and throw herself at the mercy of the prince all to be disqualified so quickly. But her struggle was fruitless. Her heart hammered helplessly. She was impossibly bound.

Unless ...

She went still.

The clock ticked down to one minute.

Cold sweat broke out across her brow.

Magic wasn't safe. Magic corrupted her mother. Magic killed her father. Magic destroyed Briar's life. It was the chaotic, angry sky. The monster in the closet. She swore she would never use it. But then a flash of lightning pierced through the dark and illuminated her brother, sick and starving inside a prison cell.

Whatever it takes.

Even if the High Prince was there to witness it.

Even if she ended up on that stage in Guillotine Square.

So long as it wasn't Lyric.

Briar squeezed her eyes shut, trying to recall a charm she hadn't used in over a decade. Long before they moved to the capitol city of Antis. Long before her mother got a job inside Castle Davenbrook. Back in the forests of Silva when Mama was still good.

Tick.

Tick.

Tick.

Thirty seconds.

Think, Briar.

What were the words?

But Briar couldn't remember them. They were part of a different life. And the clock kept ticking. Louder. Faster. And Briar was failing all over again. She could feel the heat of the fire against her hand. The searing pain as she let go and her brother fell into the inferno.

Ten seconds.

She had ten seconds before Lyric fell, too. Before she failed him like she failed Echo. She pictured him all alone, in chains like these. Her easygoing, quick-to-laugh, roll-with-the-punches little brother. Would he know that she'd tried? Or would he feel every bit as abandoned and confused as Briar had felt when Mama made the sky so angry?

The clock ticked from two ...

To one ...

To zero.

A loud, prolonged beep filled the chamber.

Followed by a silent void where the ticking had been.

All around, contestants exchanged uncertain glances. Even Iris had gone quiet. Was this it? Were they already eliminated? Had the contest gone from twelve to two so quickly?

A door in the wall slid open one foot up from the ground.

Water gushed inside.

Iris screamed as it swirled across the floor and with it, a

hysteria every bit as contagious as Parox. It spread from Iris to an Illustrian named Thomas. It caught hold of Posey in her scarf. Sunk its teeth into Garrick with his birthmark. It took Dr. Margaret and Officer Ferro and the clergyman named Sam Poe, too. The chamber was filling with water. The clock was gone. And Briar was still bound.

Then two words rose above the chaos—calm and whimsical.

"Wood floats," Aurora said, dressed the same as the rest of them, but exhibiting none of the fear. She spoke like one happening upon an interesting fact in a book, impervious to the rising water. Impervious to the infectious hysteria.

Briar fixed her attention upon the podium.

Aurora was right.

Wood didn't sink.

And wood was tied to the pick.

The water rose above her knees.

Prince Leo's eye caught hers—sharp and focused.

Beside him, Garrick continued some useless attempt at contortion.

The water rose to Briar's middle and crested the podium.

The piece of wood lifted with it.

Officer Ferro kicked.

The key bobbed left.

Sam Poe and Thomas did the same, creating a chaotic current that sent the key into a confused circle.

Briar closed her eyes.

She pushed aside the fear, the confusion, the escalating panic all around. She gathered every ounce of her energy and focused on Lyric and a long-ago memory of her mother, smiling encouragement as Briar made a leaf float up into the sky.

"It's not so much an incantation. It's a feeling. Right here." Mama placed her hand over her heart. "Imagine that feeling lifting the leaf straight up into the clouds."

With her eyes squeezed shut, Briar called the key to her as she grasped for that same feeling now.

Wonder.

Lightness.

Joy.

She pictured her brother, healthy.

Her brother, smiling.

Her brother, free.

Her chest went warm. Her locket, too. And something brushed against her knuckles. Everything came crashing back in a deluge of shouts and screams. Briar closed her fingers around the piece of wood and opened her eyes.

She had it.

The pick was in her hand.

With trembling fingers, she found the hole of the lock

and shoved the pick inside. She twisted and turned and jammed until the lock clicked.

Garrick raised his chin to keep his mouth above the water.

Iris wailed and writhed.

The restraints fell away from Briar's wrists. She pulled them off of her submerged body where they slowly sank to the steel floor. She was free and nobody seemed to know but the High Prince. He was no longer struggling. No longer kicking. He sat completely still, staring at her intently as the water rose to his neck as though waiting to see what she would do. Leave them behind and swim under the door, ensuring she would face only two competitors instead of eleven, or stay and save them? The choice paralyzed her. She could go right now and there would be nine less people standing between her and her brother. But Posey was choking on her wet scarf, Iris on her own panic. And Aurora was craning upward to take her final breath. Briar tried to steal herself against them. Tried to think of Lyric and only Lyric. He was her responsibility. Not them. She commanded herself to swim to the door.

But her body refused to listen.

She would die for her brother, but she wouldn't murder for him. Isn't that what she'd be doing if she left them here now?

Briar lifted herself off the chair, inhaled long and loud,

and dove beneath the cold water. She swam around the podium to Garrick, the first to be submerged. She made quick work of his lock, then moved to Posey beside him. By then, everyone was under water, watching with wide eyes, cheeks swollen with air. Only Iris continued to thrash, too panicked to realize Briar was free.

Her lungs burned as she moved to Margaret. As soon as the doctor was loose, Briar swam up to the surface with her. She grabbed another lungful of air and dove back down. She freed Officer Ferro, then Thomas, then Aurora, working her way around the circle. She went up with Aurora, who offered to stay and help. Briar urged her to go. The chamber was running out of air. So off Aurora swam as Briar kicked herself down to unlock the final three. The clergyman, the prince, and Iris, who had gone frighteningly still.

Briar's fingers shook as she fumbled with Sam's lock. She twisted. It clicked. She moved to Leo. As soon as he was free, he swam up to grab air like the others. Only he didn't swim to the door. He joined Briar as she unlocked Iris. He untangled her unconscious body from the restraints, wrapped his arm around her waist, and kicked up.

Briar, too.

"Are you good?" he said, his lips wet, his blue eyes as serious as she'd ever seen them. Gone was the devil-may-care prince she'd met back at Ambrose's manor. Replaced now by a young man who looked ready to help her fight the world.

"I'm good," she breathed.

"You sure?"

"I'm fine."

He took a deep breath, then disappeared beneath the water.

There was hardly any space at all between it and the ceiling. She smashed her nose against the steel and took whatever breath remained, then plunged down one last time and slipped through the opening out into the murky darkness. She hadn't tarried, but Leo was already gone, a much faster swimmer than she, even with Iris.

There was nothing but the faintest light above.

Briar swam toward it.

She kicked as hard as she'd ever kicked before, her boots like weights strapped to her ankles, her exhausted lungs screaming for oxygen, her mind begging for a surface that refused to come. The water was winning. Her boots were winning. But Briar would not quit. Her vision went black around the edges. She strained and kicked until she broke through the surface and gulped at the sunlit air. She swallowed it into her lungs as she paddled to a ledge made of brick and stone.

The prince lifted her onto the cement like she weighed nothing at all. Briar collapsed, dripping wet, coughing and sputtering as Dr. Margaret bent over Iris Grout. She placed one hand over the other on the girl's chest. Briar watched, a yawning chasm of shock and horror stretching wide inside of her as the doctor pumped Iris's chest, administered breath, checked for a pulse.

Iris's skin was blue. Her lips purple.

But the doctor kept working like she might save her. She didn't stop until a sound split the air. A loud, long beep as a dome rose up around the girl's lifeless body. With a whirr and a clank, it covered Iris completely and swallowed her into the ground.

CHAPTER 14

LEO

Water dripped from Leo's hair and rolled down his face. He scrubbed it away like a squeegee, his suit plastered to his body. The doctor sat back on her haunches while everyone stared—open-mouthed—at the wet spot where Iris Grout had been. Sam the clergyman took a knee and bowed his head, his lips moving in a silent prayer for the girl who was no longer.

Irritating, inept Iris.

Gone.

Snuffed out.

Like all of them would be if not for Briar.

Leo peered at the girl—her face ashen, her mouth grim, her dark braid dripping with pond water. This cipher from The Skid with a brother in Shard who didn't bother to hide her dislike for him, the High Prince. And yet she saved him. She saved all of them. He narrowed his eyes, wondering *how*. Had he really seen what he'd seen down below—that chunk of driftwood bobbing in her precise direction? Or had the very real prospect of death by drowning caused some weird, stress-induced hallucination? As though reading his thoughts, her golden eyes slid to his. Then looked quickly away.

"Congratulations," a voice said, drawing Leo's attention up, where a ghost-of-a-woman hovered above them. The lady from the portrait in Squire's study. The old man's first wife, Anna. Only it wasn't really Anna, but a hologram. She smiled proudly down at them as if they hadn't just been staring their own mortality straight in the eye, as if they hadn't just witnessed Iris's. "You passed the Trial of Restraint. You will now have five hours to escape the city."

As quickly as she came, Anna the Hologram disappeared, replaced by another countdown in the sky.

Escape the city.

Leo ran his fingers down his face again, removing as much water as possible, and looked from the reservoir surrounded by brick and stone to the network of fractured streets beyond, with rusted vehicles strewn about like a child's scattered toys and buildings in varying states of destruction. Some lay in piles of rubble, others rose stalwartly into a strange, blunted sky. Like it wasn't really a sky, but a—

"It's a dome," Ferro said.

Chills broke out across Leo's skin. They marched all

the way up into his hair. He looked down at his water-logged boots, lifting each one in turn. He pivoted in a slow, disbelieving circle, the air stagnant in his lungs as he took in the large compass rose embossed in the stone at their feet. He knew exactly where they were, for only one domed city existed within Korah and nobody—not even the highest government official—was allowed inside. They were standing inside the Domed City on the Forbidden Isle. The land that had cradled his mother. The land that had killed Ambrose's wife and son. The land that had turned into a desolate waste. How in the world had Squire gotten them here?

"We're inside the City of Kruse."

The officer's comment elicited a strong reaction.

The poor clergyman looked ready to faint. "That's impossible."

It should have been. But somehow, it wasn't. Leo had studied maps and poured over pictures. Even in its annihilated state, he knew this city better than he knew most in Korah. And here he was, standing in its center. A fact that filled him with equal parts excitement and foreboding.

There was a reason this place was forbidden.

"It's supposed to be toxic," Sam said.

"It's not the toxicity I'm worried about," Ferro replied.

The clergyman drew closer to the group. "You're not talking about—you don't mean—surely that's ..."

Stammering, skeptical Sam.

The poor guy's mouth was stuck in a loop.

"Of course not." Dr. Margaret cut him off with a no-nonsense side-eye. "That's nothing but rumor. Scary stories meant to frighten little children."

Leo thought about his bed-wetting cousin and his big brother's cruel cure.

"What is everyone talking about?" Garrick asked.

"The repercussions of Magic," Leo said, his attention returning to Briar.

Anyone with any schooling and plenty without knew about the Cambria Disaster. It was the greatest in Korah's history and it only happened twenty-five years ago, when his grandfather received intel that Magic was gathering on the island, assembling in the woodlands, readying for attack. The Great King Casimir sent the First Guard in the dead of night. They descended upon Cambrian villages in full force, tearing families from their homes. Hordes of people were herded inside the military city of Kruse where they were to be detained and interrogated. In hindsight, a dire mistake. So much power should never have been allowed to gather in one place, for it released its fury in a cataclysm of epic proportions.

Tornados toppled buildings and uprooted trees. Earthquakes split the ground and swallowed families whole. Lightning rained from the sky, a deluge of voltage that set fire to whatever was left. And in the midst of all that ruin, the city's radioactive arsenal began to ignite. In the end, the disaster killed more people than it spared. A perfect picture of what happened when Magic was allowed to gather and use its power collectively.

"After the disaster, the city was contaminated with chemical waste. Magic, too." Ferro shifted his weight as if merely mentioning the word made him uncomfortable. "It was everywhere. In the water. The air. The ground. The First Guard evacuated the whole island, then erected this dome over the worst of the contamination."

The Domed City of Kruse.

The *Doomed* City of Kruse.

Left to rot like the rest of the island.

"So what's the rumor?" Garrick pressed, referencing the doctor's words.

"They evacuated *people*," Leo replied.

In perfect timing, a howl split the air. An unholy, inhuman shriek of a sound that had the hair on the back of his neck standing on end and the nine of them drawing nearer.

"What was that?" Garrick asked.

"The city's wildlife," Leo replied.

For while human survivors were evacuated, the animals were not.

They remained—trapped.

Breathing the contaminated air.

Drinking the contaminated water.

Burrowing into the contaminated ground.

Turning into whatever it was they were now.

Another bone-chilling howl carried from the distance.

They stood with their backs together, Briar's shoulder slight but strong against Leo's. Adrenaline coursed through his veins as he looked up at the clock in the sky. Five hours should feel generous when compared to what they'd woken up to down below. But the reality of the situation was slowly dawning. They didn't just have to escape a city, they had to escape one that was completely enclosed. And they had to do so without calling attention to whatever it was prowling the streets.

"We should find cover," Ferro said.

"That's a good idea," Sam agreed. "We're too exposed right now."

"The city is surrounded by a wall?" Briar asked.

"And this dome," Ferro replied.

"How do we get out, then?"

Leo looked at her—still dripping wet. All of them were soaked. But while the others resembled drown rats, Briar stood with her shoulders fiercely squared, her jaw set in the same determined way it had been at dinner when she attacked the quohog with her knife. She didn't want cover. She didn't look like a girl eager to hide. Instead, she looked like a warrior ready to sprint headlong into battle. He couldn't help but admire her for it. "Right now we're standing in the city center," Leo said. "The wall should be roughly six, seven miles out in all directions. The main gate is east." Although he wasn't sure what good getting to the gate would be. It ran on electrical power, which had been shut down ages ago.

"Is there a chance it could open manually?" Briar asked.

"A small one."

"So we will probably have to climb it," she said.

"And cut through the dome," he replied.

Briar looked around, as if considering. Her attention followed the compass rose east and stopped on a line of shops across the reservoir, their windows dark and broken, signs askew. She stepped toward them.

"Where are you going?" the doctor asked.

"To find something sharp."

Leo went after her, a thrill running through him.

The others followed, too. He could hear their footsteps, quick and quiet.

Debris crunched underfoot as he followed Briar through the broken storefront window of the first shop—a ramshackle building overgrown with weeds that had at one point been something like a souvenir-boutique-amenity-store hybrid. Inside, half the shelves were toppled, their contents spilled across the floor. Briar looked around as vigilantly as she had in the woods outside the Squire Estate. Aurora stepped in behind him—her intricate braids no longer swept up into a crown, but wet and long down her back as she cast a forlorn look from one end of the dimly-lit shop to the other. "It's so strange seeing it all in person."

Leo looked at her.

She picked up a runaway glass bottle that must have rolled across the floor. She twisted off the lid and sniffed the contents inside.

Ferro nudged a pile of rubble with his boot.

Briar grabbed a knapsack with a Cambrian logo off an upright shelf and gave it a shake, sending twenty-five years' worth of dust motes into the stream of sunlight pouring in from the broken storefront window. He watched her as she looked covertly at the others. When she glanced his way, he feigned interest in a wire rack filled with postcards, maps, and brochures. He gave it a spin. Its joints let loose a squeaky moan that made Dr. Margaret hiss. It was obvious she didn't want to call any attention to whatever it was doing the howling.

"This could be useful," Ferro said, taking one of the maps.

It was cartoon-like. Meant for sightseers exploring the city.

Leo's attention returned to Briar.

She slid the knapsack over one shoulder and slipped down an aisle.

"So what are we looking for exactly?" Thomas said.

"Something that can cut through a dome." Leo clapped the gentleman on the shoulder, then crept quietly after the wooded assassin, careful to avoid debris as he went.

She walked on silent feet. Observant. Focused. Pausing only once to break open a moldy parcel of pouched water. She pulled a few free and stuck them inside her bag. Leo hid in the shadow as she reached the far side of the aisle, where Cambrian apparel hung on a rack. She removed a thick pullover and pressed the fabric against her nose. He had to imagine that after all these years, it smelled similar to Squire's study. She shook it out like she'd shaken the knapsack, then used it like a towel to dry her face, her hair, her suit. When she was finished, she slung the damp pullover over the metal bar of the rack and grabbed another. She pulled it over her head, then stepped toward a back exit like she might bolt.

"Going somewhere?" Leo asked, stepping out of the dark.

Briar startled, then pressed her gloved palm flat against her chest. "Are you trying to scare me to death?"

"No, actually. I'm more interested in being allies."

She eyed him suspiciously as he closed the gap between them.

"You don't need to look at me that way. I'm not tricking you." Wasn't he? He couldn't stop seeing what he saw down below. Briar closing her eyes. The wood bobbing in her direction. He thought his biggest competition would be Ferro or the foreigner, an assumption that would have earned him a slap from Sabrina. Now it seemed this girl with the golden eyes might be his biggest threat and Leo knew the old adage well. Keep your friends close, your enemies closer. He unzipped his suit and peeled off the wet sleeves, the air cool against his bare skin.

Briar looked quickly away, the ear he could see going pink.

He bit back a grin. Briar the Thorn Patch, unafraid of radioactive mutants. Mortified by a half-naked man. Most girls didn't look in the opposite direction when he undressed. He reached past her for one of the pullovers.

She leaned away with her chin slightly lifted.

He pulled the garment over his head. "So what do you say?"

"No."

"Why not?"

"We're competing in a contest with only one winner."

"Right. But we need to get to the end of the contest to be that winner. We could help each other get there."

"No."

Her rejection was so quick, so without consideration, he was slightly insulted. He could feel something rising up in him. A strong desire to meet the challenge before him. "Do you not accept help as a rule or is it mine in particular?"

"Allies only work when they can trust each other."

He cocked his eyebrow wickedly. "You don't trust me?"

"Not with my brother's life."

He had the feeling she didn't trust him with hers, either. "How am I supposed to repay you then? You saved our lives down there."

Her golden eyes went dark, hooded. Like the saving of lives left her feeling conflicted instead of proud. Maybe it did. Maybe she regretted her choice.

Still. "I owe you one."

"You don't owe me anything." She turned to leave.

He grabbed her elbow.

She stopped, her eyes zeroing in on his hand.

"But I do. And I can't repay you if you go out there on your own." He let go, his fingers tingling. He stretched them by his side. "Look, I know this city. I know how to reach the main gate. How are you going to get there—with a cartoon map?"

"I'm fully capable of walking east without help."

"And the wall? Are you fully capable of climbing it?"

"I'm thin enough. Years of laboring for food will do that to a person. Maybe I can slip through a crack." She stepped away.

He stepped, too. Her eagerness to leave him was aggravating. "I'm a good climber. I've spent the last two years with my cousin, exploring some the most death defying cliffs in the commonwealth." Which meant he might actually have a skill that would come in handy.

"And you're offering what, exactly? To carry me up on your back?"" Her eyes smoldered with the dare.

His blood went hot with the desire to take it.

"Thanks, but I'm better off on my own." She slung her newly acquired knapsack over her shoulders and turned away, so keen to get rid of him that she didn't see what he very suddenly did.

A horrible, awful something lurking in the aisle.

CHAPTER 15

BRIAR

The prince's hand clapped across Briar's mouth. His strong arm wrapped tight around her waist. Her nostrils flared. A scream hurtled up her throat. But his hand clamped harder, trapping the scream inside as a thousand frightened thoughts exploded in her mind like hot kernels of corn.

A contest with only one winner.

The coin in Prince Leo's jar.

A crumpled figure on the floor.

Guilty hands.

Nobody can know!

But the prince already knew.

He witnessed what she'd done down there at the bottom of the reservoir.

And now he was going to make her pay.

She refused to go down without a fight. He might be

bigger. He might be stronger. But she was scrappy. She was determined. He pulled her back and away, dragging her behind the rack of apparel as she kicked and scratched and clawed, then stopped. Her eyes went wide, her popping thoughts silent and still. The air in her lungs, too. The prince was not trying to eliminate her. The prince was not trying to punish her. The prince was protecting her.

From whatever that was skulking down the aisle directly in front of them.

A two-legged creature the size of a small bear with gray, almost translucent skin. It was creeping away from them, closer and closer to the girl standing with her back to the beast, obliviously rummaging through items on a shelf.

Posey.

The scream trapped in Briar's throat came back to life.

But Leo's broad palm was fastened tightly over her mouth.

The creature made a noise—an awful, gurgling click.

Posey went still.

The clicking stopped.

The creature lifted its ugly head and loosened a screech so hair-raising, Leo let go of Briar to cover his ears.

Someone ran.

Not Posey, but the Illustrian named Thomas.

He bolted for the door from the next aisle over.

Briar watched in frozen terror as the creature released

another piercing howl and sprang. So fast and powerfully, Thomas didn't have a chance. It leaped over Posey and tackled him to the ground in one fell swoop. Then it ripped out his jugular.

Briar's trapped scream exploded into the air.

The prince grabbed her arm and together, they fled, spilling a path of obstacles behind them. Whatever they could grab. As if tumbled boxes could stop whatever that was. Briar sprinted faster than she'd ever sprinted before. Even faster than she'd sprinted that day from Guillotine Square.

They pushed through the back exit, out into the evening air just as something caught Briar's foot. Her ankle twisted, then exploded in a burst of white, hot pain. She sprawled to the ground, the rough cement scraping the skin on her hands and knees. Leo pulled her up, lifted her into his arms, and for a moment, Briar thought he was going to run with her. But then he heaved her inside an industrial-sized trash receptacle, leaped in, pulled the top closed with a resounding clang, and threw himself long on top of her, where she burrowed deep into the crevice where the receptacle's floor met one of its walls.

Inside was dark and empty. There was nothing but their heavy breathing and their crashing heartbeats as his body covered hers.

Then that horrible, clicking gurgle as the creature jumped on the receptacle's top. Briar clamped her hands over her ears. The metal bent beneath the creature's weight, the hinges of the lid groaning. Metal crunched as the beast jumped off. She could feel Leo's heart pounding all the way through the bag on her back. Was it gone? Had they escaped Thomas's fate? On the cusp of her desperate thought, the lid opened and the creature jumped inside.

Briar did not move.

Could not move.

The monster drew closer.

Its snout touched her hair. She could smell its rancid breath.

She held her own.

It made another click. Released another shriek.

Briar swallowed a shout. It escaped like a whimper in the back of her throat. Leo's heart crashed harder. His body pressed tighter. She squeezed her eyes, positive this was it. This was the end. She and the High Prince of Korah were going to die at the hands of a mutant while her brother languished in Shard Prison. But then another sound came —a deafening howl from somewhere outside the receptacle.

The creature lifted its head and gurgled louder. Then it released a shriek and bounded away, leaving them alone.

Briar stayed portrait-still.

The prince, too.

Neither of them moved.

Neither of them spoke.

Briar hardly breathed.

They remained paralyzed, pressed together, until his heart stopped crashing and their suits were almost dry and the pain in Briar's ankle brought tears to her eyes.

When Leo finally moved, he did so like one rusted with time. The air felt cool against her shoulders and arms. Unnaturally exposed after being so tightly swaddled. He pressed up onto his knees, then onto his feet—slowly, carefully—the metal floor making a sound that felt much too loud in the surrounding silence. Briar wanted to tell him to stop. Get down. But he peeked over the receptacle's top, first checking the alleyway, then the sky, which had deepened from soft peach to a dusky blue as the clock ticked overhead.

Three hours and fifty-three minutes.

With six, maybe seven miles between them and the wall.

In a city crawling with monsters.

While Briar's ankle screamed.

Hopelessness wrapped around her like a blanket dipped in icy water. She fought against its oppressive weight. Lyric couldn't afford such feelings to undo her now. She shrugged free of the knapsack and sat up, gritting her teeth through the pain, refusing to let it be her master like she had once before when she let go of Echo. She glared at her gloved hand and forced herself to stand.

Her knees buckled beneath her weight.

The prince caught her around the waist.

Pain and frustration swelled. She pushed him away and sank down the receptacle wall, thinking of another wall. Six, maybe seven miles away. How in the world was she supposed to get to it like this? How in the world could she climb it when she did? How serious did an injury have to be for elimination? Fury and panic billowed in her soul. *No*. An injured ankle would not take her out of this contest. She'd already upset the hornet's nest. What was the harm in upsetting it more? What other choice did she have but to use Magic again? Briar wondered if this was how it happened—the slippery descent toward corruption. Was this how the monster got her mother?

She squeezed her eyes tight, unable to believe any of this was a coincidence. The contest, here on this island, where her mother and his grew up together. Ambrose was up to something. This location felt personal. A place destroyed by Magic, a perfect depiction of what it had done to all of them. Ambrose. The prince. Herself. Their families. And here she was, in need of using it again. Only this time, it wasn't some silly charm. This would be advanced Magic. She probably wouldn't succeed. But she had to try and she couldn't in front of him. The prince needed to go. If her attempts at healing didn't work, she would have to find another way. She wouldn't quit. Even if she had to hop all seven miles on her left foot. She glanced up at the clock, hopelessness closing in.

The prince crouched in front of her. "How bad is it?"

"I'm fine."

"Briar."

Hearing him say her name so familiarly was disorienting. Bewildering. She mashed her teeth and closed her eyes.

"Are you going to look at it or do you want me to?"

"I said I'm fine." She pulled in a deep breath through her nose, trying to figure out the best way to get him out of here.

"You should take off your boot," he said.

"The boot's staying put."

"It'll only get worse if you leave it on."

"Better for the swelling to leave it be."

"That's actually a myth."

She opened one eye, glaring at him through it.

"May I?" he asked.

"May you leave? Yes. Please."

"I'm not going anywhere."

She could see that he meant it. For whatever confounding reason, he would stay until she took off her blasted boot. Sucking in a sharp breath, she attempted to undo the laces. The pain came so acutely, the whole trash receptacle spun. Sweat broke out across her brow. And the frustration in her chest blossomed into straight-up rage. Her lungs seethed with it, pain once again the dictator.

Why must it always have its way? She pressed her cheek against the wall and nodded her permission.

Leo's touch was soft and featherlight as he lifted the pantleg of her suit and began unlacing her boots. "I sprained my ankle really bad once. Our doctor said I should have taken my shoe off as soon as possible. My cousin was convinced I was supposed to keep it on."

"Hawk." An appropriate name for a wingman, on the news almost as much as the prince. He had dark hair like Leo, but hazel eyes and a pointier nose. She sucked in a sharp breath as the prince pulled her boot free.

When he rolled down her stocking, they found an ankle so mangled and bruised, it didn't resemble an ankle at all.

Nausea rolled in her stomach.

"This makes getting to the wall a little trickier," he said.

Tears stung her eyes.

Leo rubbed the back of his head in a rare display of uncertainty. "I could carry you."

"I'll be fine." She gritted the words between her teeth.

"You keep saying that. Makes me question your definition of the word."

"We aren't allies."

"You're not getting to the wall without one."

"You underestimate the iron nature of my will." But even as she said it, a tiredness descended. Not from the contest. Not from using Magic. But from a whole decade of having to be unflinchingly strong. Of facing impossible choices.

She raked her teeth over her bottom lip, then bit the inside of her cheek. Ambrose said this contest would be a reflection of life. Well, a reflection it was. Briar thought of Iris Grout's purple lips. Was the girl dead because she hesitated? Was Lyric going to die because she acted? She had been cursed with an unrelenting conscience that made choices like steal or starve confounding ones. Echo used to tell her she was too noble to be an orphan. She should have been born a queen. To which she would always reply, "I'd rather be king."

Now here was the High Prince of Korah, kneeling in front of her inside a giant garbage can. He saved her life. Twice. First, by pulling her behind that clothing rack. Then by picking her up and getting her inside this receptacle. Unlike herself, he'd exhibited zero hesitation. He'd swooped her into his arms without a second thought and tossed her into safety. And he was still here, looking at her like he might actually be concerned, which was every bit as disorienting as him saying her name. Which was the real Leo? The flirtatious daredevil portrayed by the media? The eight year old on the dais? Or this one in front of her now? Did it matter? Whichever he was, she needed him gone. She couldn't do what she needed to do with him here. Her small charm might have gone unnoticed. This would not. If it worked, the truth would be irrefutable.

Briar Bishop was Magic.

"We're even," she said. "Whatever debt you thought you owed me has been more than paid."

He didn't budge.

The muscles in her jaw tightened. "You can get to the wall a lot faster without me."

"Of course I can, but I'm not leaving you here."

"I can take care of myself. I've been doing it for most of my life."

"What happened to your parents?"

Danger.

Danger.

Danger!

The pain was pounding.

The clock was ticking.

She wanted to yell at him to go.

Leave.

Stop looking at her like that!

"My parents are dead."

Leo studied her in a way that made the warning bells ring all the louder. "Do you know which one of them was Magic?"

And just like that, all the air went deathly still.

His eyes bore into hers. "I saw you do it," he said. "You closed your eyes, and the key came to you."

Deny it, Briar.

Act confused.

Tell him he's crazy.

Threaten him.

She wasn't the only one with secrets, after all. The proof was there in her pocket. She still had the coin from his jar. She thought of the crumpled figure on the floor. He'd done something. Something horrible. Something he didn't want anyone to know. She brought the coin with knowing it might give her an advantage. Was now the time to pull it out?

"Can you heal yourself?" he said. "Is that why you're trying to get rid of me?"

She glared.

He glared back. "Magic killed my grandfather."

"I know."

"It killed my mother."

She knew that, too. Better than he might imagine.

"It destroyed this entire island."

"You don't hear me arguing."

"I would have expected Magic to leave me and everyone else to die down there at the bottom of the reservoir. But you didn't." He sat down against the opposite wall, set his elbows on his knees, and studied her like she was a puzzle piece in the wrong puzzle. "I'm not leaving. I will carry you over my shoulder if I have to, which will probably be uncomfortable for the both of us."

Briar's heart pounded.

He had her trapped.

Pinned against a proverbial wall.

He wasn't leaving. She couldn't make him. The clock was ticking. And she was already a dead man walking. There was nothing for her to do but get on with it. Briar set her mind on healing. She had been on the receiving end three different times. Once, when she fell out of a tree and broke her arm. Again, when Echo dared her to catch a porcupine. And one last time—the most serious of all—when she tumbled out of the third story window of their cramped living quarters on Tenement Row. Her mother had struggled, then. She had a much easier time healing in the forests of Silva than she did in the crowd and pollution of Antis. She'd needed something to help her. Power from which to draw.

She had used Briar's necklace.

Briar reached up to touch it. She pulled it from beneath her suit, then wrapped her hand around the locket. It wasn't from a scrap market. It was from this very island, forged from a magical tree. Might it help her now? Closing her eyes, she exhaled long and slow—pushing out every drop of fear, confusion, anger and pain. Then she inhaled just as slow—determination, grit. And that thing that drove her doggedly onward. *Love*. The reason she worked so relentlessly to survive. So Lyric wouldn't have to alone. Briar imagined exhaling every exhausting, negative emotion into the farthest recesses of her mind, then fixed her energy upon Lyric and called forth healing like she'd called that key.

Warmth radiated in her palm, as if the locket had turned into a ball of heat. It seeped through her glove, into her skin, and traveled up her arm. It flooded her chest and rolled like a wave down her body. A rising tide of heat. A fevered swell that crested and crashed in her ankle before pulling back out into the sea.

The heat was gone.

The pain had gone with it.

When Briar opened her eyes, she saw that the bruising was gone, too. Her ankle was straight and new.

She sank back, exhausted.

Spent.

Diminished.

The healing had sapped all of her strength.

This, at least, was a lesson her mother had taught her.

Magic wasn't free.

It always came with a price.

CHAPTER 16

LEO

Chaos spun like a cyclone in Leo's mind.

Not only did he just witness Magic, the bracelet in his possession had scalded his thigh while it happened. His *mother's* bracelet. He pulled it from his pocket. The mysterious material was still warm, a pool of thermal energy in his palm. Why had it just responded like that? Why did it respond at all? What was his mother doing with a Magic bracelet?

His tornadic thoughts spun faster.

It wasn't the only Magic thing in his mother's life. Turned out, she had a Magic chambermaid, too. He looked at Briar and the familiarity of her slammed through him fresh and new—a puzzle piece sliding into place.

A crazy theory took shape.

A wild, preposterous hypothesis.

This girl had a locket the same rare material as his

mother's bracelet. She did Magic, clutching the locket as she did so. And his mother's bracelet went hot in response. His mother was killed by her chambermaid, who turned out to be Magic. Her dark-haired, golden-eyed chambermaid.

He pressed himself against the receptacle wall. "Who are you?"

Briar blanched. What little color left in her face drained completely away.

The chambermaid had children. A decree had gone out in search of them, but they were never found. "You're her daughter, aren't you?"

Briar didn't answer.

Leo's mind spun faster.

The wooded assassin—this girl who looked at him outside Squire's gate with murder in her eyes.

And a plot to kill the royal family.

"What's going on?" he breathed.

"I don't know."

"Is this a trap?"

"I don't know."

"Is this a trick?"

"I don't know."

"How are we here together?" he demanded.

"I don't know!" she shot back, a lock of dark hair falling loose from her braid. She shoved it behind her ear and shook her head. "I was just as alarmed when I first saw you."

"Your mother killed mine."

"Your family killed mine."

"Because they were part of a plot to kill *mine*."

"My father was innocent! He had nothing to do with any of it. And I was *seven*. I wasn't part of any plot."

"You're Magic, though."

"Not by practice."

He looked incredulously from her locket to her ankle.

"Not before this contest anyway!" She pinched her lips together. Jabbed again at the lock of hair that refused to stay put. "I didn't ask to be born this way. It's not a choice I made." She delivered the final statement with such defensiveness, a cord of rebellious sympathy pulled tight within him.

He knew all too well what it was like. To be born without a choice.

Leo shoved his hand into his hair and stared hard at Briar the Thorn Patch. She looked depleted of all energy, like one strong gust of wind might blow her away. Was it real, or was it an act meant to slip past his defenses? He knew better than most that Magic was cunning. Her mother, the most cunning of all.

She picked up her boot and shoved her foot back inside.

Leo nodded at her locket. "You obviously didn't get that at a scrap market."

"No."

He raised his eyebrows at her, waiting for her to elaborate.

She yanked on her bootlaces. "My mother fashioned it from a bracelet."

"Like this one?"

Briar nodded.

"What is it made out of?"

"A vine tree." At his confused look, she continued. "They no longer exist. Most were cut down and burned during The Purge. The only ones remaining were here on this island and they were destroyed in the disaster."

"Why were they cut down and burned?"

"They were said to be Magic."

Leo ran his hand down the length of his face. All this time, he'd been carrying Magic around in his pocket. His father had given it to him on his eighteenth birthday. "My mother couldn't have known what this was."

Briar looked at him meaningfully, like he was missing the obvious.

"What?" he barked.

"They grew up together on this island."

He blinked at her. The chambermaid grew up on the Forbidden Isle?

"They were childhood friends."

Leo had no idea. His mother had never told him. Or if she did, he'd forgotten. He knew his mother and her chambermaid shared a special relationship. Even at a young age, that much had been clear. His mother loved the chambermaid in a way that defied position. The two didn't act like mistress and servant, at least not in the privacy of his mother's chambers. It had made the chambermaid's betrayal all the worse. That same sense of betrayal stabbed him all over again. They'd known each other since they were children.

"Do you have any childhood friends?" Briar asked.

His mind slid to Sabrina.

There wasn't much he didn't know about her. In turn, there wasn't much she didn't know about him.

"Do you really think your mother didn't know mine was Magic?"

He shook his head. No. His mother couldn't have known. She never would have trusted the chambermaid if she did. She certainly wouldn't have allowed her in their home, near her son. The truth of the chambermaid's identity didn't come out until later, after his mother was already dead. Then Grandfather was killed, and it was discovered that the chambermaid wasn't the only palace employee hiding Magic. He shook his head again, his hand closing into a fist around the bracelet. She couldn't have known about this either.

It was plausible enough.

She'd lived on this isle for the first seventeen years of her life, and this isle turned out to be a hotbed of Magic. Wasn't it feasible to conclude that she'd acquired the bracelet with her friend while living here without understanding its makeup?

Briar pulled a pouched water from the knapsack. She tore off the tab and downed the entire thing, sucking it back like a parched sailor, the bag shriveling as she did.

"Thanks for sharing," he said dryly.

She tossed him another, then slowly stood from her spot.

"Where are you going?"

"To the wall," she said. She bore weight on her right foot—tentatively at first, as though testing it out—then all the way. Her face was still pale, her posture spent. She looked up at the countdown in the sky.

Leo stood, too. "Do you think you can make it?"

"Are you going to stop me?" When he made no move to apprehend her, she zipped up the knapsack, slung it over her shoulder, gave the alley a thorough check, then jumped down.

"You looked at me like *I* was the villain," Leo said.

She looked up at him.

"In the woods outside the old man's estate." How could she have looked at him like that knowing it was her mother who killed his?

But Briar offered no reply. Instead, she began quietly rummaging through the detritus in the alleyway.

Leo jumped down after her. "Like *I* was the bad guy in this equation."

She picked up a scrap of metal and examined it.

"How do I know that you aren't here to finish what your mother started?"

"Because I'm not her!" She dropped the metal, her words vehement. Her face a mask of conviction. "I'm *not* my mother."

She said it like someone who fiercely needed those words be true.

It was a need Leo understood all too well.

He didn't want to be his father.

Her golden eyes grew thick with moisture. She quickly blinked it away. "I know what she did was unforgiveable to you. But it was unforgiveable to me, too. Her choice got my father killed. My grandparents and my uncles killed. Her choice left me and my two brothers orphaned and all alone in a world that has not been kind."

"Two?"

Briar looked down. "Echo died when we were thirteen."

We.

The implications of the word sunk in slowly. It shouldn't surprise him. He knew all too well that twins and Magic often went hand-in-hand. "He was your twin?"

She shrugged.

Leo huffed.

"I had no idea you'd be here. I came because I was invited and my brother needs my help. If this is a trap, I'm not setting it. You can lock me up when this is all over. You can send me to Guillotine Square. Just please let me try and rescue Lyric first."

"Lyric is Magic."

Her eyes flashed like lightning. "If I win, you can't touch him."

The wooded assassin was back—fierce. Formidable.

Another rebellious cord pulled tight within him. Here was a girl fully prepared to die for her brother. Her love was that relentless. Her loyalty that unwavering. She might claim to have been on her own all these years, but Leo didn't have anyone like that in his corner. Nobody he'd die for. Nobody who would die for him. Certainly not his father.

Briar pulled up two long pieces of scrap wood, jagged at both ends.

"What are you looking for?" he asked.

"Something to use as a weapon." She shoved one against his chest and crept to the mouth of the alley, where she peered out into the empty street.

Leo joined her.

All was quiet.

Ominous.

There was no sign of the other contestants.

No sign of the creatures, either.

Up above, stars began freckling the sky, their twinkling muted by the translucent dome.

"At least we know how they hunt," he whispered.

"We do?"

"That thing didn't attack until Thomas ran. I'm pretty sure the clicking noise is some sort of echolocation. Like bats."

Briar looked appalled

He couldn't blame her.

If they wanted to advance further in the contest, they needed to move. And he strongly suspected the mutants hunted via movement.

"East is that way," he said, nodding.

"I know which way east is." With a scowl, she checked for signs of life, then crept across the ruined street.

He watched her navigate around the wreckage. Collapsed metal beams. Piles of crumbled brick and stone. The place looked like a war zone. When she reached the other side, she stopped and looked back at him. Like a game of strategy, and it was his move.

Leo was wary. Full of suspicion.

She was the chambermaid's daughter.

She claimed betrayal every bit as passionately as he felt it in his heart. She also claimed not to practice Magic. And yet she seemed more than competent back in the trash receptacle. Not to mention down in that reservoir. He'd be a fool to trust her. But he'd be every bit as foolish to let her go. This was a competition and she had an unfair advantage. Better to keep her in his sights. With adrenaline coursing once again, Leo took up the rear.

They made their way quickly and quietly, winding east through a maze of decimated backstreets and alleyways, skirting around craters, eyes wide and searching in the dark lest they stumble upon a mutant or fall headlong into a fissure. Several were frighteningly deep, so much so Leo wondered if they had a bottom. His eyes remained on the ground. Briar's kept lifting to the sky, where the clock ticked.

An hour in, Leo decided to break the silence. "How did your brother die?"

"Infection."

"From?"

"Third degree burns. He fell into a fire."

"That's awful."

"Tell that to your father."

"What does he have to do with it?"

"He was the one who ordered all the derelict buildings in Antis burned, even though a lot of people were using them for shelter to keep warm in the winter. He never bothered checking them first. When we woke up, we were surrounded in flames. The floor collapsed beneath us. I tried to pull him back up, but the flames got to my hand and I just ... I let go."

"Your hand was on fire."

"My brother's life was in that hand."

Leo checked over his shoulder to make sure nothing was creeping behind them. Briar said her brother died of infection. She didn't say he died in a fire. "How did he get out?"

She stepped over a pile of debris. "Somehow, I dragged him out. I don't even really remember it. I'm not sure how I survived or escaped without third degree burns of my own, especially when Echo was ..." Briar shook her head as though shaking away the memory. "He lived for a couple more days, but without any way to treat him, he died."

"You couldn't bring him to a doctor?"

"Doctors treat patients with money. We've never had any."

Leo stared absently at her backside, the Cambrian logo on her knapsack blurring in and out of focus. He might have asked why she didn't use Magic to heal him. But then, she seemed sapped of all strength after fixing her busted ankle. Third degree burns covering a person's body would have to be infinitely more difficult. Leo tried to imagine it —the horror of losing a sibling in such a way. Was it any wonder she was so determined to save the brother she had left? He frowned. If the universe was doling out punishment, she'd received plenty.

"How were you never caught?" he asked.

"I don't know."

The First Guard had apprehended the chambermaid's parents and her twin brothers within a week. Meanwhile, her children had up and vanished. But they'd been in Antis this whole time. It seemed every bit as impossible as healing third degree burns. And yet, here she was.

"In the beginning, a clergyman took us in."

"He didn't hand you over?"

"He didn't know who we were. And he considered it his life's mission to rehabilitate street kids. Echo hated it there. But not me. It was nice, not having to steal for food."

"Why did you leave?"

"Echo let it slip to one of the other kids that we were twins. So we had no choice. That's when we started staying in abandoned buildings."

They stopped at the mouth of another alley, checking the crossroad before them. Briar pointed up ahead at a railing near the street.

"What is that?" she asked.

Leo peered at it. "I think it's a UTS station."

"A what?"

"The Underground Transit System." Leo crept out into the open. "With tunnels that will lead right out of the city. Underground. This might be our way out."

He tiptoed closer. To the place the railing might have descended if not for the large sheet of metal placed over the opening. Someone had sealed it shut with a thick strip of adhesive. Leo picked at one corner, then began pulling the adhesive up in one long segment as Briar watched him from the alley.

He waved for her to join him, then pried his fingers beneath the sheet of metal. Once he had a good grip, he planted his feet wide, gritted his teeth, and lifted. Slowly—the tendons in his neck pulling with the effort—he pried up the makeshift door. It landed in the rubble and sent a spray of dust into the air. They looked around nervously.

All remained still and quiet.

Leo wiped the back of his arm across his forehead and stared down into the dark cavern. The stairs had crumbled. Roughly seven feet below was a landing made of concrete. He jumped down onto it.

Briar peeked over the opening—slightly panicked, considerably exasperated. "What are you doing?" she hissed.

"Looking for an easier way out."

"How do you know those things don't sleep down there?"

"The First Guard sealed this entire city which means there are doors like this at every UTS entrance. Unless those *things* have opposable thumbs, I'm safer down here than you are up there."

That was all the convincing it took.

Briar sat down on the edge of the entrance.

Without thinking, Leo dropped his wooden stake and reached up to help her down. His hands slid from her hips to the narrow part of her waist as she landed in front of him.

She stepped back and yanked at her pullover.

Leo cleared his throat.

Briar took a shaky breath, then leaned over the railing and peered down into the dark abyss. The faint light of the moon and stars afforded them a view of a few stairs before all faded into pitch black.

"This could lead us out of the city," he said. There'd be no wall to climb. No dome to cut through. There'd be no way to see anything either. "You don't know how to make light, do you?"

"Yeah sure, let me just consult the book of spells I keep in my back pocket."

He twisted his lips to the side. The underground transit was a system of leveled tunnels. The deeper the level, the further the tunnel went. Back on the mainland, Leo could take a conveyor lift five levels deep and get from Antis all the way to Military Ridge in less than six hours. On foot in the dark, they could get lost in the depths for much longer. Possibly forever. As much as he hated to say it, their odds were better continuing the way they'd been going. "I think we're better off up there."

"With radioactive mutants."

"Maybe there aren't very many." They hadn't heard any

more shrieks or howls or clicks. The night had been eerily quiet.

"Or their appetite has been temporarily satiated."

Because they'd just finished feasting.

On the other contestants.

With a shudder, Leo retrieved his stake and tossed it up out onto the street, then lifted himself up, back out into the open. He pulled Briar up easily. The second her feet touched solid ground, she yanked her hand from his. It was the one she kept tucked inside a glove. He knew now what was underneath. Scars from a fire.

"I'm sorry about your brother," Leo said.

She looked up at him with round eyes. Surprised eyes. That same lock of hair had fallen loose again, framing the side of her face. Only she didn't rush to tuck it away. She swallowed and looked down, then spoke so softly, he almost missed it. "I'm sorry about your mother."

Something stretched wide in Leo's soul. A longing that had been in hibernation. They were such simple words. Such obvious words. And yet, nobody had said them to him before. About him, sure. Around him, yes. But never *to* him. Back then, he'd been treated much less like a human being, and much more like a tragically gripping headline. How ironic that the person speaking the words he needed to hear was the daughter of his mother's murderer. Unsure whether to frown or smile, Leo picked up his stake.

And for the first time, Briar spoke his name.

The alarm in her voice stopped him dead in his tracks.

Slowly, he turned as a gurgling rattle shot ice through his veins. Something large and grotesque stepped out into the moonlight.

Leo stopped breathing.

He stared hard at Briar, her eyes glued to his.

Don't move.

But he couldn't say the words. He couldn't even mouth them.

That required movement.

His grip tightened on the wooden stake in his hand.

The creature lifted its snout and clicked faster.

To Leo's horror, something gurgled in reply.

His eyes darted left as two more mutants skulked from the shadows.

And then another straight ahead, right behind Briar.

It made a loud sound that had panic pooling in her eyes, and there was absolutely nothing he could do but stare back at her, exuding all of the authority he could muster, commanding her to *stay still.*

Do not move, Briar. Do not *move.*

He imagined sending the command like a laser beam from his mind to hers.

The creature to his right let loose a howling shriek.

Briar squeezed her eyes tight as the mutant behind her circled slowly around, its snout inches from her ear.

Don't move.

Blood pounded through his body.

Don't move.

The creatures began a chorus of clacking—loud and aggressive—as two more slunk out from an alleyway.

Then a different sound came. From the mutant beside Briar. A hissing breath that caught the hair framing her face. In horror, Leo watched as the lock undulated in the current.

Movement.

Before the mutant could react, Leo lunged forward and rammed his stake straight through its middle.

A fountain of hot blood sprayed into the night and splattered on the ground as the creature howled and writhed.

Leo tried to pull the stake free, knowing the others would pounce, a clatter of awful shrieks echoing all around. But no attack came. The mutants fled. They scurried away, disappearing into the shadows, leaving Leo and Briar alone in the street with the impaled mutant twitching and groaning before going still and silent.

Briar stared, frozen in place, her chest heaving.

Leo wrenched his stake free.

A dark, viscous blood covered the wood.

He stared at it, a slow and glorious discovery sliding into place.

Briar bent over the mutant, then looked up at Leo, the same discovery reflected in the golden light of her eyes.

"I think it's the blood," she whispered.

They scattered as soon as Leo drew it.

She set her hand in the puddle on the ground, then smeared it in an arc over the Cambrian logo on her pullover.

The clock ticked down to two hours in the sky.

They had several miles left to go.

But they knew the mutants' weakness.

They had found repellent.

CHAPTER 17

BRIAR

At first, Briar thought she was staring at fog. A low-hanging cloud beyond the line of trees ahead. The change from pitch black to dull gray made no sense otherwise. Several steps closer, she grasped what her eyes were seeing.

It was the wall.

They'd finally reached the edge of the city. With forty-six minutes to spare. And they weren't alone. A group of contestants had gathered in front of it. Despite the inescapable exhaustion dragging at her body, she began to jog, eager to distinguish faces in the moonlight. She counted seven. One was wearing a scarf. *Posey*! The girl was alive. Relief bowled Briar over—sharp and unexpected. She didn't realize how heavily the fate of one girl was weighing upon her until now.

"Evander," Leo muttered.

The foreigner was there, too, wearing a long overcoat he must have acquired along the way. Officer Ferro, Sam the clergyman, Dr. Margaret. Aurora and Garrick. Everyone was there but Nile the politician and the two who had already been eliminated. Via death. As Briar and Leo approached, Dr. Margaret's expression stretched with alarm, no doubt in response to their savage-like appearance.

"What happened to you?" she asked, looking from the smeared blood across their pullovers to the dried splatters on their faces to the wooden stakes in both of their hands.

"We killed one," Leo said.

"*He* killed one," Briar amended.

She still couldn't wrap her mind around it. He'd saved her all over again, only this time he'd done so knowing the truth. The cat was out of the bag. Leo knew who she was —*what* she was—only instead of condemning her, he impaled a mutant on her behalf. Briar glanced at Posey, amazed that she was alive. Posey's eyes lifted to hers, then darted self-consciously away.

"We're pretty sure the scent of their blood repels them." Leo's attention slid to the foreigner. "Where's Nile?"

"We went our separate ways after he tried drowning me in the reservoir."

Briar gaped. "He tried drowning you?"

"Awful, isn't it?" Aurora said. "I know we're supposed to

be competing against one another, but trying to kill someone like that ..." She wrapped her hands around her elbows and shuddered.

Briar turned back to Evander. "How did you get out?"

He muttered something about being double jointed.

"And Nile?" Leo pressed. "Is he a contortionist too?"

"I am not sure. He was already free when I awoke."

"You left us down there to drown," Leo said.

"I left you down there to be disqualified. I did not think anyone would drown."

"The water gushing inside didn't tip you off?"

"I shut the door which was more than the politician wanted to do." His dark eyes went darker. "You cannot blame me for playing the game. If you want to be upset with someone, be upset with the man who designed it."

Ambrose Squire.

What kind of sicko was he?

"I did not know anyone would die." Evander sounded truly remorseful. "I am sorry to hear about Iris."

"Thomas is dead, too," Officer Ferro said.

"We saw," Leo replied.

A bone-chilling shriek split the air. A chorus of others followed. Like birds calling to one another, only these were not birds.

The group edged closer.

"How long does that repellent last?" Garrick asked, eying the smear of blood across Briar's garment.

It was the same question that had been running on a loop through her mind as she and Leo made their way here. Approximately once every ten seconds, Briar regretted not having dragged the carcass behind them for an extra measure of protection.

Leo looked up at the sky. "Hopefully longer than forty-six minutes."

Briar's stomach twisted.

They were running out of time.

"Did you try opening the gate?" she asked.

"It's not budging without power," the officer replied.

Briar's attention ran from the gate to the wall in search of spaces big enough to squeeze through. But there weren't any. Not even for Garrick. Her stomach twisted tighter. Could she climb such a wall? On a good day it would be challenging. But now, with such relentless exhaustion stacking itself upon her shoulders? It only seemed to be growing worse. She suspected she needed food to replenish her strength, possibly sleep. She had nothing in her knapsack to satiate the former and she didn't have time to entertain the latter.

Leo set his hand on one of the stones and stared up the wall's face, studying the crooks and crevices as though mapping a course.

"Can you climb it?" Briar asked.

"Climbing won't be the problem. Cutting through the dome will be, though." He lifted his wooden stake. It might have impaled a mutant, but it wasn't going to slice through whatever see-through synthetic material stretched above them.

"What about this?" Dr. Margaret reached inside her pocket and pulled out a small blade.

Leo brightened. "That's perfect."

"I took it from a groom kit inside the shop."

"How are the rest of us supposed to get up?" Garrick asked.

"Some rope would come in handy," Leo said, to which Posey began to wave. When she had their attention, she got down on her knees and pulled up something from the ground.

Briar lifted one of her boots, noticing a tapestry of weedy vine underfoot. Briar grabbed a handful and yanked them up. They were thin, but strong. All around, the clicking grew louder, closer. Reminding Briar of the short-horned grasshoppers that came every summer. Never visible, but ever present—evidenced by their buzzing chorus, a sound that got louder the more intently one focused on it.

Blood pounded in her ears as she dropped to her knees and began pulling up as much of the vine as she could. Everyone joined her, no longer competitors, but working together against a common enemy. It was them against the clock. Them against the mutants gathering in the shadows. Together, they twisted and tied. Twenty-two precious minutes later, they had two lengths of viny rope long enough to be of use. Two because Evander insisted he could climb, too.

Leo pulled off his boots and stockings. He said it was easier to grip with bare feet. Evander did the same. Leo tied his laces together, shoved his stockings into his boots, and slung them around the back of his neck. He grabbed one end of a rope and looped it around his waist, then asked the doctor for her blade.

"No way," she said, shaking her head. "I give it to you and you have no reason to throw the rope down."

With an unoffended shrug, Leo picked up his stake and pulled Briar off to the side, the space between his dark eyebrows etched with two deep lines. His hair disheveled. The smooth, tan skin of his neck splattered with dried blood. The prince of Korah, her comrade in arms. They had hardly anything in common, and that which they did reflected horribly upon her. But somehow, over the course of the last few hours, an undeniable connection had formed between them. They had gone to battle together and they had survived together, too. His piercing blue eyes slid to the others, then back to her. "Try to get to the rope first."

His words seemed to confound him as much as they confounded her. He handed her his stake, then found his place on the wall as a loud, haunting howl rent the air.

She thought Leo would leave Evander in the dust.

She'd seen the cliffs he'd climbed all over the news. They were nothing compared to this wall. But the foreigner kept up, even as Leo climbed quickly, almost recklessly. Neither seemed to give any heed to their alarming distance from the ground or the fact that they had no protection should they slip and fall. Every now and then, one would glance at the other and climb faster. Even though her feet were firmly planted in the grass, Briar felt dizzy. Lightheaded. She hated heights almost as much as she hated the Illustrians who toured The Skid.

She didn't exhale until they reached the top, Leo winning by a hair.

There was a moment of unadulterated relief, out-of-place delight.

Seeming to forget herself, Posey clapped.

Aurora wrapped her arm around the girl's shoulder and squeezed.

An Illustrian and a deformed cipher, celebrating together.

The two looked up to the top of the wall and Briar wondered if they were all idiots foolishly hoping, watching for a pair of ropes that wouldn't come. Surely, Leo and Evander didn't need a tiny blade to find a way out of this city. Maybe the two of them were fighting now, scrambling to be the first one to escape.

The clock ticked.

The clicking escalated.

Briar glowered at the dark edges of the clearing, wondering if it was her imagination or if she really could make out shapes now. Surely there couldn't be that many. She should have asked for Leo's pullover. One half of their repellent was gone. Her grip tightened around the stakes in both hands as two ropes cascaded through the night and dropped to the ground side by side.

Briar stared in disbelief.

"Who's a fast climber?" Officer Ferro asked, stepping forward to take charge.

Garrick shoved his hand into the air and grabbed one of the ropes.

Dr. Margaret grabbed the other.

Leo told Briar to get to one first, but if she went now there'd be no repellent left. The image of that mutant tearing open Thomas's throat would be forever seared into her memory. She didn't want any more of them. As Garrick and Dr. Margaret climbed, Briar stepped further into the unknowing dark and puffed out her chest like the streak of blood might scare the monsters away.

Garrick was a scrappy climber.

Dr. Margaret could barely climb at all.

Leo had to do it for her, one hand over the other as he pulled her up.

She was only halfway to the top when Ferro handed the free rope to Posey, who was hardly any better than the doctor. And when Leo finally got her up, something horrible happened.

Posey let loose a strange, warbling shriek as she dropped several feet then jerked to a stop, dangling precariously.

Briar's heart seized.

The vine was coming undone, fraying before their eyes.

Officer Ferro didn't hesitate.

He grabbed the rope Leo had tossed and climbed even faster than Garrick, the muscles in his arms bulging against the black fabric of his sleeves as he went.

Posey plummeted downward again and let loose another warbling shriek. The mutants hooted and screamed in reply like a troop of agitated monkeys.

Briar took another step toward them and plunged Leo's stake into the ground.

Aurora and Sam cheered as Posey was saved. Evander and Leo pulled the officer and the girl up. There was only one rope now, and nine minutes to go. Briar slipped off her knapsack and removed her pullover as Sam urged Aurora to go first. And hurry. Briar hung the pullover over the wooden stake she'd plunged into the ground. Sam came to stand beside her. Aurora crested the wall in less than a minute thanks to the line of contestants at the top all working together to pull her up.

Then Leo shouted.

A lone mutant had broken rank.

Ice shot through Briar's veins.

She screamed at Sam to run as the army of monsters charged and the rope came sailing through the air.

Briar seized it, twisting the vines around her left arm. She was yanked upward just as Sam leapt and snagged the very end. The mutants snarled and scrabbled, gnashing their teeth in a mass below. One jumped and snagged Sam's foot.

His hand slipped.

Briar caught him, his sudden weight wrenching the ligaments in her shoulder, the vines wrapped around her arm squeezing painfully tight.

With a great kick, Sam sent the mutant into the swarm below.

Briar's body was stretched out like a T, one hand holding onto the clergyman and the other tangled in the vine. She yelled at him to grab the rope, but it was no use. No matter how hard he tried, Sam could no longer reach the rope's end. And all the jerking and flailing was making the rope unravel an arm's length above them.

She heard shouts—Leo yelling commands—as all around, the chaos morphed into smoke and heat, the mutants into flame, and Sam Poe into a thirteen-year-old boy holding on for dear life. A thirteen-year-old boy who would plummet to his death if she let go.

Briar strained, her shoulder and forearm screaming,

the socket in her elbow pulling. She clenched her teeth, growling against the pain as she gripped his hand tighter.

She would *not* fail.

"The rope is breaking!" Sam hollered, his light brown irises two rings of panic.

"Hold on!" she shouted back.

She would fix it.

Like she fixed her ankle.

But his hand was slipping and he wasn't trying as hard as she was.

"Hold on!" she screamed again.

A look stole across the clergyman's face. A look Briar recognized. Like he had something to prove every bit as much as she did. Some failure to rectify, one that haunted him the same way Briar's failure haunted her. And this was his one chance at redemption.

He would not fail either.

She didn't let go.

But Sam did.

And there was nothing she could do but watch him fall.

In the absence of his weight, Briar flew up the wall and fell into Leo's arms.

His chest heaved.

Her chest heaved.

Their eyes met and held, their hearts crashing in unison.

And then, with fifty-six seconds left on the clock and the makeshift rope in hand, he pulled her through the crude opening in the dome Margaret had sliced, wrapped his strong arm around her waist, and rappelled them both down the other side of the wall.

CHAPTER 18

LEO

As soon as Leo's feet touched the ground, the awful sounds fell away, muted by the thick stone between them and the feasting mutants on the other side. For a moment, it was just them. Hearts pounding. Breathing ragged.

He couldn't believe she was alive.

In light of what he'd just witnessed, it didn't seem possible. Nor could he ever unsee it—the beast breaking away, hurtling toward her from the dark. Briar running. Briar jumping. Briar catching Sam, a full grown man, and holding on with a strength that defied logic. Maybe it had. Maybe she used Magic. Or maybe she used the sheer grit that was uniquely hers. All he knew was that as she dangled between life and death, he found that he desperately wanted her to live. He had used all of his strength to pull them up and had shouted at the others to do the same. *Pull. Pull, dammit. Pull.* And now, here she was. Warm in his arms.

Awe and relief stretched through him. All for the chambermaid's daughter. A cipher. Magic. The wooded assassin. He let go and stepped away, then dragged his hand through his hair. Was this part of her trickery? Was she putting him under the same spell her mother had put his? She tucked that stubborn lock of hair behind her ear. Tiny specks of blood had dried on her earlobe.

Barbaric, bewitching Briar.

The alliteration started with his mother—a fun game that helped him memorize names and enhance his vocabulary. When she died, the game continued in Leo's mind. Until it became habit. An ode to his mom, who was no longer living because of Briar's. Now, here *barbaric, bewitching Briar* stood. Shivering. Her pullover gone. Her knapsack, too. Her face ashen. Her pupils dilated, turning her irises into thin golden rings encircling two pools of black. He wondered if she was in shock. How couldn't she be, after reliving such a traumatic event from her past? He remembered the story she told him. The twin brother who fell because she couldn't hold on. The reason she wore her glove. Before he could say anything—before he could drum up any words of comfort—if that's what he was going to do—the others rappelled their way down.

They'd been waiting on the other side of Dr. Margaret's carved opening, outside of the city but stuck with no rope to get down. He and Briar had gone first. Officer Ferro came last. He dropped to one knee and bowed his head like one honoring a fallen soldier—a moment of silence for the vanquished Sam as they stood in a clearing surrounded by barren trees, their spindly branches reaching up into a sky freckled with stars. Millions and millions of them, no longer obscured by a dome overhead. The view was even more magnificent than the one he and Hawk had at McKinley Pass, a stretch of cliff entirely uninhabited. Standing there in silence, it was as if they were the last people in the entire world. Getting picked off one by one.

"Congratulations," a familiar voice crooned. "You have escaped the city."

Anna the Hologram was back. She hovered in the dark like an apparition, smiling down at them in the same misplaced way she had before, entirely unaware that such a smile was not appropriate at this moment in time. But then, of course she was unaware. Anna the Hologram was nothing but well-crafted technology designed by an old man to resemble his dead wife.

Ambrose Squire had a screw loose.

More than one.

Ferro clambered to his feet.

The hologram opened her mouth, but her voice glitched. She continued speaking, but the disjointed sound warbled and pitched like a broken simulcaster.

"What's going on?" Garrick asked. "What's she saying?"

The hologram cut out. For a blip of a second, Anna completely disappeared. When she returned, she did so only part way, and that part was every bit as warped as her voice. Leo couldn't understand a word, and yet it was obvious by the length of the message that she was saying a great deal.

Garrick waved his hands. "Hellooo! We can't hear you!"

Anna cut out again.

Leo shifted, anticipating her return.

Several seconds of nothing ticked by.

"Hey old man!" Garrick picked up a small rock and chucked it into the sky. A flock of birds took flight, their wings glowing white in the moonlight. "Did you hear any of that? Because we sure didn't!"

His words returned on an echo.

And then it was gone and there was nothing but the sound of chirping insects.

Garrick let a curse fly and kicked the wall.

Beside him, Briar clutched her shoulder and shivered again as wind rustled through the trees. There hadn't been even a breeze inside the Domed City. Now that they were out, the night was chillier. Leo yanked off his pullover, his bare skin prickling. But before he could so much as offer it to her, she pressed her lips together and shook her head. If he had to guess, he'd say her revulsion stemmed more from the blood than the pullover itself. Despite the chill in the air, Leo couldn't bring himself to put it back on either. He shoved his arms into the sleeves of his suit and zipped himself back up.

Surely by now Ambrose had realized the faulty connection. So why wasn't he resending the message? Judging by the alertness of his competitors, they were making the same assumption. All of them except for Ferro, who stood with the unmistakable air of an officer, even without the uniform.

"He told me why he was here," Ferro said, pointing his words at Briar. "I was with him as we made our way to the wall."

Briar blinked.

"He got into a motor accident when he was eighteen. It killed his brother and paralyzed his friend, who has had to live with chronic pain ever since. Sam was driving. And he was intoxicated."

Leo lifted his eyebrows.

The *saintly Sam* had not always been so saintly.

Garrick sneered. "Let me guess. The Illustrian walked free."

"If being wracked with guilt is your idea of walking free, then I suppose he did."

"Guilt is hardly justice." The boy's words were filled with contempt. They seemed to come from somewhere deep and personal.

And yet, they struck Leo as true.

Guilt wasn't justice.

Shard Prison was justice.

Guillotine Square was justice.

Briar's brother was getting both for theft.

Meanwhile, Sam Poe walked free.

Ciphers weren't the only ones committing crimes. They were simply paying the steepest penalty for them.

"He sacrificed his life to save another," Ferro continued. "I think it was an honorable way to go."

"He didn't have to sacrifice his life at all," Briar said.

"The rope was coming undone."

She pressed her lips together and looked away, the angry pulse in her throat ticking in the moonlight.

A patch of wispy clouds rolled overhead, casting strange shadows on the ground. Leo sat against the wall to pull on his stockings and boots as the doctor asked Briar if she could examine her arm. Briar conceded, wincing when the examination reached her elbow.

"It's not dislocated," Dr. Margaret finally said. "The ligaments are sprained. Apart from fashioning some sort of splint, I'm not sure what can be done."

Leo's attention wandered to the place Briar's locket hid.

The doc had no idea.

He finished tying his laces.

By then, it had become clear.

For whatever reason, Anna the Hologram wasn't

returning. There wasn't a new countdown in the sky, either.

"What now?" Garrick said.

Leo set his elbows on his knees. "We wait, I guess. Sooner or later, the old man's gonna have to resend it."

The boy shoved pale wisps of hair from his beady eyes, the moonlight turning his birthmark pink. "And we're just supposed to let the politician get further and further ahead?"

"Maybe he didn't get out," offered Aurora.

"The dome wasn't tampered with before I got to it," Dr. Margaret added.

But that wasn't the only place a person could escape. If Nile could climb a wall, he could have gotten out anywhere. Leo eyed Evander, standing silently in an over-coat that reached to his knees. Then Posey, who had wandered from the group, stopping occasionally to pick something off the ground. Nile had escaped the restraints down in the reservoir, which meant he was slick. Then he tried drowning his one and only opponent, which meant he was ruthless. He was proving to be a much more dangerous opponent than Leo expected. The man probably escaped. But what did it matter, really? Whether he made it or not didn't change *their* circumstances. Leo leaned back against the wall. Forging ahead in the middle of the night without any direction didn't seem like the wise thing to do.

Posey returned to the group.

She took a step toward Briar and held out her hand. At first glance, she appeared to be holding grass. Upon closer inspection, Leo saw that it was honey clover. Posey lifted the foliage higher.

Briar took a stalk.

Posey pantomimed eating it.

Briar did so hesitantly, surprise stealing across her features as she did.

At the sweetness, no doubt.

Posey crouched to the ground and dumped the small pile. She reached inside her pockets and pulled out more. Leo realized suddenly that he was famished. And thirsty. A proper meal would be preferable, but for now, this would have to suffice. The eight of them formed a circle around the meager sustenance, Garrick glaring daggers at the clover like it personally offended him while everyone else cast glances toward the sky. If hope could resurrect the digitalized Anna, she would have been back by now.

"Do you want to hear something crazy?" Dr. Margaret said to nobody in particular as she nibbled on a leaf.

Everyone looked at her.

"My father was born on this island."

Leo's attention slid to Briar.

They exchanged a narrow-eyed look.

Posey began gesticulating. She nodded enthusiastically, then motioned all around and pointed to herself. She was too young to be born here. "Yours too?" Leo said.

She nodded.

He and Briar exchanged another look.

"My mother lived here for a time."

The surprising declaration belonged to Evander, who sat with his knees up, his arms draped over them.

"I thought you were from Nigal," Leo said.

"I am. But my mother is originally from Korah. Her parents died when she was very young. She came to this island to live with her aunt—a very unkind woman. She was the only family member my mother had left. When she died, my mother was sent to Antis to live in a home for unwanted children."

"That's a horrible thing to call it," Aurora said, looking truly horrified.

"How did you end up in Nigal?" Leo asked.

"She moved there when she became pregnant with me. My father had no interest in children, and since she knew what it was like to be unwanted, she decided to take me far away from such rejection."

Leo peered east, where the earth climbed steadily upward, the trees slowly rising higher into the sky. His mother's village was that way, not too far from where he sat now. Apparently, she'd grown up there with the chambermaid.

"Your mother was from here," Aurora said, as though

reading his mind. It wasn't classified information. The most rudimentary of research would disclose the connection. Aurora inhaled deeply—tranquilly—through her nose. She looked younger, with her braids spilling down around her face. "Maybe my mom and dad were born here, too."

"Wouldn't you know?" Dr. Margaret asked.

"I was adopted," Aurora said, twirling a stalk of clover between her fingers. "My parents used to say that they wished me into existence. They wanted a baby so badly, the Wish Keeper created me and dropped me on their doorstep. According to them, I began with their desire. A couple years ago I found paperwork I wasn't supposed to find. It said I was abandoned at a train depot." She wrapped her arms around her knees. "I have a story, I just don't know it. Maybe this island is part of it."

Leo wondered if this was why Aurora found the ceiling so fascinating. Every story had to be precious when you didn't know your own.

"That's a lot of connections to this island," Ferro said. "Do we think it's a coincidence?"

Leo doubted it. "The old man has a connection, too. His wife and son were killed here."

"His second wife killed them."

Leo balked.

Evander, too.

"What?" they barked in unison, equally bowled over by

Aurora's wild, but simply stated declaration. They exchanged matching looks of befuddlement. This information had been nowhere in Leo's research. It seemed to have been nowhere in the foreigner's either. He turned to his classmate. "They died in the disaster."

"Which his second wife was responsible for."

Leo made a face. "You think one person could be responsible for what happened here?"

"That's what the ceiling said," Aurora answered with a shrug.

"The ceiling?" Garrick shot.

"In Ambrose's manor. The paintings on the ceiling. They told a story. The Cambria Disaster took up an entire hallway." When she looked up from her twirling clover, she seemed surprised by everyone's attention. "Apparently, his second wife was the one who notified King Casimir that Magic was congregating on the isle. When all of that Magic was herded into the city, gathered in one place, she had plenty to draw from."

Across from Leo, Briar peered at Aurora from narrowed eyes.

"What motive would she have for doing something so awful?" the doctor asked.

"I wondered the same thing. Motive was hard to puzzle out. The only theory I could come up with was that she wanted the Wish Keeper for herself."

"That's a lot of trouble to go through for love."

"I don't think it was for love," Aurora said. "I think she wanted power."

"If what you say is true," Evander cut in, his voice soaked in a skepticism Leo felt himself. "Why would Ambrose Squire go on to marry her?"

"And why would she leave?" Leo added.

"That's a mystery to me, too. As far as why he married her, I don't think he knew the truth then. It explains why the style and the coloring of the paintings are so different. The bit about his second wife was added later."

"Maybe that's why she left," Ferro offered. "Her husband discovered the truth and she fled."

"Or maybe she didn't leave at all," Garrick said drolly. "Maybe he killed her when he found out and her bones are buried in the walls."

Aurora scrunched her nose. "That wasn't on the ceiling."

"I doubt he'd paint a confession," Garrick muttered in reply.

Leo plucked a clover leaf off a stem, trying to make sense of it all. What was the old man up to? Why did he set this contest here, of all places? Why was he holding a contest at all? And what had happened to the second wife?

Overhead, another patch of wispy clouds passed by.

Evander tossed his clover dispassionately on the grass, then stood up and dusted his hands.

"Where are you going?" Dr. Margaret asked.

"This is a contest. I am not going to sit by and swap stories while the politician wins. Perhaps the old man left us a clue."

~

All eight of them searched the woods by starlight. For what, Leo wasn't sure. He only knew that he felt twitchy, like at any moment, one of his competitors might find an advantage and race away with it. The feeling reminded him of the scavenger hunts he used to go on while part of the Royal Adventurer's Club, a patriarchal custom spanning back through the centuries which included, among its many highlights, a weeklong camping trip in the wilderness of Petram. Nine-year old Leo had earned two badges his very first time, which happened to be two more than Hawk. The Compass Badge for his keen sense of direction and the coveted Fire Badge for his ability to start them so quickly.

He picked up a small rock beside a jutting tree root and rubbed away the dirt with the pad of his thumb. Quartz. If nothing else, he could start a fire to keep them warm.

Nearby, the foreigner swept the uneven terrain with a walking stick, digging through thick patches of thistle with a concentration bordering on desperate. Leo had been thoroughly impressed with the young man's climbing skills. He was unaccustomed to anyone giving him such a run for his money. Not even Hawk, who had an athletic build and just as much experience as Leo. "You almost beat me to the top of the wall," he said, interrupting Evander's intense reverie.

The foreigner blinked as though startled by Leo's presence, the darkness in his eyes giving way to something less dour.

"Where'd you learn to climb like that?"

"Mountains are not unique to Korah," Evander replied, parting another bush with his stick. He was reserved, the foreigner. Observant, too.

Leo watched him curiously, wondering what he'd written on the parchment of paper Squire gave them in his study. What wish had he etched in his own blood? "What star led you here, Evander?"

"Star?"

"What wish are you willing to die for?"

The young man pursed his lips and continued searching, darkness returning to his eyes. At first, he didn't answer. He just swept aside another patch of weeds with his walking stick. But then, "My father is a wealthy man. I am his only heir. I came for my rightful inheritance."

"He doesn't want to give it to you?"

"He would rather bury himself with his gold than give me or my mother one crumb."

"Sounds like a swell guy." Leo pocketed his rock.

"Maybe your father and mine should get together sometime."

Evander cut him a surprised look. Leo's father was the king.

Leo squinted past a group of dead trees, where Briar and Posey searched like the rest of them. Leo knew his father to be cold. Aloof. Controlling. Sometimes severe. Until recently, however, he wouldn't have considered him cruel. But what other adjective could there be for a man who burned derelict buildings without clearing them first? His mind stewed over her twin brother's slow, agonizing death—stretched over the course of two days. He would have been better off had Briar left him in the fire.

"It's ironic," Leo said, picking up another rock. "You're here to take what is rightfully yours. And I'm here to get rid of what's rightfully mine."

"You do not want to be king?" the foreigner asked in a tone bloated with skepticism.

Leo understood. From the outside looking in, nobility *was* the wish. His position as prince was coveted. Fancied. Glorified. He didn't know the kind of hardship Briar and Posey and perhaps even Evander knew. Unlike them, he could have anything he wanted. Except, of course, a choice.

"Are there amusement bazaars in Nigal?" Leo asked.

"One traveled to my hometown a few times when I was a boy."

"Did it have lions?"

"They were my favorite."

Leo thought about the last time he'd gone with Hawk and Sabrina and his entourage of body guards—the Grand Bazaar on the north end of Antis, which had everyone's attention thanks to their most recent acquisition of a white lion. The exhibit already drew the biggest crowds, the most admiration. Lions were beautiful creatures—powerful and sleek as they prowled their cages between performances. Thanks to the white lion, the exhibit had become a national sensation, drawing a constant stream of gawking spectators who would gasp and applaud whenever the lion's handler commanded the albino beast to roar. Sabrina and Hawk had been thoroughly entertained. Leo had lost his appetite. "To be the High Prince is a lot like being a lion in a bazaar."

"Powerful and admired?"

"Trapped in a cage."

Evander chuckled, but Leo wasn't joking.

"Powerful in theory. Fetishized more than admired. Constantly under the spotlight with zero privacy. Every facet of life on display for public consumption, tragedy included." Tragedy *preferred*. A truth that festered. Most children grieving the death of their mothers didn't have that grief exploited for mass entertainment. They weren't dressed up for the media and paraded about at funerals and executions. Leo's jaw tightened. He didn't want to be a lion in a cage. He wanted the freedom of a wide open savannah. His heart longed for it, but a piece was fearful, too. What if after so long in captivity he was ruined for the wild? He dropped the rock. "How about this? If I win, you can have *my* inheritance. Then we can both stick it to our fathers."

A flash of desire sparked in Evander's eyes, but didn't ignite. "Something tells me it would not work that way."

"No, unfortunately." If Leo somehow won the contest and thus his freedom, his uncle would be next in line. Followed by Hawk's older brother, followed by Hawk. They would be thrilled. "I have money though, more than I know what to do with. I can't promise I can give you as much as your inheritance is worth, but if things don't work out for you, if we make it through this alive, I'd be happy to make your life and your mother's a little easier." As soon as the words were out, Leo found that they were true. The prospect of helping another in such a way made him feel lighter. Less constricted in his cage.

Evander smiled uncertainly, like he might be foolish to believe such a promise.

And a loud *boom* split the night.

They looked up as another resounded.

Then another.

And another.

Off in the distance, through the treetops, a dazzling display of fireworks exploded in the sky.

CHAPTER 19

BRIAR

Explosions of color illuminated the sky—sparkling red and gold falling like glitter through the dark—each one announced by a soft but sharp *pfft*, quickly followed by a resounding boom.

Briar ran out into the clearing.

Somebody was setting off fireworks in the distance.

Her stomach turned to stone.

Fireworks meant celebration.

Had the politician won?

Her heart rejected the question. *No*. She hadn't let the monster out of the closet, she hadn't outed herself to the High Prince, she hadn't watched Sam the clergyman fall to his gruesome death or relived the horror of failing Echo all over again to lose like this. Aimlessly wandering about in a patch of dead wood while she searched for Keeper knows what.

Her brother was *not* going to die in Guillotine Square.

Briar marched toward the display.

Leo and the rest followed—beneath scattered patches of trees, up a gradual hill that got progressively steeper, until she began to hear noises between the resounding booms. Impossible noises. The nonsensical nature of it propelled Briar faster, until she crested the hill and beheld the valley below.

Leo stopped on her left. "It's a carnival."

Filled with *people.* On a desolate isle that had been devoid of human life for the past quarter of a century.

"The Merivus Carnival," Aurora said, stopping on Briar's other side.

"The Merivus Carnival?" Briar and Leo said at the same time.

Aurora mistook their surprise. "It is strange timing. Merivus is still months away. And yet, that sign is pretty clear."

Briar followed Aurora's gaze to the sign in question.

Welcome to the Merivus Carnival

Briar stared at it, her mouth ajar. Her mother used to go to this carnival every year as a little girl. She used to go with Leo's mother. Judging by his expression, he was as familiar with the festival as she was. Maybe Princess Helena used to tell him about it at night before bed like Briar's mother used to tell her and Echo once upon a time.

"How is this possible?" Dr. Margaret said behind them.

It wasn't. That was the obvious answer.

But neither was being here at all, on this island. Neither were the coins on their wrists. Neither was the Wish Keeper himself. And yet, here they were with Magic all around. Briar could feel her locket vibrating in response to such a flagrant display. Bright lights. Jaunty music. Whirling rides. And people. So many people—standing in lines, riding the rides, playing the games, eating the food—all of them cast in the reddish, smoky haze of the firework display overhead.

Posey pointed at a man in a top hat, pedaling himself on a unicycle while juggling a set of flaming knives. A crowd had gathered to admire him, then broke apart to make way for a garish lady ambling past on dangerously high stilts.

"Are they holograms?" Officer Ferro asked.

There was only one way to find out.

Briar advanced down the hill, straight to the closest booth where a pockmarked teenager with a weak chin called from inside. "Tickets! Tickets heeeeere! Get your tickets!"

"Excuse me." Briar stopped in front of the counter.

The boy quit hollering.

If he was a hologram, he was a much more realistic one than Anna.

"Did the politician win?"

The kid pulled back his chin. It practically disappeared.

"Nile Gentry," she clarified. "Did he win?"

"I don't know. What game was he playing?"

"Not a game. The contest."

Her words only seemed to confuse the boy further.

"Is that what the fireworks are for?" she pressed. "Is it over?"

"I'm not sure what contest you're referring to, but I'm sure it's not over. The night's too young. All the more reason to get your tickets."

"Where is Squire?" Leo cut in. "Does he know the hologram didn't work?"

"The holo-what?"

"The hologram!" Briar snapped, smacking her hand on the countertop.

The young man jumped.

"How is all of this here?" Leo said. "What are we supposed to do?"

As if in answer, a breeze came. It swept through the grounds, rustling up the scent of deep fried dough, sweet sugar, and frizzled turkey.

Briar's mouth watered.

Garrick's stomach let loose a loud growl.

Briar inhaled deeply, her eyes going heavy with bliss. Ever since healing her ankle, she'd been weak. Depleted.

Honey clover did little to renew her strength. But this. This would fix everything.

Leo took her arm. "What are you doing?"

With a blink, all of the commotion came screaming back in technicolored brightness. The young man was calling again, adding his voice to the cacophony. "Tickets! Tickets heeeere! Get your tickets!"

The others were wandering away in different directions, as though inexplicably drawn by the hypnotic swirl of sights and sounds and smells until only Briar and Leo and Aurora remained.

"Is this a new trial?" Leo asked.

Briar searched the dark, hazy sky where fireworks continued to explode. There was no clock counting down the time anywhere she could see. No clear objective either.

"Maybe the Truth Teller will know," Aurora said in a voice even more breathless than usual. Before Briar or Leo could object, she crossed the busy path to a tent with a sign that wasn't flashy or gaudy but read simply, The Truth Teller.

Carnival goers jostled Briar and Leo to the side as they joined the queue to get their tickets. The ticket peddler had been no help at all. Maybe the Truth Teller would be.

They followed Aurora.

The tent was made of nothing more than thin canvas, and yet as soon as they stepped inside, all the noise fell away. A pair of matching lanterns flickered on either end of a crude table made of wood. A woman sat behind it dressed in a robe with a hood that cast her face in shadow. Briar could only see the hint of a profile and a salt and pepper braid much like her own. Next to one of the lanterns, a stick of incense burned. A thin ribbon of smoke curled from its wick—the scent extra cloying inside the confined space.

The woman inclined her head. "Welcome to my tent," she said in a hypnotic voice. "I am Katya, the Truth Teller. Which of you would like to play first?"

"What are we playing?" Leo asked.

"A game of truth, where I will tell you two along with one lie and you decide which is which."

"I'd like to try," Aurora said.

Katya extended her hand, inviting Aurora to take the empty chair in front of the table.

Aurora sat.

There was no crystal ball or flashy theatrics. Just the incense, Katya's questionably dramatic cloak and hood, and a deck of cards she shuffled in her hands. They were old hands with bulbous knuckles and long, yellowed nails. She flipped the card on top over—revealing a frantic swirl of dark colors on the other side—and set it in front of Aurora. "You don't know who you are." She flipped over the next card—two balls of bright yellow—and placed it to the left of the first. "You did not start alone." She flipped over one more, this one all black. Impossibly so. Like it wasn't a card at all, but a hungry, rectangular hole and if Briar got too close, it would swallow her inside. Katya set it to the right of the first and said, "Your worst fear is true."

Leo snorted. "That's it?"

Katya turned her hood in his direction.

"I'm sorry," he said. "But those sound like they came straight from a wise cracker. 'The answers you seek come from above.' 'It's never too late to change your mind.' 'A dubious friend might be an enemy in disguise.'"

The key to moving forward is surrender.

Briar remembered hers all too well.

"Did Squire give them to you? If so, would you mind telling him his hologram didn't work? If there's some task we're supposed to accomplish here, we have no clue what it is."

"Would *you* like a turn?" Katya asked him.

"Aren't you going to finish with Aurora first?"

"We are already finished. The truths are for her to determine."

"How convenient."

Katya swept the three cards into her hands and shuffled them into the deck. Aurora stood, worrying her lip in a way that suggested Katya's statements hadn't been generic at all. Not to her.

Leo took her spot.

Katya paused, then straightened the deck, and set it in front of her. She cast a long look at Leo, who sat with all the flippancy of the High Prince. Here was the eighteen-year old the tabloids loved. Katya turned the first card—two balls of bright yellow. "You did not start alone."

Leo laughed. "How original."

Katya flipped the second card. This one wasn't a repeat. On its face were two M's—one stark and upright, overlayed with one smaller and inverted. The symbol of Korah. "Your mother wished for your freedom."

Leo's flippancy disintegrated.

The second statement had not been generic.

The second statement was about Leo's mother.

Only it didn't make sense. Why would she wish for her son's freedom? Leo wasn't a slave. He was as far from one as a person could possibly be.

Katya flipped the third card—a picture of the symbol bursting into three-dimensional pieces. "Freedom will be yours."

Silence filled the tent.

Briar looked from the Truth Teller to the High Prince, trying to decipher the meaning, her heart thudding dully in her ears. Freedom would be his?

"Would you like to play?" Katya asked, turning her hooded face to Briar.

Her thudding heart picked up speed. She imagined falling headfirst into Aurora's black card. She imagined Katya's words.

Your mother was a murderer.

The monster will get you, too.

Lyric will live.

Two truths.

One lie.

Briar's mouth went dry as bone.

She didn't want to hear whatever Katya the Truth Teller might say. She didn't want to see any more of those cards, either. With a shake of her head, she fled the booth, escaping out into the clamor and noise.

Several strides up the path, Leo grabbed her shoulder. "Wait."

She rounded on him, her fear erupting into anger. "Is that your wish? Freedom from the throne?"

His face was tight, his mouth stern. "Yes."

She raised her eyebrows, surprised to hear him admit it. "And it will be yours? Was that a truth or the lie?"

"I don't know."

Disgust blistered in her throat. He wanted freedom from his responsibilities. Meanwhile, she was doing everything she could to keep her brother's head safely fastened to his neck. "What are you doing here if that's your wish? Surely you don't need a contest to walk away."

"A Davenbrook has never abdicated from the throne."

"So what? Be the first."

"I can't!" he yelled, a storm raging in his eyes. A conflicting swirl of anger and agitation, shame and helplessness. And beneath it all, a glimpse of the little boy on the dais. Visibly frustrated, he took her elbow and ushered her off to the side, away from all the people—the *impossible* people. Then, to her immense bewilderment, he unzipped his suit like he had in that busted-up store back in the Domed City.

"What are you doing?" she asked. Seeing his bare upper half was not something she needed right now. Unlike his lust-filled groupies, it wasn't something she needed ever.

He yanked the top of his suit to one side.

She followed the deep line running down the center of his chest. His olive skin smooth and tan and perfect, except for the place over his heart where the symbol of Korah was etched. The same as the symbol on Katya's card, only this was not made of black ink. But thin, white scar tissue she hadn't noticed inside the store. Probably because she'd looked away too quickly. "Do you see this?"

Of course she saw it. At the moment, it was impossible not to.

"This is why I can't walk away. At least not with my life." He exhaled a mirthless laugh. "It's ironic, isn't it? The Davenbrook family has done its best to eradicate Magic, and yet we use it. Every single time a new heir is born, *this* is what he gets. Branded, sealed, his life irrevocably bound to the throne in a secret ceremony dripping with the forbidden."

Briar should be shocked. Appalled. But somehow, she

wasn't surprised at all. Those in power would use anything to get ahead. To secure their advantage. Why should Magic be any different? She looked Leo dead in the eye. "Boo hoo."

His face flushed.

"Am I supposed to feel sorry for you, stuck in your poor life of privilege and wealth? All the power of kingship is at your disposal. You have a chance to do good. To make real change. Do you know what I would give to have such an opportunity?" How many nights had Briar and Echo whispered under their covers, retelling each other Papa's bedtime stories. The kind where the hero prevailed and good always won. How much had Briar longed to be one of those heroes? If only she could be, she would do what everybody in power couldn't seem to.

She would make the right choice.

She would do what was good.

Instead, the whole world seemed so tragically shortsighted. It was the age-old problem, the one with a capital P. The one that inflicted the entire race of humanity from the top all the way to the bottom. She thought of old Rosco, selling to the Illustrians as they toured The Skid. He had to make a living, didn't he? Oh well if it fed the cycle. Survival ruled the day for those on the bottom. Greed, for those on top. "For once, I'd love to see someone in power put aside personal gain and think of the common good."

"You're speaking like Korah is a monolith. Over half the country is happy with the way things are."

"Not the half dying of preventable diseases. Not the half being sent to Guillotine Square."

"For *crimes*."

"Petty crimes."

"They're still crimes! They wouldn't be going to Guillotine Square if they followed the rules."

"Like you have your whole life?"

His cheeks flushed harder.

"You have no idea what it's like living at the bottom. You've never had to break your back working twelve hours a day only to earn barely enough money to buy bread. You've never had to watch diseases like Parox sweep through your neighborhood in some twisted form of population control. It's so easy for you to say, 'follow the rules' sequestered away in your palace when you don't know the first thing about hardship!" Briar clamped her mouth shut, but it was too late.

The words were out, spoken with the same fiery conviction with which her mother had spoken all those years ago, the night before she tore Briar's world apart. "She's become a token, Fynn! A shiny coin the King takes out of his pocket and flashes about anytime anyone tries to fight against this oppression."

"Maybe it's time to go, my love," Papa had said in that

gentle rumble that was uniquely his. "We can move back to Silva."

Briar's small heart had swelled as she eavesdropped from the hallway.

Silva! Oh, please let them go back to Silva, where Mama had smiled and laughed and showed Briar how to make flowers fly. Antis was crowded and cramped and smelly and so miserably hot in the summertime, and Mama worked and worked so much Briar never saw her anymore. *Yes*, she'd wanted to shout. *Let's go back to Silva!*

But they didn't go back to Silva.

How differently might everything have gone if her mother would have listened?

A ride zipped past in a rush of clanging metal and ecstatic shrieks. A burst of loud that came and went as fast as the carts hurling around the track. The fireworks had stopped, but the smoke remained. Briar felt as though it had seeped inside her ears.

"I'm sorry," she said. "I know that's not true. I know you—"

"Know a thing or two about hardship?" He looked down at her, his blue eyes flat. Hard. "I guess I have your mother to thank for that."

"I'm sorry." Briar lifted her chin. "But her actions don't excuse you from doing what's right."

"Right according to whom?"

"Right according to *right*."

"Says the girl who is Magic."

Briar's ears caught fire.

"What exactly do you want me to do, Briar? The Monarchy is a centuries-old, well-oiled machine operating within the confines of unyielding ritual and tradition. Don't even get me started on Parliament. What exactly is right in this situation? Getting rid of Guillotine Square? Freeing every prisoner in Shard? There'd be anarchy within the week."

"You don't know that."

He shook his head like she was asking him to do the impossible. "If I become King, I will have one primary duty. Keeping law and order in the commonwealth. As much as I don't like it, Guillotine Square ensures that law and order is kept."

"My brother stole in order to get medicine for our neighbor, who died by the way. Of a disease that could have been treated with a simple antibiotic." She jerked her hand toward the scar on his chest. The symbol. *Eleos Partim Pentho Omnis.* Mercy for Some. Misery for All. "You think you're keeping the people of Korah from experiencing misery, but those of us at the bottom are drowning in it."

Leo's mouth turned grim.

"Your mother was a cipher," Briar said.

"My mother was killed by one."

The woman on stilts came rambling up the path.

People laughed and jumped out of the way.

The prince ran his hand down the length of his face. When he looked up from the ground, his eyes were no longer flat and hard, but two deep oceans of misery. “She didn’t want this life for me. She saw what it was doing to my father. She knew it would do the same thing to me. That was one of Katya’s truths. She wished for my freedom.”

He said it so dejectedly Briar wanted to take his hand. Instead, she caught sight of something that yanked her attention straight out of the moment.

Leo noticed. “What?” he said, following the direction of her gaze.

“It’s Nile.”

The politician was playing a game across the path. He used a padded mallet to smash the heads of two animatronic rodents rising simultaneously. *Wham-bam!* Three more took their place, and three more after that. Nile couldn’t keep up. The game went dark. She and Leo hurried over as he dropped the mallet and gave the machine a violent shake.

“Nile,” Leo said.

The politician looked at them with crazy eyes—manic eyes—his face in dire need of a good shave. “Do you have any money?”

Briar drew back.

Nile gave the machine another shake, then dug deep

inside his pockets and pulled them inside out. A whirling light from a nearby game caught the coin on Nile's wrist. He touched it as though noticing it for the first time.

"Nile," Briar said this time. "It's us. From the contest."

But Nile wasn't listening.

He was removing the coin from his wrist.

Briar turned to Leo, alarmed. But Leo's focus had gone cloudy. No longer paying attention, he took a few steps to the left, peering into the milling crowd.

"What is it?" Briar asked.

He took another step, almost right through her.

She placed her palms flat against his chest to keep him from barreling her over. "What are you doing?"

"It's her," he said, looking down at Briar with the same wild eyes as Nile. "It's my mom. She's here."

CHAPTER 20

BRIAR

Before Briar could process the impossibility of such a statement, Leo left her. With an uncertain glance at Nile, who was now plugging his coin into the machine, she went after the prince. She navigated her way around the carnival-goers—the *impossible* carnival-goers—her gaze trained on Leo's broad shoulders, the distance between them widening, the crowd thickening.

"Leo!" she called.

But he didn't look back. He was getting further away from her. She shouted his name again, louder this time, craning to see over the tops of heads when someone crossed her line of vision that ground her to a halt.

Another impossibility.

But there he was with that achingly familiar profile.

The crowd jostled her from behind.

Briar's heart leapt as she changed course. She pinned her attention on this new set of shoulders like her life—like *his* life—depended on it. She squeezed through a cluster of people and watched him disappear inside a small building—the entrance made to look like the stretched mouth of a giant clown.

"Lyric!" She sidestepped a pair of rowdy children and hurried in after him only to discover a myriad of Briar's blinking back at her. Tall Briar. Short Briar. Thin Briar. Wide Briar. Wavy Briar. Upside down Briar. She was standing inside a house of mirrors.

"Lyric?" she called again—tentative, unsure. How could Lyric be here when he was in Antis, locked up in Shard? She turned in a circle—infinite Briar's all around, reflections within reflections—each one looking confused. Each one looking hopeful.

A laugh echoed around the room and bounced down a hallway.

Briar chased the sound. She wound her way through the disorienting maze. Her pace grew faster, more frantic with every corner she turned until she reached a dead end and the boy she'd been chasing stood there at the end of it.

She stopped.

The boy was not Lyric.

The boy was ...

"Echo?"

He smiled that mischievous smile. The one she hadn't seen in over four years. Briar squeezed her eyes tight—her breath bottled in her chest, her heart galloping beneath her ribcage. This had to be a trick. This had to be an illusion. But when she opened her eyes, he was still there. Her second half. Her counterpart. Her best friend. Her echo. With the same black hair and the same golden eyes. Alive and smiling. The exact age he'd been when Briar let go of his hand. The same age Lyric was now.

"Echo," she said again.

He nodded encouragingly, as if beckoning her to come.

Briar went—slowly, haltingly—convinced if she moved too fast he would disappear. Vanish into thin air. But he didn't. Echo remained. And when she choked on a disbelieving cry and snatched him up in a hug, he was solid and warm. "How is this possible? How are you here?"

Echo laughed.

Briar laughed, too. She grabbed his arms and held him out in front of her to get a better look. It was him. In the flesh. With that light spray of freckles across the bridge of his nose and the cowlick he was perpetually trying to smash flat. He made a gesture—like a trickster reaching up his sleeve—and winked.

"Magic," he said.

Magic.

The truth she tried so desperately to hide. The truth

Echo would have rather embraced even though he'd been there, too. The night Mama stormed into their living quarters and confessed to murder. But he hadn't been at Guillotine Square. They'd drawn straws for that. His was shorter, which meant he stayed at the junkyard with Lyric while she crept her way through the streets of Antis to the place their parents were to be executed. Echo wasn't there when the Imperial Magistrate condemned their mother's heart. Echo wasn't there when the wind blew cold and the panic so sharp. He didn't see Mama turn that sky black and he didn't see the fear in Papa's eyes when he yelled at Briar to run.

Echo wanted to play with the monster.

Briar wanted to lock it up for good.

Now here she was, in the middle of a contest frothing with it. If such Magic could grant wishes. If such Magic could make carnivals appear in the middle of a desolate island. Was it really so crazy to think that Magic could bring her dead brother back to life?

"Can you believe it?" he said.

No.

Yes!

Another laugh bubbled up her throat. Tears blurred her eyes as the past four horrible years melted into a nightmare and suddenly, she was awake again. Echo was *alive*. She didn't have to live this impossible life alone any longer.

She didn't have to keep carrying the load all by herself. She had a partner once again.

"It's the Merivus Carnival, Bri." His smiled stretched wide.

Briar smiled back.

How often had they dreamed of this in their cramped, shared bed in Antis? How often had they stayed up way past their bedtime, whispering under the covers about the food they would eat and the rides they would ride and the games they would play if they ever got to go to a carnival like the one outside their mother's village on Merivus Eve?

"Did you see the Swirl-A-Whirl?" Echo asked.

"There's a Swirl-A-Whirl?"

"And powdered cake and cloud candy and frizzled turkey leg!"

Her mouth watered.

"And the Trolley Tower! Did you see it? I say we go on that first. There'll be more fireworks soon. We can watch them from the very top."

"Maybe we can touch them."

With an excited nod, Echo took Briar's hand. "C'mon. Let's get our tickets."

"Tickets?"

"To ride the rides. We can't ride them without tickets."

"But we don't have any money."

They never had any money. How could they when every spare coin was spent on food? Still, Echo rooted around in his pockets like he might find something. When he pulled his hands free, they were empty. Just like always.

Briar frowned.

"What about that?" Echo nodded at her wrist.

To the coin tied there with twine.

"I bet that'll be enough to get us on the Trolley Tower." Echo grabbed her hand again. "Let's hurry, before the fireworks start."

But Briar resisted. Something tingled in the back of her mind. A niggling thought that kept circling the coin. She wasn't supposed to use it to buy tickets, was she? She looked down at the glove on her hand, then up at one of their reflections. She looked different in the mirror. She looked younger. Thirteen, like Echo. Her gloved hand bare and unscarred.

Annoyance puckered her brother's forehead. "Don't be greedy, Bri. This is our chance to ride the Trolley Tower together. At the Merivus Carnival!"

She pressed her thumb against the strange symbol stamped into the gold and like a whisper on the wind, she remembered. Another boy. Another brother. "I can't use this for tickets."

"Of course you can."

"No, I can't. This coin is for Lyric."

"Lyric?"

"He's in prison, Echo. The constables locked him up in Shard."

"Don't be ridiculous. Lyric's too young for Shard." He squeezed her hand tighter and gave her arm another tug.

Briar dug in her heels.

Echo's expression hardened at the edges. She recognized that look. He'd made it a million times before, whenever obstinance strong-armed reason. He crossed his arms. "You don't want to ride the Trolley Tower with me?"

"Of course I do." She would love nothing more than to ride the Trolley Tower with him. To lose herself in this moment. To forget all about her problems. For once in her life, to set the burden down. But if she did that, who would help their little brother? She shook her head, trying to clear away the fog. "But I'm here for Lyric. I came here to save him."

"Don't you want to save me?" he asked.

"I can't." Briar pulled her hand from his. Her gloved hand. Her scarred hand. A daily reminder that she had already tried. And she failed. But Lyric. Lyric was still alive. "You're already dead."

Echo's expression morphed from hurt to hostile.

The room morphed with it.

It was as though someone was wiping away the shine and veneer of the carnival only to reveal rot and mold underneath.

"Why am I dead, Briar?" Echo's golden eyes sparked.

She took a step back.

"Whose fault is that?" he asked, taking a step forward.

She watched in horror as his flesh bubbled and melted, transforming into something awful. The boy from her nightmares, his body scarred like her hand. Scarred beyond recognition while flame danced in the blacks of his pupils.

Briar took another step back and Echo lunged.

CHAPTER 21

LEO

The woman stopped at the end of a line. Leo stopped, too, the muscles in his jaw going slack. He wasn't seeing things. It was her—*really* her—even more beautiful than he remembered. For no picture could do her justice, and Leo had taken to studying every one he could find to keep her face from slipping away. Now here she was, staring back at him, smiling a radiant smile that made his heart swell to such a size it was almost painful.

She held out her arms in invitation.

Leo closed the gap between them in four long strides. He stepped into her embrace, wrapping his arms around her waist, his ear pressed against her heartbeat. Somehow, the tight hug made him small. Like an eight-year old boy.

"Do you like it?" she asked, her voice a vibration against his ear.

Leo couldn't speak. His throat had tied into a knot. All he could do was absorb the steady thrum of her heart. She stepped back and placed her hands on his shoulders. "It's the carnival I used to tell you about. We're here together, sweetheart. We're here because of *you*."

"Me?"

She beamed. "You did it, my love." At his confusion, she tipped back her head and laughed a laugh he'd forgotten. The kind of laugh that wrapped around him like a warm hug and made him feel like he might float up into the sky. "You won the contest. It's over!"

He blinked several times rapidly, trying to process what she was saying. But digesting anything beyond the reality of *her* was like trying to eat a horse after swallowing an elephant. With a shaky breath, words bubbled out of him. Long-trapped, cankerous words. "I'm sorry."

His mother's expression faltered. "For what?"

"For not staying in your lap longer." The day before her birthday, when he saw his parents arguing in his father's study. When his father stormed out and his mother sank down the wall and wept. He'd been embarrassed by his mother's need. Confused by her tears. Afraid of her words. *I wish we could leave this place. I wish we could get away from the poison in these walls.* "You wanted to go but I couldn't. You stayed because I had to."

She squeezed his shoulders tight and shook her head.

"Don't be sorry. All of that is in the past. We're free now, my love."

His skin prickled. He slid his hand inside the unzipped front of his suit and felt smooth skin where his scar should have been. His eyes went wide. His mother tipped back her head again and laughed that melodic, wonderful laugh as the Truth Teller's words swelled in his mind.

Your mother wished for your freedom.

Freedom will be yours.

Two truths.

His breath stalled in his chest. A carefree lightness washed over him. Like gravity letting go.

"It's time to celebrate!" His mother took his hand and pulled him closer to the front of the line. "How about we start with some taffy?"

Taffy.

She used to tell him about this taffy. Every year she saved as much money as she could find or earn, then spent it on a bag of freshly stretched taffy at the Merivus Carnival. She would eat three different colored pieces—a mouthwatering workout for her jaw—and hide the rest under her mattress in the white crumpled bag it came in. Every morning for many mornings to come, she would unwrap one and pop it into her mouth. When the bag got low, she'd take to splitting the pieces in half to make the candy last for as long as possible. Now here they were—together—at the Merivus Carnival, waiting in line for the taffy his mother loved. Leo was finally going to get a taste of it.

She frowned.

"What's wrong?" he asked.

"I forgot to bring my money."

Leo patted his pockets to see if he might have some. When he reached inside, his hand curled around a bracelet. He pulled it out.

"Oh," his mother exclaimed. "How did that get there?"

"Dad gave it to me." On his eighteenth birthday. Because his mother was dead. But how could that be when she was right here beside him?

"I don't think the taffy man will take my bracelet. But I do think he will take that coin."

The coin. It was tied around his wrist with twine. Leo touched the smooth skin where his scar had been.

Freedom will be yours.

But then, what about the girl? Who wanted him to fight for good. Who thought he could actually make change for better. *Beautiful, brazen Briar*. Her brother was locked up in Shard, headed for the guillotines—the last person left in her family. Leo was free, but Lyric was doomed. He shouldn't care. Lyric's mother had killed his. But no. She couldn't have. His mother was here with him. Leo shook his head, grappling for clarity.

His mother gazed toward the horizon where the navy sky had softened into something lighter. The first hint of dawn. "The carnival will be over soon. I'd love nothing more than to share some taffy with my son before it ends."

Leo touched the twine. "I think I'm supposed to give this coin to Ambrose Squire."

"Ambrose Squire? Why, he has plenty of coins. He doesn't need that one."

"But it's part of the contest."

"The contest is over, Leo," his mother said, her affectionate tone going slightly brittle.

He took a step back.

His mother cocked her head. "Leo?"

He took another step, and as he did, a searing pain carved through his chest. Wincing, he pressed the heel of his palm against the spot. When he lifted his hand, his breath stuck. The scar on his chest was back and everything around him began to fade like shine wiped away.

"I'm not free," he said.

"Of course you are."

"The contest isn't over."

His mother rolled her eyes. "Stop being silly, son. Come here so we can get some taffy."

He shook his head.

They couldn't get taffy.

His mother was dead.

The truth of it pounced with vicious aggression.

And suddenly, it wasn't his mother anymore. Suddenly,

he was standing face-to-face with the chambermaid, her gruesome neck mangled.

Leo stumbled, bumping into someone behind him.

His muttered apology fell dead on his lips, for that someone was the chambermaid's husband, his neck just as horrific.

The two of them closed in—glaring, angry, dead.

Terror laced up Leo's spine as he turned and ran. But they were everywhere. All around. Living corpses from Guillotine Square, grabbing at him, snatching at him with cold, clammy hands. Wailing for their lives. Leo ducked and yanked free. He shoved and kicked. Then he sprinted, knocking over the lady on the stilts who screamed for his coin. He shoved past the man juggling knives, who caught two and threw them at Leo. He tore past the Truth Teller's tent and nearly collided with Aurora who had burst outside.

They skidded to a halt as Garrick tore past, Briar right behind.

The carnival-goers amassed into a legion of zombies as Ferro, Evander, and Posey came tearing around a corner.

Leo ran.

Aurora, too, as the horde made chase, gnashing their teeth behind them.

He passed Garrick. He passed Briar. He slammed into the iron bars of the carnival gates, swinging them open. The other contestants burst through the exit, Posey the last of them, and together, they heaved the gate shut just as the rising sun crested the horizon and stretched its light into the valley below, silencing the chaos.

Everything stopped.

All that remained was the sound of their heavy breathing and the chirping of birds as the pale pink light of a new day spread across a barren field where the Merivus Carnival had once been.

"What *was* that?" Garrick choked as Anna the Hologram appeared in the sky. "Congratulations," she said. "You have passed the Trial of Confusion."

CHAPTER 22

LEO

Anna the Hologram didn't glitch. She spoke in a calm, measured tone uninterrupted by malfunction while Leo caught his breath and Garrick retched into the grass. They had done well, Anna said. They had made it far. It was time to rest and regain their strength in preparation for the second half.

"The second half?" Ferro panted.

"Regain our strength?" Garrick spat. "With what—more clover? Maggots disguised as something edible?"

Anna did not answer either of them. She continued as if there'd been no interruption. She would return tomorrow morning with further instruction. Then she disappeared.

Garrick dragged the back of his arm across his lips, looking desperately like he wanted to scrub out his mouth but had nothing to scrub it out with. "A radioactive city filled with mutants. A disappearing carnival filled with zombies. What's next—a burning forest filled with crazed birds?"

"That's caused by a disease spread by mammals," Aurora said. "I don't think birds can get it."

Garrick shot her a mutinous glare.

Leo looked out over the barren field where his mother had been, his heart twisting painfully in the wake of her. He glanced at Briar, remembering the mangled state of the chambermaid. Bile churned in his stomach. For a moment he thought he might retch like Garrick.

Posey pushed sweaty tangles of bright red hair from her face. Evander had smudges of dirt on his cheeks. Briar's braid was a mess. Dried blood still speckled her neck and ears. Each of them looked like soldiers after battle. Dr. Margaret wasn't a part of the group. Neither was Nile. Leo pictured the politician attacking the robotic rodents, the greedy way he'd pulled off his twine bracelet and loosened his coin. Had he been eliminated—his wish gone because of a silly carnival game? And what of the doctor?

"It looks like there's nothing left for a fire to burn," Ferro said.

The officer was right.

There was the hill a couple hundred yards behind them, which they'd walked down before entering the carnival, and a flat wasteland in front with a line of scorched fir trees standing at half-mast alongside the charred remains of what was once a village. Leo walked toward it, knowing exactly where he was, his arms lead weights at his sides as he beheld the destruction.

Blackened tree stumps. Homes mostly reduced to crumbling foundation. And a lone steel pole at the edge of the wreckage. It was the only thing standing—empty and barren where the Cambrian flag had once flown. He imagined the First Guard—officers like Ferro—marching through the streets in the dead of night, tearing families from their homes, herding them toward the City of Kruse. He could hear the ghosts of their screams. Their panic like a specter. Their fear haunted the air—more real out here than it had been inside the dome. Perhaps because he knew his mother's screams had been part of the fray.

An emptiness stretched wide within him—terrible and sad. He looked at Briar, wondering if she knew where they were. Wondering if their mothers evacuated the island together. Wondering if her mother had been a part of the destruction. Or did Squire's ceiling tell the truth? Had all of this been carried out by his second wife? A sudden burst of anger exploded into the emptiness. A flash of rage—the kind he'd seen in his father. How could the chambermaid have done it? They grew up here together. She used to sing Leo to sleep at night. She was nice. She was kind. But somehow, she'd been part of a plot to kill his family. To kill him. He couldn't make sense of it. But then, it was Magic. Chaos by definition. Impossible to make sense of.

"What's that?" Aurora pointed to a wall of mist past the line of fir trees.

A wind ruffled what remained of their needles, bringing with it a succulent scent—mouthwatering like the carnival food, only this didn't fill his brain with fuzz. If anything, the smell made him more alert.

Garrick lifted his nose into the air like a hunting dog on point and inhaled deeply. "Somebody please tell me that's real."

The seven of them moved ahead uncertainly. After having been through—as Garrick so aptly put it—a radioactive city filled with mutants and a disappearing carnival filled with zombies, nobody was quick to race toward the unknown. Or put much stock in Anna the Hologram. Perhaps they were entering the Trial of Fools, and only a fool would rest in the middle of such circumstances.

As they approached, it became clearer that the mist wasn't rising from the ground. The ground up ahead fell away. Nearer still, Leo could see that it wasn't a cliff, but a craggy slope giving way to a large body of water surrounded by rock and pine. The mist was steam, coming from the very spring his mother used to swim in with her friends when she was only a few years younger than himself. Was the chambermaid one of them?

"Food!" Garrick exclaimed. Throwing caution to the wind, he scrabbled down the craggy slope and hurried along the bank, which curled around the steaming water toward a flat beach with two picnic tables. An impressive spread of food lined them both. Towels were stacked on one of the benches. Folded blankets on another. Beyond them, brand new obsidian-colored suits hung on a line.

"Clean clothes," Aurora said.

Garrick reached the food. He seemed to check it first—maybe for maggots—then promptly dug in. Since nothing had lurched out of the water or sprang from the pines to snatch him, the others made their way toward the unexpected bounty, albeit more prudently than their hungry counterpart.

Briar remained.

Leo watched as she made her way down the steep, rocky embankment to the spring. She crouched into a squat and held her palm flat above the water's surface. She skimmed her fingers over the top, then dipped them all the way in and sighed. She sat down on a nearby rock and began unlacing her boots. She pulled each one off in turn, then unzipped her suit—filthy and bloodstained from their battle inside the city—and let it fall in a puddle at her feet. She was wearing only her undergarments.

Leo swallowed.

He'd seen plenty of girls in considerably less, dressed in lingerie made of fabric much more provocative than cotton. Girls eager to flaunt themselves, constantly peeking in his direction to see whether or not they had captured his attention. Briar, however, seemed altogether unaware of his presence. He felt as though he were intruding upon a moment of privacy. A gentleman would look away, but his eyes refused to be gentlemanly. They were too busy tracing the smooth curve of her shoulder, traveling along the delicate contour of her waist, lingering on the narrow set of her hips. She didn't possess the voluptuous curves to which he was accustomed, and yet an undeniable heat stirred deep down in his abdomen.

Arousal was an old friend. A familiar friend. Almost always an uncomplicated, straightforward friend. But this? This was tangled. Taboo. Briar was forbidden. Off limits. Magic. The chambermaid's daughter. He shouldn't want her. The fact that he did had everything swirling into an attraction stronger than any he'd felt before. An attraction that transcended the physical, although there was plenty of that, too. An attraction intertwined with wariness, intrigue, and a confounding admiration for this girl so filled with unflinching courage, dogged determination, and a deep devotion to the people she loved. A complicated snarl of emotions that made his veins throb with desire. His fingertips tingled with the need to touch. He balled them into fists as she lifted her arms above her head and dove into the water. When she came up, she pulled her braid loose with long, graceful fingers, then sank again beneath the misty surface.

Leo tugged off his boots. This time he was not going to scale a wall. There was no ticking clock counting down precious seconds or a hive of monsters gathering in the shadows. Just this edict to rest, a crystal clear pool, and this girl he wanted but shouldn't. He quickly shed his suit and dove in after her.

The warm, soothing water enveloped him. He swam several submerged lengths, then came up to a pair of startled, golden eyes. Briar's attention dipped to his bare chest. She looked away, color pooling in her cheeks, tiny droplets of water beading on her long, dark eyelashes as steam rose around them. Her face was clean, all of the blood and grime from the last two trials washed away. But her vigilance remained. Leo imagined finding her body beneath the water, his fingers fanning wide around her hips. He imagined slowly pulling her toward him ...

"Did you really see your mother?"

Briar's question yanked him back to reality. He blinked away his wayward thoughts. "I saw something that looked like her," he said. But then that something turned into Briar's. The memory of her mangled neck made him shudder. Leo dragged his hand down the length of his face. He didn't want to think about their mothers.

"I saw my brother," she said.

"Echo?"

She nodded.

His attention traced the silver chain around her neck, the locket submerged. Her arms undulated beneath the water's surface, the coin on her wrist visible but warped as it refracted snatches of morning sun. Even now, she was still wearing her glove.

"We used to dream about going to that carnival together," Briar said.

"I used to dream about it, too."

Her gaze lifted to his—her eyes a swirl of warm honey. "That destroyed town was their village, wasn't it?"

"Yes."

Briar caught her bottom lip between her teeth.

Leo sank lower, his eyes level with hers, his hands pulsing with the desire to touch. He shifted closer as the sound of chattering in the distance trickled across the water. Briar looked over at the others gathered around the two tables. Ferro. Evander. Aurora. Garrick. Posey. Meanwhile, he couldn't look away from her lips and the heart-like shape of them.

"Do you think Nile and Margaret are dead?" she asked.

"I hope not."

Her attention slid through the water, down to his chest. "How does it work?"

"How does what work?"

"Your scar."

Leo considered. "I don't know the particulars. Only

that there was a private ceremony when I was seven days old. My mother wasn't allowed. Not even my father. Just the current High King, which happened to be my grandfather, and the Royal Priest. When it was over, I was branded with the Korish symbol and my life was bound to the throne."

"What does that mean—*bound to the throne*?"

"When the time comes, I become king or my heart stops beating."

Her mouth gave a grim twist. "So that's your wish. The freedom to abdicate with a beating heart."

"That's my wish."

"It's a little ironic, isn't it? Your willingness to die for the freedom to ... not die."

He ran his hand down his face and laughed half-heartedly. When she put it that way, it did ring with a definite note of irony.

Briar narrowed her eyes at the coin tied to his wrist, then gave him a strange look—one Leo didn't understand. She peered toward their clothes, then back at him, her head slightly tilted. It was as though his features had become puzzle pieces and she was trying to put him together.

He pulled back his chin. "What?"

"I have one of your coins."

"One of my coins?"

"I took it from your jar in that chamber."

"You found my jar?"

With a nod, she sank deeper into the water, her nose just above the surface.

He remembered the frantic way she'd sprinted from the room. He remembered going after her to check to see if she was okay. A bemused grin tugged at the corner of his mouth. "Is that what made you run?"

He meant it as a joke.

But color pooled in her cheeks.

"Briar?" he said, his voice husky.

"What is it that you don't want anyone to know?" she asked.

"What do you mean?"

"The coin I took. Your wish. When I held it, those were the words that came. *Nobody can know.* And there was someone laying on the floor."

The statement gave him whiplash. "What?"

"You were staring down at your hands. It was almost like ..." She squinted, her nose slightly scrunched as if searching for the right descriptors. "It was almost like you strangled someone."

His mind zoomed to his grandfather, strangled to death inside the castle. In a plot to kill his family. A plot her mother was a major part of. Was Briar messing with him? Leo stood taller, the air cold against his exposed upper half. "I have no idea what you're talking about."

"I have it."

"The coin?"

"It's in the pocket of my suit."

Leo didn't hesitate. He dove under the water and swam. When he came up, he pulled himself onto the rock and rooted around in her pocket. As soon as his hand closed over the coin in question, the vision slammed through him. Uncontrollable rage. Someone crumpled on the floor. Someone with hair as white as Grandfather's. Guilty hands spread wide in front of him. Followed by a dawning sense of terror and three loud words.

Nobody can know.

Leo dropped the coin.

It fell into the dirt.

"What *was* that?" he said.

"I thought you would know," Briar said, having swam over.

He stared at the coin like it was a scorpion ready to strike. "You took *that* coin from *my* jar?"

"It had your name. Leopold Davenbrook."

But he wasn't the only one with that name. "The second?"

She looked at him with confusion.

"Did it say Leopold Davenbrook the Second?"

"Your father's name is Alaric."

"My father's *middle* name is Alaric." Which he officially took upon coronation, as kings were sometimes known to do.

Briar stared, realization dawning across her features in a slow wave.

"You didn't find my jar. You found my father's." He looked from Briar to the coin glinting on the ground. How did this bring any clarity? His father hadn't strangled his grandfather. Had he? The uncertain question had an absurd laugh pushing its way up Leo's throat. Was Briar trying to confuse him? Was this all part of her Magic? He looked across the spring toward the others. Eating. Oblivious.

His attention zeroed in on Posey.

Leo dove back into the water and swam across the spring to the other side. When he came up onto the shore, he strode to the girl with the scarf, water dripping down his body, rocky sand sticking to his feet.

She shrank back from his aggressive approach, the top half of her face turning the same shade of red as her hair. If he had to guess, he'd say she wasn't overly familiar with the male form, especially not one so disclosed. Leo was wearing nothing but a pair of snug undershorts. "The coin you showed us from your jar. That memory. Or the wish. Did it belong to you?"

Everyone stopped eating.

Briar came up behind him, panting. She grabbed one of the towels folded on the bench and wrapped it around her body.

"What are you doing?" she asked.

"Posey's coin," he said. "What did you see when you picked it up?"

"I dropped it too fast to see anything."

He returned his attention to Posey. Her scarf trembled. Leo took a deep breath and as calmly as possible, told her everything he'd seen. The enraged man. Posey on the ground. And himself—a bystander watching helplessly from the shadows. That coin had been inside Posey's jar, but that coin was not Posey's wish. It couldn't have been. It belonged to whoever the witness was, begging for her life.

"It was like I was holding someone's wish *for* you," he said, his thoughts tangling into a knot. Even if this was true —even if the coins in the jars weren't wished by the person but *for* the person—how did that explain the one Leo left in the dirt on the other side of the spring?

Posey shook her head and patted her chest.

"It *was* your wish?"

She nodded.

"But how can that be? I was watching you, on the ground." Unless she was wishing for someone else with a head full of bright red hair.

Posey shook her head harder.

Leo's tangled thoughts twisted tighter. "That wasn't you?"

More adamant head shaking.

"But the girl on the ground looked exactly like you. It was like she was—"

"Your twin," Briar said.

All around, everyone went still.

The only movement was Posey's fluttering scarf. She was breathing quickly, fearfully.

"It's okay," Briar said. "I'm a twin, too."

A hunk of meat fell from Garrick's fork.

Posey's terrified eyes snapped from Briar to Leo.

He didn't blame her.

Briar had just confessed something that could earn her a one-way ticket to Guillotine Square, right in front of someone with the authority to send her. He could feel each of their stares, watching to see what he might do. "I already knew this about Briar," he said, his voice sharp with aggravation.

Calmly, Briar sat beside Posey. "His name was Echo. He died several years ago. He was my twin brother. My best friend."

Tears pooled in Posey's eyes. She reached into Briar's lap and squeezed her gloved hand. The two looked at one another—an understanding solidifying between them. Then Posey nodded bravely.

Leo stared in shock.

Briar had guessed right.

It wasn't Posey on the ground. She'd been the one watching from the shadows, desperately wishing for someone to save her *twin*.

"I'm a twin, too."

Leo turned.

The words belonged to Ferro.

He said them vehemently, his prominent chin lifted in defiance—like the confession was a long time coming and now that he'd made it, he refused to be ashamed or afraid. "We were raised apart. I, by my father. She, by our mother. I became so good at hiding what I am, I think I started to believe the lies myself." He shook his head, the deep rumble of his voice filled with contempt. "After my time stationed at Shard—"

"At Shard?" Briar cut in.

But Ferro didn't respond. He pressed on like a man determined to get the words out. "I was transferred to Military Ridge. For four years, I was stationed there. Do you want to know what I did in service to the High King?"

Nobody answered.

"I tortured and killed Magic." He spat the words. "I tortured and killed my own kind."

Leo thought about the man's extended furlough. Often times, soldiers took them for physical injuries. Or mental health.

"What's the random chance that three of us would be twins?" Briar asked.

"Astronomical," Aurora replied.

"Make that four," Garrick said.

Leo gaped. Water dripped from his hair onto his neck and rolled down his chest. He looked at Evander, who stood silently. Stalwartly. When Leo caught his eye, he neither shook his head nor made any confessions. But Leo remembered his story. His mother fled to Nigal when she became pregnant with him. He claimed it was his mother's way of protecting him from his father's rejection. But now Leo wondered if she'd been protecting him from more. His attention turned to Aurora.

Adopted Aurora.

"I didn't start alone," she said, as if realizing the possibility at the same time. "The Truth Teller said I didn't start alone. What if that's why I was abandoned? What if that's my story? What if I'm a twin?"

"It would make sense," Briar replied. "It's very dangerous, raising twins. Especially if you were identical. Maybe it was the only way your parents could protect you."

"You said you were left at a train depot," Ferro added. "Those are busy places. Whoever left you there would have known you'd be found quickly."

Aurora's eyes grew bright and glossy. Almost orb-like inside her face. As though she'd been handed a gift instead of a curse. Then she turned to Leo. "Katya said the same thing to you."

He blinked, remembering the card. Two balls of yellow.

"Maybe you're a twin, too."

He scoffed at the statement. He was the High Prince of Korah. A crucial member of a royal family that had spent the better part of a century eradicating Magic. Leo shook his head. "That must have been the lie."

As soon as he said it, his gaze slid to Briar.

If that was his lie, then freedom was his truth.

He would win the contest.

And her brother would die.

HE DIDN'T START ALONE

YEAR OF KORAH: 506

LENA

Lena could not believe her eyes. Or her arms.

Phoebe!

She was hugging Phoebe. A fact that was so impossible to reconcile, she was afraid to let go—convinced that once she did, she'd wake up and this impossible reality would be nothing more than a realistic dream. So she held on. And for the first time since her pregnancy six years before, she let go, too. Tucked inside the safety of her friend's embrace, the cork popped. All of the grief and the fear and the confusion she'd kept locked inside came spewing forth like a shaken bottle of fizzy lemonade.

Phoebe held on tight and let Lena cry.

As if she knew.

As if she'd come for this exact purpose.

"I tried to get to you sooner," Phoebe said. "But you're not a very easy person to get to ... *Princess.*"

With a snort and a sniff—the idea of being princess remained such a ludicrous thing—Lena finally allowed herself to pull away. To behold this friend she had grieved. This friend she thought dead. This friend she had not laid eyes upon since she was thirteen. The years stretching between then and now shrunk into nothing. Here was the one person—the only person—Lena could trust with the strange and tragic truth.

"They were twins," she said.

Phoebe's expression hiccupped, jerking from concern to confusion as she processed Lena's words. *They were twins.* Her familiar golden eyes searched Lena's, looking from one to the other. "Twins?"

"A boy and a girl." Lena's voice broke over the final word.

Girl.

The forgotten one.

The erased one.

Her daughter.

Lena cupped her hand over her mouth to trap the sob.

Phoebe took her by the elbow and guided her to the bed. They sat down together in the center, knee-to-knee, and through her tears, through the oddest mixture of sadness and joy—for Phoebe had found her, Phoebe was alive, Phoebe was *here*—Lena told her everything.

Her whirlwind romance with the High Prince. The surrealness of becoming princess. How much she'd longed to be a mother. The crushing blows from the tabloids, constantly speculating over a potential pregnancy when pregnancy eluded her. The flood of euphoric happiness when her wish finally came true. The delight in her husband's eyes to see her in such bliss. The wonder of hearing that fast, healthy heartbeat for the first time—*one* heartbeat, for they'd only been searching for one. The joy of sharing their news with the public.

Then the shocking blow of her first visual examination.

A few minutes into the procedure, with her hand entwined with her husband's, the nurse sucked in a sharp breath and dropped the medical apparatus she was using to pull up a digitalized videocast of the baby. The nurse brought her fingers to her lips and lurched back as if a snake had come snapping out from the screen.

Lena's husband stood abruptly, demanding to know what was the matter while all the warmth seeped from Lena's body—an icy cold stretching from the top of her head to the tips of her toes. As exciting as this time had been, it came with an undercurrent of gnawing anxiety.

Yes, life had finally taken hold inside of her. But Lena knew—as every expecting mother did—that life taking hold did not mean life keeping hold. When the nurse stepped back, Lena had been certain her worst fear was true. That precious life—that miraculous heartbeat—was no longer.

But that was not the case.

Lena did not lose her baby.

Lena was carrying two.

Her husband's face blanched as white as the sheet folded across her lap.

The impossibility left her reeling.

But there it was on the screen.

Two distinct heartbeats.

Her husband stepped away like the nurse, and for the first time since they met, he did not look at her with affection or desire. He looked at her like he didn't know her. He looked at her like she was something to fear.

The nurse fled the room in search of the doctor.

"How is this possible?" Alaric demanded.

Lena stuttered and stammered like she did when she was young, her heart pounding erratically. "I-i-it isn't. It shouldn't b-b-be. I'm nnnot—"

"You're carrying *twins*, Helena." He whispered the words accusatorily—as if she'd done something deliberately deceptive behind his back. As if she wasn't every bit as shocked as he. But before she could utter her defense, the doctor stormed into the room with the nurse at his heel.

Lena was escorted to her bedchamber and locked inside, where she paced the floor. She was pregnant with *twins*. But only Magic conceived twins. Lena was not Magic. Lena had never been Magic. That had always been Phoebe. She was the one who made flowers fly and leaves dance. She was the one who could heal an injured animal and create light without fire or electricity. The only Magic thing about Lena was *Phoebe*.

And the bracelet around her wrist.

She had stopped then. She'd stood there in the center of the room, clutching her wrist with the bracelet to her chest, wondering if its essence had somehow seeped into her skin and turned her into something she wasn't. Princess Helena, future queen. Pregnant with twins. Something that sent most people to Guillotine Square. She could be beheaded. The two lives growing inside of her snuffed out. Her hand curled protectively around her abdomen, and Lena knew only one thing for certain. No matter how this had come to happen, no matter how confusing or impossible, she would do whatever it took to protect those lives.

In the end, she failed.

Her daughter's life had been lost.

Lena's attention lingered on the spot she'd stood all those years ago, when she had longed—desperately longed—for her old friend. Phoebe would have known how this had come to be. Phoebe would have known what to do. Phoebe always did. Now, here she was, back in Lena's life listening attentively.

"What happened?" Phoebe asked.

"Exactly what I knew would happen. The Royal Doctor went straight to King Casimir." Lena wiped the tears from her cheeks. "After the initial shock wore off, Alaric believed me. But by then, it didn't matter. His father already knew and that knowledge convinced him that I was a seductress. A witch who'd cast a spell upon his son. My husband defended me, but he was no match for his father's fury. I made plans to run. There was no other choice. Alaric begged me to stay. He swore he would protect us. He was convinced the public would be on our side. If his father did anything to hurt me, he'd have a mutiny on his hands."

Lena sniffed and picked at a thread in the duvet as one final tear tumbled down her cheek. "In the end, running wasn't possible. I became very ill. The doctor said it was the pregnancy. The toll of something so unnatural as twins upon my body. I was too weak to do anything but stay in bed, sequestered away like an outcast. I knew I couldn't stay, but I had no strength to run. Then one day, the doctor came to check on the babies and there was only one heartbeat."

It was a moment forever carved in Lena's memory.

Her husband by her side, their cold, clammy hands fiercely interlaced as the doctor delivered the news. Devastation had rocked her. It had rocked Alaric, too.

"We could not remove the child without risking the life of the other, so the child remained. For two more months, I carried them both. Life and death inside my womb. And when it was time, I bore them both, too. A little boy. And a little girl."

Lena could still feel the tiny weight of her. The precious dip of her nose. The beloved curve of her cheek. The tiny form of her fingers. She mourned when the doctor took that precious bundle away. Oh, how she had mourned. Even while cherishing the life of her son.

"The King let you and Leo stay?" Phoebe asked.

"What else could he do? He couldn't send me to Guillotine Square. Not without risking an uprising."

Phoebe's eyes flashed, like an uprising would not be an unwelcome thing.

Lena shifted uncomfortably.

"And all of it was kept secret?"

"Alaric's father went to great lengths to ensure nobody would find out." Lena exchanged a dark look with Phoebe. After that visual examination, she never saw the nurse again.

"And you felt safe?"

"Of course I didn't feel safe. For the first year of Leo's

life, I lived in a constant state of terror. You know how much King Casimir hates anything to do with Magic."

"And now? Are you still afraid?"

"Now ... the King pretends I don't exist. And he treats Leo as if he'd never been a twin."

Phoebe looked skeptical.

"My husband never talks about it." Lena picked at the bedspread. "Sometimes it's like he's forgotten the whole thing ever happened."

Sometimes, Lena wondered if it really had. Maybe she imagined the twins. Maybe they were a dream. But then she'd feel the ache in her arms where the tiny weight had been, and she knew no dream could ever be so real. Lena looked up from the bedspread, the unanswerable question that had haunted her these past six years finally having a placc to go. "How was it possible, Phoebe?"

"I think you already know."

"But my parents weren't Magic. My parents *feared* Magic. You of all people know how much they feared it." As girls, they'd had to hide their friendship from Lena's parents.

"Maybe it wasn't Magic they feared, but what was happening *to* it." At Lena's confusion, Phoebe continued. "They could have used a suppression charm to keep you safe. They wouldn't have been the first to do so. My father told me that parents used them all the time during The

Purge as a means of protection. Spells of that nature do not outlive their caster. When your parents died in the Cambria Disaster, the suppression charm would have died as well."

"But that would mean—"

"Your parents were Magic. At least one of them."

Lena's mind spun. "So it wasn't the bracelet?"

"No, it wasn't the bracelet." Phoebe reached into Lena's lap and squeezed her hands. "It's you. You're Magic, Lena. You're Magic like me."

CHAPTER 23

BRIAR

Briar's thoughts reeled as Leo snagged a clean suit off the line, his well-sculpted biceps taut with agitation. Water dripped from his dark hair. It rolled over his broad chest, down his chiseled abs—his expression dark and angry. Only Briar didn't understand why. He couldn't possibly be a twin. And if that was his lie, freedom was his truth. Katya the Truth Teller had all but told him he was going to win this contest—a fact that made Briar's stomach tie into a thousand horrible knots.

"What lie are you talking about?" Garrick said.

Aurora explained. As Leo dressed in gruff, jerky movements—not bothering with a towel—Aurora told them about Katya and her tent and the game she invited them to play. Briar watched Leo stalk away. He strode toward the other side of the spring where they had shed their soiled clothes. Where he had left the confounding coin that turned out to be his father's.

Nobody can know.

"How did the prince know you were a twin?" Officer Ferro asked.

Briar tore her gaze from Leo. Everyone was staring at her. "I hurt my ankle inside the Domed City. We were together when it happened. I had no choice but to heal myself."

"You healed yourself?" The startled, heavily-accented question belonged to Evander. His dark eyes swept over her like he wasn't just reconsidering an opponent but seeing her for the first time. His underestimation grated.

"Yes," she said.

"That is very powerful Magic," he replied. "It takes years of study and practice to perform successfully."

Briar pulled her towel tighter—a shield against everyone's sudden and suspicious interest. She didn't have years of study or practice. Briar had made a point to avoid both. And yet they were all looking at her now like she possessed a highly valuable and unfair advantage.

"Who trained you?" Evander asked.

"Nobody."

His attention dipped to her locket and there remained.

Briar covered it with her palm. The foreigner was making her feel naked, exposed. The foreigner was turning her further around than she already was. But before she could say anything—before she could insist that she had no advantage—Leo returned. He strode over, his blue eyes ablaze, and thrust his mother's bracelet toward her in his fist. "Show me how to do it."

Briar blinked at him—several times in quick succession.

"There is no way I'm a twin. The fact that I'm even entertaining the idea is lunacy. But it's in my head now and I can't get it out unless we do something to disprove it."

"Do something?"

"Twins are Magic?"

"Yes."

"Then if I'm a twin—" He delivered the word with a derisive laugh. As if there was no other way to deliver it. "Then I should be able to *do* Magic."

Briar bit her lip.

"Right?"

"Not exactly."

"What do you mean?"

She hesitated, unsure how to explain. Magic didn't come with a list of incantations. Despite what he might think, she didn't actually have a spell book.

He clutched his mother's bracelet, his eyebrows arched with impatience. "Will this help?"

"Maybe," she said. Her mother's locket had helped her. The bracelet was made from the same material. Maybe it would help him. But then, he'd have to be Magic for it to help him and Leopold Davenbrook could not be Magic. He was right. This was lunacy. A trick of the contest meant to break them mentally just as Ambrose Squire warned it might do.

His arched eyebrows rose higher.

Her cheeks flushed. "It doesn't just happen automatically. Magic is something you have to learn."

"Then teach me."

"I don't know how to teach you."

"Why not?"

"Because I've spent the last ten years of my life suppressing it!" It was a curse that got her parents killed. A curse that ruined her entire life. The monster in the closet. Magic wasn't safe—not for her, not for her brothers. Yet somehow, here she was on the Forbidden Isle using it. In front of His Royal Majesty the High Prince, who wanted her to show him *how*. "I barely understand it myself. I have no clue how to teach it to you."

"I can," Evander said.

Leo turned on the foreigner. "You're Magic?"

"How else do you think I climbed that wall?"

"You said—"

"There are mountains in Nigal, yes. But none that I have ever cared to climb." His attention dropped to the bracelet in Leo's hand. He looked again at Briar's locket. Did he somehow know they were connected? Did he know what they were made of? "May I?"

Leo didn't object. He handed the bracelet over, then dragged his hand through his hair as the foreigner let the delicate silver spill across his fingers.

"Most Magic takes years of study. It is a wild and mysterious thing."

Aurora sat up straighter. Like a little girl at story time.

Garrick paused from his eating.

"As old as time itself, infused with creation at the very beginning," Evander continued, turning the bracelet over in his palm. "Some were given the ability to harness this power—a gift passed down through bloodlines. Years upon years of persecution, however, has weakened the gift. Only the Wish Keeper has remained unscathed, his power protected."

"Why?" Briar asked, wondering why the Wish Keeper should receive protection.

Evander returned the bracelet, then helped himself to an apple. "His power binds the Davenbrook family to the throne."

"What?" Garrick barked.

Officer Ferro gaped. "The royal family uses Magic?"

"You're talking about the room, aren't you?" Aurora said. "The secret room inside the palace."

"How do you know about that room?" Leo asked.

"It was on the ceiling," Aurora answered.

"Of course it was," Briar muttered.

Garrick propped his knobby elbow on the table. "What room are you talking about?"

"The inner room in Castle Davenbrook. Only the High Priest, the High King, and the newest heir are permitted to enter. A ritual is performed that binds the child's life to the throne, ensuring the Davenbrook family remains in power forever." Evander took a bite of his apple, flecks of juice spitting from its flesh.

"You know a lot about the inner workings of my family," Leo said darkly.

Evander shrugged. "I have always possessed a robust curiosity about this country from which my mother took refuge."

A sparrow hopped along the ground, then flew up onto the far table where it jabbed at a piece of bread and flitted away.

Leo sat down across from Evander. "Go on."

"It comes in a variety of forms. There is power over nature. Power over the body. Power over the mind. And power over the inanimate." He ticked each one off on a finger. "Power over the inanimate is the easiest to wield." He made a show of setting his apple on the table. He fixed his attention upon it and the fruit rolled toward Leo.

Posey gasped.

Leo jerked away.

"It is a simple trick. Easily done with the right concentration." Evander retrieved the apple and returned it to the center of the table. "Set your mind on the fruit and command it to move. Inanimate objects have no will of their own. If Magic runs in your blood, the apple will not resist."

It was exactly how Briar had gotten the driftwood and the pick. She commanded it to come and since nobody else was commanding it at the same time, the driftwood listened.

Leo looked down at the apple skeptically. "This is stupid."

"Perhaps," Evander said. "There is no harm in trying though."

After a moment of consideration, the prince seemed to agree. He held his mother's bracelet in a white-knuckled fist and narrowed his eyes at the fruit. As he focused, Briar's locket went warm against her skin. And the apple clumsily rolled Evander's way.

Leo stood and stumbled back.

Briar gawked.

So did everybody else.

The High Prince of Korah had just done Magic.

Which meant the High Prince of Korah *was* Magic.

So was Evander and Posey and Officer Ferro and Garrick and quite likely Aurora. Katya's three statements circled Briar's mind. If the prince was Magic, maybe he really didn't start alone. And if that was true, then only one statement remained that could be the lie. Freedom wouldn't be his. Because maybe, just maybe, it would be Lyric's. A ferocious hope burrowed into Briar's soul.

Leo sat against a tree with his elbows on his knees, all ten fingers shoved into his hair. He had separated himself from the others, close enough to hear them murmuring, far enough to miss the words, his mind spinning itself into exhaustion as the sun made its way across the sky.

He was Magic.

Malignant, malevolent Magic.

The very thing he'd been taught to despise. The greatest threat to the peace and wellbeing of Korah. A terrible stain upon the commonwealth. It didn't just carve a scar over his heart. It coursed through his veins. A curse passed down through bloodlines. A curse he inherited from his mother—born on this island, with a Magic chambermaid and a Magic bracelet, too. How could she have been so foolish as to marry the eldest son of King Casimir, a man who began his reign with The Purge?

No reason made sense other than one.

She didn't know.

Wasn't Leo proof that such a thing was possible?

Aurora, too.

A person could be Magic without knowing they were

Magic. His mother must not have known. Until she became pregnant.

With twins.

Leo's stomach twisted.

He imagined the confusion she must have felt. The debilitating fear. The realization that her life was in grave danger. The lives she carried even more so. Did she use her Magic to hide it from King Casimir? Did she use her Magic to fix the problem? But then, if she didn't know she was Magic, she wouldn't have known how to use it. At least not according to Evander. Leo thought about his father. They'd always had a dysfunctional relationship. Was this why? His son was Magic. His son was forbidden. But then, so was his wife. Leo's father did not treat his wife like a disease. Leo's father would have died for her.

His head throbbed with confusion.

He felt like it might split his brain straight in two.

If Leo had a twin—if that really was his truth—what happened to his twin? And what was that coin in his pocket—the one Briar had taken from his father's jar? He didn't want to touch it. It was worse than Posey's by a thousand. He gripped his head tighter, his fingers digging into his scalp. But he couldn't stop seeing the white-haired figure on the floor. Leo's grandfather had white hair. Leo's grandfather was strangled to death in his own palace.

Leo stood and began to pace. Was this more trickery? Squire's attempt to spin him so far around he'd stumble right into elimination? The old man said the contest was designed to stretch—even break—the contestants. Was this how Leo would fracture? No. The coin couldn't be his father's. Briar must have misread the name on the jar. As if to prove it, Leo plunged his hand into his pocket, bracing himself for impact. The scene rolled through him like an icy wave. He didn't resist it. He let it come with gritted teeth and searched for details that would exonerate his family. There was the white-haired man on the floor. An all-consuming rage. And two hands stretched wide in front of him with a familiar signet ring and three loud words soaked with debilitating fear.

Nobody can know.

Leo let go of the coin like it was a hot ball of fire.

He jerked his hand out of his pocket and stared down at the signet ring on his left pinkie. One passed down from High King to High Prince every coronation. Leo had worn his on a chain around his neck until his fourteenth year, when the ring finally fit.

His stomach heaved, but there was no food to expel.

There was no denying it. The hands were his father's. The coin was his father's. The white-haired man, his grandfather. Which meant Leo's dad had committed treason. A crime punishable by death. A crime that made no sense. His father didn't want to be king. His father had been too consumed by grief to even consider it. Agony had wrapped him up in a dark and inescapable cloud. When he took the sacred oath on coronation day, he'd still been reeling from the brutal death of his beloved wife.

Leo's mind spun faster.

His mother was killed. Poisoned by her chambermaid. A fact that never made any sense either. The chambermaid was his mother's friend. The chambermaid was Leo's friend, too—a fact that had him throwing a fit well past the appropriate age. For he would not—could not—watch her be executed in Guillotine Square. Grandfather had stopped his emotional outburst. He'd grabbed Leo by the arms and knelt in front of him, then spoke sharp words Leo would never forget.

"This woman murdered your mother. She is an evil that must be extinguished. You will be there when justice is served. And you will not cry."

So Leo had gone.

Leo had watched.

Leo had seen the chambermaid and her husband put to death while his grandfather stood behind him, his heavy hands clamped over Leo's shoulders like a vise, locking him into place.

Two weeks later, Grandfather was strangled to death.

Magic was blamed.

But Magic was innocent.

The Great King Casimir was killed by his own son.

In a fit of rage that could have only been brought on by one thing.

A picture started to form—clear and horrible.

His mother, Magic.

His father, madly in love.

The whole commonwealth, too.

Everyone adored Princess Helena.

Everyone but Grandfather.

The two interacted sparingly. Hardly ever in the privacy of the castle. Was that because Grandfather knew? He knew Leo's mother was Magic. He also knew he couldn't send her to Guillotine Square. Not without looking the fool. A doddering old man unaware that the very thing he was trying to eradicate had infiltrated his family. His home. If there was anything Leo remembered about his grandfather, it was that he would not be made a fool. No, Grandfather would not have had her publicly executed. Nor would he allow her to keep on living. To keep his reputation intact, to preserve peace and order in the commonwealth, he would have had to think of another way to get rid of her. A more creative way. One that would require patience and cunning. One that wouldn't risk an outbreak of sympathy for something so abhorrent as Magic, but instead, solidify the public's tightly held opinions.

The chambermaid.

A wave of nausea pummeled him.

He needed to breathe.

He needed to be somewhere other than his own skin.

With his arm clutched across his abdomen, he turned and startled.

Posey stood in front of him with a plate of food in her hands. A cipher. So disfigured that she covered the bottom half of her face. Here was a girl standing in the very epicenter of Hawk's disdain. And yet, she held out the plate of food to Leo like the kindest of offerings.

My mother was a cipher.

Your mother was killed by one.

His words.

Hawk's words.

False words.

Leo had no appetite. But he took the plate and thanked the girl. Then he walked to the table where Aurora, Evander, and Briar sat talking. She was no longer wrapped in a towel, but wore a clean suit, her hair neatly braided.

"Can we speak privately?" he asked in a tone that was short and clipped.

"Sure," she said.

He set the plate of food on the table and strode back into the woods, the foreigner's stare hot on his back as they went. When he turned to face Briar, his attention caught on her gloved hand and another wave of nausea gripped him. She lost everything because of his family. Her parents. Her grandparents. Her uncles. All of them were executed for a crime he was pretty certain his grandfather committed. For a curse that ran through his own veins.

Briar and her brothers were left alone to fend for themselves in a cruel world with a bounty on their heads. And if that wasn't enough, his father ordered the fire that killed her twin brother.

Bile rose up his throat.

He swallowed hard and forced himself to look her in the eye when he said it. "It's about your mother."

Confusion flooded her eyes. Whatever she'd been expecting, it hadn't been this. "What about her?"

"I think she was innocent."

THE FIGHT

YEAR OF KORAH: 508

LENA

Lena had never craved the spotlight. She would have been happy to marry, have children, and live in obscurity on the Isle of Cambria forever. But life had other plans. Ironic plans. The kind that drop-kicked her onto the mainland, orphaned at seventeen, then thrust her into notoriety. The fact that she'd fallen in love with the High Prince of Korah was an irony not lost on her. For Lena, living her life under constant appraisal—a pendulum that swung from wild adoration to harsh critique—was not a sought-after thrill, but an unavoidable byproduct. One that turned every milestone into public consumption.

Her heart, however, could not help who it fell for, and fall it did for the prince. With such a fall came a title and a crown and a whole host of obligation. One of which was the annual hullaballoo that became her birthday. It seemed a silly thing for the entire commonwealth to celebrate. The ball held in her honor was excessive. The speech she was expected to give, anxiety-inducing, for what if her stutter returned? Captured and broadcasted to the whole of Korah. The very thought stole her sleep, stole her appetite, stole her peace until the blessed affair was over and she could put it behind her until the following year.

This year, she was turning thirty-three. Tomorrow was the big day, which meant her private quarters were a bustle of activity. She was wound impossibly tight as the speechwriter and his assistant stressed the proper delivery of specific lines and her stylist fussed over the finer details of her wardrobe and Phoebe stood at Lena's vanity organizing the discarded jewelry, her movements sharp and jerky. Phoebe didn't like the birthday bash the first time she had to endure it as Lena's chambermaid. She liked it even less this second time around.

A knock sounded on the doors.

At Lena's invitation, two more people swept inside—the event coordinator and the media director, come to inquire about the transition from dinner music to dessert.

Phoebe shut the jewelry box with a sharp snap, her palpable irritation winding Lena all the tighter. She loved having Phoebe here. But sometimes she hated having Phoebe here. Increasingly more often, her friend didn't seem to understand the position Lena was in. Lately, a tension had grown between them, one that frayed at Lena's already fraying nerves.

She extricated herself from the stylist, who was measuring her waist. "Please," Lena said. "If you wouldn't mind stepping out for a moment, I'd like to rest awhile."

The event coordinator looked up from the papers she and the media director were shuffling through. "Are you unwell? Should we call for the doctor?"

"I'm fine, thank you. It's just a slight headache. Nothing a few hours of quiet won't cure." She ushered them to the door, allaying concerns and politely declining offers of food, drink, and a masseur until the room was clear and only Lena and Phoebe remained.

Her friend had moved to the portable armoire brought in by the stylist and was hanging various gowns on the rack.

Lena leaned back against the closed door and heaved a sigh. "One more day and this will all be over."

Phoebe rounded on her. "Is that really what you're going to say?"

Lena pulled back her chin. She closed her mouth,

unsure how to respond. The silence only seemed to aggravate Phoebe further.

"Have I told you the latest rumors circulating?"

Lena winced. Recently, her friend had become a fount of depressing news.

"Do you want to know what's been happening up at Military Ridge?"

"Would you keep it to yourself if I said I didn't want to know?"

Phoebe's eyes flashed. "Torture, Lena. Human beings are being tortured. Do you want to know why?"

Lena rubbed her temples. Why did Phoebe bother asking if she wanted to know when what Lena wanted never mattered? Phoebe was going to tell Lena regardless, even though Lena knew very well what was coming.

"They're torturing people for being *Magic*."

"Alaric assured me that such torture is no longer happening."

Phoebe shook her head.

"I talked to him about it, Phoebe. He gave me his word."

"Your head is in the sand, Lena. Ciphers are dying of starvation. They are being put to death for petty crimes. The brutality of the constables in Tenement Row is appalling. I've heard it's worse in The Skid." She shoved another gown onto the rack. "Life isn't the way it was when we were kids in Cambria. Poverty is no longer just a hardship. It's a torment. I myself didn't understand how bad things were until we came here to Antis."

"So you have told me." Again and again and again, until Lena wanted to stop up her ears so she could hear no more.

"Then *do* something about it."

"I am! I go to Alaric with every bit of news that you give me. He takes it and he does with it what he can."

"He does nothing."

"He tries, Phoebe. But he isn't King and his father won't listen. What more do you want him to do? What more to you want me to do?"

"Give a different speech."

Lena laughed.

"I'm serious."

"I don't write the speeches."

"Of course not. You just give them. You stand there in your fancy dress like a shiny token in King Casimir's pocket."

"A token?"

"He uses you. And you let yourself be used. You've become his convenient shield, one he holds up against every accusation of bias and discrimination flung his way. How can he possibly be against ciphers when his own daughter-in-law is such an exemplary one? He lays the condition of our suffering squarely upon our own shoulders and you help him do it."

Lena drew back, her hand pressed against her cheek as if the words had physically slapped her.

"I'm not trying to hurt you. I'm only trying to get you to see." Phoebe took Lena's ice-cold hands in her own and squeezed. "You are so much more than a token. I believe that with all of my heart. You were put in this position for a reason, Lena. It's time for you to *do* something with it."

"What can I possibly do? I have no power in this place."

"You have the heart of the High Prince."

"Who has the devil in his ear!" Lena pulled her hands away, fear grabbing her by the jugular. Debilitating, all-consuming fear. One that had dogged her ever since the nurse revealed two heartbeats in her visual examination. She wasn't the brave one. She wasn't the rule breaker. That was Phoebe. Not her. And she was so sick of being afraid. "He *knows*, Phoebe. King Casimir *knows*."

He knew what she was. He knew what her son was.

They were living with a predator.

She and her little boy were two gazelles inside a lion's den.

"And he's done nothing," Phoebe said. "For eight years. Don't you think if he wanted you gone, he'd have arranged it by now?"

"Don't you think if I do what you're asking, he will arrange it still?"

"No, I don't. You're safe, Lena. Your son's safe. Alaric's love protects you. The people's love protects you. Your son's scar protects him. I'm not asking you to start a revolution. I'm merely suggesting you make a few tweaks to a speech."

Lena's stomach clenched into a fist.

"I know you worry about Leo, but he is heir to the throne. As the firstborn son, he's safe. He's untouchable. If only your daughter had been so lucky."

The words came like another slap. "What are you suggesting?"

"Come on, Lena. Do you really think King Casimir was going to let you have twins?"

Lena stared, sucker-punched by Phoebe's suggestion—not at all sure what to do with it. "What do you mean?"

Phoebe only gave her a knowing look.

Lena swallowed, unable to believe what her friend was implying. She attempted to breathe, but the air stuck stubbornly in her lungs. She pushed it out, then drew a rattling breath back in and shook her head. "Alaric would *never* have allowed it."

"You were going to run. If there's anything I've learned these past two years, it's how madly your husband loves you. He wasn't going to let you run, Lena."

"You think he had something to do with it?"

The pity brimming in Phoebe's eyes was all the answer Lena needed.

Shock morphed into fury. Alaric had been crushed when the doctor delivered the news. Every bit as crushed as Lena had been. "How *dare* you."

"You deserve to know the truth."

Lena marched to the doors and yanked them open. "Get out."

"Lena—"

"Get out!" she bellowed, so loud the words rang through the palace corridors. So loud, the event coordinator came running.

"Is everything okay, Your Highness?"

And just like that, Phoebe put on the subservient mask. With eyes down and head bowed, she curtsied and obeyed Lena's command. Phoebe exited the room.

"Your Highness?" the coordinator asked, looking in perplexed, concerned confusion from the princess to her retreating chambermaid.

"I'm f-fine. It's fine."

But it obviously was not. Lena's entire body shook. Great seismic waves from head to toe. How could her friend make such an accusation? Alaric was not the cruel king. He was her husband. The father of their children. A man who had been wrecked over the loss of their daughter. Sometimes Lena wondered if that grief was what drove a wedge between him and their son. Leo was a walking reminder of the child they'd lost.

Or a walking reminder of his own guilt.

The sinister statement coiled like a snake in Lena's mind. No! She would not think such a thought. She would not allow Phoebe's lie to slither its way inside her mind. She would cut off its head, and she would do so immediately.

"Your Highness?" the event coordinator asked again.

Lena didn't answer.

She was already marching down the hall.

She found her husband in his office, hunched over his desk.

"What happened to our daughter?" The question escaped without censure. It filled the cavernous room—ugly and bloated and startling. But Lena saw no other way to ask it. She needed Alaric to look up from his papers in absolute confusion and deny the unfounded allegation with an outrage that equaled her own.

Instead, he went very still.

"Alaric?"

Slowly, his eyes lifted to hers—the blacks of his pupils expanding.

Lena waited for his confusion.

Lena waited for his denial.

Lena waited in vain.

"Helena ..." He was using his calm voice, his reasoning voice.

She took a step back, her heart plummeting.

He stood from his desk, set down his pen, and came to her—his face breaking, his eyes anguished.

Lena took another step back.

"Please," he said, taking her arm.

She yanked it free. "What did you do?"

"What I had to in order to keep you safe."

Monster!

The word rose up inside of her as her heart crashed and shattered. She couldn't believe it. Phoebe had guessed right. Phoebe had spoken the truth. Lena took one last step away, her back coming against the wall, her hand pressed against her abdomen—the place her daughter had been. *Their* daughter had been. She could still feel the tiny weight of her. The memory of it had carved a permanent ache in her chest. Her precious baby girl. A sob rose in her throat. Tears sprang to her eyes. "How could you?"

"Twins are an abomination."

Lena raised her hand to slap him.

He caught her wrist and thrust his face toward hers. "Stop this, Helena." A vein throbbed in his temple. "It is over. It's in the past. I did what I had to do and we will never speak of it again. Do you hear me?"

She stared in frozen horror, no longer recognizing the man in front of her. There was poison in the walls of this place. That poison had poisoned him. With one last angry look, he let go of her wrist and stalked away.

Lena sank down the wall and wept.

Not until later—after she hugged her son and cried her tears dry—did she send word to Phoebe. She needed her chambermaid. She needed her friend. Her *sister*. They had changes to make to the speech she would deliver tomorrow.

CHAPTER 24

BRIAR

The fire popped and crackled. Flames flickered as everyone but Briar slept. She lay on her back wide awake, gazing up into the clearing. A black canvas dusted with glittering stars, fringed by a border of towering pines. The beauty of it pinched deep inside her heart. It was the kind of picture her brother would see and immediately want to paint.

Lyric.

So named because Mama couldn't stop singing when he was growing in her belly. Often, Briar joined—brimming with excitement to hold her baby brother. Before Antis and Castle Davenbrook became a part of their lives, their small cottage had been filled with song. Such memories were painful things. Confusing things. So Briar smothered them until they suffocated altogether. She didn't want her heart to soften toward Mama. It was easier to be angry.

For it was Mama who uprooted them from their life in Silva. Mama who brought them to the stinking, crowded streets of Antis. Mama who disappeared inside the castle. Then came home one night in a frenzy and confessed to killing her best friend.

"I did it, Flynn. I killed her."

Briar hated the High King. She hated the nobility. She hated the entire Illustrian class. But deep down in her heart of hearts, she hated Mama more. Because Mama was supposed to love them. Mama was supposed to protect them. Instead, Mama got Papa killed. Mama got her parents and her two brothers killed, too. She left her children all alone in a cruel world with nobody to care for them. And for what? To murder her childhood friend? To take part in some plot to exterminate the royal family? Briar didn't know. Briar never understood. So she locked it all away behind the impenetrable wall she built around her heart. A wall that protected her from whatever thorny emotions awaited on the other side of her anger.

Now, as frogs croaked and the fire crackled and Posey softly snored, Briar wanted nothing more than to resurrect the sweet sound of her mother's singing. She gripped the locket in her gloved hand as tears slid down her temples and into her hair.

It turned out, Briar believed a lie. The coin she'd been carrying around in her pocket wasn't Leo's wish, but his father's. The crumpled figure on the floor, his grandfather.

When Briar asked Leo why his father would do such a thing, Leo had one word. Revenge. For it was his grandfather—not Briar's mother—who killed his. According to Leo, Mama was innocent.

Why, then, did her mother confess?

Beside her, Leo inhaled sharply and jerked awake. He sat up. Then he scrubbed his eyes, dragged his palms down his face, and let his arms rest over his knees as firelight danced along his profile—straight nose, full lips, a strong jawline, his dark hair disheveled. He jammed his fingers into it, the signet ring on his pinkie finger resting at his hairline.

Briar wiped her temples dry and sat up quietly.

He glanced at her over his shoulder—his expression dark and shadowed.

His theory changed things between them. If true, her mother was not the guilty party. His family was. They killed hers. They blamed Magic. All the while, they were the murderers. The stigma of guilt was no longer hers to bear. Briar pulled the sleeves of her suit over her hands and scooted forward. "Bad dream?"

Leo stared at the fire despondently. "Have you ever watched a coronation ceremony?"

"There's only been one in my lifetime that I could have watched." And she didn't exactly have access to a simulcaster at the time.

"Well, there's this box that's a part of it. The future king presents it to the priest right before he takes his oath." Leo pulled at his chin, his palm scratching against the stubble on his jaw. "Every night for a year straight after my father's coronation, that box gave me nightmares."

"Why?"

"I thought my dad's heart was inside of it."

"Yikes."

Posey turned over, her soft snores quieting—her scarf shifting in such a way that revealed a glimpse of the girl's scarred neck.

Leo picked up a stick and poked the fire. "For the longest time, I actually believed that when I became king, I was going to have to carve out my heart and put it in the box."

"What's really inside?"

"A golden iustus."

The symbol of Korah, in sculpture. They were sold on nearly every street corner of Antis—large and small, cheap and expensive. The most impressive being carved from marble in the center of Guillotine Square.

"Of course," she said dryly.

"Eleos partim pentho omnis," he replied, a bite in every syllable. A muscle in his jaw pulsed in the firelight as he turned to look at her. "I don't understand how you can sit here talking with me knowing what my family has done."

Briar looked back at him—the High Prince of Korah—

and found that when it came to this mind-blowing theory of his, she couldn't muster any anger. Not toward him, anyway. Maybe because he'd been there, too—at Guillotine Square, stuck up on the stage, looking every bit as frightened and powerless as she'd felt under the stands. "If it wasn't fair for you to hold me responsible for my mother's actions, then it's hardly fair for me to hold you responsible for your grandfather's."

"But your mother didn't do anything."

"Neither did you."

His mouth flattened into a grim line.

A log popped.

Officer Ferro murmured something, then rolled onto his back. An officer who had spent the past four years torturing his own kind. And before that, stationed at Shard. Where Lyric was. Where her mother had been.

"Do you remember her—my mother?" Briar asked, the disembodied question hovering in the air. Hollow. Without inflection. And yet, her heart throbbed in the wake of it. Leo looked like his might be throbbing, too. A broken beat that somehow tied their hearts together.

He scrubbed his face and sighed. "I remember her voice. There was a lullaby she used to sing to me whenever I couldn't sleep."

A lump rose up into Briar's throat. She looked away, a surge of heat swelling in her chest. That lullaby belonged to her and Echo and Lyric. Instead, the High Prince got a piece of their mother that was meant for them. For the last two years of Mama's life, she'd spent more time with Leo than she had with her own children. Briar wiped an errant tear, embarrassed that it should come while he watched.

"I'm sorry," he said, his voice ragged.

"It's fine. It's just ... I wish I could remember it, too."

Another log popped.

Leo cleared his throat and in a low, rumbling voice, he began to sing. Words she'd forgotten. A familiar melody resurrected from the grave in a tone so rich and warm, it wrapped around Briar like one of Papa's hugs.

He stopped a little jarringly as though unable to remember the rest.

"I'm not much of a singer," he said, "but I think I got most of the words right." He looked bashful—uncertain as he wrapped his hand around the back of his neck. Here was a version of the prince the public never saw. A version who would sing her a song to help her remember what had been stolen.

Briar swallowed. "Thank you."

He seemed to relax then, as though her gratitude released an invisible pressure valve. The fire crackled as he set his hands behind him and gazed up at the sky where the stars sparkled liked diamonds. This boy—royalty—raised in the lap of luxury, never in want of anything. She—an orphan—scrapping and scraping to survive, always in want of everything. They shouldn't have a single thing in common. And yet, their lives intertwined in the most irrevocable and intimate of ways.

Briar wrapped her arms around her shins and looked up at the stars, too. "Lyric would love to paint this view."

"He's an artist?"

She nodded.

"A good one?"

"Sir Wellington Ferris said his paintings were good enough to hang in Castle Davenbrook."

"Sir Wellington Ferris?"

"A curator from Hillandale."

Leo arced an eyebrow at her.

"There's an old man named Rosco who runs a booth in The Skid. He makes money by selling artwork to the Illustrians who come through. I didn't want Lyric to have any part of it, but we needed medicine so Lyric gave Rosco one of his pieces. The curator came through while visiting his cousin in Antis. When he saw Lyric's painting, he offered to sponsor him at *L'Eclat Ecole D'Art*."

"That's a really good school."

"So said Sir Wellington." The mere memory of the man made Briar's lip curl. "For a mere sixty percent of all paintings sold, he would be happy to take Lyric under his wing."

"That's robbery."

"He seemed to think his offer was more than generous."

"I hope your brother took his offer and told him where to shove it."

"My brother never knew. He was working a job out in the countryside when the offer was made. When he got back, I couldn't bring myself to tell him." Briar scooped up a handful of rocky sand and let it tumble through her fingers. "If I had, none of this would be happening. Lyric wouldn't be in Shard. Mrs. Simmons might be alive. And I wouldn't be here." Sitting beneath a star-strewn sky on the Forbidden Isle with Prince Leopold Davenbrook.

"You wouldn't know the truth, either."

Briar frowned, unsure what to make of that statement. She looked at the others sleeping soundly. Evander under the cover of his long overcoat, the furthest away with his arm slung over his face. All of them, Magic. She thought about her connection to this place. Leo's connection. Evander's connection. Ambrose's connection. So many connections. "My invitation came before Lyric was arrested."

Leo narrowed his eyes.

"Do you trust him?" she asked.

"Squire?"

Briar nodded.

Leo's brow furrowed. "I don't know."

"Did you know it was his power that bound you to the throne?"

"I knew it was Magic. But I didn't know it came from the Wish Keeper."

Briar twisted the twine around her wrist, Katya's words to Leo circling in the back of her mind. *You did not start alone. Your mother wished for your freedom. Freedom will be yours.* "If his power bound you to the throne, then his power can unbind you."

"Maybe," Leo said. "But it isn't going to."

The circling stopped. The air inside her lungs went very, very still.

"Freedom is the lie, Briar. It's not going to be mine." His attention lowered briefly to her lips, making her stomach dip. "If I win this contest, I'm not submitting my coin. I'm going to submit yours."

Her eyelids fluttered. Hope, too. "Why?"

"I don't want to be a monster." The space between them crackled and hummed as his ocean-blue eyes filled with conviction. "If I took my freedom knowing what I know now, if I let your brother go to Guillotine Square, then that's exactly what I'd be."

CHAPTER 25

LEO

Anna the Hologram arrived early the next morning and told them to travel east. That was it. The entirety of her instructions. Leo knew the layout of the island. The Domed City sat on the western shore where most of the island's population once resided. They escaped over the east gate. Had Anna told them to travel north or south, they'd reach the ocean in fifteen miles either way. Straight east, on the other hand, left seventy plus miles of increasingly wild and uninhabited terrain stretching before them. The kind that had become—thanks to the disaster—a landmine of sink holes, schisms, and sudden, unexpected drop offs.

Leo would feel more comfortable leading the way, though he could not object to his current view. Briar walked in front of him, a makeshift knapsack she'd fashioned from one of the blankets slung over her back.

Having no idea how long or far they were supposed to travel, they decided to pack as much food as possible. They had no reliable means of carrying water, however. An unfortunate predicament that left him uneasy. He kept one eye out for sources of hydration and the other trained on the girl in front of him while behind, Garrick jumped at every squirrel and chipmunk that scampered across their path. Leo couldn't blame him, given the wildlife they'd encountered in the first trial.

They stopped midday to eat. They stopped again when they came upon a crystal clear lagoon. Now they were trudging along a flat stretch of terrain, Leo passing the time by making inanimate objects move. A pebble here. A twig there. Each one cementing the truth. He was Magic, something he inherited from his mother. A secret uncovered by his grandfather, who poisoned the princess and blamed the chambermaid, then met his end at the literal hands of his enraged and grief-stricken son. Magic was blamed for both deaths. Both times Magic was innocent.

Leo's attention traveled to the narrow of Briar's waist where the fabric of her suit cinched. When he confronted her yesterday, when he forced himself to look her in the eye and explain exactly what his family had done, he expected her wrath. Braced himself for her hatred. Perhaps even a physical attack. When she left him in a state of shock to process the bomb he'd dropped, he assumed her simmering silence was slowly burning toward fury. Instead, he woke up from a nightmare he hadn't had since he was nine only to encounter a Briar not filled with accusation, but clemency. She didn't grovel when she thought her mother was guilty. Not once had she simpered or begged for pardon. She refused to take on her mother's guilt and now it would seem she refused to sack Leo with his grandfather's.

Up ahead, the ground gave way—a fog-filled gorge carved into the earth. On the other side of the chasm, a collection of stark rock formations reached into a darkening sky like castle turrets made of granite. A stone watchtower leaned precariously over the precipice and beside it, a narrow rope bridge with wooden planks stretched long from one side to the other. Leo crept to the edge and looked down as the wind blew cold and the bridge creaked and swayed.

"Where are we?" Briar asked behind him.

"Catbirds Bridge," Leo said, eying the curtain of dark clouds rolling in over the rock formations straight ahead. A storm was brewing. The temperature, dropping. There'd been no sign of Anna. If they looped down the rocky path along the escarpment, he was almost certain they'd find an overhang to shelter under through the night. "I don't know about you, but I'd rather not be on it when that storm hits."

The wind blew again. Briar wrapped her arms around

herself, a few strands of hair blowing across her face as she peered up at the sinister sky.

"I agree," Ferro said. "We should stop for the night. We can gather wood and find shelter before the rain comes."

Nobody argued. Everyone was cold. Tired. Eager to rest and get warm.

Leo had the flint from their previous campsite tucked in his pocket. Starting a fire wouldn't be difficult so long as their wood wasn't soaking wet. "There's a path there," he said. "I'm going to follow it and see if I can find an overhang. Maybe a water source." He looked at Briar. Survival Basics, never go off on your own. "Want to join me?"

"*Down*?" she asked as another gust of wind came. The storm was approaching from the east, which meant the wind was blowing in from the west. Things would be a lot calmer—and warmer—with the rock at their backs.

"There's no way to go *up*."

She hugged herself tighter and peeked over the edge, her face paling. The wooded assassin. A girl who glowered at him when most would salute. A girl with the guts to give the High Prince a piece of her mind and had done so on numerous occasions even though he had the authority to punish her for it. That girl, it would seem, was afraid of heights. Or maybe storms. Or maybe the pair of them together.

"I'll make sure you don't fall," he said.

His attempt at encouragement only made her scowl.

"And for what it's worth, the rock will block the wind."

That did the trick.

While the others headed toward an outcropping of trees in search of wood, Leo took Briar's knapsack and began directing her carefully downward. He was right. With the cliff behind them, the sharp bite of wind disappeared. They could only hear it howling overhead as Briar's teeth chattered. Whether from cold or fear, he couldn't tell.

"You don't like heights?"

"They're not my favorite," she grumbled as she edged along the rim, her back pressed against the rock wall. "How far are we going?"

"To that overhang there." Leo pointed out the jut of rock a few switchbacks below them, right above the cloud-like fog, then pulled Briar to a stop. There was a gap in the path ahead of them. An arm-length of space where the rim fell away altogether.

Briar's face blanched.

"It's just one long step," he said, inviting her to go first. She went with a glare. His hands moved instinctively to her waist. His fingers touched the subtle flare of her hips and a rush of heat pooled deep in his torso. On the other side, the ledge widened. Leo let go reluctantly and noticed a tangle of vines growing along the cliff's face, twisting in and out of cracks and crevices. Pink berries hung from them in tiny clusters.

He picked one and popped it into his mouth.

Briar smacked his arm. "What are you doing?"

"Tasting the local flora."

"It could be poisonous!"

"It's not. Look." He held the cluster in front of her, pinpointing the familiar heart-shaped sepal. "It's ardorberry. Perfectly safe. And perfectly sweet." He offered her one.

She crooked her eyebrow at him.

"What?"

"I'm just trying to figure out how a guy with his own personal attendant and an entire royal guard picked up survival skills."

With a laugh, Leo told her about the Royal Adventurer's Club while they continued along their steady descent into the foggy canyon. When he finished listing his impressive array of badges, she frowned at him over her shoulder. "It's *only* for boys?"

Leo grinned. "That rankled Sabrina, too."

He watched for her reaction, wondering what a girl like Briar might think of Sabrina. She made the tabloids more than Hawk. Half the commonwealth loved her. The other half wanted to be her. But Briar was moving forward carefully ahead of him, climbing over rocks, groping for handholds, her reaction completely hidden. He was beginning to think she wasn't having a reaction at all until he heard her say, "Lebrina."

His grin widened. *Lebrina*—the ridiculous conjoined name the media created last year, when Sabrina accompanied him to the Merivus Ball after his dramatic breakup with *covetous, capricious Contessa*. After the theatrics of such a rocky split, he'd wanted the stability of an old friend. "Sabrina thought her half of the name should come first, being a lady and all. I have to admit, Sabreo does have a nicer ring to it."

"Is she your girlfriend?" Briar asked.

"She's a regular friend. Who happens to be a girl." Leo ducked under a protrusion of rock, thinking of the one and only time they'd kissed. His eighth school year on a dare. By then, Leo had kissed a handful of girls. Enough to know that kissing Sabrina was all wrong, like kissing Hawk's little sister. Something told him kissing Briar would be very, very different. The heat in his torso stirred hotter as his attention meandered from the back of her neck—bare with her thick braid swept out of sight in front of her shoulder—down the length of her spine ...

He took a careless step. Fragments of sediment broke loose and tumbled down the cliff. Briar shot him a look that could kill, as if tumbling to his death wouldn't make her sad so much as irate. "Are you trying to give me heart spasms?"

He held up his hands, eyebrows lifted.

Hers lowered in a severe line. She took a shaky breath, then climbed over a rock.

He did his best to avoid admiring her backside. Now was not the time for unchaste reveries, no matter how pleasant. He fixed his attention stalwartly on the path and searched for a conversational distraction. He'd told her about the Royal Adventurer's Club. It was time for her to share something equally benign with him. "What about you?" he said. "What does Briar Bishop do for fun?

"Fun?" She said the word like it was foreign.

"You know. Enjoyment. Pleasure. A hobby for one's own amusement." He ducked under another protrusion. "Your brother paints and you—?"

"Make sure we have food to eat."

"That's not very fun."

"Fun is a luxury."

"Fun is a necessary part of life."

Briar stopped. They'd reached the overhang. Working their way under it would require a bit of navigating. It would be best if he went first. He maneuvered his way down, then helped Briar follow, letting her know where to step and what to grab. When she got low enough, he took her waist again and the pool of heat in his torso returned. She was all too quick to step away, wiping bits of dirt and dust from her suit.

The cavern was deep. A cave set in the face of the cliff. A perfect shelter to ride out the storm. Leo set the knapsack of food against the cave wall. Briar finished her visual inspection, then sat down and began unlacing one of her boots as the wind howled over the mouth of the gorge.

"My father was a storyteller," she said begrudgingly in response to his question about fun. She yanked off her boot and tipped it upside down. Two tiny pebbles spilled out from inside. "He used to tell us stories before bed and Echo and I would spend the next day reenacting them. Does that count?"

"Depends on the kind of story. Tragedies. Cautionary tales. Those are less fun. More dire."

"His were adventure. The epic kind where good battled evil and good always won. We'd run around with wooden swords, pretending to be the heroes. Once, we got so invested, I fell out of the third floor window of our living quarters on Tenement Row."

"That explains your aversion to heights."

"Two broken ribs and a shattered wrist will do that to a person."

Leo watched as Briar shoved her foot back inside her boot. He pictured young Briar and her twin brother, fencing with wooden swords in a cramped tenement. He pictured the chambermaid using Magic to heal her daughter's injuries. And something inside of him pulled with longing at the picture his mind had conjured. Briar finished tying her laces. Leo took her hand to help her up.

It was silly, the shock of heat that came with such a simple touch. And yet, this golden-eyed girl was setting his skin on fire. Making his heart ache. Turning his breath ragged. Piercing him straight through with a longing so acute, it made every muscle in his core contract.

A flash of lightning skittered across the sky.

Briar pulled her hand away, her attention darting nervously upward.

"Are you afraid of storms, too?" he asked, his voice low —intimate—as the clouds let loose a prolonged grumble.

Briar looked up at him, flecks of dark amber swimming in the gold of her irises and said something he didn't expect. "I was there that day."

Leo blinked. "What?"

"My brother and I drew straws. He stayed with Lyric. I went to Guillotine Square."

His stomach twisted. Briar was there? Briar had seen? He tried to fathom it—choosing to go to such a horrendous event. Leo never would've set foot in that square had his grandfather not forced him. His grandfather, the actual murderer. "Why?"

"Echo and I were hoping for a miracle. This was back when I still believed in a Wish Keeper. Maybe he would grant my wish and save my parents. Maybe our mother would use Magic to break her and my dad free. Instead, she turned the sky black. Even though she knew how much I hated storms." Briar tucked a lock of hair behind her ear, her attention fixed on the encroaching darkness outside—her brow furrowed. Leo needed to climb up so he could guide the others down before the clouds unleashed. But he was impossibly glued as she turned her eyes upon him. "Are you really going to help me save my brother?"

Leo stared down at her, his conviction solidifying. He was standing at the bottom of McKinley Pass, having mapped out a course of his own choosing. Not trapped, but locked in. Committed. His whole body buzzing with anticipation. "Yes."

"You're not going to wish yourself free?"

"If I survive this contest, I will be the next King of Korah. For better or worse." He attempted to insert some levity into the statement, but all he felt was ill. Leo was good at mayhem and mischief. An expert at providing fodder for the tabloids. He knew how to party. He knew how to play. But rule?

"For better," Briar said.

Her words were a cool drink in the heat of summer. He drank them in like a man who didn't even realize he was parched, then gently plucked a burr from Briar's braid. A tagalong from their hike earlier in the day. Her eyelids fluttered—her attention darting quickly from his hand to his eyes to his lips. The space between them hummed with an energy that was hot and potent. But before he could do anything about it, she took a decisive step back.

"We need to start a fire," she said, her cheeks red.

He stood there—jarred by her sudden retreat—trying

to recover from the blow. They didn't need a fire. They already had one crackling between them.

But she took another step back, her chin slightly lifted. "You should go get the others."

A second bolt of lightning lit up the sky, followed by a loud clap of thunder and the soft pitter-patter of rain.

"Right," he replied. Disappointment tangled with desire as Leo stepped out into the cold.

CHAPTER 26

BRIAR

Briar trudged through the weeds, her unease expanding with every passing hour. Entirely too many of them had passed. Seven days of trekking eastward. Six days since the storm and the moment that preceded it. A moment that left Briar feeling hot and disjointed. Out of sorts. On the fritz. Her wires impossibly crossed. For in that moment, she had wanted to kiss Leo. She'd wanted to be kissed by him. She'd never been kissed by anyone. At least not in the way she wanted Leo to kiss her. The whole thing was reprehensible. Her little brother was stuck inside Shard. Meanwhile, she was turning into every other fawning girl in Korah. But reason didn't cool her attraction. Nor did time. If anything, her growing frustration with Anna's radio silence only seemed to magnify it.

Was it the heightened circumstances of the contest?

Witnessing death together. Facing death together. Or was it his promise to help her? After four years of being on her own—of carrying not just her weight, but the weight of her brother, too—she couldn't deny how nice it was to have a partner again. One so completely capable that at times it bordered on exasperation. Crossing Catbird Bridge had been an utterly terrifying experience. Meanwhile, Leo walked behind her like he was taking a casual stroll, ready to steady her should she need it. She'd made sure not to need it, and when she reached the other side, her hands ached with having gripped the ropes so tightly.

For two days after, they hiked the kind of death defying terrain she hoped she would never see again. Then the landscape flattened. They lived off a diet of berries and nuts. They always managed to find water just when they needed it. Leo had ample opportunity to show off his survival skills. And all the while, Briar tried dousing her growing attraction—attempting to focus every ounce of her attention on Lyric—but no matter how many figurative buckets of water she poured, the embers continued to burn. For seven nights, they shared intimate talks by the fire. For seven nights, she learned things about him—things about all of them—that she would prefer not to know about her competitors. For seven nights, the moon deepened into a shade closer and closer to red. And the thick vegetation started to look alarmingly the same. A combination that made her want to scream. Where was

Anna the Hologram? Why hadn't she returned? Didn't Ambrose realize Briar's wish came with an expiration date? The Red Moon was approaching, and with it, Lyric's execution. With every passing hour, he remained in Shard. A place that still haunted Officer Ferro, and he'd only ever been a guard. According to him, the agonizing cries of the prisoners at night still frequented his nightmares. Full-grown men begging for their mothers. Her brother was only thirteen and he'd been there for close to two months now and she could no longer check the list of the dead.

Briar wanted to crawl out of her skin. She was tired and hungry, increasingly convinced Ambrose had forgotten them altogether. Lyric would go to Guillotine Square and she would still be here, trudging east. Leo said the island was roughly eighty miles across. After seven days of travel, they should be approaching the shore. She kept searching for evidence of a nearby sea—the hint of brine, the faraway crashing of waves. But there was nothing to smell but pine and moss, and nothing to hear but their own heavy footsteps and Garrick's aggravating complaints.

She, at least, kept her frustration to herself.

Leo stopped in front of her.

Briar stopped, too.

She followed the direction of his gaze to a broken bough hanging over a path of bent reeds and trampled brush. The kind that looked as though it had been walked through recently. Briar's heart plummeted.

"We are lost," Evander said—a statement of fact.

Garrick kicked at the weeds. "I thought you said you knew the way."

"The hologram said to travel east." Leo flung his hand toward the bits of sun visible through the canopy of trees above. "According to that, we've been going east."

"According to that," Garrick retorted, shoving his own hand toward the broken bough, "we've been walking in circles."

A muscle pulsed in Leo's jaw—a visible sign of his own frustration. It was obvious he was every bit as confounded as the rest of them. Maybe more so, given the Compass Badges sewn onto his Royal Adventurer's uniform.

"Maybe this is the third trial," Aurora said.

"Maybe we'll never get to the third trial," Garrick muttered.

"Maybe we should stop whining and come up with a plan so we can reach the third trial," Officer Ferro retorted.

By *we* he obviously meant Garrick.

The boy's thin chest puffed with indignation and in seconds, the group was not only lost but arguing. It wasn't the first time. The tension grew thicker by the day. But arguing would get them nowhere. Nor would it help her brother. Briar extricated herself from the group, looking for what, she didn't know. She only knew that she hated feeling so helpless. Hated, hated, hated. With the passion of a thousand burning suns. It was, hands down, the worst feeling in the world. Like watching Echo slowly die from infection all over again. She approached the broken bough, searching for a clue. Something, anything that might give them some sense of direction. She set her hand against the tree as Leo stepped beside her, having extricated himself from the group, too.

"Are we lost?" she asked—quietly, without accusation.

"We shouldn't be," he said, heaving a sigh.

"Maybe if we had a better vantage point," she suggested, her attention traveling up the length of the tree her hand rested upon. It was tall. So tall in fact, it rose above the rest, disappearing out of sight above the canopy.

Leo looked at her like she'd just turned on a light, then grabbed the limb overhead and pulled himself up easily.

The arguing petered out as Leo climbed to an impressive height. Briar's stomach turned cartwheels. With every new branch he grabbed, she kept picturing him plummeting to his death—a vision that had her muscles going rigid. She didn't exhale until he was climbing back down again. When he reached the bottom, he dropped to the ground and dusted off his hands. "There's something up ahead, that way."

Without any further explanation, he set off in a different direction. Not an exact about face, but enough of a shift that she didn't think they'd have found this mysterious *something* had Leo not climbed the tree. Briar clambered after him. They tramped through the brush with an amplified sense of purpose, and when they came to a clearing that they most certainly had never come upon before, Garrick muttered an *I-told-you-so* that made Briar want to smack him.

Officer Ferro stepped out onto what must have been a road once-upon-a-time, now overrun with weeds and vegetation.

Posey pointed up ahead.

Briar and the others hurried forward, then stopped in front of a sign for the Underground Transit System. There was a vine-covered bench and a railing around the same type of sealed entrance she and Leo came across in the Domed City.

Posey found something tangled in the vine. An envelope. She tore it open, pulled out a piece of parchment eerily similar to the invitation they had each received, and gave the words a quick scan before shoving the parchment at Briar. As soon as her eyes caught sight of the first word, a wave of relief crashed through her.

"Congratulations," she read on an exhale. "You have reached the third trial."

Aurora clapped.

Posey, too.

"Finally," Garrick grumbled.

Briar cleared her throat and continued to read. "How do you act when you cannot see? When darkness encroaches and you want to flee. Go down below to the absence of light. Don't lose your head or rely on your sight. A platform awaits; more will be revealed. Find it quickly lest your fate be sealed." Her words tapered into uncertainty as everyone looked from her to the sealed entryway.

Posey shifted uncomfortably.

Leo picked at the sealant, then began pulling it up in a long line like he did before. Then he and Officer Ferro pried their fingers beneath the solid metal. Briar joined. Evander, too. Together, the four of them heaved the metal up easily. The door fell to the ground with an echoing thud and the group stood over the entrance, staring down into the black abyss.

"It feels like a tomb," Aurora said.

"You don't think it'll actually be ours, do you?" Garrick asked.

Briar wished she could laugh. She wished she could roll her eyes at such a dramatic question. But after witnessing Iris drown in the reservoir. After seeing Thomas and Sam devoured by radioactive mutants. After running from a horde of hostile zombies inside an impossible carnival and the disappearance of Nile and the doctor, Briar wasn't sure anymore.

"I hate the dark," Officer Ferro said.

"In all honesty, I'm not a big fan of it myself," Leo replied.

Evander raised his hand and snapped, creating a ball of light that hovered above his fingers, then led the way down, the dark creeping closer behind them with every stair they descended. When they reached the bottom, a resounding clang made Briar jump.

Garrick spun around. “What was that?”

Briar peered toward the pitch blackness where the shrinking box of daylight had been. “The door.”

“Who closed it?”

The question went unanswered.

Did there really need to be a physical *who* at this point? Did the *how* matter when faced with the immediate threat before them? The words from the rhyming note circled in Briar’s mind as Leo came to stand beside her, his nearness comforting. Evander explored the space. Slowly and methodically, his light revealed a large vestibule with automated ticket machines and turnstiles rusted over with disuse. The only sound was his shuffling steps and the hollow plink of dripping water somewhere beyond the light’s reach.

“We’re not supposed to rely on our sight,” Aurora said.

“You are free to go ahead without it,” Evander replied, lifting his light to reveal a cockeyed poster hanging on the wall—an advertisement for a twenty-five year old theatrical performance.

Aurora looked uncertainly at the tracks below.

There were two sets of them.

“How are we supposed to find the right platform?” Garrick asked.

It was a valid question. One that loomed large in Briar's mind. Surely the Underground had a myriad of platforms. How were they to know which one to look for?

Leo looped his thumbs into his pockets and turned in a slow circle, scanning the vestibule as far as Evander's light would allow. "That tunnel heads west," he finally said.

"Are you sure?" Garrick challenged.

Leo's expression tightened, but he pressed on, nodding at the tunnel going in the opposite direction. "Which means that one would take us east."

"The way Anna told us to go," Aurora said.

"She never said to change direction," Officer Ferro added, stooping over to pick something up off the ground. A large chunk of crumbled cement. He hopped off the platform, onto wooden boards supporting the tracks, and used the cement like chalk to mark the tunnels with the appropriate directional letter—E and W. "Just in case we get turned around."

Something about it made Briar's uneasiness grow.

Aurora was right. The directions had been clear. They weren't supposed to rely on their sight. But it seemed even more foolish to proceed blind when Evander was sharing such a clear advantage. He joined Officer Ferro at the tunnel entrance where he'd scratched the E. He stopped and crooked one dark eyebrow at the rest of them, his light reflecting off the drip of water. "Shall we?"

Briar and Leo took up the rear, slightly apart from the

others.

As they wound down the tunnel, Officer Ferro and Evander leading the way, a sound joined the shuffling of their boots. A twitchy scratching. Evander lowered his light. It glinted off a pair of red, beady eyes and a pale pink nose.

"Rats," Aurora said.

Briar wasn't sure how they were alive. This Underground had been sealed off for the past twenty-five years. Her nose wrinkled, imagining them breeding and feeding off one another to survive. Like ciphers in The Skid.

Her stomach churned.

They continued onward—whether straight or veering off in a particular direction, Briar couldn't tell. Down there in the dark with nothing but Evander's faint light and rats skittering over their boots, she'd lost all sense of direction. So when they reached a branch in the tracks, and Officer Ferro used his makeshift chalk to mark the tunnel veering right with an E, she couldn't help but wonder if he was simply guessing. But on they went—the tracks splitting three more times before coming out into another vestibule —larger than the first one, with six platforms and a network of tracks that veered off in three different directions .

Evander walked to one of the tunnels.

Posey shivered.

Aurora ran her fingers along a nearby concrete wall,

then stopped, her head cocked in the same curious way it had been when she studied Ambrose's ceiling.

"What is it?" Briar asked.

Before Aurora could answer, the chamber plummeted into darkness.

There were several gasps.

A strangled noise.

A *choking* noise.

The unmistakable sound of a struggle.

"Evander?" Briar called, ice zipping through her veins.

Something sharp pinched the back of her neck.

She slapped her hand against the spot. "What the—?"

"Evander!" Garrick shouted.

The others, too.

His name echoed all around in the darkness.

What happened?

Where was he?

Then a gurgling rattle rose above the din—hauntingly, horrifyingly familiar. A sound Briar hoped she would never hear again. A sound that made the hair on the back of her arms stand on end.

Everyone went still.

Even the cannibalistic rats.

For the span of a heartbeat—for the span of their nonexistent breaths—there was nothing at all but the debilitating, paralyzing weight of fear. They were not alone. The mutants were down here.

"What was that?" Garrick hissed.

Then it came again.

Someone grabbed Briar's arm, fingernails sharp.

"Nobody move," Leo said, his voice even. Close. Impossibly calm.

But the rattle turned into an agitated click that filled the cavern.

Followed by another that came from the other side.

Despite Leo's warning, everyone scattered like leaves in the wind. A flurry of movement that gave Briar no choice. She could stay in the center of that giant bulls-eye or she could run.

Briar ran.

In pitch blackness, with no sense of direction, she fled as far and as fast away from the clicking as her muscles would allow. She sprinted along the tracks, turning blindly into tunnels. She didn't stop until her lungs were heaving and her legs on the verge of collapse. And then they did. Her knees buckled and she fell to the ground. She pressed herself against the wall—her eyes wide in the pitch black, blood whooshing as her ears rang. She beat her fist on the ground, chest heaving, heart railing.

Against the dark.

Against the monsters.

Against this contest that was too much.

She pounded her fist again. "You could save him without this mess!"

Her haggard voice returned on an echo.

She shoved her hands into her hair and gripped her head between her palms. He could save Lyric right now if he wanted. It was no longer a question of if he could. But if he *would*. And why should she believe he would when he never had before? Not Echo. Not her grandparents. Not her uncles. Not her father or her mother.

"Do you trust him?"

The question she asked Leo seven nights ago taunted her. She wasn't sure then what to think of Ambrose Squire. But she was sure now. The Wish Keeper was not someone she could trust. Pain wrenched her heart as she stomped her boot against the ground. It was better when she didn't believe in a Wish Keeper at all. Easier to think there was nobody there than someone who didn't care. Someone as cruel as the world in which she lived.

"She was innocent!" Briar shouted, then dragged the back of her arm across her eyes, a sob bubbling up her throat. She groped for her locket but touched only collarbone.

Briar pressed her palm flat against her chest.

Nothing was there.

Her locket—the only thing left she had of her mother —was gone.

Lost in the dark.

Lost like Briar.

Completely and utterly alone.

ARRESTED

YEAR OF KORAH: 508

PHOEBE

Phoebe raced up the fetid stairwell, her heart shattered. Her panic, swelling. She ran down the length of the third story corridor, a light flickering as she skidded to a stop in front of her tenement door and attempted to fling it open. The door caught. Phoebe pounded her fist against the worn wood as a baby wailed across the hall.

The lock clicked.

The door opened.

Her husband Flynn's face appeared, his features pinched with confusion. "Phoebe? What are you doing home?"

She was supposed to be tending to the princess. She was supposed to be offering moral support as her dear friend took the first brave steps toward reform. But Lena didn't even get a chance to make her speech.

"She's dead." Phoebe swept past him into their cramped living quarters where their three children sat wide-eyed at the kitchen table, half-eaten bowls of porridge in front of them, their small faces scrubbed clean from their bedtime wash. Phoebe went to the window and looked down at the dark street below.

"What do you mean she's dead?" Flynn asked.

She closed her eyes, unable to unsee the scene unfolding in her mind. Prince Alaric, lifting his goblet in a toast to his beloved wife. Lena, smiling bravely as she lifted hers, too, a tremble in her hand as she brought the drink to her lips and took a sip. The goblet falling, shattering to pieces against the marble floor. Red wine splattering like blood. Lena collapsing. The guests inside the ballroom gasping. Phoebe caught her head before it hit the ground. Lena spluttered and choked. Alaric dropped to his wife's side and shouted into the rising din. "What's happening? Somebody help my wife!"

Phoebe tried to help her. Phoebe tried to heal her. But she didn't know where to focus her Magic and Lena couldn't breathe and her lips were turning blue and she grabbed Phoebe's hand in a death grip and wheezed Phoebe's name. Lena's hazel eyes locked onto hers with a single-minded ferocity that cut through the chaos. It was just them—Lena and Phoebe. Holding hands. Best friends. *Sisters*.

"Tell my son," she choked, her grip tightening. "Tell him, Phoebe."

"What Lena? What do you want me to tell him?"

"Tell him ... to b-be brave."

Then her hand went slack and her eyes went unseeing and Phoebe screamed and screamed and screamed.

"Who's dead?" Flynn asked.

"Lena," she whispered.

Dear, beloved Lena.

"What?"

"She was poisoned. From a drink *I* poured." Phoebe wrung her hands. Lena had tried to tell her. She'd been afraid, and with good reason. It wasn't safe. It was too risky. But Phoebe hadn't listened. She'd dismissed Lena's fears, thinking Prince Alaric's love would keep her safe. She pushed her best friend—her sister—into dangerous territory, and now she was dead. *Dead*! Phoebe pulled her hair. She promised to love and protect Lena and tonight, Phoebe broke that promise. "I killed her, Flynn. She's dead because of me!"

He crossed the room in three long strides. He grabbed hold of her shoulders and gave her a sharp shake, as though to rattle her from her rising hysteria. "Stop it, Phoebe. You're scaring the children."

Lyric began to whimper.

The children.

With a fierce look at all three, she marched to their chest of drawers and began removing clothes. "We have to go. We have to go right now."

"Sweetheart, slow down."

"We can't, Flynn! There isn't any time." Was he not hearing her? Didn't he understand? Lena was dead. Phoebe poured her drink. And they fought the day before. So loud the event coordinator heard.

A siren began to wail.

"Papa!" Briar yelled.

She was standing at the window, clutching the sill.

Down below, the street was no longer dark but a parade of light as uniformed officers poured from a line of vehicles.

Phoebe shoved a handful of clothes into her husband's arms. "Take the kids and go."

"I'm not leaving you."

"The Royal Guard is here."

"Exactly. I'm not going to let you face them alone. If they intend to make an arrest, they will do so with a witness present." His voice shook with conviction as he picked up a blanket from their tattered sofa and wrapped it tight around Briar. "Take your brothers to the junkyard and hide. Stay there until we come for you."

There wasn't going to be a *we*!

But Briar raised her pointy chin, her golden eyes large inside her thin face. Lyric's whimpers turned into a cry. Flynn pulled two more blankets from the pile and wrapped up each of their sons. "Take care of Lyric and wait for us to come find you."

Screams sounded from below.

Phoebe's heart jumped into her throat.

Blood thrashed in her ears.

Lyric cried harder.

She bent down and clutched her children to her in a tight, desperate hug and did the only thing she could to protect them. With a kiss upon the crown of each head, she cast a charm of protection. Until Phoebe removed it or until Phoebe died, they would be unseen, unheard by anyone set against them.

Flynn unlatched the window and lifted all three onto the escape hatch outside. Echo's fear turned into panic. He tried to claw and kick his way back to them.

A loud knock came on the door.

Flynn pried his son from his arm and pushed him out into the night. "Be brave. Stay together. Now go!"

Phoebe tried to say she loved them.

She tried to say she was sorry.

She tried to say so many things.

But she couldn't speak past the hard, hot knot in her throat.

And another loud bang came on the door. "Open up, by order of the Royal Guard!"

Flynn shut the window just as the door crashed open, hinges splintering. A burly man in uniform stepped inside. "Phoebe Bishop, you are under arrest for the murder of Princess Helena."

Two other officers advanced toward her, their hands set on the hilts of their batons.

Flynn stepped in front of them.

They shoved him aside.

He recovered quickly, thrusting himself between them and his wife.

One of the officers removed his baton and delivered a violent blow that knocked Flynn off his feet.

"No!" Phoebe shouted.

But she couldn't go to him. The two officers already had her by the arms.

"Flynn Bishop, you are under arrest for the aiding and abetting of Magic," the burly guard declared. Two more swept inside and grabbed hold of her unconscious husband.

"No!" Phoebe shouted again.

"Search the home," the burly guard said. "They have children."

Yes, they did. All three of them were currently pounding on the windowpane, their tear-streaked faces wild with fear.

But the guards did not hear.

The guards did not see.

Only Phoebe could as she and Flynn were bound and dragged away.

CHAPTER 27

LEO

Leo panted, his eyes groping in the dark—reaching for some trace of light when there was none to be found. It was as though he had no eyes at all, his sense of sight completely removed. There was only the cement wall behind him and panic closing in all around. The mutants were down here. They were prowling the Underground like the stuff of nightmares and he had no idea what happened to Briar. The two of them had been separated.

He set his palm against his chest and forced his breathing to calm. When the crashing of his heart subsided, he strained to hear—attempting to scoop up any and all sound—but there was nothing beyond the scritching and squeaking of scampering rats. No mutants. No contestants, either.

Leo had lost her. He'd lost her in the commotion and

not even the most impressive sense of direction could help him now. Not when he didn't know which way she'd run. Not when he wasn't even sure if—

No.

He squeezed his eyes shut as though to squeeze away the possibility, the muscles in his chest tightening. Briar was alive. She had to be. And he could not lose his head. That was part of the instructions. *Don't lose your head or rely on your sight.* Which meant he had to keep his wits.

This was a test.

A trial.

Squire had to have given them the tools necessary in order to pass it. What tools did Leo have at his disposal? There was Magic. But what good would that do him? He didn't know any locator spells, if such a thing existed, and moving inanimate objects from point A to point B was hardly going to help him find Briar. He had the bracelet. A piece of jewelry that went warm when Briar healed her ankle. Could that help him somehow?

He pulled it out and squeezed, willing it to do something. *Anything.* The delicate chain remained lifeless in his palm. He shoved it back in his pocket and pulled out the flint. He struck the rock against the wall. Sparks flew. A small burst of light. But without anything to grab hold of, the sparks fizzled and died. Leo heaved a frustrated sigh.

He would not find Briar by standing here like this.

He needed to move.

Even if moving would draw attention.

He reached for the wall to feel his way forward. His palm rubbed against something thin and defined. Something raised. Leo stopped. His fingers fumbled over the marking and made out the unmistakable shape of an arrow pointing in a specific direction. He sparked his flint to get a better look, but the flash of light revealed nothing but concrete.

"Don't rely on your sight," he muttered.

The arrow wasn't visible.

He moved in the direction the arrow pointed, feeling his way further down the wall. Sure enough, there was another one. He sparked his flint again. More concrete. He stepped back, the tightness in his chest releasing ever so slightly. There were directions on the walls only noticeable by touch.

Would they lead him to the platform?

Leo didn't want to get to the platform. Not without Briar. *Bound-and-determined Briar.* Maybe she was already there. Maybe she discovered these markings, too. Maybe by following them, he would find her. He continued along the wall, doubling back whenever the arrows stopped. In such circumstances, he would grope his way backward until he found a missed turn and the arrows resumed. He moved quickly and quietly. Until sounds stopped him. A grotesque, slurping gobble and sharp, frantic squeaks. Leo didn't have to see to know.

A mutant was up ahead, dining on rats.

He took a step back.

His boot caught on something. He stumbled, the wall catching his fall. But it was movement all the same.

With a blood-curdling shriek, the mutant was upon him. Leo stood stock still—his back pressed against the cement, his heart pounding—as the creature's rancid breath brushed against his face. It released a gurgling click. Cold, slimy flesh pressed against his cheek. He suppressed a shudder as a rat scuttled past. The mutant shrieked again and pounced, following the trail of rodents, leaving Leo alone and motionless.

He let out his breath.

Wiped his cheek.

Then crouched down to feel whatever it was he'd tripped over. His hand touched a leg. Terror shot through him. He groped upward—past a torso, over a shoulder, then a scarf. With a sharp exhale, he grabbed Posey's arm and gave her a shake.

She didn't respond.

He felt the bare skin of her hand—cool, but not cold—then up to her neck where he felt puckered skin and the faint tapping of a pulse. Something warm, too. Leo rubbed his thumb across the dampness on his fingertips. *Blood*. He searched for an injury, trying to find the source. When his hand reached the back of her head, it came back wet.

Leo tried to rouse her.

But she refused to rouse.

And time was slipping away.

He could not stay. Nor could he in good conscience leave. With his jaw set, he grabbed Posey by her elbows, then heaved her up and over his shoulders and found the arrow on the wall. He followed them up and down tunnels —the weight of Posey heavy over his back—making wishes while he went. He imagined each one sinking to the bottom of Squire's fountain—demanding, persistent.

Come on, old man. Help me find her.

And let her be alive when I do.

A soft shuffling sounded ahead.

Leo stopped.

So did the shuffling.

There was no squeaking rats.

No gurgling mutants.

Just the pitch black and the uncanny sensation that he wasn't alone. That he was participating in some sort of silent faceoff. With someone or some*thing*. The mutants hunted by movement, not sound.

"Hello?" he said, his lips motionless.

Nothing but quiet.

And then, "Leo?"

"Briar?"

"Leo!"

The sound of her voice unglued him. It must have unglued her, too. He set Posey on the ground, strode forward, and she slammed into him. Her arms wrapped tight around his neck. One of his caught around her waist. He inhaled the woodsy scent of her hair as their hearts crashed against one another.

He'd found her.

She was alive.

His hand reached up to touch her braid, her face. His other pressed hard against the small of her back as he did what he'd been dying to do every night since that cave. He curled his fingers around the back of her neck and kissed her like he was a dying man and this was his final kiss. When she kissed him back, his entire body exploded with heat. Wave upon wave of it.

Briar Bishop tasted like heaven.

He wanted more of her.

He wanted *all* of her.

The need consumed him as his hand ground against her hip, then spread wide up her ribcage, his lips traveling to her jaw. When she tipped her head back to give him access to her throat, he groaned and pressed her against the wall.

Her fingers dug into his hair. "I can't believe you're here," she whispered on a ragged breath.

Briar, unleashed.

Briar, unbound.

Briar, alive. Rousing his desire into something so acute, it was painful. He buried his face in her neck to catch his breath as her hands moved to his shoulders, then his chest. She patted him like he wasn't real. Like he might disappear. "I thought you were—I thought ..."

He could imagine what she thought.

He'd been working hard not to think the same thing.

He could feel her shifting away. He set his hand over hers, unwilling to let her retreat now that she was here. He didn't want Briar to stop touching him. He didn't want to stop touching her. "I found Posey."

"What?"

"She's hurt."

"Where?"

He threaded his fingers with hers and felt for the girl he'd momentarily forgotten. She was behind them. On the ground. Unmoving.

"Is she—?"

"There's a pulse." Very faint. "And she's breathing." But only just. "The back of her head's bleeding."

"What happened?" she asked.

"I don't know," he said.

He could feel Briar beside him, her hands exploring Posey's injury in the same way his had.

"Maybe I can heal her."

Something inside of him protested. The last time Briar used Magic to heal, it had taken a serious toll. What if this depleted her strength altogether? What if they ran into another mutant? But it seemed she was already trying. And failing.

She pushed out a breath. "I need my mother's locket."

"What happened to it?"

"I don't know. It's lost somewhere down here."

Leo frowned. How did she lose her mother's locket?

"Maybe I can use your bracelet."

His frown deepened, but Briar was insistent. He reached inside his pocket and let her try. It didn't work. She gave the bracelet back. Leo could feel her frustration. She voiced it, too. Namely, why wasn't the bracelet helping if it was made from the same material? Leo had no idea.

"We need to get her to the platform," he said.

"How?"

"We can follow the markings on the walls."

When she didn't know what he was talking about, Leo took her hand and guided it to the concrete, then gently pressed her fingers flat against one of the arrows, her body warm and close in front of him.

"It's an arrow," she said.

"They took me to Posey. Then they took me to you. Maybe they'll take us to the platform."

"Whoa." Briar pulled her hand back.

"What?"

"The arrow just ... moved."

Curious, he felt for himself. The arrow once pointing

left now pointed right. Just like Magic. Leo lifted Posey back up again. He hefted her over his shoulders.

Time was of the essence.

The instructions said so.

He had no idea how long they'd been down here already. A fact that made him want to move quickly. A fact that made him want to take Briar's hand and run. But they weren't alone. They had to be careful. He only hoped such caution wouldn't be their downfall.

CHAPTER 28

BRIAR

Behind her, Briar could hear Leo readjusting Posey. So far she hadn't stirred, a fact that twisted Briar's stomach into a knot. Over the course of this contest, she had come to care for Posey. If not for Lyric to consider, Briar might have forfeited her wish to see Posey's come true. She strongly suspected it had something to do with her voice. Ciphers were invisible enough even with the ability to speak. Never mind without it.

Leo pulled Briar to a stop.

Her heart pounded as she listened intently.

Not to rats. Not to mutants. But the indistinct murmur of voices.

She groped the wall, sliding forward until it gave way, opening into something larger. She could feel it—a change in the air. With a gasp, she realized she could see it, too. The faintest of impressions.

Light.

She held her hand in front of her. She could see the outline of her fingers. And when she turned to Leo, she could see him, too. His eyes wide. His hair a mess. Posey draped over his strong, broad shoulders like a fallen soldier. He carried the full weight of her—a cipher so disfigured she had to cover the bottom half of her face. Leopold Davenbrook—the High Prince of Korah—refused to leave such a girl behind.

The memory of his warm lips on her neck, his strong fingers in her hair sent heat racing through Briar's body. For several glorious seconds, nothing had existed but that kiss and the feelings Leo roused inside of her. Feelings she'd never felt before in her life. Feelings that had nothing to do with survival or practicality and everything to do with ... pleasure.

Pure, unadulterated pleasure.

And belonging, too.

They stared at one another for a moment—processing the change from pitch black to this less extreme dark—then hurried forward, Briar's eyes leading the way. They reached and strained like starved street urchins compelled by the scent of food. The light grew, balancing out the dark until she could see not only the outline of her hand, but the laces on her boots and rust on the tracks and rat droppings on the wooden planks and when she looked back, the determination on Leo's face burgeoning in the blue depths of his eyes. They rounded another corner and found it. A platform bathed in light.

"Evander," Leo said.

And Officer Ferro. And Aurora, their eyes rounding as Leo came all the way forward and set Posey on the platform.

"What did you do to her?" Evander asked.

"I carried her here," Leo shot back.

Aurora dropped to Posey's side. Briar knelt next to her, taking the girl's cold, limp hand and squeezing it. Now that she was in the light, the pallor of her skin was alarming. The only sign of life the faintest fluttering of her scarf. Briar scanned Posey for more injuries. Finding none, she focused on the blunt force trauma to the back of Posey's head where her hair clotted with blood. It was as if someone clubbed her with a rock. Briar pulled her trembling hand away from the injury and wiped a red stain down the pantleg of her suit. She peered from Evander to Ferro—an officer like the ones standing guard at Shard Prison, laughing cruelly as she begged to see her brother. An officer who admittedly tortured his own kind at Military Ridge. If he was capable of that sort of brutality, then certainly he was capable of this. "Where'd the rock go?"

His face went hard like flint. "What rock?"

"The one you were using to mark the tunnels."

"Are you suggesting I used it to attack Posey?"

"That injury isn't from a mutant."

"Nor was it from me. I dropped that rock as soon as Evander's light went out."

"My light went out because I was attacked."

Briar whipped around. "You were attacked?"

"Someone tried choking me."

"Choking?" Briar and Leo exclaimed, their attention catching, no doubt thinking of the same thing—the coin now in Leo's possession. The coin from his father's jar.

The foreigner rubbed his neck and nodded.

Suspicion sank deep down into the marrow of Briar's bones. Someone tried choking Evander. Someone had bashed Posey's head in with a rock. There was an enemy in their ranks.

"What about you?" Ferro spat at the prince.

"What about me?"

"You have flint in your pocket. That's a rock, too, isn't it?"

Leo's face lost some of its coloring. "I carried her here."

"So?"

"So I wouldn't have done that if I was the one who attacked her."

"It allows you to eliminate a competitor and look like a hero at the same time."

The two glared at one another—the prince and the officer—squared off and seething, societal hierarchy long forgotten. It was such a stark difference from the Ferro who saluted outside Ambrose's manor the night they arrived.

"Can you heal her?" Aurora asked, her intricate braids tied into a thick knot on top of her head. She was still kneeling on Posey's other side.

"I already tried," Briar said.

And failed.

But maybe the light would help. Maybe now that she could see Posey's injury. Maybe now that she wasn't reeling quite so aggressively from that kiss.

A loud clatter jarred her thoughts. A whirring mechanical sound she'd heard once before, after they came up out of the reservoir and Iris Grout was dead. Briar scrambled back as the same dome that took Iris rose up over Posey and took her, too. It sank back into the ground and just like that, Posey was gone. Posey was eliminated. Was Posey also dead?

"Garrick," Evander said.

Indeed. The boy was sprinting toward them, casting glances over his shoulder, his hair sticking up in every direction, the red stain on his face extra bright, the other half extra pale. He scrambled onto the platform, then set his hands on his knees to catch his breath while Briar's suspicion grew. What about him? Could he have done it? Could he have bludgeoned Posey? He didn't ask where she was. He simply sucked at the air, then nodded toward a ticket booth.

"Is that it?" He winced, grabbing his side. "Is that the 'more to be revealed'?"

Leo stepped forward and tapped the monitor. "It's a code."

Briar came beside him. There was a picture of a key at the top with nine dashes in the middle with letters and numbers at the bottom.

"With nine characters," Briar added.

Aurora leaned over her shoulder. "The chances of guessing are statistically impossible."

"It's not going to be random." Briar cast her attention around the platform. It was small, enclosed by a railing. There was a pile of crumbled cement where the staircase had once been, two benches, and the ticket booth. "There has to be a clue."

The six of them began to search. But they found nothing—no notes to read, no buttons to push, no levers to pull.

Leo returned to the monitor. He stood with his hands braced on either side. "Should I start typing in words from the instructions?"

Briar recited the note from memory. She got stuck twice. Aurora filled in the gaps and Leo plugged in words from the rhyme while Ferro peered into the dark from which Garrick had come. He'd found two pieces of broken cement, holding one in each hand like he intended to club the mutants in the same way Posey had been clubbed. Briar eyed him distrustfully while Leo went further back and began plugging in words from the mysterious invitation. Most of them didn't fit nine characters. He often had to add extras at random. All of which made the whole thing feel increasingly impossible.

Leo rubbed his jaw and looked at Aurora. "There wasn't anything on the ceiling about a key, was there?"

Aurora narrowed her eyes as if thinking while something in Briar's mind shifted into place.

A key.

Hearing the word out loud was different than seeing a picture of it on the monitor. They were looking for a *key*. Briar squinted at the nine dashes. Somewhere along the way, a key had been mentioned. She was sure of it, for the word tickled like an invisible strand of hair. And then suddenly, it clicked. The words tumbled out in a rush. "Beware of holding on too tight. Sometimes *the key* is surrender."

Leo and Aurora stared.

She let loose a disbelieving laugh. When she first opened that wise cracker and read those words, she'd wanted to throw them away. To spit or scoff, for she would never surrender. Not when her brother's life was on the line. But now it seemed that Ambrose had given her a clue before she knew what it was.

Leo tapped in the letters.

When he typed the ninth—a perfect fit—a sound came. Another loud clank and whirr, like the dome that had swallowed Posey. She spun around in search of the noise to find that the railings around the platform were closing into a solid wall and rising all the way up to the ceiling, completely shutting them, the benches, and the booth in. A clock appeared like the one down in the reservoir. Like the one in the city sky. Only this one did not give them five hours. This one didn't even give them ten minutes. But an astoundingly short ten seconds.

"What are we supposed to do now?" Garrick asked.

Nobody knew.

How could they?

Nothing more had been revealed.

All they could do was stand there and watch in helpless horror as the clock ticked down to zero. Briar braced herself as though water might start flooding the enclosure. Instead, there was another loud clank, a metallic groan as the walls shifted, closing in by two feet.

The clock reset itself.

Ten more seconds.

Briar's eyes went wide as Ferro set his hands against one of the walls and pushed.

It didn't budge.

Briar's heart began to thud.

Had she entered the wrong word?

Did Ambrose trick her?

Were they all going to be crushed to death?

The clock ticked to zero again. The walls lurched closer. With a loud shout, Ferro called for help. Evander and Leo joined. The clock reset. And floating between all of that hollering came Aurora's breathless suggestion. "I think we have to surrender something."

Briar stared down at her.

She was crouched beside the booth, running the tip of her pointer finger over a slot. "It's for coins."

Like the ones on their wrists.

Another clank.

A loud groan.

The space shrunk.

The clock reset.

Aurora unwound the coin from the twine on her wrist.

"He said not to lose them," Ferro said, his feet planted wide in a squat as he shoved his back against the wall.

"We're not losing them," Aurora replied. "We're surrendering them." Without another thought, without any warning at all, she slid her coin into the slot.

"No!" Briar yelled.

But it was too late.

Aurora disappeared.

The walls pressed tighter.

"Where'd she go?" Leo shouted, his face ashen—as

though here was finally a situation that genuinely frightened him. Not heights or storms or radioactive mutants, but being trapped inside a shrinking box.

Briar spun around.

Aurora was nowhere.

The clock ticked overhead.

Garrick began unraveling his coin.

Evander already had his free.

Briar looked at Leo.

Leo looked at Briar, the muscles in his jaw tight.

This was Lyric's life.

Was she really supposed to surrender it? What if doing so eliminated them from the contest?

The walls clanked and groaned.

Briar sucked at the air. She couldn't breathe. The room was closing in and she couldn't breathe.

Greedily, in the same hungry way that he ate his food, Garrick shoved his coin into the slot and disappeared, too. Evander paused. He looked from Briar to Leo to Ferro, then did the same. And only three of them remained. They stood back-to-back as the benches scrapped and slid together.

"Where are they going?" Briar asked.

"I'm sure they've been eliminated," Ferro said, gritting the words between his teeth. "You don't win a war by surrendering."

But this wasn't a war.

This was a contest.

Ambrose said to take care of their coins.

The carnival tried stealing them.

Was this the same? Were they in some twisted game of dare and the last one standing would win? Was this the final trial?

Leo grabbed Briar's shoulder. He had his coin free. "What do you want to do?"

The room squeezed tighter. So tight one of the benches splintered and Ferro wedged his back against one wall and pushed his boots against the other, as if his bulky body had the strength to keep the two apart.

Twenty more seconds and they'd be crushed.

Beware of holding on too tight. Sometimes the key is surrender.

She hated that word. It required trust. And she didn't trust Ambrose Squire. But then, the arrows had led Leo to her. The arrows had led them here.

Was the advice inside her wise cracker a trick or a clue?

Trick or clue?

Trick or clue?

"Briar," Leo said, his voice cutting through the spinning chaos in her mind, his eyes holding her steady, staving off the fear that so obviously threatened to overtake him.

With four seconds to go, she made her choice.

"Coins in," she said, pulling hers free and sticking it inside the slot.

The clock disappeared.

So did the room.

She was thrust back into darkness.

And then, there was a bright and blinding light.

CHAPTER 29

BRIAR

Briar squinted against the onslaught of light and sound as wind and fresh air whipped through her hair and waves crashed below. She no longer stood on a shrinking platform underground, but out in the bright open on top of a cliff overlooking the Afrean Sea with Leo beside her. Aurora, Evander, and Garrick were there, too. The five of them stood in a circle looking around uncertainly with no sign of Officer Ferro when Anna the Hologram appeared.

"Congratulations," she said in the same serene voice as always. "You have passed the Trial of Loss. Welcome to the end."

The words rang in Briar's ears.

The end.

She'd made the right choice. The advice inside her cracker wasn't a trick. Ambrose had given her a clue. And because of it, she was here. She'd made it to the end. This was the final trial. She was still alive. She was still competing. Hope carved a crater inside her chest.

Lyric, I'm coming!

"Find what you have lost, be the first to toss it into the well, and victory will be yours." Anna smiled at each of them, then dissolved into nothing.

All that remained was the bright, sunless sky and the wind and the crashing waves and an alabaster lion perched near the cliff, so lifelike in size and detail that for one shocking second, Briar thought it was real. With a gasp, Aurora crept toward it, her posture so soaked in reverence, Briar half expected her to prostrate herself in front of the albino beast. Instead, she stepped right past like she hadn't noticed it at all, then stopped in front of whatever was behind. From Briar's vantage point, she could see nothing remarkable.

Leo pivoted beside her, surveying the panoramic view. Behind, a tangled forest of behemoth trees reached their twisted limbs toward the sky. In front, a series of tall, stark cliffs bent around the sea like a giant's staircase.

"It's the Guardian of the Well," he said, his voice tinged with disbelief as he stepped toward Aurora, the wind making the gnarled tree branches groan.

"What well?" Garrick asked.

"That one," he said, nodding past the lion as he set his

hand on top of its white mane. "The Well of Good Hope. The lost wonder of Korah."

The Well of Good Hope.

The name rang a vague bell, like something Briar had heard a long time ago but she couldn't remember from when or where.

"It doesn't seem very wondrous," Garrick said.

Briar couldn't help but agree. From where she stood, the well seemed like nothing more than a crevice set into the cliff, surrounded by a crude formation of rock and stone. But as she approached, the same humming energy she'd felt near the fountain outside Ambrose's manor prickled her skin. Like the air was electric.

"People believed that whoever tossed a coin inside and made a wish would receive their heart's desire," Leo said.

The tiny hairs on Briar's arms stood on end. She looked down into the dark cavern of the well, then rose up onto tiptoe to peek over the cliff's edge. Large rocks jutted from the sea below, surrounded by foamy surf as the waves crashed over their tops.

"Who made it?" Garrick asked, edging closer.

Evander, too.

"According to legend, nobody. The well's existed since the beginning of time."

Briar brushed her fingers across the lion's smooth back. Perhaps one could argue that such a well might occur naturally. The lion, however, was wholly out of place in such wild, untamed terrain.

"This was commissioned by King Korah's grandson, the High King Orion, who hired a Cambrian native to render it." Leo slid his hand down the lion's mane, his fingers stopping just short of hers. Her stomach dipped. She could feel the heat of his skin every bit as palpably as the strange energy emanating from the well. "Sojourners from all across the world would travel here. It was a dangerous journey that claimed many lives and drove more than a few crazy."

"Crazy?" Briar said.

"A lot of people got lost. Turned around. They wandered in circles for days, sometimes weeks, never finding the well at all. That's why King Orion had this commissioned." Leo patted the lion. "It made the well easier to find."

"And it kept the evil spirits away," Aurora added.

A shiver rippled up Briar's spine. It felt silly. Like she was a little girl again, enraptured by one of Papa's stories.

"Enemies of hope," Aurora continued. "Malevolent forces who wanted to steal the wishes. King Orion had this guardian made to keep them away."

"An alabaster scarecrow," Leo said wryly.

Aurora set her hands on the stone and bent her ear over the well's mouth. "Do you hear them?"

Briar shifted closer, her brow furrowed.

So did Evander.

"Hear what?" Garrick said.

"Wishes from long ago. They whisper from the depths."

Goosebumps marched across Briar's skin. She heard *something*. Whether it was the crashing of waves rippling up the cavern of the well or wishes of old, she couldn't tell.

Leo disentangled himself from the well's hypnotic pull and wandered off to the side. The wind tussled his hair, accentuating a profile every bit as strong and distinguished as the lion's. He crept to the precipice and stared down the cliff's face. It wasn't like the cliff at Catbird Bridge. It could not be hiked down. There was no slope or rocky path. Just a sheer drop into the foamy sea. Briar fought the urge to grab his arm and yank him away from the edge as he cast his attention from cliff top to cliff top, to the brink of the highest one, where a stone tower rose up into the sky.

"Our coins could be anywhere," Garrick said.

It was the nine-digit code all over again.

But that hadn't been random.

Ambrose provided a clue.

Aurora began exploring the nooks and crannies of the well. She got down on her knees and felt around with her hands. Garrick reached inside the lion's mouth, then toed the dirt around its hind legs. A shot of panic zipped through Briar's arms. She imagined Garrick unearthing his coin and tossing it into the well. The contest over. Lyric doomed. Just like that. Whatever tenuous truce might have arisen among them as they trekked east blew away with the wind. It was no longer them against the contest, banding together to stay alive. But then she thought about Posey's injury. The attack upon Evander. The truce had only ever been an illusion. Now they had reached the final trial, and not even the pretense of an alliance remained. The first person to find their coin and toss it inside the whispering well would win.

Briar squinted at the stone tower.

Leo was looking at it, too, his eyes narrowed.

For some reason, it had another vague bell ringing in her mind. Like the Well of Good Hope. Like the key on the monitor of the ticket booth.

Clues.

Breadcrumbs.

She groped through her memory and found it—two large paintings encased in golden frames hanging on the walls of Ambrose's dining room. Illuminated watchtowers casting bright beacons of light through inky black sky. Illuminated watchtowers that looked identical to the one on the clifftop before her now. She remembered the dinner. She remembered Ambrose lifting his goblet in a toast. Someone tried poisoning him. Who and why? And what was it that he'd said? The contest would be a reflection of life. There would be peril. There would be confusion.

When such times came, he advised that they look to the *light*.

Her eyes went wide.

Leo stared back at her, his own smoldering.

The dots had connected for him, too.

Their coins were in the watchtower.

They had to be.

Briar's mouth went dry as she looked from Garrick to Aurora, both immersed in their search. Evander, however, eyed her dubiously. She quickly looked away, her pulse skittering. She did not look again at the watchtower. She didn't want to call any attention to it. He was at the dinner. All of them received the same clue. How long until Evander or Garrick or Aurora figured it out, too?

Urgency grabbed her by the throat.

She needed to get away from the group. She needed to do so unnoticed by the others. As if reading her mind, Leo wandered from the cliff. He kicked up rocks and weeds like he was searching at random. Briar did the same, hoping they didn't look suspicious, knowing they did. She could feel the heat of Evander's stare boring into her back. Her breathing went shallow. She pictured the five of them in a mad dash to their coins. She pictured Posey, bludgeoned. She pictured Posey, dead.

Her heart twisted.

She needed to get away. She needed to get to that tower.

Aurora dusted the dirt from her hands and moseyed away from the well. Evander's attention slid after her and Briar made a calculated choice. She darted for the trees. Leo darted after her. They sprinted into a tall thicket of weeds and dropped flat against the ground. Evander came crashing through seconds later, but the brambles were so dense, he stomped right past them. They scooted further back, ears cocked as brush crunched underfoot. Then Evander stepped back out into the open, kicking off a vine wrapped around one of his legs, his eyes searching the dark tangle of forest where Briar and Leo hid.

With a curse, he stomped toward Garrick and Aurora.

Carefully, Briar pushed herself up into a crouch and as silently as possible, the two of them made their way north toward the watchtower. Leo walked in front as Briar shot glances over her shoulder, convinced that Evander would come flying upon them at any moment. She became so fixated on what was behind, that she hardly noticed the thickening fog ahead. By the time she did, there was so much hazy white, she could no longer see Leo.

She hissed his name.

He didn't answer.

She turned around, startled to see that the fog was every bit as concentrated behind her. Somehow, she had walked straight into the center of a cloud.

"Leo!" she called again, louder this time, batting at the air as if the fog were a curtain to be parted. She coughed, the damp seeping into her lungs, and hurried forward. Was this a part of the contest, or some weird weather phenomenon—a patch of peculiar fog she would escape so long as she kept moving? But the more she moved, the thicker it grew until she couldn't even see her own hands groping in front of her. She was back in the Underground, only instead of pitch dark, she was surrounded in a cloying white that seeped into her pores and filled her body with cold. Except this time, it wasn't just her sight that was gone. But sound, too. She couldn't hear the blustering wind. She couldn't hear the creaking tree limbs. Gone were the crashing waves and Leo's steady footfalls. She couldn't even hear her own frantic heartbeat. So when the whisper came—not from far away, but right beside her—Briar jumped and spun around.

The whisper came again.

"Leo?" she hissed as a vaporous, bodiless voice slid into her ear.

"Lyric is dead."

Briar stumbled back. She shook her head.

"Lyric is dead just like Echo," the ethereal voice crooned.

She shook her head harder, searching the mist. Eyes straining to see. *No.* He couldn't be dead. She was here in the final trial. She was still competing.

"You cannot save him."

The words slithered around her chest and pulled tight.

Briar tried to take a breath. But the mist fell so heavy over her shoulders, she couldn't breathe at all.

"You cannot save anyone."

She squeezed her eyes shut.

And the whispering multiplied—no longer one voice, but dozens. Behind her and in front of her and over her, like a hundred ghosts flying and swooping—faster and faster, louder and louder until they were wailing banshees and Briar was crouched in a ball with her hands clamped tight over her ears. "Stop it, stop it, stop it!"

But they didn't stop.

They weren't going to stop.

She had to get away.

So Briar stood and ran.

Then collided with a hard, strong body that was running, too.

She fell with a loud *oomph* and the mist evaporated.

The voices, too.

Leo knelt in front of her, the tree limbs groaning all around.

Briar shrank back. "Did you hear them?"

With a disquieting nod, Leo pulled her to her feet and held on to her hand as they continued onward, quicker than before, as if they were trying to outrun the strange mist that vanished as quickly as it came. They reached a steep, craggy path filled with loose rocks. Halfway up, the path split in two.

"This way," Leo said.

They didn't slow down until they reached the peak and the briny wind whipped at Briar's hair and they were standing on top of the world. She didn't pause to enjoy the view. She ran to the watchtower entrance and found a spiral staircase so steep it was more like a ladder. She began to climb. She gave no heed to its warped, rickety condition. She'd become a runner at the end of a race, her mind fixed on the finish line.

Lyric, I'm coming!

A rotted stair gave way beneath her boot.

Leo caught her. His hands on her hips, his lips by her ear as they breathed in unison, his body warm and solid behind her. "You okay?"

She nodded. Swallowed. Then resumed her climb, all the way to the top, where the wind gusted cold and violent and a large lantern that once shone like a beacon sat dark and dormant. And there in front of it, on a metal beam, rested four shiny coins—a fact that had Briar's heart slamming into her throat. "Why are there only four?"

There were five contestants remaining.

There should be five coins.

Did someone beat them here?

How long had she been trapped in that fog?

Leo swept his hand along the beam to scoop the coins into his palm, but only one cooperated. The other three remained. He tried again; they didn't budge.

Briar tried.

One of the three fell easily into her hand. With it came a crystal clear memory. She was sitting in a chair inside Ambrose's study, scrawling her wish in blood. Briar touched the other two and similar images rushed through her. Different hands. Different wishes. Same setting. *I want what is rightfully mine. I want to know my story.* Evander's wish. Aurora's wish. Where was Garrick's?

"We need to go," Leo said.

Without hesitation, Briar pocketed her coin and flew down the stairs. She spilled out into the open air and without looking to see if Leo was close behind, she sprinted down the path from which they had arrived.

Lyric, I'm coming!

She was so consumed with frenzied need she hardly heard Leo calling for her to slow down. So consumed with panicked urgency, she didn't notice the mist creeping at her heels.

CHAPTER 30

LEO

"Briar?" Leo strode down the overgrown path, alarmed at the speed with which they'd been separated once again. One second she was racing ahead of him into the woods. The next, she was gone. Like the forest swallowed her.

Leo shuddered, trying not to think of that fog. But he could still hear the voices. It was almost like the strange mist had slipped into his ears and spread inside his brain. He rattled his head like a diver trying to expel trapped water, then stopped in front of the forked path. He peered in both directions—an attempt to gain his bearings, drum up some sense of direction. Two things he'd never had to work to gain or drum up before. Not until this blasted contest.

"Briar?" he called again, listening intently.

No response.

No footfalls.

No fog, either.

He looked around at the knotted trees, their arthritic limbs stretching into a canopy of claw-like hands through which shone patches of hazy, bright sky. He knew all about these cliffs and the forests that surrounded them. His obsession had reached such heights over this particular stretch of island, Hawk's mother gave him a book on his twelfth birthday entitled *Forbidden Folklore: Mysteries of the Isle*. A book that divulged things his mother had censored. She told him about the Well of Good Hope, but she never told him so much death surrounded it. She never mentioned how many had perished during their pilgrimages and how many more had disappeared altogether.

Evil spirits.

Malevolent forces.

It was the stuff of myth and legend. Stories to tell around a campfire. At the age of twelve, he wanted to take the journey, not because he believed in such stories, but because he was convinced that he could make it when so many others hadn't. Now, knowing the Wish Keeper was an old man named Ambrose Squire, the line between myth and reality had gone impossibly blurry.

A bird twittered in a tree limb above him.

Insects chirped—an evening sound.

Leo squinted up at the patches of sky, trying to locate a

sun that refused to show itself when a blood curdling scream split the air.

Briar!

Terror surged through him. Leo ran toward the sound. He crashed through the weeds, branches scratching at his face and his hands as he sprinted down the rocky path. Just as it leveled out, his boot caught. He sprawled to the ground with a loud grunt. Then sucked at the air like a guppy on dry land. He turned to see what tripped him and stopped his gulping.

It wasn't a root.

It wasn't a rock.

But a boy with a port wine stain on half of his face, laying belly up. As still as death.

Leo crawled forward and grabbed Garrick's thin shoulder. The boy's head lolled to the side. Leo jerked back with a sharp intake of breath. Garrick's eyes were open and unseeing, bloodshot and bulging from their sockets, his mouth frozen in a twisted scream. His lips an unnatural, purplish gray. The skin on his neck mottled with bruises.

With a gag, Leo lurched away.

Garrick hadn't been eaten by a mutant. He didn't drown in a reservoir or disappear in a vanishing carnival or receive a sharp crack to the back of his head in the dark of the Underground Transit System. Garrick had been strangled to death. Strangled like the High King Casimir.

By Davenbrook hands.

A familiar voice flitted past his ear.

It sounded like his father.

Leo turned, eyes wide.

Was he here?

Had the king finally come for his son? Did he do to Garrick what he'd done to Grandfather?

Leo peered into the shadowed wood like his father might step into view. But it wasn't his father who came. It was the mist. It rolled over the ground, creeping closer to Garrick until it covered him completely.

Leo scrambled back on all fours, then clambered to his feet and ran.

~

Briar didn't notice the mist at her heels, stalking her like prey. But she heard the high-pitched scream. It whipped through the trees like its own gust of wind. She ground to a halt. The scream tore through the air again and Briar ran. She bolted toward the noise and didn't stop until she crashed into a clearing and spotted Aurora, writhing on the ground, clutching her throat. Briar sprinted to her side and dropped to her knees, trying to get Aurora to stop, but she rolled around like one wrestling with an invisible opponent.

"Aurora!" Briar grabbed her by the arms. "What's happening?"

Aurora wheezed and choked like she couldn't get any air, then scooted away from Briar with feral eyes, her braids spilling loose and wild around her face, until her back met the trunk of a large oak.

An icy fist grabbed Briar by the middle as she scurried closer.

Aurora reared back, her face twisted in fear.

"I'm not going to hurt you. I'm going to—" The words stopped dead in her throat.

Bruises.

Aurora's neck was covered in bruises. Aurora's neck was horribly swollen. Someone had crushed the girl's trachea with bare hands and if Briar didn't do something right now, Aurora would suffocate. Briar's gloved hand fluttered to the worst of the swelling.

Someone had tried choking Evander.

Briar suspected Ferro, but the officer wasn't here.

Someone had bashed in Posey's head.

Briar suspected Ferro, but he wasn't the only one with a rock.

"Who did this to you?"

Aurora couldn't answer.

Aurora could barely breathe.

"Was it Garrick?"

Aurora shook her head.

And Briar's stomach rolled.

That left Leo. But surely he couldn't have. Wouldn't have. Would he? Did he try to kill Aurora in order to help Briar win? She shook her head, unable to think straight. She didn't want anyone to die. He didn't have to do that for her.

Was something so violent really for you?

The question slithered into her frantic thoughts—a snakelike intruder. The cold fist seizing her middle clenched tighter. She could trust Leo. He was her ally. But then, she believed she could trust her mother, too. Trust her not to leave them alone. Trust her to use Magic to rescue. To save. But all Briar remembered was wind and chaos and fear and Papa yelling at her to run. Like she should run now.

Leo had his coin. He had his coin and he knew how to get to the well and she didn't know where he was.

Lyric, I'm coming!

But Aurora was gasping and gagging—sucking at the air, clawing at her throat. She couldn't leave. If she did, Aurora would suffocate and die. Briar groped for a locket that was no longer there. A locket that was lost forever. She squeezed her eyes shut in an attempt to summon strength, but panic came like waves—one after the other, crashing over them like rocks in the sea. She couldn't heal Aurora. She couldn't heal Posey. She couldn't save Echo. And now Lyric ...

Was it too late? Was he already dead?

I saw it happen, Briar. You're going to be the hero. You're going to save us all.

Echo's final words tormented her, twisting with the memory of that whispering, screaming mist. She wasn't the hero. She couldn't save anyone. Death and suffering followed her wherever she went. Death and suffering were as inescapable as oxygen all around. Oxygen Aurora couldn't get into her lungs.

"Come on, Aurora. Breathe!"

Something snaked around Briar's leg.

She slapped it, expecting to see a snake. But it wasn't a serpent; it was a vine. They were everywhere, tentacle-like as they crept and crawled over Aurora.

Briar tore at them.

One wrapped around her wrist.

She shook it off and jerked back as the vines snaked around Aurora's waist, her legs, her arms...

"Aurora!" Briar screamed.

But it was too late.

Aurora was wrapped up like a fly in a spider's web.

And the fog was back.

It rose up from the ground, whispering voices roiling within.

~

Weeds snagged at Leo's legs.

Twigs snapped underfoot.

The fog chased him.

The bruises on Garrick's neck, too.

The ground dropped away.

Suddenly, Leo was falling, tumbling head over heels—weeds and brambles scratching his face, snagging his suit. Something sharp and hard jabbed his ribcage. His shoulder slammed against a rock. He rolled twice more, then slid to a stop.

Black spots danced in the periphery of his vision as Leo groaned, the pain in his side so sharp it took his breath away. He propped himself up on his elbow. A patch of thistles surrounded him and glinting on the ground beside it—a golden coin. It must have slipped from his pocket when he fell. Leo picked it up and cold fear barreled through him. A wish so visceral it felt like his own.

Nobody can know!

The words screamed in his head. He looked down at his hands—guilty hands—rage cooling into a horrible paranoia. The memory of flesh and sinew pulsed in his fingers, the memory of them tightening, tightening, tightening as life slowly leaked away and there was nothing left but those bulging, bloodshot eyes. Leo shook his head.

But he couldn't stop seeing it.

Garrick's face.

Garrick's neck.

Guilty hands with a signet ring.

The Davenbrook ring.

And Leo, the only Davenbrook on this island.

He scrambled to his feet, fog and fear all around. He swatted at it. He needed clarity. He needed his eyesight. He needed something tangible to hold onto so he could work out what was real and what wasn't. He spotted another coin on the ground. Another wish. Leo grabbed it.

A thrill of excitement shot through him.

Sitting in a study with a small piece of parchment in front of him.

Curiosity.

Disbelief.

Hope.

Freedom.

"Take it," a voice whispered.

Leo turned one way, then the other.

"Take it before it's too late."

The well.

He needed to get to the well.

Leo squinted into the fog, then raced along the ravine he'd fallen down. Voices flew at him—hissing, invisible things—the fog a writhing beast he couldn't escape. He hurdled bushes and dodged trees until he came crashing into the clearing. He ran for the vague shape of the alabaster lion—barely visible through the mist as the voices reached a crescendo of wailing shrieks.

"Monster!"

"Murderer!"

"Magic!"

"What have you done?"

"Nobody can know!"

Chaos swirled around him, a fever pitch of noise as the world spun and he stared down into the depths of that well with a coin clutched in each hand. Debilitating fear in his left. Freedom in his right. He didn't want to be a monster. He didn't want this to be his fate. He didn't want to be trapped. He wanted a choice.

"Poison in the walls!"

"Poison in your veins!"

"Freedom is yours!"

"Take it!"

With a great roar, Leo slammed the coin in his left hand down. Not into the well, but against the mouth of it. There was a resounding whoosh, a ring of wind that raced outward, chasing the voices and the fog away until all was silent and still. The only sound, Leo's heavy breathing as his chest rose and fell.

He stared at the coin.

Stamped with a *W*.

A wish that wasn't his.

Because the coin wasn't his.

It was his father's.

And Leo wasn't him.

Holding it might have made him feel guilty, but he wasn't guilty.

He didn't strangle Garrick.

His father had strangled his grandfather. Because his grandfather murdered Leo's mother, framed Briar's, and ordered her parents executed. Then her grandparents, and her uncles, too, leaving a young girl all alone with nothing to her name but a bounty on her head. Then her twin brother died. In a fire his father started.

So much greed.

So much corruption.

So much fear.

Leo's nostrils flared, his eyes narrowing at that coin.

Nobody can know.

Because of that wish, his father exiled an entire palace staff. His father allowed Magic to take the fall. A plot was fabricated. One Leo had spent the better part of his life believing.

He shook his head, hatred for all that was rotten welling within him. Maybe the mist was right. Maybe there was poison in the walls. Poison in his veins. His heart might end up in a box and he, one more corrupt king on the throne. But before that happened, he could do one right thing. One *good* thing. He could make sure that

Briar's last remaining family member did not die because of a Davenbrook.

He looked down at the coin in his right hand—his wish —the weight of an entire commonwealth heavy on his shoulders. It was a weight he never wanted. A duty he didn't ask for. But he finally had a choice. Freedom was his for the taking, right there at his fingertips. His entire body longed for it—an ache ten times worse than the pain in his ribcage. But there was something that burned even hotter. Something he wanted even more.

To make that one good choice.

For her.

For Briar.

With guttural cry, Leo hurled his wish into the sea.

CHAPTER 31

BRIAR

Briar crashed through the forest. Away from the voices. Away from the fog. Away from the traitorous evidence nipping at her heels. Aurora, with bruises on her neck, gasping for air. Posey, bludgeoned in the back of the head with a rock. Leo, with flint in his pocket. She ran harder, faster. Hating her suspicion. But also propelled by it.

She needed to get to the well.

She needed to get there before he did.

Briar sprinted out into the clearing when a blast of cold, white mist pummeled her. It blew back her hair. It bent trees. It snapped branches off their limbs. A tumult of hissing, screeching voices tumbled within.

"What have I done?"

"Nobody can know!"

"Freedom is yours!"

It roared past like a tempest, and when it was gone, so was the fog. All that remained was the alabaster lion. The Well of Good Hope. And the High Prince of Korah. Already there, his broad back to her as he leaned over the well. Had he thrown in his wish?

Briar's heart thundered.

Her lungs heaved.

Her knees buckled.

But before she could fall, someone grabbed her around the waist and shoved a hardened point against her neck.

Briar inhaled sharply. She tried to fight free. She tried ramming the back of her head into the person's nose. But the grip around her waist was too tight.

"Step away from the well."

Leo turned around slowly, his eyes going wide as he looked from Briar to her captor.

"I said get away from it!" Evander shouted.

Leo stepped back, grabbing something gold as he did. A coin. *His coin.* He still had it. He hadn't thrown it in. The contest wasn't over. Warmth ricocheted through Briar's body. The blade dug deeper into her neck. She winced against the hot sting as a drop of blood rolled down her throat.

Leo thrust his hands into the air. "Stop!"

"Drop the coin and I will," Evander snarled.

Leo spread his fingers wide. The coin dropped to the ground.

"Let her go," he said, a current of distress swirling beneath the steady, deep timbre of his voice.

Evander's grip tightened.

"I understand you want to help your mother. But you don't have to hurt her to do it." Leo's attention moved from the blade against Briar's throat to the arm wrapped around her waist to the young man who held her captive. "You don't even have to win this contest. I can help you. I have more than enough money to ensure that you and your mother will never be in want again. You can have all that you want. I give you my word."

"We do not want your money."

Leo frowned.

Briar tried to press away from the blade, but there was nowhere to go.

"We want what is rightfully ours," Evander hissed.

"Which is?"

"My inheritance!" The foreigner trembled as he spoke, his voice high-pitched. Deranged. "And all that comes with it."

Leo's brow furrowed.

"This contest is a joke, concocted by an old man who refuses to die. An old man who would go to any length to keep me from what is mine. The blood be on his head!" Evander pushed the blade harder.

Briar swallowed, her mind spinning.

Someone put poison in Ambrose's goblet.

He'd confirmed that it wasn't the first time.

Was it Evander? Had he been trying to kill Ambrose Squire?

But why?

"That's why she left," Leo said, as though to himself. Like he was thinking aloud.

Another drop of blood rolled down Briar's throat.

"The second wife." Leo's eyes were bright. Disbelieving. "She's your mother. Ambrose is your father."

Evander scoffed in Briar's ear.

"That's why she fled to Nigal. She was pregnant with the Wish Keeper's son. Squire's only heir. She wanted to hide you from him."

"She wanted to protect me from him!"

Briar stopped breathing.

Leo had guessed right.

Evander was the Wish Keeper's son.

"He didn't want me. He didn't want her!" The blade dug deeper. A whimper bubbled up Briar's throat, her nostrils flaring. "He married my mother to soothe his own pain, but she could never measure up to Anna. Just as I would never measure up to Collin."

"Your mother killed them."

"That's a lie!" Evander's overcoat billowed with the wind. It billowed with his fervor. Pockets lined the inside and out from one spilled a familiar, silver chain.

Briar's locket!

It wasn't lost in the underground, but right there in Evander's coat. Nobody attacked him. He extinguished his own light. He stole her locket in the dark. He pretended like someone was choking him. Then he hit Posey and he strangled Aurora. Briar thought about the philandering politician, Nile Gentry. Had he really tried drowning Evander, or was that a lie, too?

Evander dragged her closer to the well—closer to victory—the bite of his blade sharp and insistent.

She had to act. She had to do something.

But what?

Could she reach inside her own pocket and throw her coin into the well before he stopped her? She had no doubt he'd slice her throat wide open before the coin reached its mark. She would be dead, but might Lyric live? The chances of getting the coin into the well were minimal. Evander's ability to stop her, staggering. She couldn't toss anything without being noticed. But perhaps she could take something.

The locket had power.

The locket gave her strength.

She wasn't sure how or why, only that it was true.

The locket enabled her to do things she couldn't on her own.

And over the years—honed out of necessity—she had acquired the skill to take it. For it was either picking pockets or watching her brothers starve.

Evander edged closer to the well.

"I know what it's like to be lied to, Evander," Leo said, holding his ground. "My father has been lying to me my whole life. I think your mother has been lying to you, too."

"Ambrose is the liar!" Evander's voice exploded in Briar's ear—wild and deranged. "This whole contest is proof. He's not being honest about what this is. He's not telling the truth about what he's doing."

"What is he doing?" Leo asked.

"I already told you. He's trying to keep me from what is mine. Now shut up and move to the side, or so help me I will gut her in front of you."

"Go right ahead."

The unexpected words came like a hiccup.

They distracted Evander.

They distracted Briar, too.

But not before her hand closed around the locket.

"Or maybe it would be smarter to let her go and get this!" The coin on the ground flew up into the air. Leo used Magic. Magic the foreigner had taught him.

With an animalistic scream, Evander let Briar go and lunged at the well. Briar watched it unfold in slow motion. Leo's coin traveling in a high arc. Evander diving. His hands missing. His boots sliding. His body wobbling precariously as he pawed at the air, scrambling for a hand hold but finding none. With his eyes wide and his arms flailing, he fell over the edge of the cliff just as Leo's coin dropped into the well.

This time the scream came from Briar. It rent loose inside her chest and tore up her throat. She dropped to her knees, the locket falling to the ground. She dug her fingers into her hair and doubled over her thighs. Leo might have stopped Evander from winning, but he'd sacrificed Lyric in order to do it. The contest was over and she wasn't the victor. She hadn't succeeded. Lyric was doomed.

The wind blew.

The trees groaned.

The waves crashed.

And a gentle hand took hold of Briar's wrist. Another lifted her chin. Leo knelt in front of her, his eyes bluer than they'd ever been. He had tiny scratches on his face and neck. His suit was shredded at the shoulder. A bruise darkened his right cheekbone. The wind tousled his hair as he smiled.

Briar wanted to scream at him. She wanted to pull up the earth under her knees and heave it at the sky. The contest was over and Leo had won. He'd won with *his* coin. *His* wish. What a fool she was to think it would go any other way. What a fool she was to think that the story would end in victory for someone like her. Hot, angry tears welled in her eyes.

"Briar," Leo said. "That wasn't my coin."

His words came like another hiccup.

She blinked.

"I threw my wish into the sea."

"But—" She looked past the lion. She saw it with her own eyes. Leo's coin sailing through the air and dropping into the well.

"That coin was the one you took from my father's jar."

"You mean—"

"It wasn't part of the contest. It wasn't mine." He wiped the tears streaking her face with the pads of his thumbs, his attention flicking to the trickle of blood on her neck, then ever so gently he drew her up onto her feet, his smile widening. It was just them. Her and Leo, in this contest that wasn't yet done. "It's time to free your brother."

Lyric.

Leo walked with her to the well.

With her legs shaking, he wrapped his arm around her waist and helped her stand.

Briar reached inside her pocket and removed the coin.

Her wish.

Lyric, we're coming!

A disbelieving laugh bubbled past her lips as she held her hand over the well and dropped the coin inside.

CHAPTER 32

LEO

A swirl of wind and water surrounded him, only somehow Leo could breathe and there were no sinister voices whispering from inside of it. It lifted him, carried him, supported him. And then, just as suddenly, let go.

He was sitting in a cushy chair.

There was no more Forbidden Isle. No more Well of Good Hope or alabaster lion. But a warm study and a crackling fire and a gold coin in a porcelain dish beside a small velour pouch on top of a desk where Ambrose Squire sat. His velvet coat was a deep plum, the cuffs of his sleeves stitched with fleur-de-lis trimming. Beneath, he wore a brocade vest over a striped taffeta shirt with black buttons. His long fingers were steepled in front of his grizzled goatee and a myriad of emotions swirled in the depths of his eyes.

"Congratulations to you both," he said, inclining his head. "You did impressively well."

Next to Leo, Briar sat on the edge of her chair, her golden eyes ablaze, her black hair a wind-swept tumble over her shoulder. Tears stained her dirt-smudged cheeks as she looked from the gold coin to the velour pouch, then cast her attention around the study like her brother might be hiding in the curtains. "Where's Lyric?" Her voice was so breathless with hope, the warmth of it welled inside Leo's chest. "Is he here? Is he free?"

"Rest easy, my dear. Your brother is alive. We will get to your wish very shortly, I assure you."

Her white-knuckled grip on the upholstered armrests eased, but only just. "And Aurora? What about Posey? Are they—"

"Both alive. If not well, then certainly on the mend. And very eager to see you, I am sure. The officer is here as well, however I don't believe your connection with him was quite so strong. Garrick, unfortunately, did not make it."

Briar's mouth fell open.

She'd never seen the bruises on his neck.

"Thanks to your son," Leo said. The shock of it swept through him, the debilitating fear he'd felt when Evander had the doctor's blade pressed against Briar's throat morphing into anger. "You put us inside that contest with a lunatic."

"Not a lunatic, Leo." The old man's voice rang with grief when he said it. "But a very loyal, brainwashed young man who was raised to believe that everyone was his enemy."

"He killed Garrick. He tried killing Posey."

"And Aurora," Briar said.

Leo narrowed his eyes, the old man's evident sorrow only serving to make him angrier. "He's been trying to kill you, too, hasn't he?"

Squire nodded regretfully.

"She almost died!" Leo flung his hand toward Briar, his eyes finding the trickle of dried blood on her neck. If his half-baked plan had gone sideways, she would have. He suppressed the shudder making its way up his spine. Watching her bleed in such a way had been—without a doubt—the most terrifying experience of his life.

"I do not excuse his behavior. We are responsible for our own choices. But I do hope you can understand that Evander was raised by a woman who indoctrinated him to believe a certain way, and those beliefs led him to act accordingly." The hollow beneath the old man's cheeks seemed to deepen with the words. "When he sought me out last year, I tried explaining what his mother had done. He refused to listen. I hoped seeing such destruction with his own eyes might persuade him to change his mind."

"Is that what all of this was about?" Leo stared incredulously. "You hoped to *change his mind*?"

"I was hoping and continue to hope for a great many things. And I would never have put you inside such a contest had it not been necessary." With a deep and mournful sigh, Squire motioned to the coin in the porcelain jar, engraved with the same symbol stitched on the velour pouch. "You understand what this is."

"My wish," Briar said.

"And the room with the jars?"

Shelves and shelves of them, each with a name. Squire had called it his *burden to bear.* From one of those jars came the coin Briar had given Leo. A wish made by his father that hadn't come true. He didn't want anyone to know what he'd done, but Leo knew. Briar knew, too.

"Wishes you couldn't grant," Leo answered.

Squire opened a desk drawer and pulled out a small brown case. The inside was lined with black velvet and contained three slits arranged like the points of a triangle. Tucked inside each of the slits, a coin. Squire removed the one on the bottom left. He paused for a moment, as though letting the power of it sweep through him. "I have kept these in my desk for some time." He looked up at Leo. "This one belonged to your mother."

Everything went silent and still.

Even the fire seemed to stop crackling.

Squire turned the coin over in his hand. "It was the last one I ever received from her. A wish made with you in her arms."

The muscles across Leo's chest pulled tight.

He knew this wish.

He'd thrown it into the sea.

"I'd like you to have it."

Leo pressed back in his seat, his hands curling into fists. "Why, so I can carry it to that room for you?"

"This coin doesn't belong in that room."

Leo could feel his brow wrinkling. *Freedom would be his.* That was Katya's lie. But Squire nodded at him encouragingly and held out the coin. As soon as the old man dropped it into Leo's upturned palm, the deluge came.

In a flash, Leo experienced it. A collection of thoughts and emotions and words and images that didn't come in a line, but all at once. The anger at what had been done. The piercing betrayal. The horrible truth. The desperation to flee. Sadness and grief, desperation and shock, hope and worry and conviction. And undergirding them all—every emotion and thought and word and image—was the strong, all-consuming heartbeat of love. For this child in her lap. This child that was Leo. His eight-year-old self in his mother's arms, seen through her eyes.

In that flash, she wanted to run. She wanted to take her son and go far, far away, to a place that was safe, free from the toxins that corrupted her husband. Free from the fear all around. For her son. For herself. For what had been done and what could still be. It was the kind of fear that debilitated and permitted and justified and destroyed.

Fear was the poison.

Not Magic.

But hadn't she always known? Since she was a little girl and her best friend made the flowers fly and healed that which was broken. The same Magic that enabled Phoebe to do something so good flowed inside her. Inside her son. Alaric kept saying he was helpless. Change, impossible. But it was fear that made him say such things. Fear that kept evil in power. Fear that kept her quiet for far too long.

In that flash, her hand moved to Leo's chest, covering his heart, covering his scar, and for one bright and shining moment, love overpowered fear. More than she wanted to run, more than she wanted to hide, she wanted to be brave. She wanted to do the right thing. For her son. For the child she lost. For the children she wasn't allowed to have. For Phoebe and her family and everyone else who had to run and hide because of that poisonous, pernicious fear. She would stay for them and she would stay for her and she would show her son how to be the king he was born to be.

Give me courage so he can have it, too.

All of it rolled through Leo like the loud refrain of a resounding gong. His mother's deepest and truest wish. Not for his freedom. That was Katya's lie. And yet the truth of her wish set him free. Leo looked up, his eyes burning, his throat thick. Squire stared back at him like the wish resting in Leo's palm—his mother's wish—was every bit as intimately the old man's. In a way, maybe it was. "She wanted me to be king?"

"Sometimes what our mouth speaks is far from what we cry in here." Squire set his hand over his heart.

"And the other two?" Leo said, his attention dropping to the small case, the coins bright against the dark backdrop. "What are those?"

"This one," Squire said, his thumb traveling to the coin at the top, "wasn't a final wish, but a first. Made by two little girls who loved each other deeply. I felt such joy to find it in my fountain." With a dewy-eyed smile, Squire reached inside the pocket of his coat and pulled out a familiar, silver chain. "It so happens that this came to be on the very same day."

"My locket," Briar said. She took the jewelry, looking both pleased and relieved. "Why did Evander take it?"

"Because he knew it wasn't just a locket." Squire removed the third coin, the one on the bottom right, and with a long, slow breath, turned it over in his scarred palm. "It has been more than that for some time now."

HER LAST

YEAR OF KORAH: 508

PHOEBE

Someone shoved Phoebe from behind, but the chains shackled around her ankles prevented her from going any faster. For three days, she languished in a cell awaiting her fate, hoping and praying that somehow—some way—Flynn had been released. Flynn was with their children.

Her heart pounded.

"Step up," a gruff male voice muttered.

Something sharp bit into her shins.

With a wince, she groped in front of her and crawled up onto a metal floor.

The guard shoved her down onto a seat and cuffed her in place. Then he pulled the sack off her head. She blinked against the onslaught of light—the darkened figure sitting across from her inside what appeared to be some sort of carriage crate coming into focus. *Flynn.* His cheek bruised, his lip split, his left eye swollen shut. She lurched toward him and he toward her, but their restraints kept them apart.

"I'm not supposed to let you see each other," the guard said. "But final moments ought to be seen."

"Where are you taking us?" Flynn asked.

"Guillotine Square." The guard slammed the back doors shut, leaving the two of them alone.

Phoebe struggled.

Flynn struggled.

But it was no use. Neither could move and her Magic had been rendered ineffective. Just as she couldn't use it inside Shard, she couldn't use it now. An engine rumbled to life and they were carried away from the prison yard.

Tears sprang into Phoebe's eyes as all hope died, every bit as dead as Lena. Her husband had not been released. He was here with her in the back of this vehicle. Which meant their children were out there alone. Waiting for Phoebe and Flynn to come for them.

"Can you save us?" Flynn asked.

Phoebe shook her head, a hot tear tumbling down her cheek. "Oh, Flynn. I'm so sorry. I'm so, so sorry."

He stared back at her—nostrils flared, eyes aglow. "This isn't your fault."

But it was. "I should have listened to you. We should have gone when you wanted to leave. We should have packed up our belongings and left."

"On the cusp of change?"

"What change? It was killed before it could happen."

"We had no way of knowing that."

"I never should have brought us here. We should have stayed in Silva."

"Where we lived our lives in hiding? In perpetual fear of being discovered? You said it yourself, love. That is no way to live."

"But now we won't live at all. Everything is lost." Tears wet her cheeks, but she couldn't wipe them. They fell freely. They fell generously. And each one seemed to tear her husband's heart in two, his face a mask of anguish. "Lena is dead. And now our children—"

"Are going to be okay," he said fiercely, as though saying it with enough conviction might make it true. "Briar and Echo are survivors, Phoebe. They have the same tenacious spirit as their mother. They will find a way."

Phoebe sniffed.

If only she could touch him.

If only she could feel him.

Flynn, her ardent protector.

Flynn, her eternal optimist.

Briar and Echo were *seven*.

What hope was there for them in a world so cruel?

"And they have your protection," he added.

"You know as much as I that my protection dies when I do."

His optimism slipped.

Her agony grew.

Oh Keeper, help us.

She strained against her manacles, trying once more to call forth Magic. But it was no use. She let her head fall. "I'm so sorry," she whispered.

"I'm not."

She looked up into his eyes.

"I will never be sorry, do you hear me? I will not let them make me sorry. You are the best thing that has ever happened to me. Our life together, the very best thing. And no matter what it looks like right now, I refuse to believe all is lost. I refuse to believe this is it. Even if this is our end, Phoebe, it is not *the* end."

The vehicle stopped.

They had reached their destination.

Phoebe drank him in, unwilling to look away from the man who had been her sun and her stars. The man who had given her a cottage in Silva and three perfect children. The man who had loved her and supported her and now would die with her.

The guard opened the doors. He unlocked them and shoved them outside into the fresh air, where Phoebe fell into Flynn's arms, his strong, steady heart beating against her ear. They were torn apart too quickly, the sacks returned to their heads as the guard ushered them up onto the stage to a booing jeering crowd.

When the sacks were torn away, she saw King Casimir standing on the dais. His son, Alaric, stood beside him, his face ravished in pain, twisted in agony as he seethed with the full force of his hatred. He was glaring at the wrong person. His wife's murderer was standing beside him, holding tight to his son's shoulders.

Prince Leo.

The king had killed the princess, but he would never kill her son—heir to the throne, with a scar on his chest to prove it.

And Magic in his blood.

Leo didn't know. Maybe he would never know.

But the truth was the truth and the undeniability of it fluttered in her soul like the wings of a baby bird. Prince Leo may be the spitting image of his father. But his heart was pure Helena. Her dying wish that he would be brave and despite everything, Phoebe still believed in wishes that came true. Flynn was right. This wasn't the end. It couldn't be.

The torch in the center of the marble iustus was lit.

The verdict was read.

The drums began to beat.

And the crowd cried for blood.

Phoebe searched the frenzied mass as if she might find an ally among it. The Wish Keeper himself come to save them. But she did not find the Wish Keeper. Instead, she found her daughter. Her precious, brave Briar, hiding beneath the stands.

Afraid.

But alive.

The executioner dragged Phoebe forward. Flynn, too. He forced them down onto their knees and secured them into place as the drum beat louder. Faster. In tune with her heart as the manacles bit into her wrists. Phoebe looked up, past the hateful crowd, drinking in her daughter's face, the wings of the baby bird flapping harder. She set her eyes upon the locket. Once a bracelet. A gift she'd given Briar on her fifth birthday.

Phoebe could not use Magic to free herself or Flynn.

Their fate was sealed.

Their end had come.

But Keeper help her, she could use Magic to protect her daughter.

She looked at Prince Leo, a little boy with his mother's heart. She looked at her daughter, a little girl with her mother's tenacity. She ached to tell her everything. Why they'd come to Antis. Why they'd stayed. The change Phoebe hoped it would bring—for her children and everyone else like them. But that was an impossible wish. So with all the love inside of her, she wished one that wasn't impossible. Phoebe wished that her power and protection could outlive her. It was Magic too big to accomplish on her own. Magic that defied nature.

Which was why that nature was protesting.

The sky grew dark.

The wind blew hard.

The clouds began to churn and roll black up above.

The crowd stirred, their hunger for vengeance shifting into alarm.

Keeper, grant me success.

Give me the strength.

Let my aim be true.

Phoebe could feel it swelling—life and love and Magic and grit growing into a force more powerful than the wind and the clouds.

The crowd screamed.

Flynn yelled, "Run Briar! Run!"

Something inside Phoebe gave way. Opened wide. And with a laugh, she knew her wish was being granted. She wasn't alone. Neither was Briar. *The story isn't over, my daughter. The story isn't over.* With one great and final heave, Phoebe expelled the life inside of her. It hurled through the chaos and hit its mark just as the blade came down.

But the blade didn't take her life.

Phoebe Bishop was already gone, reunited with her dear friend. The rest of the story belonged to their children.

CHAPTER 33

BRIAR

Once upon a time, Briar hopped a train—long before Guillotine Square, when her family was still intact, and Papa wanted to take her on a special adventure. Just the two of them. He scooped her onto his back. She wrapped her legs around his waist, her arms tight around his neck as he grabbed hold and jumped aboard. She burrowed into Papa's lap, her whole body vibrating as the train rumbled into a tunnel, sunlight flashing through cracks as they barreled through.

Holding her mother's coin was like that.

Only instead of sunlight flashing, it was the final images of Mama's life. Papa's face. The blade of the guillotine. Black clouds. The screaming crowd. And a little girl hiding under the stands. Mama's wish barreled through Briar like a train through a tunnel. And when it burst through, Briar was left breathless, sitting in a chair, staring down at the locket in her hand. "I don't understand," she said, looking up at Ambrose. "Protection charms die with their caster."

"They do."

"Then—"

"Your mother found a loophole, Briar. She didn't cast a protection charm. She cast her life. She anchored it to that locket, and in so doing she not only offered you protection. She offered you her power, too."

"That's why I could heal myself."

Ambrose nodded.

A low buzzing rose in her mind.

She didn't die in the fire. Somehow, she dragged Echo from the flames with smoke and heat closing in around her. She remembered thinking they were going to die. Both of them would perish and their little brother would be all alone. One second, she was collapsing. The next, a soot-covered Lyric was shaking her awake, the sky a cerulean blue above him, a severely injured Echo clutched tight in her arms. It never made any sense, how she escaped so unscathed. But now ...

Her fingers curled around the locket.

It shouldn't have been possible. Not just the fire, but all of it. Two seven-year old kids with a three-year-old to care for? They shouldn't have been able to survive. And yet, despite having a bounty on their heads, despite their grandparents and uncles being arrested within days, they'd never been caught. They'd never gotten sick. Briar had given her bread to Lyric on numerous occasions, and yet she never starved. She always had strength to keep going.

Tears welled in her eyes.

It was because of her mother. Mama wasn't a monster. Magic hadn't corrupted her. She didn't kill her best friend, and she didn't choose vengeance over her children, either. She had loved them until the very end, with her dying breath. And because of that love, Briar had never been alone. Even when she felt alone. Hope crashed like waves. The contest was over. The locket helped her win. It was time to go get her brother. She had so much to share with him. So, so much.

Lyric, I'm coming!

She wanted to stand from her seat. She wanted to go right now, straight to Shard. But Ambrose pushed the porcelain dish on his desk forward and the velour pouch with the half-finished symbol of Korah stitched in gold, too. He had tears in his eyes. "I am afraid it is time that I speak with you about another loophole."

The softly spoken words sliced through her soaring hope.

They seemed to grieve the old man as much as the death of his murderous son, and with that grief, came a suspicion that twisted inside Briar's chest.

"I hope you can understand that this was a necessity," Ambrose said.

Beside her, Leo shifted in his chair.

Briar's heart began to pound in her ears. "What are you talking about?"

"Being Wish Keeper of Korah is a great responsibility. A grave responsibility. It comes with immense power and is passed down from generation to generation through the firstborn."

Briar glanced up at the portrait of Anna and Collin.

His firstborn was dead.

"If it happens that the firstborn cannot fulfill the role, the position falls to the next, and so on and so on. There have been rare occasions wherein there was no next of kin. Or the next of kin was not fit for such a responsibility." Ambrose picked up the embroidered pouch. "In such a case, it is up to the Wish Keeper to find someone to inherit this."

Briar swallowed. "What is it?"

"The Wish Keeper's coin. It will not go to just anyone. The benefactor must, of course, be Magic. And if the benefactor is not part of the natural succession, he or she must prove his or her worth through a series of trials."

"A contest," Leo said.

Ambrose inclined his head. "My father, Rubin, entered such a contest and came out the victor. This coin went to him and the power of the Wish Keeper transferred to our family line. My father was a lively man who thoroughly enjoyed adventure, and so he decided to hold similar contests. For fun. They became something of a sport. An exciting competition. When one of the contestants died, my mother convinced him to stop for a time, but his thirst for excitement was too strong. Eventually, that thirst for excitement would kill him. I inherited the responsibility of Wish Keeper at the age of twenty and the contests ceased.

"Several years later, I met and married Anna. We had our son, Collin." Ambrose's voice broke over the name. He cleared his throat. "She had the kindest, softest heart, my Anna. When her path crossed with Mara's—a young woman with a very tragic story—Anna was overcome with compassion."

"What was the tragic story?" Leo asked.

"Mara's parents were killed in the Purge when she was very young. She was sent to Cambria to live with her aunt. In the very village your mothers lived, in fact, although she preceded their time."

Briar and Leo exchanged a startled look.

"Mara's aunt, though Magic herself, was afraid of the girl. She had uncommon powers. Strange powers. Instead of loving Mara and treating her kindly, she was harsh. Perhaps even cruel. Rather than finding acceptance amongst her own people, Mara met rejection and ridicule." Ambrose stroked the silver whiskers of his goatee. "Her jar is a difficult one for me to visit. I carried many of her coins there."

"Couldn't you have granted any?" Briar asked.

"No, unfortunately. There was a disturbing darkness to them, even at so young an age. A thirst for revenge that I could not accommodate. Rejection leaves a very deep wound, you see. It is the kind that can twist a soul. It twisted Mara's most egregiously." Ambrose heaved a heavy sigh. "When the girl turned eleven, her aunt died in a gruesome, peculiar way and she was sent to Antis to live in a home for troubled girls. When Anna's path crossed Mara's years later, she was a young woman with no family. No support system. No place to call home. My wife insisted on bringing her into ours. To this day, I'm still unsure whether Mara knew who I was and so arranged the encounter with my wife, or if she discovered my identity later."

"Why did you let her in your home if you knew what she'd done?" Leo said.

"Ah, but I didn't. Mara stopped making wishes long ago, even before her aunt's death. By the time she came into our lives, she'd learned a great deal about the ways of the world and how to manipulate it. I didn't know her mind."

"Then how do you know all of this?"

"It's been a slow process—putting the pieces together." Ambrose folded his hands. "Mara was a very becoming young woman. Very demure. Much closer in age to Collin than myself, and outwardly smitten with him. Anna thought we might give Mara the family she never had, but I became a bit of a sticking point. There was something off about the girl, though I couldn't put my finger on it. And Collin was still young. Impressionable. There was no hurry for him to get married, and so any engagement that might have been made was put off.

"I believe her original idea was to kill me. I was the barricade standing between her and the heart of the future Wish Keeper. So she concocted a plan. One that might achieve two ends at once. Revenge upon the people who rejected her. And an unobstructed route to the power she so greatly craved."

"The Cambria Disaster," Leo said.

"Mara was the anonymous informant. She tipped off King Casimir. With the right skill set, Magic can be drawn from. There was plenty of Magic to draw from that day. When the wishes came flooding in, when I started to get a clear picture of what was happening—that people were being rounded up and arrested—I believe Mara thought I would come. Of course, my place was here, with the wishes. But not Anna. The only way she could help was to go. It wasn't safe to be a sympathizer of Magic, but we had great influence and wealth. I could not have kept her away had I all the strength in the world. Collin insisted on going with her and I never saw either of them again."

"She killed them," Briar said.

"Then swooped in to console an old man in his grief." His eyes went dull and lifeless. "It was her fast-thinking contingency plan. By then, she had plenty of time to study Anna's personality. Her mannerisms and quirks. I believe she even used Magic to subtly alter her appearance and voice to resemble and sound like my late wife. Foolishly, I found comfort in her presence. In an attempt to stave off my loneliness, I married her. She wanted a child. I didn't. Eventually, she left. Before doing so, she made an attempt on my life and I realized her true colors. I had no idea when she disappeared that she'd gotten exactly what she wanted."

"A child," Briar and Leo said together.

"My only heir. With total control over his mind, his heart, his upbringing. Had he been raised here, I believe I would have loved him." He said it a little too desperately, like he was trying to convince himself. "I believe I would have taught and prepared him as I taught and prepared Collin. But she fled to Nigal and I remained in the dark about his existence until a year ago, when he arrived in Antis and has been attempting to assassinate me ever since.

"I knew immediately what was at stake. I knew that I had to act quickly. For if any of his attempts succeeded, he would become Wish Keeper. The coin in this pouch would be his, and all the power that comes with it." Ambrose turned the pouch over, then leaned back in his seat. "You are right, Leo. I hoped Evander might change his mind. I hoped that seeing what his mother did might set him on a different course. Alas, Mara's influence was too strong, her hooks too deep. I never intended for him to die."

"What did you intend, then?" Leo asked.

"To protect Korah from the terrible fate of a Wish Keeper under Mara's control. The contest was established not only to find an heir should none exist, but to replace an heir should such a necessity arise."

"Your loophole," Leo said, his voice low.

"Either my son would see the truth and change his mind, or he would be defeated by a worthy opponent." Ambrose looked at Briar, whose pounding heart had gone loud in her ears.

"Are you saying *I'm* the replacement?"

"If you choose to be."

"What does that mean?"

"Winning the contest was the first step. The choice you must now make is the next."

"What choice?"

"You have defeated the current heir. The only thing left now is to prove that you do not seek the position for selfish gain."

Briar hadn't sought the position at all.

"You must sacrifice your heart's greatest desire."

Leo came out of his chair. "*What?*"

"It is the only way."

Briar's mind spun.

The room spun.

Everything spun.

"And if I choose my brother?" she breathed.

"As the last living relative of the heir, the power of the Wish Keeper will pass to Mara upon my death, which I suspect will be sooner rather than later, given her thirst for the position."

"What's to stop us from killing her first?" Leo said. "I can wish her dead right now."

"I will not use the Wish Keeper's power to take human life."

"You took plenty of life in that contest!" Leo kicked the chair.

It tumbled over with a loud crash.

Briar wanted to join him. She wanted to pick up every stupid trinket on the old man's desk and hurl it at the walls. She wanted to grab the porcelain dish and heave it into the fire. She wanted to grab every book and tear out their spines.

"You saw what she did to Cambria, Briar," Ambrose said with a calmness that made her want to scream. "That is only a fraction of what she will be capable of as Wish Keeper."

"Why didn't you tell me this from the beginning?"

"Would you have started the journey had you known what it would entail?"

"If you would have freed Lyric, I would have given you anything!"

"If I had freed Lyric, this wouldn't have worked."

Briar seethed—her breathing shallow, her thoughts racing. She pictured the ruins of Cambria. The destruction Mara had wrought. All the lives she had taken. All the vengeance in her heart. There had to be another option. Some way to keep Mara from such power while saving Lyric, too. "If I make this choice, can someone else wish my brother free?"

"If you make this choice, your wish will be sacrificed. No matter who wishes it."

A ball of scorching heat rose up Briar's throat.

"I will not be able to use the power of the Wish Keeper to save your brother. But I do have power of my own, separate from the position in which I hold. And I promise to do whatever I can to help you."

"When have you ever helped me?" Briar snarled.

The words rattled the room.

Ambrose Squire had the audacity to look hurt by them.

It only fueled her rage. "My parents. My grandparents. My uncles. Echo." Her mother's locket protected her, but who protected *him*? Her parents had been innocent. Her grandparents and uncles had been innocent. And still, all of them ended up dead. "How can I possibly trust that you'll help save Lyric when you didn't save any of them?"

"You can trust *me*," Leo said. He knelt in front of her. "Listen. Briar, you do not have to make this choice."

"Yes, she does," Ambrose interjected.

The muscles in Leo's jaw ticked angrily. He looked like he wanted to yell at the old man, tell him to shut up. Instead, he fixed his gaze on her, his eyes blue flame. "But if you do choose, and it isn't your brother, *I* will help you. I will go to my father. I will demand a pardon."

"You said it wouldn't help. You said it would only make the situation worse."

"That was before I knew what I know now."

Briar squeezed her hands into fists.

It was happening all over again.

Lyric was dangling above a raging inferno.

She could save him. His life, guaranteed. A sure thing.

But then what? Mara would be Wish Keeper. Unimaginable suffering would ensue. Briar had the power to stop that from happening. Here was the opportunity she'd been longing for her entire life. To do something good. To bring actual change to the commonwealth. But in order to do so, she would have to let go of Lyric's hand. She would have to trust that Leo would catch him. Trust that Ambrose would help. But how could she trust something like that when she'd spent the vast majority of her life on her own? Hating the Wish Keeper. Not even believing in him.

The hot ball of heat in her throat throbbed.

She imagined choosing Lyric. The devastation that would come at the hands of a woman like Mara. Everyone from top to bottom would feel it, but ciphers would suffer the most. Those at the bottom always did.

The future roared through her—two distinct paths.

Her brother.

Or an entire commonwealth.

The sure thing.

Or trust.

According to Papa, the good guys always won. Against all odds and logic, Papa believed this was the way of the world. Good would win. Good had to win. And if good wasn't winning, then it wasn't the end. Papa's belief had been so strong—so ingrained—that those had been Echo's final words.

I saw it happen, Briar. You're going to be the hero. You're going to save us all.

They were words that tormented her, for how could she ever be the hero of the story—an orphaned cipher from The Skid? She had no power. She had no money. She couldn't change anything. The years had taught her that Papa's stories were just stories. The world didn't care about good. But maybe that was only true so long as people kept making the easy choice, the short-sighted choice, the personally advantageous choice. Maybe that was only true so long as people kept feeding the corrupt cycle. Maybe it took one person—just one person—to step up and do what was right. Do what was best. She held onto Lyric's hand with tenacious ferocity. Here was the chance to break that cycle. Here was the chance to make the right choice.

The fire raged.

The pain was unbearable.

Letting go, excruciating.

Yet that was exactly what Briar had to do.

For her mother and father and Echo.

For every cipher stuck in misery at the bottom.

For every parent watching their children starve.

For every big sister trying desperately to save their own Lyric.

Briar made her choice, praying it was the right one.

She let go.

She chose trust.

With the back of her eyes burning, she looked up at Ambrose. "What must I do?"

CHAPTER 34

LEO

Leo paced outside the study beneath the painted ceiling. He had no idea what sort of ritual was happening inside. No idea what blood Briar might yet have to spill. He only knew that she had made her choice.

Brave, benevolent Briar.

Korah had done absolutely nothing for her and she was sacrificing everything for it. The muscles in his arms tightened with readiness. They might not have the power of the Wish Keeper at their disposal, but they did have information. There were things Leo knew now that he didn't before. Things that would make his father cooperate. Leo was prepared to bring all of it out into the open if need be.

He paced faster, feeling as though he might come out of his skin. Outside, rain started to fall. A light pitter-patter that ran like rivulets down the tall windowpanes. Leo came to one of the sills. He looked down at the fountain, then up at the sky. The day had already sunk into evening. Clouds hid the moon, but Leo knew its color—a pink so deep it was nearly red. Tomorrow was execution day.

He dragged his hand down the length of his face.

The door to the study opened behind him.

Leo turned.

Squire stepped out into the hallway, Briar right behind.

Leo searched her for signs of injury. But there were no gashes on her palms. No blood anywhere that he could see other than the dried trickle on her neck, drawn by Squire's son. The only sign of distress was the storm raging in her eyes.

Leo's heart squeezed.

He wanted to touch her. Grab her up in his arms and never let go.

As if sensing his need, Squire cleared his throat. "If you'll excuse me, I will find you a raincoat for your travels."

As soon as he turned the corner out of sight, Leo stepped closer, his blood pounding. "My father has to pardon him, Briar. If he doesn't, I'll go straight to the media and tell them everything."

She looked up at him, a knot dimpling the space between her dark eyebrows. "He strangled your grandfather."

"Exactly. He committed treason. It's a crime punishable by death, no matter who he is."

Her golden eyes swirled in a way that made him think he missed her meaning. In a way that made him think that perhaps her distress wasn't all for Lyric.

She swallowed.

He could see the subtle bob in her throat. The rapid tapping of her pulse in the hollow of her clavicle. Unable to help himself any longer, Leo closed the space between them in one sure step and covered her mouth with his.

Her breath hitched.

Then her lips parted and Leo's entire being caught fire. His hands spread wide up her ribcage, then slid around to her back. He lifted her off her feet, desire consuming him, consuming her, consuming them both. He could never—would never—get enough of this, and yet he had to tear himself away. He set his forehead against hers, his chest heaving, her lips swollen.

"I could come with you," she whispered.

"No." His response came thick and hoarse. In that contest, they'd lived a lifetime together. Gone through war together. He didn't want to separate from her any more than she seemed to want to separate from him, but he wasn't going to bring Briar anywhere near the castle. Not when she still had a bounty on her head. He brought his hand to the side of her face, the tips of his fingers touching the nape of her neck. "It'll be quicker if it's just me. I'll go as fast as I can and when I come back, I swear I will have Lyric with me."

"Be careful," she said.

With a nod, he kissed her one last time—soft, chaste. The kind that made his heart feel broken and somehow whole. Then he let her go and strode away.

Leo's boots slopped through puddles. Cold, fat drops splattered against his musty coat. The thing had not seen the light of day in decades, evidenced by the flying dust motes when Squire gave it a good shake. Leo cared less about staying dry and more about staying undercover. He couldn't afford the time that would be wasted should he be ambushed by fans or media hounds. The raincoat had a large hood and was so old, nobody would suspect the High Prince might be hiding inside. So he'd taken the offering and hurried out into the rain without a clue as to what might be happening in the capital city.

He had no idea what the media was making of his absence. He imagined all the messages from Sabrina and Hawk on his vox. What did they think happened to him? And what would be the hardest to explain when he got the chance—the contest, the truth about his mother's death, or Briar?

A groan unfurled at the thought of her.

Leo had wanted girls before. But never like this—desire mixed with such tender feelings of care and the highest of esteem. Sabrina wouldn't believe it. Someone had finally captured his heart. When all of this was over, when Lyric was safe, he couldn't wait to introduce them. Two of his favorite people in the whole world.

Up ahead on the street corner, two men with recording equipment stepped out of a white vehicle. Leo ducked into a nearby tabloid stand, the response to his disappearance staring back at him from an array of bold headlines ranging from inaccurate to entirely bizarre.

Trouble in the Palace

Addiction Strikes Again: Leo's Secret Battle

Sick or Dead? The Royal Coverup

This headline featured two side-by-side images, both of himself. In one, he looked pale and bedraggled, taken a few months ago the morning after one of Hawk's raucous parties. The other four years earlier, when Leo's face still possessed more boy than man. According to this, the High Prince was not sick, as some were speculating, but long dead. A look-alike had been posing as Leo for some time. He rolled his eyes and turned away, but the cover sliding past at eye level stopped him.

The Prince's Ultimatum: Me or Her

There wasn't an image of him under this headline, but one of his father and a woman, her arm looped around his, her face pointed away and obscured by a fashionable head scarf. Leo picked it up, flipped to the article inside, and began to skim. Apparently, in Leo's short absence, his father had fallen in love and the romance had opened old wounds. It was ridiculous. Not because of the time frame —Leo understood more than ever how quickly love could strike—but because his father was incapable of it. The king's heart might not be in a box. But it had died in his chest alongside his wife.

"She can't replace my mother," Leo was quoted to have said before storming out of the castle.

He never said it.

Nor did he know who *she* was.

He flipped the page, hoping for more information about this mystery woman, but found a different article instead.

Tomorrow at Guillotine Square: Will the Prince Come Out of Hiding?

"Hey, buddy!"

Leo startled.

"This ain't free reading. You read it, you buy it." The tabloid peddler, a rough-looking man with a large belly, eyed him suspiciously.

Leo pulled his hood further over his eyes.

But not before the man narrowed his. "Hey—"

Leo stuffed the tabloid back into the rack and exited hastily. With his hood up and his head down, he raced through the streets of Antis, straight for the castle, not stopping until he could see the horde of reporters waiting outside the front gate. He considered slipping into the woods, re-entering the castle grounds the way he exited that fateful night a lifetime ago, but by now, the media hounds were most likely surrounding the entire castle perimeter, and there was no time for slinking and climbing.

Leo marched to the front, setting off a commotion of massive proportions. Reporters swarmed him—exclaiming and saluting and calling his name. They descended, scrambling to get closer, shoving recording equipment in his face with no bodyguards to keep them away.

"Your Highness, where have you been?"

"Your Highness, how is your health?"

"Your Highness, have you come to make amends with your father?"

Leo pushed through them.

When he reached the front gate, two guards stepped forward to bar the horde. The gate groaned open. Leo hurried through the grounds, inside the portico, and into the Great Hall. He was a mess, soaking wet in Squire's coat, his hair tousled beyond repair. Every palace slave he passed did a double take before jerking to a halt—bowing, curtsying, saluting, gaping at his sudden and disheveled appearance.

Leo ignored each one.

He strode to the cabinet chambers in the west wing. At this time of day, his father would be finishing up his meetings, the kind Leo was forbidden to interrupt as a child and forced to attend more recently. He swept into the antechamber, where his father's chamberlain sat working at a desk. The pair of guards manning the double doors remained still and statuesque upon Leo's entrance. The chamberlain, however, leapt to his feet.

"Leo!" he choked, the chair scraping on the marble floor as it lurched backward.

"I need to speak with my father."

The chamberlain gawked, then looked at his watch as though considering whether or not to interrupt the meeting.

"Now!" Leo barked.

"Yes, of course." He quickly bowed, then opened one of the double doors and hurried inside.

Leo paced.

Moments later, the doors burst open.

The High King came striding out. "Excuse us, please," he said, grinding the words between his teeth, sparks igniting in his eyes.

Leo glared back, completely unafraid.

The chamberlain scurried away like a frightened rat.

The guards remained.

"Out!" the king bellowed.

And the guards—who never left their posts—startled

and slunk away, too. The antechamber crackled with tension as the High King's attention swept his son. Then he lunged. He grabbed Leo by the lapels of his wet raincoat and slammed him against the wall, no longer sparks in his eyes, but a raging fire.

Leo didn't flinch. He stared back at his father defiantly and asked in a voice that was eerily calm, "Are you going to strangle me, too?"

His father blinked, as if processing the words. Then slowly, the color drained from his face. Every last drop.

"I know," Leo said. "I know *everything*."

His father's pupils expanded—large and black as night. He let go of Leo's coat. His hands fell to his sides. He gave his head a small shake, his larynx bobbing as he swallowed. Then he cleared his throat and straightened his suit. "What are you talking about?"

Leo looked him dead in the eye. "You killed Grandfather."

With a sharp, hissing shush, he glanced over his shoulder. "I don't know where you heard such a thing, or what you think you know—"

"When did you learn that he poisoned Mom? Before or after the chambermaid took the fall?"

His father stepped back, his face going whiter.

"Did you let her die and her husband die and her parents and her brothers die while you patiently waited for your moment of revenge?"

"I didn't know!" he said, his voice choked with emotion. "I swear I didn't know he killed her until they were already dead."

"But you knew Mom was Magic. You knew I had a twin."

His father took another step away.

This time, Leo grabbed *him* by the collar. "Twins means two, Father. I'm only one. What happened to the other?"

"How do you know all of this?"

"What happened to the other?" he growled, shoving his father against the opposite wall beside the desk.

"Sh-she couldn't have twins."

Leo let go.

His father sank into the chair. "She couldn't. She couldn't have them. And he made so much sense. So much blasted sense." He pounded the desk with his fist. "And he swore to me. He swore that no harm would come to her. If I agreed and we had no more children, he swore he would drop it. He swore she would be safe."

"What did he do?"

"He ordered the Royal Doctor to get rid of one."

Leo's whole body went cold.

"He gave her a sleeping drought and he—he took care of the problem. The doctor assured me she would feel nothing. He assured me that the procedure was safe. It was the only way to protect her. And they weren't even—they weren't ..."

"Babies?" Leo felt sick, like he might hurl right there on the marble floor. He turned away from his wretch of a father and shook his head in disgust. He was one of those *not-babies*. Had he survived simply because he was least accessible in his mother's womb? Or had the doctor chosen carefully, knowing the importance of preserving an heir? Selecting the one that was bigger. Stronger. Male. "Was it a boy or a girl?"

His father didn't answer.

Leo slammed his hands on the desk. "Boy or girl?"

"Girl," his father whispered.

The muscles in Leo's throat tightened.

A girl.

A sister.

Leo was supposed to have had a sister.

"You killed your own daughter."

"No! *I* didn't do anything. It was your grandfather. I just—"

"Let it happen?"

His father crumpled, then. He slumped face down over the desk as though he could not bear the weight of his guilt any longer. Eighteen years of lies and deceit spilled forth in the form of a wrecked and weeping man. "I didn't know what else to do. Keeper help me, I thought it was the only way."

"Why did Grandfather wait eight years to get rid of her?"

"She found out. She found out about the baby. The night before her birthday. Somehow, she found out." His father wiped at his face. "Your grandfather had eyes and ears all over the castle. Someone must have seen. Someone must have heard."

"So he decided to silence her forever."

"I thought it was the chambermaid." His father dug his fingers into his hair. "I swear to you, I thought it was the chambermaid. She was Magic."

"Your *wife* was Magic." *Leo* was Magic. "They were friends. Childhood friends. Did you know that? She was like a sister to Mom and you killed her."

"I didn't know she was innocent until it was too late."

"Too late for the chambermaid. Too late for her parents and her brothers, but not for her children. Why did you keep a bounty on their heads? Why didn't you make it right? How could you exile an entire staff knowing the truth?"

"I had no choice."

"There's always a choice."

"*You're weak, Alaric!*" His father pounded his desk again—this time with both fists. "*You're a coward, Alaric. Be a man, Alaric!*" He raked his fingers though his hair, his face contorted. Tortured. "Do you want to know the only time he ever looked at me with pride?"

Leo leaned away, not at all sure he wanted to hear the answer.

"When I was strangling him to death."

Leo's stomach clenched, revolted.

This was sick.

Messed up.

Twisted.

He wanted no part of it. No part of it at all.

"Right now," he said, his voice low. "There is a thirteen-year-old boy in Shard Prison headed to Guillotine Square."

A knot formed in his father's brow.

"You can pardon him."

"Why would I do that?"

"He's the chambermaid's son."

His father's eyes went wide.

"Mom saw something in you. She loved you." It was true. Leo couldn't understand how or why, but his mother had loved his father. She had made him a better man. At least while she was alive. "If you don't want to be a coward, if there's any piece of you that still loves her—"

"I will always love her!"

"Then do what's right. Do something she would be proud of. Pardon the boy. Exonerate the innocent. Welcome them back to Korah. Stop the unwarranted persecution of Magic."

"I can't do that."

"Why not?"

"Parliament would never allow it."

"Screw Parliament. You're King."

"Which means—as you well know—that I am bound by process. Drastic changes at the very least require an explanation."

And that explanation would indict him.

If Magic didn't kill King Casimir, then who did?

Disgust blistered up Leo's throat. Lies and deceit. Fear and cowardice. All of it was poison in the walls. Poison that needed to be eradicated. "You have the chance to do something right. You can be strong and brave. You can be a man. Prove Grandfather wrong." Leo spread his hands on the desk and ground his teeth. "Or so help me, I will go straight to the nearest reporter and tell them everything."

His father blinked.

"I'll give you some time to think it over." But not much. Not much at all. Briar was waiting and he wasn't going to make her wait long. He pictured escorting Lyric from Shard. He pictured bringing him to the Squire Estate. He imagined a reunion overflowing with relief and joy. It would be one of his greatest honors. With that thought firmly in mind, Leo turned to leave.

They were no longer alone.

A woman stood in the entryway.

She didn't salute or curtsy. There was no golden bracelet around her wrist identifying her as a castle slave.

She leaned alluringly against the doorway, studying Leo with dark, fathomless eyes. It was the woman from the tabloid. "You've returned."

Leo faltered.

"See, Darling. Didn't I tell you he'd be back?"

She looked neither embarrassed nor flustered at having witnessed such an intense altercation between father and son. She sauntered seductively toward them, then extended her hand with all the regality of a queen.

A feeling of unease wrapped up Leo's spine.

"We haven't had the pleasure of meeting. You have however met my son, may he rest in peace." Her smile turned as cold as ice. "My name is Mara."

CHAPTER 35

BRIAR

The ornamental clock chimed for the third time since Leo left. Briar had bathed. Changed into clean clothes. And now she couldn't stop pacing. Or wringing her hands. With every minute that ticked past, the tighter the knots in her stomach tied and the more she wanted to claw out of her skin. Peg, the grandmotherly housemaid, brought a platter of tea and biscuits into the sitting room where Officer Ferro, Posey, and Aurora sat, porcelain clattering and clinking as they helped themselves.

"What is taking so long?" Briar asked, not for the first time. How long did it take to get to the palace, confront the king, and procure a pardon for a prisoner in Shard? Worry was flooding her. She kept thinking about his father's coin. She kept remembering the rage she felt when she held it. What if Leo confronted his father and the king responded with that same rage?

"Maybe they're drawing up the paperwork," Aurora offered. Her neck was no longer swollen, but the bruises were an angry purple. Posey's head was wrapped in gauze. Injuries obtained at the hands of Evander. Whenever the old man looked at them, the evidence of his son's brutality seemed to cause him pain, making Briar wonder why he didn't just heal them both.

A squeaky wheel sounded from somewhere down the hallway, growing louder as it approached. Ambrose returned from his short absence pushing an old cart with an even older simulcaster. The kind with knobs and a crank that harkened back several decades, at least. "Perhaps we can glean something useful from the media. They seem to enjoy reporting on the young man's whereabouts."

Judging by the thick layer of dust on the monitor, Ambrose didn't typically glean his information in such a way. An inference that could only be true after the length with which it took him to get the contraption running. Finally, after Officer Ferro twisted the crank in just the right way, they found a simulcast.

Ambrose was right.

Leo's face filled the screen. He was wearing the moth-eaten raincoat, his hair a mess, in need of a shave with tiny scratches on his cheekbones as he pushed his way through a crowd with the help of two burly bodyguards at the front gate of Castle Davenbrook. Which meant he hadn't been hit by a taxi-van or attacked by a stray dog or fallen into a hidden ravine. He was home. So why hadn't he sent them word?

The simulcast warbled and pitched.

Officer Ferro twisted the crank again, then turned one of the knobs. He found another program with better reception. They, too, were dissecting the prince's arrival and all of the minutiae surrounding it. A pair of female media correspondents swooned over his sudden appearance. He was so obviously wrecked by the rift in his family. So clearly tortured, his sexiness at an all-time high, for who knew the prince was such a family man? A woman was mentioned. Apparently, the king had a girlfriend. An image of her filled the monitor and Ambrose made a strangled sound.

Briar looked at him.

He stood with his hand pressed against his sternum. His face had gone pale, concerningly so, and for one alarming second, Briar thought he might be having heart spasms. He was going to collapse right there in the sitting room, leaving her to take on the responsibility of Wish Keeper when she still had her brother to save. He sank into a nearby sitting chair.

"Sir?" Officer Ferro said, noticing too.

The old man didn't answer. His eyes remained locked on the monitor as the correspondent talked about the

High King's whirlwind romance and Prince Leo's reaction to it. Where had he gone when he stormed out of the castle, where had he been hiding, and what prompted him to return now? The two women discussed whether or not this meant peace or war. All of it dripped with gossip and conjecture. The King's romance had nothing to do with Leo's absence. Ambrose knew that. So why then was he so riveted?

"It's her," he whispered.

"Who?" Briar said.

"Mara." The answer did not come from Ambrose. It came from Aurora. She, too, was looking strange—less horrified, more surprised—with her cup of tea frozen halfway between the saucer and her mouth.

The name sent a shiver up Briar's spine. She looked from Ambrose to the woman pictured on the monitor. The woman pictured on the king's arm. "What is she doing?" Briar asked. "Why is she here?"

"She always made a contingency plan."

Briar wanted to grab Ambrose by the shoulders and shake him. Make him stop gaping at the simulcast and focus. What did this mean for Lyric? What did this mean for Leo? She pictured him storming into the castle and confronting his father. She pictured Mara showing up—a woman who had killed Anna and Collin, the destruction of an entire island collateral damage. Her blood went cold.

Did she kill Leo, too? Was that why he hadn't sent any messages?

Her mind started to spin.

She was back inside the contest. The clock was ticking. Twelve more chimes to complete her task and if she failed, her brother would die. She pressed her hands against her stomach, trying to settle the frenzied panic. She didn't think they could count on Leo any longer, a likelihood that squeezed her lungs. She shook her head, unwilling to go there. She could only focus on one person at a time. Leo was strong. Leo was capable. She'd seen it all for herself firsthand. Lyric, on the other hand, had been locked in a cell for nearly two months now. Briar turned off the simulcaster. "How do I get him out of Shard?"

"You can't."

She turned on the officer. He was no longer dressed in contest apparel, but wore a clean, crisp uniform once again.

"It's impossible," he said.

"It can't be."

"Shard is the highest security prison in the world. Nobody gets out. Not without a pardon or a trip to Guillotine Square."

Briar wanted to pull out her hair. She wanted to gnash her teeth. What Ferro said couldn't be true. There had to be a way. Just like everything else, there had to be a loophole. The coin that would pass to her upon Ambrose's death was proof. The locket she wore was proof. Briar's spinning mind stopped.

The locket.

For the past ten years, it had protected her. Without even knowing, it had been a shield against death. Lyric was facing death. Briar wrapped her gloved hand around it, her heart taking off like the wings of a hummingbird—light and fluttery in her chest. They couldn't get him out. "What about getting something in?"

Officer Ferro's brow furrowed.

Briar pulled the necklace over her head. If it saved her from a burning building, couldn't it save Lyric from the guillotines?

"What good will that do?" Ferro asked.

"It's a protection charm."

"More than a protection charm," Ambrose added.

Right.

More than was a good thing.

The officer shook his head. "Magic doesn't work inside Shard."

"But it works in Guillotine Square." The locket was proof. Magic was done there before. Magic that had kept Briar alive. She held it up higher. "Is there any way we can get this to my brother?"

Ferro considered. "You would need to find a guard willing to give it to him."

"You're a guard."

The two stared at one another, their gaze locked and unflinching. Briar's unspoken request was clear. She was asking him to put his life on the line for a boy he didn't know. She was asking for his help when she'd all but accused him of attacking Posey back on that underground platform. He seemed to be wrestling with the same thoughts.

"My wish was to forget," he finally said. "What I did at Military Ridge. The cries of torment in Shard Prison. I wanted those memories wiped from my mind."

Briar could understand that wish. There was plenty she wanted to forget herself.

"But then, maybe if I forgot, I'd go on making the same mistakes. The same cowardly choices." A look stole across his face. A look Briar recognized, for it was the same one that had stolen across Sam Poe's before he let go of her hand and fell to his death.

A chance at redemption.

A chance Ferro was going to take. "I guess we need to find a way for me to get inside."

And so their contingency plan began.

As an officer of the First Guard, he already had the right credentials. Shift changes happened twice each day, promptly at the sixth and eighteenth hour. The opportunity for him to transfer tonight had already passed, which meant they had one shot tomorrow morning. If he succeeded, Ferro would have two hours to find Lyric and deliver the locket before he was loaded into a vehicle that would take him to his death. And that was only the first step. They needed to figure out a way to get Lyric off that platform once the locket saved him. They would still need to break her brother free—an impossible feat inside Shard, a dangerous and complicated possibility outside of it.

They would need to create a massive diversion. They would need to get Ferro counterfeit transfer papers. And they would need to do so without the assistance of the Wish Keeper's Magic. That wish had been sacrificed—forged with the Wish Keeper's coin. They did, however, have their wits, Ambrose's wealth, and a whole night to plan.

Lyric, I'm coming!

CHAPTER 36

BRIAR

Briar crouched in the shadows beneath the stands in the same place everything unraveled, her heart thrashing every bit as wildly as it had ten years ago. Their plan was in motion. Officer Ferro left the manor early this morning. He sent word that he had successfully gotten inside. Forty-two minutes later, word came again. The locket was in Lyric's possession. A fact that flooded Briar with more relief than she'd ever felt in her entire life. Her brother was protected. Her brother knew that she hadn't forgotten him. He knew that she had a plan and was doing everything in her power to carry it out.

Now here she was experiencing intense déjà vu with thirty minutes to go until the execution ceremony began. Despite the damp, gray weather, Guillotine Square thrummed with life. Spectators filed inside the gates.

Vendors hawked their wares. Reporters milled about the growing crowd, extra-large because of the circulating rumors. Not only was the High King bringing his new mistress, his son would be accompanying them. If true, Leo was alive. Mara had not killed him or locked him in a dungeon in the bowels of Castle Davenbrook. If true, this would be the prince's first appearance at an execution in a decade.

Briar didn't know what to think about the rumors.

If true, what was Leo doing? Why hadn't he contacted her?

Footsteps clanked loud overhead.

She pressed herself flat against the ground. This wasn't a déjà vu. She was no longer the terrified, filth-covered, street-urchin of a girl she'd been the last time she found herself here. Back then, she had been all alone, her brothers waiting for her in the city junkyard. Back then, she had been without a plan, helpless and confused. Now she had a plan. She had allies to help her carry it out. Aurora. Posey. And an officer of the First Guard. They were out there, getting into position, doing their part, risking their lives to help save her brother's.

They also had the locket on their side.

Briar peered through the square to a far set of stands and found him—sitting by himself, hidden beneath a heavy cloak. People walked right by without a clue who they were passing. Ambrose Squire, the Wish Keeper of

Korah. She didn't understand why he let her parents die ten years ago. She didn't understand why he let Echo fall into the fire. She still felt angry and manipulated at the choice he'd given her. So much about him remained a mystery, but she did know this—he had been there that day. Maybe not in person, but in spirit. He granted her mother's dying wish, and even though that particular power could not play a part in their plan now, somehow his presence bolstered her.

Briar stayed in the shadows as various members of Parliament arrived, each one playing to the media, posing for pictures, offering up soundbites for the reporters, shaking hands with the public. The Imperial Magistrate garnered the most attention until the Royal Cavalcade arrived—a full procession of flagged vehicles that turned the humming crowd into a buzzing hive. Spectators and reporters alike pushed for a prime vantage point. Everyone wanted the first glimpse of their High King and his handsome son and the mysterious woman, together in public for the first time.

All night long, as Briar and Ambrose and Ferro and Posey and Aurora planned, they had kept one ear to the news—a never-ending stream of speculation. The mystery woman would be the Guest of Honor. She would be lighting the iustus. According to the media, this was a sure sign that she was being groomed as Korah's future queen. Had the High King already proposed? What did Prince Leo really think about the whirlwind romance? Could this woman possibly fill the beloved shoes of Princess Helena? The public was hungry for answers. They were hungry to love her. They were hungry to hate her. But inside the Squire Estate, none of them were fooled.

Mara did not come to fill Princess Helena's shoes. She came with a plan. And although they were unsure about the particulars, they knew her aim. It was no different than it had been twenty-five years ago, when the Cambria Disaster unfolded.

Power with a side of revenge.

Trumpeters blasted their horns, heralding the Royal Family's arrival as the High Attendant rolled a red velvet runner to the main gates and an entourage of bodyguards exited the vehicles, talking into voxes, vigilantly surveying the bustling square for signs of danger. They had no idea the true danger was right next to the king.

Briar strained to see. Was Leo really here?

The crowd raised their hands into the air and shouted, "Izar!" as King Alaric stepped outside. Recording equipment snapped and flashed as he reached into the grand carriage and drew out a long-legged woman, stunning in beauty, dressed in fur, a picture of elegance and grace with her arm draped over the king's. Nobody would have guessed that her son died only yesterday. Was it possible Mara didn't know? Or was Evander such a puppet in her grab for power that she simply didn't care?

There was a pause—a note of crackling anticipation.

Briar's heart thrashed harder.

And the High Prince appeared.

She wasn't sure what she expected. Whatever it was, it hadn't been this. Leo—well-dressed, unharmed—looking neither distressed nor distraught as he filled the large holographic screen above the platform where the prisoners would soon stand. His thick hair—longer on top, shorter on the sides—was neatly styled. His face, freshly shaved. His smile, straight and white and charming as ever. The only evidence that he'd been through any ordeal at all, the tiny knicks and scratches marking his cheekbone.

Briar tried to make sense of it, but she couldn't figure out how. Even if Leo was acting—playing along in an attempt to protect himself from the monster on his father's arm, he was doing so to the detriment of her brother. Her lips pulsed with the memory of yesterday's kiss. Only the second in Briar's entire life, but even with such limited experience she knew it was real. It had to have been. But Leo didn't know they'd come up with a contingency plan. When he left the Squire Estate, confronting his father and procuring a pardon for Lyric was the only plan they had. So what was he doing now?

Briar willed him to search the crowd, to give her some sort of sign. But his expression remained unbothered—inscrutable—as the security guards ushered them inside. They stopped in the center of the square beside the iustus to pose for reporters. Devices clicked greedily, hungrily, as Mara slid her free hand on top of the marble podium where Korah's motto was engraved.

Eleos Partim Pentho Omnis.

Mercy for Some, Misery for All.

The words circled a golden torch that was lit at the commencement of every execution, a ritual that represented the meeting of justice, a necessary part of any civilization seeking to uphold peace and prosperity. Smoke and mirrors, all of it. Corruption disguised as lawfulness. A move to keep power in the hands of those who already had it, the oppressed in their oppression, and the masses preoccupied. The spectators who came to these executions did not do so as sober witnesses, but debased revelers looking for their next fix of entertainment.

A bustle of excitement came from outside the gate.

The prison caravan pulled to a stop.

Briar's mouth went dry as bone.

Lyric was here, in the back of that caravan. He would be led out onto the stage, hands bound behind his back with a sack cloth over his head, just as their parents had been. The moment she saw them, her heart had pounded out of her chest as she silently pleaded with the powers that be for her mother to use Magic. Her mother had, but not the kind Briar understood. Now that Magic was going to save her brother.

Spectators hurried to their seats. Security guards

escorted the Royal Family to the dais where the Imperial Magistrate was already standing. The Chief Guard unlocked the caravan doors, and one-by-one, the prisoners stepped out into the gray morning light. Frantically, Briar scoured the haggard line as the captives were led inside the square and up onto the platform, where seven guillotines and their sharp blades glinted ominously. Her attention honed in on the prisoner second from the right —tall and painfully thin, shoulders bony knobs beneath his prison garb.

Lyric.

It took every ounce of restraint to stay hidden in the shadows as silence fell over the crowd and the horns blared over the slow, rhythmic thud of the executioner's drum. It reverberated through the air, sank into Briar's bones, wholly out of pace with the frantic beating of her heart. The Chief Guard shackled the line of prisoners to the steel chain at the back of the platform.

The horns stopped.

The drum, too.

The Chief Guard walked to the first prisoner, the clunk of his boots and the creak of the wooden planks amplified thanks to the careful planning of the square's acoustics. He pulled the sack off the first prisoner's head. An old man with jaundiced skin like Rosco. Despite the clouds hanging thick in the sky, he squinted as if the barest hint of light was more than his eyes had seen in a good many days. The

Chief Guard reached for the sack on the second prisoner's head and in a single motion, snapped it off.

Briar cupped her hand over her mouth to trap the sob tumbling up her throat as the dark headed boy swayed precariously. He was so gaunt. Skin stretched over bone. The familiar lines of his face angular and severe, his eyes hollowed and dull—a ghost of the boy that was her teasing, cajoling, quick-to-laugh little brother.

Lyric, I'm here!

And Officer Ferro, and Posey and Aurora, each one of them positioned to carry out their rescue plan as soon as the locket did its job. She searched her brother's neck for the chain but found none. Her attention dipped to the pockets of his prison clothes when a piercing scream rent the air.

"My baby!"

The high-pitched outcry was followed by a commotion that wasn't part of their diversion.

Guards quickly descended.

A hum of chatter rippled through the crowd as spectators strained to see what was going on. Moments later, the guards pulled a struggling man and woman from the fray. Two Illustrian spectators, only they were no longer enjoying the show. The woman had fainted. The man struggled violently, his face twisted in horror.

"Unhand her!" he yelled, straining toward the platform. "Unhand my daughter!"

Briar's attention darted from him to the prisoners.

Her blood went cold. Her mind scrambled to make sense of what her eyes were seeing. Something that wasn't at all a part of their plan. Aurora, standing amongst the prisoners, bound like Briar's brother, watching as her parents were dragged from the square. And beside her was none other than Officer Ferro.

No.

Up on the holographic screen, Mara grinned like a cat who'd eaten a canary. She stood with one hand on the banister in front of her, the other stroking a piece of jewelry around her neck.

Briar's mind reeled.

Lyric didn't have the locket.

Mara did.

Their plan was not set in motion.

Their plan was already doomed.

Devastation slammed through her. Briar had chosen wrong. She thought she could have both—a better world and her brother, too. She chose the better world, but it wasn't the world in her care. It was Lyric. He was her charge and she had failed him. She searched the far stands, but the cloaked figure was gone. Ambrose Squire had left. Lyric was unprotected. Aurora and Officer Ferro had been caught. And the High Prince stood there on the dais looking like he didn't care at all.

The full force of reality descended upon her. Briar

couldn't breathe. She tried sucking at the air, but she couldn't get any into her lungs. Lyric was going to die and she was going to watch him. In the same spot she'd watched her parents.

Blood whooshed past her ears as the Imperial Magistrate stepped forward to the lectern to quiet the agitated crowd. An Illustrian and an Officer of the First Guard were being put to death? How could this be? His lips moved. He was speaking. But Briar only heard snippets and snatches. Phrases that tumbled over one another, lost in the tumult of panic and desperation swirling in her chest. The man was weaving a story—one of infiltrators and betrayers of the throne. Another plot. More *Magic*.

The crowd responded with cries of alarm, boos, hisses.

All the while, the world spun like a Swirl-A-Whirl at the Merivus Carnival. Briar dug her fingers into the dirt as though to keep from being flung out into the open. She stared at the prince, but he remained unmoved. Then her stomach sank further. Magic could make a person forget. Hadn't that been Officer Ferro's wish? Was that what Mara did? Had she wiped away Leo's memories so he no longer remembered the contest or the truth or *her*? If she jumped out from beneath the stands right now and called his name, would his brow pucker in confusion?

A profound sense of loss closed tight around her throat.

Briar didn't have allies. She didn't have the prince. The

Wish Keeper was gone. Her mother's locket was in the hands of their enemy. Darkness was all around, just like before. But back then, the darkness wasn't really darkness at all. What she registered as betrayal had been love—her mother and the Wish Keeper working as one to protect her, Briar. Her mother gave up her life. Ambrose enabled her to do it. Briar didn't have the locket, but she did have her mother's blood. It ran through Briar's veins. It thrummed in her ears. And it wasn't the monster. It had never been the monster. Briar let it flow, calling upon every bit of it that she could.

While the Magistrate introduced the Guest of Honor.

While the Guest of Honor lit the Torch.

While the executioner's drum commenced and the smaller torches around the platform were lit.

While the Chief Guard locked each of the prisoners into a guillotine and the Magistrate pronounced them all guilty.

The clouds swirled.

The wind blew.

The crowd stirred.

With her fingers digging deeper into the earth, Briar pulled from every loss and injustice, from every sacrifice and act of love. Papa telling her bedtime stories, encouraging her to believe in hope against all hope. Mama's melodic voice, telling Briar to feel it right here. *In her heart.* Echo and Briar, battling side by side with wooden swords, the good guys fighting the bad. The sound of Lyric's laughter. The beauty of his paintings, like those golden coins against black velvet, made all the more exquisite inside The Skid. She remembered calling for the key and unlocking the contestants. She remembered Leo grabbing her up in his arms and throwing his body over hers inside the trash receptacle. She remembered holding tight onto Sam's hand. She remembered Posey handing her honey clover. She remembered Leo finding her in the dark and the kiss that lit up her soul.

The sky darkened. The wind howled. The crowd began to cry out as the executioner took his spot on the stand and the snare drum began—a series of drumrolls that started and stopped—intensifying her fear, her love, her grit and determination. She looked from Ferro to Aurora to Lyric, the blades poised above their necks, ready to drop as soon as the lever was pulled.

The drumroll stopped.

The executioner reached.

And Briar screamed a great war cry of a scream, drowned out by the wind. She threw the Magic from her body, hurling it toward the lever as the executioner pulled.

The blades released.

Then caught halfway down, the lever stuck in place.

There was a moment—a shock of silence as the wind stopped and the crowd went still and the executioner frowned.

Mara stepped forward on the dais. She brought her hands down on the banister and bellowed, "Finish it!"

A loud blast burst through the square. A blinding flash of light that didn't come from Briar and wasn't directed at the prisoners.

The crowd screamed as the blast slammed into Mara. She flew through the air, tumbling in an arc, then recovered, landing gracefully on her feet. With her hair wild and windswept, she laughed a malevolent laugh and pinned her sparkling, flint-dark eyes on the cloaked figure stepping out from the shadows.

The Wish Keeper.

He couldn't use his Magic to free Lyric—that had been sacrificed—but he could use it to take the witch down.

The stands quaked as spectators scattered and fled.

Briar lifted herself up off the ground and sprinted through the hysteria, one thought and one thought alone blazing in her mind—she had to get to that lever before the blades fell.

CHAPTER 37

LEO

The world burned.

And Leo was trapped.

Held prisoner against his will.

Inside his own mind.

No matter how hard he tried to speak, to shout, to scream, his body remained on auto-drive and he had no access to the control panel, the past twelve hours a brand of torture he had never before experienced in his life. He tried Magic. He tried everything. But it was no use. Whatever fledgling, unexplored power he might have at his disposal was nothing compared to hers, the woman who had imprisoned him.

Monstrous, mendacious Mara.

She had sauntered into the antechamber and introduced herself in the most nonchalant of ways. By the time Leo realized who she was and the threat she posed, she already rendered him useless. As she poured seductive words into his father's ear, preying on his cowardice, preying on his paranoia, Leo made the shocking discovery that he could not open his mouth to argue. He stood there silently, indifferently, while his father stared in confusion, perplexed by his son's sudden change in demeanor. And then, to Leo's horror, he found himself walking away as if none of it mattered. He'd wanted nothing more than to stay, to combat Mara's lies with truth, to expose her for who she really was. Instead, he had walked to his bedchamber and there he had remained, locked behind invisible bars with an invisible key.

Outwardly, he bathed, shaved, then lay in his bed.

Inwardly, he thrashed and flailed, his mind turning from shock to outrage to panic to exhaustion.

All through the night, he stayed awake—waiting, hoping that once Mara fell asleep, the spell she cast upon him would fall asleep, too. But the spell remained. His vox buzzed and beeped, chirping incessantly with messages from Hawk and Sabrina. *Dude, what's up? Where have you been!? Is everything okay? Why is Aurora DuMont asking me to have you call her?* This last one tormented him most. He could only imagine what Briar was thinking. The betrayal she must be feeling. By the time the first glimpses of a gray, dull morning crept through his bedchamber windows, Leo's panic had morphed into a painful impotence. Lyric was headed for the guillotines and he was eight years old all over again, only instead of Grandfather's relentless grip holding him in place, it was Mara's. Briar would be scrambling to save her brother. Of that, Leo had no doubt. But what could she possibly do without the Wish Keeper's Magic and Leo's own influence? He had abandoned her in her greatest hour of need. Even if she managed to break her brother free, how would she ever forgive him? His family was about to kill her last remaining relative. And when he didn't think anything could get worse, he saw the necklace.

Briar's locket.

On Mara's neck.

He noticed it on the silent drive to Guillotine Square, while his father fidgeted and Mara sat with one long, sinewy leg wrapped over the other, fondling a piece of jewelry around her neck, smiling smugly—knowingly—as though waiting for Leo to realize what it was. And when he did, his panic returned in full fervor.

How had she gotten it?

Why wasn't Briar wearing it?

He'd raged like a madman rattling the bars of his prison cell. While he stepped out of the carriage. While the hungry media captured their images and the security guards led them to the dais. By the time the prisoners stood in a row and the Chief Guard began removing the sack cloths from their heads, cold fear had wrapped itself like a snake around Leo's heart and squeezed. He'd braced himself, sure that one of the prisoners would be Briar.

But Briar was not among them.

Aurora and Officer Ferro were.

Maybe it was already too late for her.

Maybe Mara had killed her in secret.

A possibility that had Leo raging all the harder.

He fought and bucked and writhed to no avail.

The invisible chains remained.

Then the clouds began to gather and the sky went dark. A replica of another scene ten years earlier. Leo had stopped his inward thrashing and searched the stirring crowd. And then, as the snare drum rattled and the executioner pulled the lever, the blades stuck. A blinding blast sent Mara sprawling through the air. She landed on her feet, eyes fixed on the cloaked figure that was Ambrose Squire stepping out from the shadows amidst a scrambling, hysterical crowd.

Hope exploded.

It ricocheted inside of Leo as he stood in place, unmoving as security guards attempted to pull him to safety. His father dropped to the floor of the dais. Another blast resounded through the square, fissuring the earth, setting the wooden stands on fire. And there, sprinting through the pandemonium—an unmistakable flash of raven hair. Briar Bishop, her face a mask of fierce determination.

Love detonated inside of him.

Briar was alive!

The bodyguards tried again—yelling at Leo through the din, urging him to get down. Even if he could move, he wouldn't have. His eyes fastened on the girl running toward the platform. The first blast had knocked the executioner off the stand. He lay on the ground, unconscious.

Yes Briar, go!

Mara saw her and attacked. Fire hurled through the air.

Briar dove out of the way and rolled to safety as the fire set the other stands aflame.

Ambrose countered with an attack of his own.

A blast of water.

Mara deflected it, then tilted back her head and laughed again—a maniacal sound that filled the entire square. "Is that all you've got old man?"

A scarfed figure scrambled up the executioner's stand.

Posey!

Mara saw her, too, and with the simple flick of a finger, sent the girl flying. She landed in a heap by the executioner as Briar pushed herself to standing.

"Guards!" Mara shouted, her amplified voice rising above the clamor, her hair wild, her eyes even wilder. "Ambrose Squire killed my son! I command you to arrest him!"

Like puppets on a string, the guards obeyed. Even the ones that were supposed to stay and protect the High King and Prince. They surrounded Squire from all sides, slowly moving in as the clouds overhead resumed their roiling and Mara sent another blast at Briar—a lightning bolt that split the sky and landed with a crash in a wall of flame that blocked her from the platform. Inside Leo's pocket, his mother's bracelet burned. It scalded his skin straight through his clothes—this piece of jewelry intimately connected to the one Mara had stolen. She was using the locket's power to bolster her own and the bracelet was responding.

Squire attacked again, launching a ball of bright light that scattered the guards.

Mara called forth more lighting. It rained down upon the square, blowing apart the marble podium in an explosion of jagged debris. Deadly projectiles catapulted through the air. One landed right next to Leo's foot. Another by his father's elbow, stabbing the dais floor. The High King stared in horror from the marbled knife to his unmoving son to the woman who was making it happen.

"Oh Executioner!" she called. "It's time you wake up and finish the job you began." She stretched out her hand and lifted it into the air.

The unconscious executioner stirred awake. He gave his head a rattle and wiped at the trickle of blood oozing down his forehead. He looked at the prisoners, still locked into the guillotines. Helpless. Trapped. Just like Leo. The executioner's attention moved to the stand, to the half-pulled lever. His job, undone. He pushed himself up slowly, his left leg twisted unnaturally as Briar found her way around the wall of flame.

Leo surveyed the scene.

A deluge of wind and fire and lightning.

The executioner, dragging himself closer.

Squire and Mara locked in battle.

The guards closing in.

Briar running.

Mara, throwing another obstacle in her path.

Briar dodging, rolling.

The marble blade stuck in the dais by his father.

The locket around Mara's neck.

Protecting her.

Empowering her.

And himself, unable to move. Unable to fight.

Unable to do anything but watch and hope and ...

Wish.

The answer came in technicolored clarity.

Briar, sprinting.

The executioner, limping.

Squire, battling.

Leo could not wish for anything that would save Lyric. But he could wish for this. The destruction of a locket that was empowering the wrong person. The destruction of a locket that had nothing to do with Lyric or his life but was protecting the only person standing between Briar and that platform.

Destroy it.

The words came quietly, vehemently.

As soon as Leo wished them, Squire's eyes locked with his. And Leo knew. Squire could see and feel exactly what Leo was seeing and feeling. It did not surprise him. It did not catch him off guard. Instead, the old man's eyes beamed with pride, as if he had been engaging in battle with Mara, biding his time until this exact moment. As if he had known all along what needed to happen and was so very pleased that Leo had caught on. Pride and pleasure swirling with ferocity and love and goodness and beneath it all, a resignation Leo didn't understand.

Squire set his attention on the locket around Mara's neck and unleashed the full force of his power.

Mara had no chance.

It blew past everything she hurled his way—the Wish Keeper's Magic—and slammed into its target. The necklace erupted in a burst of light. An effort that required all of Squire's strength, for he was undoing the very thing he created. He granted the wish that allowed Phoebe Bishop to anchor her life to the locket and now he gave his all to grant a wish that would destroy it. He had no energy left to defend himself against Mara's counter.

She sent forth a black bolt of lightning that hit the old man square in the chest.

Briar stopped, her mouth stretching wide as Squire fell.

With an unhinged laugh, Mara turned to the girl, her black eyes sparkling. "You might have been able to defeat my son, but did you really think you could defeat me? Did you really think I would not have my way?" She looked at the platform, where Lyric was bound, the blade poised, and smiled an inhuman smile.

Briar's eyes went round with horror.

She was too far away to do anything.

"First things first." Mara raised her arm to draw forth the lever and the blade hit its mark.

Not from the guillotine, but from the splintered iustus.

Not from Mara.

Not from Leo.

Not from Magic.

But from the High King as he shoved the blade in further.

Mara's mouth fell open. She stared down at the jagged marble stabbed in her chest with no locket to save her. Red blossomed across her chest like a rose in bloom. She sank to her knees, and with a bubble of blood on her lips, collapsed to the ground. The rain turned into a heavy downpour as the invisible bars imprisoning Leo vanished, the crushing weight of captivity gone.

The guards came to—blinking and confused at the charred, smoking stands, the old man on the ground, the High King's mistress laying in a puddle of her own blood, and the prisoners still shackled in place on the platform.

One of the guards grabbed Briar by her hair.

Another yanked a stirring Posey to her feet.

The executioner stepped toward his stand.

"Stop!" Leo called.

But his father beat him to it.

"Release the prisoners," he said, his posture going straight and strong. "By order of the High King."

Faster than Leo had ever moved before, he grabbed the lever and held on tight. He didn't let go until the prisoners were unshackled and Briar had her brother wrapped safe and tight in her arms.

CHAPTER 38

KORAH

The Catastrophe at Guillotine Square was reported by the media and accepted by the public as one of the worst natural disasters in recent history. The damaging winds and deadly lightning had injured many and killed two. Tragically, the High King's Guest of Honor. And one Ambrose Squire. The former remained shrouded in mystery, more so in death than she'd been in life. The latter was known and honored. Not as a fallen hero who sacrificed his life in order to defeat a woman responsible for the destruction of Cambria. Not as the Wish Keeper of Korah, either, for that remained the stuff of legend. He was, instead, honored as a long-time philanthropist who had done much good for the commonwealth once upon a time.

People had questions. Namely, why had he finally come out of hiding? What could have possibly brought him to Guillotine Square, of all places? And how hadn't any reporters noticed him upon his entrance? Between that and the High King's tragic luck in love, the public would have had plenty to speculate for months to come. But all of those mysteries fell into insignificance, overshadowed by the posthumous exoneration of the chambermaid, Phoebe Bishop, and the redaction of the Palace Exile.

The High King stood in front of his people, speaking truth and upholding true justice for the first time. Irrefutable evidence had come to light. His beloved Princess Helena was not assassinated by her chambermaid, but poisoned by the late King Casimir, who'd come to believe that her popularity amongst the people along with her humble beginnings was threatening to upend the status quo. There had never been a plot to usurp the throne. Those in exile were innocent, just as the chambermaid and her family had been innocent, and though death could not be reversed, exile could, should any of them wish to return.

No mention was made of Princess Helena's Magic, for if it was, then all of Korah would know that the High Prince was Magic, too, and while change was on the horizon and even in their midst, the carefully constructed ideologies of an entire commonwealth could not be undone overnight. The High King did, however, send out a decree that put an immediate stop to the persecution of

Magic happening at Military Ridge, deeming it a cruel and unnecessary practice. In all the shock and excitement, with so many things about which to gossip, who then killed King Casimir slipped through the cracks. If anyone suspected his son, such speculation remained behind closed doors, in the privacy of homes.

The High King experienced what he didn't deserve, what he and his forebearers had spent their rule withholding.

Mercy.

Eleos Partim, Lucram *Omnis.*

Perhaps compassion for some could be for the good of all.

CHAPTER 39

BRIAR

Briar knocked on the half-opened door. Inside, her brother sat in front of an easel with his tongue protruding in that concentrated way of his as he swept oil across the canvas, an empty tray of food on his bedside table. Two days had passed since Guillotine Square. Two days since the Wish Keeper's coin had fallen to her—figuratively and literally, right there in her pocket as soon as Ambrose breathed his last.

Over the course of those two days—sequestered in the quiet privacy of their new home—Briar had done a lot of talking. More than she'd probably ever done over the course of her entire life. She filled Lyric in. She told him the full story. Of Magic. Of friendship. Of a brave mother and a brave princess and wishes and a locket and a contest and a choice and the victorious triumph of good over evil. He listened attentively. He wandered the hallways like

Aurora. He painted. And he ate. Almost constantly. Peg, all too happy to oblige.

Briar hovered, wondering at what point Lyric would no longer tolerate her concern.

For now, he didn't seem to mind.

For now, he let her talk and check in and watch as he painted.

Her shell-shocked brother—transitioning from the hell that was prison to this, a manor that rivaled the palace in size. So far, he hadn't talked about Shard. He might not ever talk about Shard. But that didn't mean he wasn't sharing. His paintings told the story, the darkness of them troubling but necessary.

Better out than in, Peg insisted.

Lyric looked up from his creation with a ghost of a smile.

"Are you ready?" Briar asked.

He quirked an eyebrow at her doubtfully, like he didn't really believe where they were going. Castle Davenbrook. Leo suggested they bring one or two paintings along. Lyric stood—tall, lanky—and stretched his arms overhead.

Her brother, alive.

Her brother, recovering.

Slowly and steadily regaining his strength. And some of his spirit, too.

Briar couldn't help herself. She wrapped her arms around his waist, relishing the solid warmth of him.

"Want to see the latest?" he asked, draping his arm across her shoulders.

"Sure," she said. Although she wasn't, really.

She knew Peg was right.

It was good for Lyric to share.

She just didn't want to see the dark turn of his paintings getting any darker.

"It's only a start. But it's something." He leaned forward to pivot the easel. And a knot tied in Briar's throat.

The picture was not one of pain or suffering.

But a familiar invitation that showed up on the dirt floor of their shanty back in The Skid.

"I created it a hundred times in my mind. Over and over and over again."

The beauty was astounding—the golden lettering like threads of light bursting from the canvas. This was what her brother painted. Without oils. Without parchment. Locked up inside a prison cell with no idea what was happening outside of it. As days turned into weeks and weeks turned into two whole months. This was the image he'd held onto.

Hope.

"Maybe when I get it right, I can add it to the ceiling."

The knot in Briar's throat tied tighter, her arms around his waist, too. With her head resting against his shoulder, she took a deep, invigorating breath. "I think Ambrose would have loved that."

Briar stood outside Ambrose's office for the first time since the Wish Keeper's coin became hers. The light from the hallway crept across the floorboards, up the front of his desk, and pooled on top, where a jar sat in the center.

She walked tentatively inside.

Briar Bishop.

The jar was hers. Ambrose must have removed it from the room that was now her burden to bear and placed it here with the coins still inside. Except for one, which sat alone beside an unopened wise cracker.

Leo came beside her, his presence life-giving as he slid his hand around her waist. Her ally. Her partner. This boy she didn't know she needed until he was already saving her.

With a deep breath, Briar picked up the coin and let the memory sweep through her. She was little, untouched yet by tragedy though familiar with hardship. Her belly was hungry, Echo slept beside her, and somewhere not far, her mother sang and baby Lyric cooed. Briar scrunched her eyes shut, which made her nose scrunch too, and wished the same wish she'd been wishing ever since her family moved from the forests of Silva to the crowded streets of Antis.

"What is it?" Leo asked.

Briar's eyelids fluttered and with a faraway smile, she poured the coin into Leo's palm. After a moment, he smiled, too—a disbelieving, crooked grin. "*You* wished to meet the king?"

"Does that surprise you?"

"When we first met, I got the distinct impression that the king was the last person you cared to meet. Or maybe that was just his son."

"When I was little, before everything went ... so horribly, I would wish that wish every single night, positive that if I could just have the king's ear, if I could just explain to him how unfair everything was, then he would do something to make it right and life wouldn't be so hard."

Leo turned the coin over in his hand.

Maybe he was thinking what she was thinking. Leo had introduced her to the king yesterday. Lyric, too. One of his paintings hung in the castle atrium. Sir Wellington Ferris was right in the end and Lyric didn't even have to go to that stuffy, private school for it to happen.

Briar picked up the cracker and broke it open. She pulled out the slip of paper inside and read. A laugh rolled up her throat and came out half-sob. She cupped her hand over her mouth and shook her head.

"What?" Leo asked.

She handed it to him.

He read the words out loud. "Some just take longer."

Tears welled in her eyes. Somewhere along the line,

Briar had stopped making wishes. She stopped believing the Wish Keeper heard them. She stopped believing the Wish Keeper cared. Then she stopped believing in the Wish Keeper altogether. All the while, he'd held on to this one. "I guess it came true. I have the king's ear now."

"And his successor's heart." Leo took her hand and placed it flat over his chest—his muscles strong and warm and delectably well-defined.

"It's a good one," she said.

His eyes twinkled like he might never take for granted hearing her say those words. Like he truly didn't know how good of a heart it was and would need her to stick around for a long time to remind him.

Briar picked up the jar and placed it on the shelf where the former Wish Keeper's had been. Ambrose had known every single coin inside. He'd held each one in his hand—feeling them, experiencing them, bearing them. Maybe the unfulfilled ones most of all. She didn't understand what compelled him to grant some and not others. She hoped and prayed this knowledge would come to her as she stepped into this strange and magnificent role. She only knew that he carried them. Every last one.

And when it didn't feel like it—even in the darkest, most hopeless of nights—she had never, not once, been alone.

ALSO BY K.E. GANSHERT

The Gifting, The Gifting trilogy book 1

The Awakening, The Gifting trilogy book 2

The Gathering, The Gifting trilogy book 3

Luka, The Gifting trilogy companion novel

ABOUT THE AUTHOR

K.E. Ganshert graduated from the University of Wisconsin in Madison with a degree in education. She worked as a fifth grade teacher for several years before staying home to write full time. Now she's an award-winning author torn between two genres. Young adult fiction of the fantastical variety, as well as contemporary fiction of the inspirational variety. She lives in Iowa with her family and their furry dog, Gus.

For book news & updates:
www.katieganshert.com

Subscribe to K.E.'s email list to see cover art, sneak peeks, official release dates, and more!

Made in the USA
Las Vegas, NV
14 October 2021